KINCAID
and the
Furious White

To Darin & Wesley
all My Best

Curtis D. Carney

CURTIS D. CARNEY

ISBN 978-0-615-52680-5

PUBLISHED BY:
Insight Press, LLC.
Spokane, Washington

VISIT US ON THE WEB AT:
www.insightpressbooks.com

DESIGNED AND PRINTED BY:
Gorham Printing, Centralia, Washington, USA

AT THE BEGINNING OF THE 20TH CENTURY, Alaska had gained the reputation of being the graveyard of the Pacific because so many shipwrecks occurred on her shores. The problem resulted from the pinnacle rocks that were submerged only a few feet below the ocean surface. Many ships met their fate as the hulls were ripped open by the invisible rock formations that were built up from the deep. Ninety percent of all Alaskan coastlines in 1900 were not surveyed, and marker buoys and lighthouses were eventually installed to keep ships from running aground.

Logging contracts were constant but with dire consequences, as men were killed and maimed eking out a living. Well stated by a logger in Juneau, "I've never worked so hard, for so long, in such a cold and dangerous place, as these Alaskan woods."

Canneries and fishing villages were being built to accommodate the demand of the lower 48 for Alaskan salmon, and fishing areas were protected to the point of eliminating trespassers from their claimed areas.

Gold was being mined in numerous locations with boomtowns sprouting up overnight with little or no law to control the robust miner and his misbehavior.

Furs of all kinds were being taken from the coastal water as well as the interior to satisfy the world's desire for fur clothing, especially in Europe. The fur takers were greedy, and would let no laws stop them from gathering the furs that were worth great sums of money on the world market.

To these extents, I dedicate this historical novel
to the men and women that experienced
extreme hardships to exist and flourish
in such a wild and wonderful country.

Prologue

AMERICANS HAD BEEN PUSHING WESTWARD over the continent for more than one hundred years, but never had the pioneers encountered such a land as Alaska.

After the purchase of this land from Russia in 1867, there were few settlements or villages established in this desolate land, especially north of the Arctic Circle. Nomadic groups of Eskimos inhabited most of the purchased land with no governing body except their own laws and customs, and the Native tribes and customs were still quite mysterious.

Gold was discovered in 1880 in the southern stretches of the Alaskan territory, which started the first push into this great, unexplored land purchase. As miners and explorers ventured into the heart of this strange land to seek their fortunes in gold, furs, and land, they unknowingly were opening up a great frontier.

Quietly in Washington, D.C. in 1882, a few of the country's leaders were concerned with the resources of this newly acquired land. Gold had been discovered, the fur industry was flourishing, but the politicians were curious about what other resources existed there. Because of their apprehensions about the Alaskan Territory, and other parts of the country, a few forward-looking men decided to form an organization called the Wildlife Service. The duties of the individuals who were sent to the Alaskan Territory were to report on and protect the wildlife for the nation, discover what natural resources were present in this mysterious land, and establish communications with and gain an understanding of the Alaskan Native culture.

Thus, a few brave men volunteered for assignment to this last great, undiscovered land to seek out its hidden treasures, and James Kincaid was one of these early explorers that ventured into the wild, unknown land.

CHAPTER ONE

Grasping the guide handles of the sled so tightly his hands ached, the Native clothed in animal skins moved his head slowly to the left and right. His vision was blurred so badly by the harsh wind and blowing snow that he was only able to see a short distance beyond his lead dog. Encouraging the team to press on, he knew that they should be back to their village by first dark and then all would be well.

In the sled, concealed from the cold by layers of skins, were his wife and young son, and his portion of meat from a seal-hunting trip. He knew that his wife and young son were cozy and warm as they were huddled together between the sled rails, and that sent a feeling of honor through him.

He strained to see beyond his eight dogs, as he adjusted the wolverine face shield to protect his face from the torturous wind and blasting snow. The wind was gusting straight into the man's face as the team pulled hard against the heavily loaded sled, which made the sled runners cut deep into the snowy surface.

The dogs were tired and the pace was slow, but steady. The Native man knew they were a strong team and would pull them back home and to safety. When his family returned to the village, everyone would want to know about the seal-hunting trip, and all who went on the trip. It would be a fine time to tell stories.

His feet settled firmly on the back sled runners, the man shrugged his body beneath the animal skin clothing for he had felt a chill, as if something was going to happen. Hastily glancing around to see anything out of the ordinary, he abruptly felt uneasy. Hailing even louder encouragement to the team, and detecting nothing wrong, his feelings of uneasiness subsided.

Suddenly a huge white blur smashed into the side of the sled accompanied by a loud snarl that penetrated the howling of the wind. The large animal's weight of impact tipped the sled over on its side and the woman and boy were thrown free. Meat scattered on the crusted snow as the dogs stopped pulling, and the man was knocked free of the sled as he lay dazed a short distance from where the beast had suddenly attacked the sled.

The polar bear instantly grabbed the first two dogs in front of the sled and ripped them to shreds as steaming blood and body parts were broadcasted over the snowy surface. The rest of the team had stopped and they were charging toward the intruder with fangs flashing for the fight to the death.

Somehow, managing to muster enough strength to regain his feet, the Native man began staggering toward the ensuing, raging battle. He moved as quickly as he could to the fight, and realized that he could not move his right arm. His attention was caught by the movement of his wife and son struggling to regain their feet, after being thrown from the sled.

The Native man yelled and motioned, "Follow the river south to the village." Seeing them run between him and the overturned sled, he knew what his fate was to be. He must stay and fight this beast to save his wife and son. Pausing to watch his wife and child disappear into the blowing snow, he then quickly grabbed his spear off the sled and advanced to the raging battle, to kill or be killed.

Moments later, the woman stopped suddenly and jerked the boy to an abrupt halt. She hastily instructed, "Stay by the river and look toward the mountains to get to the village," and with a hard push she shoved him away from her toward the direction of the boy's travel.

Hurrying as fast as he could, Moaka briefly stopped and turned to see his mother disappearing into the blowing snow toward the raging battle. The boy pulled his hood close to his face, and ran as fast as he could along the river south to the village, to get help for his father and mother.

⋅ ⋅ ⋅

James Kincaid had always loved hunting and romping in the forests of maple and pine trees of Wisconsin. There was one thing that made this morning special; his father had finally given him his very own rifle.

Growing up on the Upper Peninsula, James spent most of his time in or around the forests when the farm chores would allow. His father's farm was surrounded by woodlands, and along with his brothers and sisters, they romped and played in the timber and meadows. His father always said James was a natural hunter because he seemed to know where the animals were, and what they were doing. His father always took him on hunting trips, saying it never hurt to have someone around that knew the animals' ways. James always knew he would somehow learn more about wildlife, and the way in which they lived.

Now in his twenties, of strong medium build, with dark hair and soft steel gray eyes, James wanted to push on with his life. He was quick to learn and showed patience to act. After what seemed like a relatively short four years of college life, he was finally a graduate of William's University, Wildlife Division, and he could now set himself to the task of doing what he'd always wanted to do, study and work with wildlife. He had volunteered to work for the Wildlife Service and they wanted to send him to the north slopes of Alaska to study wildlife, which made his blood run hot with excitement and anticipation.

Standing outside the graduation hall savoring his time at the university, James thought, *I'm glad I never lost track of what I wanted to do more than anything else; to learn about the different animals, what they ate, what kind of habitat and environment they liked to live in, where they raise their young, and how they died.*

Spotting Dean Kipley, the Dean of Wildlife, exiting from the graduation hall with the rest of the graduates and guests, James had a sense of loneliness creep over him. This old school had been a place of security and a sense of belonging, but now he would find a new life in Alaska.

As Dean Kipley approached, he smiled and asked, "You all set to go, James?"

Looking away from the large wooden hall doors James returned his smile and replied, "Yes sir, my train leaves in the morning about nine-thirty."

Sincerity gleaming from his eyes, Dean Kipley simply stated, "James, do you realize that the Wildlife Agency of the government, that you are going to work for, doesn't know any more about the north slopes of Alaska than you do? I hope they know what they're doing by sending you up there with no experience."

With a nod of his head, James replied, "That's the impression I got when I went for my interview, but I'm looking forward to the opportunity. They said I would be transported to Barrow, Alaska, by several means. I'm to go to the Wildlife Service Office in Seattle, Washington and meet a fellow named Don Nealy; then he will send me to Nome, Alaska, to hook up with a Mr. Harris. Harris is supposedly the contact up there that will break me in and show me the territory I will cover. The Service assured me that all arrangements would be made ahead of me."

As James and Dean Kipley shook hands and said their goodbyes, the two men silently acknowledged respect for each other.

Back in his one room apartment, James thought about the trip he was about to embark on to see his parents, relatives, and friends back home, then on to the North Country. Lifting his arms above his head and stretching his neck muscles, he thought, *Oh well, the visit will only be for two or three days, then on with the continuing train ride to Seattle.* James was so excited that he was having trouble settling himself to think straight.

The official James had talked with from the Department of Wildlife made it plain that he should get to Barrow as soon as possible because of cold weather in that part of the world. Because of the late start they had at college last year, the class didn't graduate as soon as scheduled. So tomorrow, on the 16th day of September 1899, James Kincaid would start his journey to the northland.

The oil lamp flickering low caused strange shadows to appear on the walls, as James began taking inventory again of all the gear that he had been issued from the department. While fumbling through all the clothing, he mentally took stock, one pair of boots, some cold weather outer gear, and miscellaneous needs of the trade, like compass and knife. As he finished going through his gear, he remembered having to sign for all this stuff. Who was going to know what happened to it anyway? He was going to be on the north slopes of Alaska. "What in the world would be the living condition in Barrow, Alaska?" James mumbled as he blew out the oil lamp.

* * *

Moaka gazed across the almost perfectly flat sun-brightened ice pack as he wondered about his new home with the missionaries of the village. He had been told that his parents had been killed by a marauding polar bear. His thoughts were still troubled thinking about that terrible day because it had been only a short time since he'd returned from the seal hunting trip with his parents. Moaka had been told he'd be living with a missionary family that came to the north slopes of Alaska, and they didn't have any children, so the Natives approved Moaka to be raised by his newly adopted family. His new parents tried to teach him English and things about the white man, and by being only seven years old, he was told it would be easy for him to learn. Moaka didn't mind, except his friends used the Native language.

Sighing, he leaned over to inspect his fishing hole in the ice, and remove some ice that was starting to form around the edges. He had used a snow knife to cut the hole in the ice about two hands wide. The ice removed, he rested back in his sitting position, and stared off across the ice sheet hoping for a fish to bite. Feeling sad, he could not remember exactly what his father and mother looked like. Shrugging slightly and scratching his head, he thought, *in time I will remember.*

Much to his surprise, the water in the hole seemed to be moving up and down slightly. Puzzled, he leaned forward and much to his delight, he could see a large fish swimming by the open hole. Firmly he grasped the line and raised the seal baited hook just to the level he thought the large fish was and suddenly the line went taut. Moaka was ready for a hard pull, as the line tightened around his small, mittened hand. He jerked back on the line with all his strength, and the only thing he could do was hold the fish from getting away.

He knew he had to do something quickly before the line was cut on the edge of the roughened ice hole's edges. Scrambling to his feet, Moaka swiftly wrapped the line around his hand, and gave the hardest jerk he could to bring the fish out of the icy water onto the ice. Instantly, the head of the fish appeared above the ice and it seemed to be stuck in the hole. Without hesitation, he flipped his mittens off and lunged at the fish that was stuck in the hole, and hooked his fingers into the fish's gills and began pulling with all his might.

Noticing that he had jerked so hard on the line that it almost pulled the hook from the fish's mouth, his grip tightened even more into the gills, knowing that this was his only way of pulling the fish from the icy water. Wild thoughts ran through his mind, knowing he would be able to show off his prize and be able to tell the story of his fishing trip. With a gushing noise, the reward suddenly slipped from the hole and out onto the ice. Moaka could not believe his eyes. The fish was as long as his leg. Lying back and resting for just a moment, he could feel the fish's slow, methodic movement as if trying to swim. Putting his mittens in his coat, he grabbed the fish in the gills and stood.

It was starting to get dark as he struggled with every step, dragging his prize, but he was determined to get it back all by himself. He would be complimented and looked up to by his friends, and they would want to hear his story of the big fish. Smiling to himself, he was proud. Then suddenly, he began to silently cry for he wondered what his father and mother would think if they were alive. Stopping, he rested from pulling his fish, and thought, *I will always miss my father and mother.*

By the time he reached the village, his new parents were anxious about his return for it was almost dark. Nearing the village, Moaka could see the missionary woman had started looking for him, and he could tell by her facial expression that she was relieved to see his small, dark figure returning from the white landscape.

CHAPTER TWO

"Coming into the City of Seattle, Washington, folks." The conductor spoke loud enough for all the passengers to hear over the noise of the train car. "We'll be there in about thirty minutes."

James rubbed his strong, narrow jaw as he turned to stare out the window, while his thoughts strayed to his family in Wisconsin. *It had been a fine visit, and I was glad to have been able to see them before taking on a job so far away. I wonder how long it will be before I will see them again.* He'd seen a lot of country not familiar to him, talked to people with backgrounds unlike his own, and was inspired by every mile of the trip. The United States was very large and would need many people to settle it.

Stepping from the train, he hoisted his grip and new Winchester rifle, and started looking for the Department of Wildlife office.

He made his way down the street by walking on the board sidewalks, and as he inquired about the office, nobody had the faintest idea where the Department of Wildlife office was located. Finally, an older shopkeeper thought he knew where the office might be, and made a suggestion which way James should proceed.

As James followed the sketchy directions to find the office, he noticed Seattle was built entirely of wooden buildings and wooden sidewalks with dirt streets. It was easy to understand why because the forests for the raw materials were very close. The town was laid out square from north to south, which made it easy for a stranger to find his way. Although James had no idea how big Seattle was, it looked like a bustling, growing town.

James felt a kind of excitement among the people in the way they hustled about performing their daily duties. As James continued, he noticed that most of the buildings were accented with special woodcarvings. Stopping to gaze at a hitching rail, James was amazed that the two wooden support posts were hand-carved to resemble naked women.

The dirt streets were busy with buggies, buckboards, and freight wagons. Dust swirled from the wheels of some of the rigs that were traveling faster than most and were probably going too fast.

It was late in the afternoon by the time James arrived at the Wildlife office. Finding the door ajar, James poked the end of his rifle barrel against the door and entered, and as he opened the door, the hinges sounded an eerie, high-pitched squeak. The large, dark room had one desk with an oil lantern sitting on it, a couple of wooden straight chairs, a wood stove with a small amount of wood stacked on the floor, and an old wooden box sitting on the floor with some papers scattered in it. The one window that faced the street was so grimy that very little light could force its way through the dirty panes. He looked around for someone to approach, but found the room empty.

Setting his bags down on the dusty wooden floor, James turned to walk outside. Just then, a large-framed man came up the steps to the boardwalk and James stepped aside to let him enter without either man saying a word.

As he passed James, he looked at him through glassy, grey eyes as he shrugged off his coat. He walked over to the only desk in the room and sat down behind it as if James wasn't there.

James studied the situation for a second, and then stepped abruptly to the desk and stated, "I'm James Kincaid and I'm here to see about transport to Alaska."

Without a word or expression, the man behind the desk leaned forward and lit the oil lamp that was sitting on the desk. The large, grizzly-looking person had a two-day growth of reddish beard and wore soiled work clothes. He leaned back in his chair after lighting the oil lamp, folded his heavy arms across his large chest, and replied with a smirk, "The hell you are. You stroll in here wanting me to jump up, drop everything, and see to your every need. I've been in the field for damn near three days, and I'm dog-tired. I come back to the office and what do I find, but some kid that wants me to jump to his every need?"

"No sir," James replied straightaway, somewhat taken back. "I meant that I've come from Boston and have been assigned to the north slopes of Alaska for duty, and I'm supposed to contact someone here for arrangements to get to Nome, Alaska."

"Yeah, Kincaid, I know all about you. I got the letter the other day from those dummies back east, telling me I'm supposed to help you get on your way. They think that's all I have to do is nursemaid greenhorns like you." Lazily reaching across his dusty desk with his large, burly hand, he demanded, "Let me see your papers."

With conviction, James stepped back to his bags. Retrieving his papers, he handed them to the rudest man he had ever met, and James wasn't surprised he didn't make an effort or have the decency to introduce himself. Stepping back from the desk, James thought, *I won't be badgered by the likes of you.*

Rifling through the papers and glancing at them for only a second, he handed the papers back to James saying, "You're in luck, kid, there's a boat leaving tomorrow at noon for the North Country."

Leaning back his chair, he continued, "I don't mean to sound like I'm against you, kid, but I just hate to keep sending young pups like yourself up to that country. We have sent seven or eight like you up there in the last year, and every one of them froze to death or just packed it in and came on back. Hell, two of them have never been heard from since, although we are still looking for them. I don't know why the department can't send experienced men up there. Can you talk Eskimo?" Without giving James a chance to respond, he waved his large arm into the air and continued, "Don't worry about the Eskimo stuff, nobody around here can speak it either."

"No, I can't," James answered, as his confidence was beginning to return. "But I plan on getting a knowledgeable guide when I get there to take care of the language problem until I can learn the language." Pausing, he continued, "I was told I could get a guide; it states that in the orders you looked at."

With a shake of his head, the hard-crusted, overweight man behind the desk asked, "What did the people back east tell you that you would be doing up there..."

Breaking in before the man behind the desk could finish his question, James interrupted, "By the way, what the hell is your name? I don't even know who I'm talking to."

With a surprised look on his face, he replied, "I'm Don Nealy."

His confidence returning, James answered, "Well, they said to observe the wildlife and terrain and report back to this station at least four times a year by mail. They also said that I should come back to this station at least once a year to check in with my supervisor. Are you going to be that person?"

"Hell, kid," he said as he waved his arms in the air, "I don't know. I don't think they've thought that far ahead yet. I guess I will be until further notice, though. The Service never worried about field supervisors until now."

"Don, can you tell me anything at all about what I might expect when I get there?"

"Kid..."

Without warning, James abruptly leaned forward and put both hands on the front of the desk and in a rather loud voice fired, "Stop right there, Don. I was told, back east, that at the Seattle Station I could depend on a guy by the name of Nealy. Now I figure you know a few ropes, but if you and I are to get along for any length of time, you're going to have to give up this 'kid' thing."

Once the burst of anger had subsided in James, he stood up straight, taking his hands from the desk, and walked slowly across the room to peer out the stained windowpane.

Following the young lad across the room with his eyes, Don knew he was different from the others—more grit.

"James," Don said, "You're right by damn. I'm sorry. It won't intentionally happen again. I've never been up to that country, but I do know that a damn good guide will go a long ways to helping you out as far as the language and where to go and how to get there." Don started to relax somewhat after James' temper flared, and he motioned for James to sit in the other chair. "I can't recall anybody else going up there ever trying to get a guide," Don explained. "That might be the edge you need. By the way, who authorized you to hire a guide and pay him?"

"It is written in my orders, like I said." James motioned with his hand toward the paperwork he'd laid on the front of the desk.

"James Kincaid, you just might make it. You've shown more spunk right here in this room than most." Smiling, Don asked, "Are you a drinking man?"

"On occasion," James replied slowly, "but other than that, I stay away from the stuff. However, I'll not fault a man for pulling a cork occasionally. My father and grandfather are quite frequent users of their home brew."

Don pulled a bottle from the desk drawer and lifted it to his lips, took two big swallows, and sat the green bottle down on the desktop. He commented as he wiped his lips, "Well, it's just as well you drink in moderation."

As James was getting up from the wooden chair, he commented, "Listen, if we are done here I'd like to get a place for the night, get washed up a bit, and take a nap before I go out and eat. Where could I take care of all that?"

Don gestured with his left hand and said, "Just down the street and around the corner. Best damn little hotel you ever been in."

"Well, Don, if you don't have anything else for me, I'll be on my way. What time should I be back tomorrow morning?"

Sighing deeply and thinking for just a moment, Don replied, "Better be back around eight o'clock or so. We need to get down some information about next of kin and the like before I get you on the boat."

CHAPTER THREE

The next morning as James arrived at the office, he saw a team and buck-board slowly rounding the corner and recognized Don Nealy sitting on the buckboard spring seat.

Don brought the team of horses to a halt in front of the office, and tied off the reins to the brake stay. Still sitting in the buckboard seat, he hailed, "Good morning, James." With a smooth motion of his large frame, Don jumped from the buckboard seat to the ground.

Once through the squeaky front door and inside the office Don and James set to the task of getting the paperwork completed. Don was selecting forms from different drawers of his desk, and James began to study Don a little closer.

This wasn't the grizzled, bad-tempered, person who sat behind the desk yesterday. This person was clean-shaven, well-groomed, with clean clothes and a very nice felt, full-brimmed hat that James admired. What a difference a good cleanup and good night sleep made for Don. James was amazed and was glad he had the opportunity to know the real Don Nealy before he left.

The papers stacked together, Don handed them to James to fill out. Don arose from his chair, walked over to the stained window, spit on a portion of one of the panes, and then wiped it off to see through the glass. Peering out intensely for just a second, Don inquired, "How long do you think you want to stay up north, James?"

Abruptly, James stopped filling out the paperwork, and he leaned back in his chair, responding, "Don, I don't know for sure. How long will the job last?"

Laughing quietly, but loud enough for James to hear, Don replied, "I'm sure the position you're going to fill will not need to be filled for a long time—meaning years. The only two reasons the Department would move you would be if you could not get along with the Natives, or you were very good at your job, and they wanted you somewhere to train other men." Don sat down behind his desk again as James finished up the paperwork.

James passed them to Don and started to get up, but Don waved him to sit back down.

Don finished the forms by signing his name to them and putting them in a large envelope for safekeeping. He raised his eyes to meet the younger man's, saying, "James, I'd like to talk with you for a bit. We aren't in that big a hurry anyway."

His large arms folded across his chest, Don leaned back in his chair. In a serious tone, he said, "James, I've only known you since yesterday, but you've shown more spunk than most that come this way. Where you're going, you'll need every bit of toughness you can muster, and there are going to be times when you're going to have to reach down inside yourself for all you have just to stay alive. Hell, we don't know anything about that country that you're going to, and there's been damn few of us that have ever been past Nome. I've been to Nome to set things up with Harris, but no further. Your idea of getting a guide will help you a lot, but be damn careful whom you hire. I guess I'd recommend trying to find a Native Eskimo who would stay with you for a while. I hear you can't trust them much either. Just don't pay any guide until you get to where your going— if that is possible." Pulling out the top drawer of his desk, he handed James an envelope explaining, "These are vouchers for government payment.

These will take care of getting any supplies or lodging you or your guide will need to be outfitted in Nome. There is more than enough to get your supplies, clothing, and equipment. Keep the rest for use as time goes along. Do you have money with you? "

Taking the envelope, James commented, "Thanks for the vouchers." Pausing, James continued, "Yes, Don, I have money with me. My family wasn't going to see me off without proper financing. How well do you know Harris?"

"He runs a grubstake store up there, and he'll sell you anything you want, supposedly on agreed prices. Anyway, he will accept those vouchers for anything you buy from him. Ray Harris, for the time being, is your contact in Nome. He will help you get pointed in the right direction, but don't count on anything else from him. When I first met him, he was a good man on that end, but ever since he has thrown in with that thieving bunch of seal hunters, and he has overcharged the Service on both supplies and equipment. When you get there, don't haggle price with Harris, he'll be caught eventually. Just get what you think you need and sign the voucher, and he'll take it to the local bank for payment. By the way, when you get a guide, I need to know his name so I can verify payment for his services through the bank at Nome." Don observed a puzzled look on James' face and asked, "Do you have a question?"

Leaning forward in his chair, James exclaimed, "Yeah, about a hundred or so!"

With a loud laugh, Don came forward on his chair as the front legs hit the wooden floor with a thud. "By hell, you're honest anyway, James. I'd suggest you stay in Nome for a couple of days just to get the feel of things, and do some talking to folks about that country. Do some looking around and see what kinds of clothing and equipment everybody else has, and believe me, there is no hurry in getting to the north slopes because that place has been there for thousands of years, and it's not going anywhere. In the packet of papers I gave you, you will find a map that locates your area of responsibility, and what you're supposed to be looking for. It's very basic: note the wildlife and their habitat, natural resources, do a little map-making of lay of land, and try to keep poaching under control, if there is any of that going on. Another thing you need to do is talk to the Natives, and try to make them understand Alaska now belongs to the United States and not to Russia. Keep a good log of what, when, and where, and send a report every quarter to this office, or whenever you have the opportunity. Your territory will be from Barrow almost as far easterly as you want to go. When you get to Nome, your biggest problem will be getting from Nome to Barrow then parts east. And hell, I couldn't begin to tell you how to do that other than a dog sled this time of year. The ice has already moved in around Barrow so all ship travel is out till next spring."

"You say those government vouchers are good for anything like food, ammo, clothing, and general supplies for me and the guide, but what about if I want to buy a dog," James inquired.

"They are good for anything you need to perform your job; if that means buying dogs…that's OK," and smiling he continued, "Probably the best way to proceed when you get to Nome is don't be in a hurry because that country moves slowly." Don lazily leaned back in the chair once more, as the wooden legs groaned in protest. "I can get you on a boat that will take you to Nome, I can give you vouchers to pay your way, and we can talk here all day, but son, you're the one that has to make the decisions when you get there. It's important for you to understand that you more or less speak for the Service up there, at least for right now. Someday we'll probably have an office in Nome, which will make things easier, but until that time you're it up there." Pausing for a moment, Don continued, "Ray Harris doesn't really work for the Wildlife Service. He helps us out from time to time in supplying and helping locate the men we send up there. Eventually you're going to hear about the northern fur seal traders, and believe me those guys don't give a damn about anything except making money. They will kill anything, young or old, male or female, just as long as the animal has fur, and I think Harris has thrown in with them."

The chair scraped on the wooden floor when Don pushed it back and got to his feet. He stretched his large arms above his head and commented, "Well, I guess we are about finished here. Let me hear from you from time to time on what you see and what you're doing about it. I've enjoyed meeting you, James, and I hope you do well. Now I think it's about time we tried to get you on that boat."

After introducing James to Captain Marks of the freighter *Hannon*, Don grasped James' hand in farewell, and with a nod of approval, Don turned and made his way down the gangplank back to the shore. Once on solid ground he turned and waved in a parting gesture of good luck and goodbye. "Keep in touch, and let me know where you are and what you're doing. Also," and raising his voice he yelled, "Be sure to put dates on reports."

Seeing Don disappear into the crowd, James turned to observe the Captain barking orders to the crew in a rough and seasoned voice. The Captain's scrutiny was then turned to James as he looked through cold gray eyes, shaded by long gray eyebrows, that made James' blood run cold until the Captain remarked, "Donald thinks quite highly of you, lad, and he seems to think you're the one that will stay in that God-forsaken country."

CHAPTER FOUR

Nome didn't have a harbor like Boston or Seattle and the *Hannon* dropped anchor some distance from shore. When all was secure, James and some other passengers climbed down the accomodation ladder into a large longboat that was rowed ashore to a small wharf.

The wind was calm, the sky was gray, and the air and everything touched with bare hands was cold. James strained to see over the men's backs who were manning the oars to see what Nome really had to offer. The shoreline was littered with seemingly hundreds of white canvas tents, but in the background he could see wooden buildings. In addition, to his surprise, there was very little snow on the ground.

As the longboat slid alongside the wharf, James and others that debarked from the *Hannon* picked up their belongings and clambered up onto the wharf. Shivering from the chill in the air, he noticed barges being rowed out to the ship to carry in the cargo.

Hefting his grip and rifle, he now had to find someone who could get him to Barrow. James was feeling anxious about what was ahead, but he could feel himself growing in confidence because Don had told him to take it easy in Nome, and not to get excited. He also said to look at what was going on in the area—try to know what you're doing before you obligate yourself.

Back on firm footing again, it seemed strange not having the movement of the ship beneath his feet. James walked up the ramp from the wharf to the main street, and he could see that the men who lived in the tents were hunters and miners. The dress of most of the people was bulkier than he was used to seeing, and these clothes were probably warmer than the tailored clothes he was wearing. Making his way through the crowd and rows of tents, he finally entered the main part of town.

Don Nealy had told him that when he got to Nome, he should go to the city hall or somewhere like that, to find a guide to take him on to Barrow. He probably should try to find a guide before he found Harris. Considering a guide, James thought, *Harris would probably try to give me one of his cronies as a guide, and the guy would leave me stranded in the middle of nowhere, when the going got rough.*

James' first and lasting impressions of Nome were all the men who lived in tents looked ragged and dirty. After seeing the way they worked, and the way in which they kept themselves, James was glad to be doing what he was doing for a living. Some way he was determined to make a go of it up here, and do well, not just survive as the men appeared to do that lived in the white tents.

The town was undeveloped and rugged as compared to other towns in the east. There were no board sidewalks, as in Seattle, let alone stone or mortar sidewalks, as in Boston. The wooden hitching rails were lined with a few saddled horses, their breath steaming in the frigid air. It was cold and the streets were frozen solid. Some snow had fallen recently, and the footing was very slick, especially for the kind of smooth sole boots he was wearing. The front of the buildings had been dressed-up, trying to make them appear what the back of the buildings were not. Between some were spaces where he could see behind the false fronts and the actual buildings were shacks with fancy fronts. Passing by one saloon, James could smell the stale beer and the rancid odor of unwashed bodies reeking from the open doorway.

He made his way along the street slowly trying to take notice of all the new sights around him, including the people's activities and their dress and habits.

James approached an old timer who was dressed entirely in animal skins, including his handmade animal skin boots, and inquired, "Say mister, can you tell me where the city hall is located?"

Without a word, the old timer slowly raised his hand and motioned down the road to the left.

James thanked him, and went on his way in the direction the old timer had indicated, hoping it would somehow lead him to the city hall.

Suddenly, James froze in his tracks. Approaching him on the snow-covered street was the first real live dog team pulling a sled he'd ever seen. Setting his bags down and letting his rifle hang loosely in his right hand, he watched the team and sled approach, trying to savor every moment. James wondered how the man on the back of the sled kept all those dogs pulling in one direction. Seeing them pass by, he marveled at the huge beautiful dog in front. He was a magnificent animal with large, strong shoulders and different color tones in his coat. The team and sled passed out of sight, and he picked up his grip and continued making his way to the city hall, and wondered if one day he might have a team like the one he had just witnessed.

His body started to protest the conditions from the persistent cold, and James knew he'd better find some different kind of clothing to wear, and soon. Looking around, he noticed that most everybody wore clothing that seemed to be made out of animal skins, even most of their footwear.

From somewhere behind him James heard someone holler, "Hey, greenhorn, where ya goen all duded up like that? Come over here so's we can take a look at that fancy new rifle you'ren packen."

James knew well the rough sounding voice was addressing him, but he was not looking for trouble so he kept walking. An instant later the same rough voice hollered even louder, "Hey, greenhorn, I'm talken to ya."

Pausing and looking back over his left shoulder, he saw three burly, unshaven, filthy-looking men all dressed in animal skins looking to give him a bad time. Quickly turning away, James continued on his way, until he heard heavy footsteps behind him. Dropping his grip, he quickly turned and was only able to move his head enough to have the blow glance off the side of his forehead. Half-dazed he plummeted to the hard frozen ground, and rolled over just in time to feel the shooting pain of the man's foot that had contacted with his rib cage. Instinctively rolling away from the blow of the man's foot, James was able to turn himself on his back, just as the intruder started coming at him again. Mustering all his strength, James kicked with his right foot at the oncoming man's shin and a loud crack sounded as James was sure that he had broken the man's leg.

James rolled to the side, away from the falling body, and jumped up ready to take on his companions, but they stopped short when they heard their fallen comrade moaning in pain. The roughneck rolled back and forth on the ground, holding his now useless leg. His two comrades rushed over to help him, as James bent down and picked up his jersey hat and carefully placed it back on his head. After straightening his clothes, he started brushing the snow off the front of his coat.

Startled, he felt someone brushing the snow off his back, and quickly turned to see who was helping him, James found himself looking down at an old Eskimo man. His animal-skin dress covered every part of him except for his upraised, smiling, brown face. His smile exposed yellowish teeth and his face was leathery and weatherbeaten, but the man seemed friendly.

In somewhat broken English, the old Eskimo pointed at James and whispered, "Do good, Brady bad."

Not wanting any further problems, James patted the old man on the shoulder, thanked him again and picked up his grip and rifle then continued on his way, still trying to find the city hall. He wasn't hurt, but did have a dull ache in his side where the roughneck's foot had caught him.

"Kincaid, Kincaid."

Hearing his name called, James turned to see a short man, dressed all in skins, hurrying toward him. Not being able to see his face because his head was bent down somewhat, James thought it might be the old man wanting to add something further, but as the figure got closer James could see that he was a much taller and stronger built person than the old man. James sat his grip down and placed his rifle atop his left shoulder, and turned to meet this person, wondering how in the world this fellow knew his name.

From a short distance, the newcomer yelled above the street noise, "Kincaid? Marks say need guide Barrow."

Watching the Eskimo hurry toward him, James wondered what the Native wanted of him, or if he was the guide he was looking for. Don had told him to go to the city hall or somewhere like that to get a guide. When he finally got within talking distance, James replied, "Yes I'm James Kincaid, and I do need a guide, but how in the world did you know my name, and I needed to go to Barrow?"

"Cap'in Marks say. Say why you here. No say pick fight."

Detecting a slight smile that appeared across the Eskimo's weathered face, James somehow instantly sensed that this stranger could be trusted, and he wondered how this person knew Captain Marks. The Eskimo seemed to be open, straightforward, and honest; besides that, he seemed to have a sense of humor. James removed his glove from his right hand and thrust it out in greeting, and inquired, "You know my name, what's yours?"

Quickly this smiling-faced, short, stocky, strong-built fellow responded, as he gestured proudly toward his chest, "Moaka."

Moaka extended his gloved right hand to meet James', and James pulled his bare hand back and quickly retorted, "I won't shake with a man whose hand I can't feel."

Instantly, silence fell between the two men who stood staring into each other's eyes, each man oblivious to the surrounding street noise and passing people. Each man determining to what extent the other would be dominant. One man being well educated and much more worldly than the other; the other man, while not formally educated, was just as wise in the ways of the world in which he lived.

Looking slightly up into the eyes of this newcomer, Moaka was determined not to break eye contact with the person who seemed to challenge him.

James studied Moaka for an instant, and was about to break the silence when he saw Moaka move, without breaking eye contact with him. Slowly Moaka removed his glove from his right hand and extended it toward James.

James smiled and nodded slightly, as he extended his hand to meet Moaka's naked one.

Without warning, Moaka grabbed James' hand and squeezed it as hard as he could, which instantly brought a grimace onto James' face, and before James could react, Moaka flung James' hand from his and quickly said, "You no tough."

In utter shock, James stood silently looking at the short man in front of him that had clenched his hand like a man twice his size. James' mind was racing as he thought, *What sort of person is this? He's certainly not afraid of me. Does he want me to make the next move? He isn't moving and that means he is willing to take on whatever I can dish out. That has to stand for good character. He may be afraid, but had guts enough to take me on, whatever the consequence.*

James' face formed a huge smile, and he responded, "By the damn, Moaka, you're right, I'm not very tough."

Instantly a grin came upon Moaka's face, and again he grabbed James' hand and shook it almost viciously, sputtering, "Kincaid, think we fight."

Finally James stopped Moaka from shaking his hand off, and in a questioning tone, James asked, "Moaka, just Moaka, no other name?"

Surprised at James' question, Moaka quickly nodded and responded, "Moaka, other you no say."

"Okay, Moaka, if that's the way you want it." As James and Moaka continued to make their way down the street, James inquired, "How is it that you know Captain Marks?"

"We know same person."

James was puzzled at the answer, but he didn't figure it to be that important, so he let the answer stand good enough.

"Do you happen to know a guy around here named Harris that has a supply store?" James asked. "He's my next contact for supplies and equipment. Also, how do we get to Barrow?"

"Stop Kincaid." Moaka turned and stepped squarely in front of James. "How know Harris? No friend hunter."

With a shrug of his shoulders, James responded, "I was told he had a stores house in Nome, and that was where I was supposed to get my supplies and equipment. Why isn't he a friend of the hunter?"

"Harris kill many seal for fur," Moaka declared. He looked James up and down and with a slow sideways shake of his head commented, "No dress right. Cold in Barrow. We go dog sled."

"Dog sled!" James exclaimed. "Someone else told me about maybe having to use a dog sled to get to Barrow, but I don't know anything about dog sledding."

"I teach. You learn?" was Moaka's simple answer.

James fired back, "Damn right I'm willing to learn. You just give me a dog team and I'll learn."

Moaka turned and gazed down the street in silence, and thought, *The things I will have to teach this stranger to exist in the North Country. The proper ways of hunting and fishing in the far north, the building of a dog team, and I will have to teach this newcomer the value of a good lead dog, and how to take care of his team. Can I do this job or would it be all for nothing, if Kincaid thought it was getting too tough would he leave?*

James stared at the people that passed—thinking. *This native seems to have some knowledge of the English language. It was plain by his speech, this newly found guide had used English to some extent, and although he left out words in his English speech, Moaka seemed to be able to speak plainly. I wonder what his background is and where he came from. Moaka seemed to be taller than the Native Eskimos I've seen so far, but shorter than me. Moaka obviously knew how to get to Barrow, and that was something. In addition, he is willing to teach me dog sledding.* James was not sure about the whole situation of getting a guide, but he seemed to trust Moaka or at least he wanted to trust him.

James' thoughts were brought back to the present when Moaka turned back to him and explained, "Kincaid, no buy team." He motioned with his hands as if building something, and continued, "Make together." He motioned with one mitten-covered hand. "Pick dog, pick more, have team." Then lifting his mittened hand and grasping James' shoulder, Moaka smiled broadly and stated, "Kincaid, ride Moaka sled. Time come build team."

James let Moaka's hand fall away from his shoulder and replied, "That suits me fine, Moaka. Now let's go see this Harris character and get me some warmer clothes. I'm about ready to freeze to death. In addition, if possible, I'd like to leave for Barrow by sometime tomorrow. I can pay you a good wage if you want to be my guide, but we can work out the details tomorrow at the bank."

"See Harris morning." Nodding his head yes, Moaka replied, "Pay okay. Got money for supplies? Barrow long way. Hard trip for all." Moaka stepped in closer to Kincaid and gently laid his hand on James' arm, stating firmly, "Kincaid, land where go hard. First must live. Must…" As he waved his hand in front of his face as if mentally searching for the right word, he muttered, "*issumayok.*" Finally, Moaka came up with the English words and blurted out, "Who thinks."

Not being able to hold his feelings, James laughed aloud and followed Moaka's last statement with, "I understand Moaka, a person has to think about what he's going to do and plan well."

As Moaka released his hold on James' arm, he smiled broadly and responded, "Yes, Kincaid, one must think." Shaking his head Moaka turned slowly and started to lead the way, but James did not follow. Moaka's mind was churning with frustration, as he considered, *The Captain had said Kincaid seemed to be a good man and that he was someone that could be trusted. I just hope that this newcomer to the North Country would listen and learn, and not go back on his word when the way became hard.*

Looking at the stature of the short, rugged man walking away from him, James was beginning to believe that this Native knew what he was talking about and had the knowledge James was looking for. Not moving, James thought, *Maybe this could be the man who would teach me to survive in the North Country? Moaka did say he would accept the wages for being a guide, whatever they were. This would be the man I would have to depend on to help me get established here in Alaska, and this Native would have to be trustworthy on all counts.*

Realizing that James was not following, Moaka stopped and slowly turned back to face James. Tilting his head to one side, they both stood silently sizing each other up. Finally, Moaka broke the silence, while shaking his head side to side slowly muttering, "Kincaid, dumb looking." With a wave of his mittened hand in the air he commanded, "Kincaid come, I teach live North Country. Stay Castle House this night. Captain say good thing for Kincaid, good for me. I see morning."

Ending his instructions for James to stay at the White Castle Hotel for the night, Moaka seemed to melt into the crowd. He figured he'd meet up with Moaka tomorrow morning, but tonight he would circulate around Nome and learn as much as he could.

CHAPTER FIVE

As Moaka promised, he was at the steps of the White Castle Hotel when James exited the hotel's front door. Moaka led the way, and they made their way to Harris' to buy supplies and equipment. James purchased several sets of loose-fitting wool and soft leather clothes that were fleece-lined and fur-trimmed. Moaka made continual checks with James, ensuring they acquired the proper supplies for the trip to Barrow. He also inventoried the supplies that would be needed for later use such as salt, ammunition, rope, traps, and snowshoes for Kincaid. They bought so many supplies, equipment, and food that Moaka was concerned about getting everything on his sled with Kincaid riding on it also.

Suddenly, James felt someone grab the sleeve of his new outer garment he had just donned, and jerked hard enough to spin him around until he was looking into the eyes of a man he didn't know. James' first reflex was to defend himself given the experience he had yesterday. James' blow to the stranger was squarely to the face, which knocked him to the ground. Instantly, three men jumped on James and started beating him with closed fists. Seeing the chain of events unfolding, Moaka jumped into the fight attempting to beat the men off from Kincaid.

The battle ensuing, all parties eventually ended up on the ground hitting and pounding on each other like a bunch of schoolchildren. Not long into the fight, the man James had a hold on started yelling for the other men to stop fighting and get away. Hearing that, James let the man go, and stood up while letting the other man get up.

As James' victim regained his feet, he started sputtering and swearing as he looked at Kincaid and yelled, "Are you that greenhorn Nealy sent up here?"

"Yeah, what of it, and who the hell are you?" James screamed back.

"I'm Ray Harris and I'm getting damn tired of wet-nursing the idiots that asshole keeps sending up here," he loudly responded.

Somewhat more calmly James rebutted, "Well in the first place I'm not an idiot and Don Nealy is a friend of mine." As James made a fist and shook it at Harris, he continued, "If you want to make something of it we can continue. I've used a voucher to pay for all the supplies that we were overcharged for so that should make you happy." In a lower tone James continued, "I don't feel right about paying you what your clerk wanted, but apparently your outfit is the contact up here at least for now, so I'll have to go along."

Belligerently, Harris retorted, "Well, take your stuff and go. I'm sick and tired of you greenhorns."

＊　＊　＊

The sled was loaded sometime after noon as Kincaid crawled on top of all the gear and Moaka hailed his team forward. At the edge of Nome, Moaka smiled to himself, and yelled down to Kincaid asking, "You want fight more?"

James could hardly hear Moaka's remark through his wolverine-rimmed hood, but the only response was to wave his arm forward.

Two hours' travel brought James to a despairing decision. "Stop this damn sled, Moaka!" James yelled, as he tried desperately to adjust his position for dismounting the rocking, rolling, contraption called a dog sled.

"*Nutkarpok, Nutkarpok*," Moaka hollered to the dogs over the top of the struggling Kincaid who was half out of the stopping sled. Putting a small amount of pressure down on the *kresuktautit*—sled brake with his left foot to bring the sled to a full stop, Moaka removed his wolverine face cover and smiled to himself and asked, "Kincaid, say?"

Moaka looked down at the struggling body form, as he watched Kincaid exiting the sled. The commotion resembled a large walrus struggling to get free from between two rocks.

Falling over the top rail of the sled, James slammed onto the frozen, snow-covered surface. Glancing up at Moaka then back to the ground, James declared, "Moaka this has got to change. We haven't been on the trail even one day, and I already feel like I will never make the trip to Barrow riding on this damn thing." Struggling to maneuver his body to a sitting position, James peered around the fur-lined parka hood at the smiling Moaka and angrily blurted, "What the hell are you smiling at?"

His arms folded together, Moaka leaned on the guide bars of the sled, and calmly asked, "What Kincaid want?"

Still in the sitting position, James gestured toward the sled with his mittened hand and responded, "Hell, I don't know. Maybe move some of that junk around so I won't be riding on a lump."

"Lump?" Moaka quickly questioned with a puzzled facial expression.

As James shook his head in frustration, he made a motion with his hand like the top of a hill and replied, "You know, a lump."

Yellow teeth shining through Moaka's wide smile he nodded and replied, "*Koksukpok*—whale hump"

"That's right," James explained, "Just like a whale's hump." James tried to repeat the word that Moaka had just spoken in his Native tongue, but it was a bad imitation.

Moaka laughed and said, "You say here," as he motioned to his chest.

James was discovering that the Native language was spoken with most of the enunciation occurring in the upper chest and throat. The language was very guttural in sound and it was laborious to speak it.

James motioned with his mitten hands, saying, "Let's move the gear around so as to flatten the load out. That way I can lay flat or sit up and lean against the back of the sled." As James was explaining what he wanted, he knew Moaka was thinking about what to do because he was watching James' hand motions showing to flatten out.

Moving from the back of the sled, Moaka began to remove the canvas tarp from the load.

James struggled to his feet and started walking toward the front of the sled.

Moaka instantly yelled, "Kincaid, stop!"

Scared half out of his wits, James whirled, "What the hell Moaka!"

"No go by dog. Not know."

With a wave of his hand into the air, James fired back, "I wasn't going near the stupid dogs."

"Kincaid, dog no stupid," Moaka sternly fired back.

Nodding his head, James' lowered voice responded, "Okay Moaka, the dogs aren't stupid, but I was just coming to the front of the sled to help out with the canvas tarp."

"Kincaid, trail short time, tired?"

Frustration starting to set in, James shook his head and replied, "No. I'm not tired. It's just that these clothes are too damn big," and as he shoved back the fur hood, he finished his statement, "And this damn hood is like looking through a tunnel."

"Clothes warm. Ride sled, no fight sled." As Moaka began to move the gear around on the sled, he continued, "Kincaid show."

James hurriedly stepped forward and began to place the frozen fish, long knife, both axes, and the coil of rope in such a manner that the load was flatter.

Moaka moved to the front of the sled and began moving gear away from the front of the sled toward the back following James' lead in flattening the load.

Once the sled's cargo was redistributed and covered, James again mounted the sled, and Moaka hailed the team and they were off again.

Listening to the occasional barking and whining of the dogs, the scraping of the wooden runners on the frozen surface, and Moaka's hailing to the dogs, James settled into his new position on the sled with somewhat more comfort. The afternoon soon became gray light, and eventually Moaka hailed the team to stop.

In the waning gray light, James could barely make out a small structure or something. Not sure, he asked Moaka as he pointed, "What is that just ahead of us over there."

"*Okkoarmisiortok*—shelter," Moaka replied.

Sliding off the sled, James straightened his body, trying to get the kinks out. "Moaka, how far did we go today?"

"One day."

In a rather frustrated voice James responded, "One day, what does that mean?"

Chuckling, Moaka replied, "Kincaid, distance by day."

"All right, Moaka, how many days to Barrow?"

"Twenty-one or twenty-two," was Moaka's somewhat tiring reply, and continuing Moaka explained, "Sled heavy for dog."

"Moaka, go ahead to the shelter and I'll meet you there after I stretch my legs some with a short walk."

Moaka immediately headed the team in the direction of the shelter, as James was left standing in the stillness. James remembered Moaka telling him that before, and he had not equated the time element into days of travel, rather he thought, *Days verses miles of travel per day. It wasn't a big deal, just a different perspective.*

Arriving at the half wooden and half snow-constructed shelter, James asked, "What can I do to help set up camp?"

Moaka's quickly answered, "No camp, skins," surprised James.

"What! No camp, what are we going to eat?"

Moaka was busy starting to unpack some items from the sled and didn't respond.

"What are we going to eat?" James inquired again.

Straightening up from his unpacking, and in a reassuring voice Moaka replied, "Dry meat. Dog eat fish."

In the diminishing light, James could see Moaka moving with such a fluid and confident motion as to reassure James that Moaka was just what he was looking for in a guide. He seemed to have his priorities in mind, for the best possible trip they could have, considering the elements they were experiencing.

"Here, Moaka, let me help you get some of this stuff out of the way," James said, as he leaned over the sled and began getting the frozen fish for the dogs.

As the food for the dogs was unloaded and stacked on the frozen, snow-covered ground, Moaka instructed, "Kincaid go shelter. Take skin stay. No help now. Help later."

Hauling the skins to the shelter, James could barely see Moaka staking out the dogs at distances away from each other for feeding. Each dog had a small chain around its neck that was hooked to a steel stake and was driven into the frozen surface. When the dogs were all staked, Moaka returned to the sled to get the pieces of fish. He then gave each dog a piece. Each dog growled low as the meat was being devoured. As Moaka returned to the shelter leading his lead dog, James wondered what was going to be required of him.

About five feet from James, Moaka stopped and in a stern sounding voice ordered James, "Kincaid, stand up. Take glove off. Hold hand out. Stand still."

Moaka led the dog to James as the lead was being held on a short leash. The animal was huge and he moved ahead slowly, smelling James' hand, and growled low in his throat. Instantly Moaka jerked the chain very hard and the dog backed away from James. Again, Moaka pulled the dog toward James. The dog again smelled James' hand and this time there was no growling sound.

Moaka pulled the dog away from James, and as he sat down on the skins that James had spread out on the frozen snow, he smiled at James, and said, "Kincaid, sit down."

Being wary of the dog that could rip him apart at any moment, James was in complete astonishment. Slowly shaking his head, he commented, "That was amazing."

James lowered himself down on the skins, and made sure that Moaka was between him and the dog. "What is the dog's name and how old is he?"

"Anore, mean wind. Two seasons," Moaka replied.

Shaking his head side to side, James chuckled and commented, "I don't know, Moaka, distance is marked by days, a guy names his dog wind, and he's not two years old, but two seasons old. Moaka, I've come to a strange land with strange people, but I'm looking forward to every day. I'm going to be counting on you to help me learn the ways of this country and its people."

"Kincaid, how long stay?" Before James could answer, Moaka further inquired, "What do here."

"Right now, Moaka, I can't tell you for sure how long I'm going to be in this new frontier, but I can tell you it will be for quite a while, and quite a while will be measured in years. As far as what I'm doing up here, well," pausing, James thought before continuing, "I'm here to scout the country, tell what is here and what is not here. I'm here to discover the secrets this land has to give. Finally, but not least, I'm here to discover what kind of wildlife survives in this cold, desolate country. This place is called Mr. Seward's Ice Box by some folks down below, and many people would like to know what we bought from the Czar of Russia. Also I need to inform the Natives that Alaska is now part of the United States."

"Much work, Kincaid," Moaka enthusiastically responded as he continued questioning, "Kincaid need guide all time? Moaka guide Kincaid. Moaka know all land."

Barely being able to see Moaka's face in the star-lighted darkness James said, "That's good Moaka, I think we can be a great help to each other. I've just got to get my feet on the ground around here."

"Feet on ground?"

"It's nothing," James responded. "It's kind of a joke that means learning what you're doing." James and Moaka ate their dried meat, rolled themselves in the skins, and let the night pass.

The next morning James was awakened with the barking of dogs, as Moaka had the team hooked up and was getting ready to go, and it wasn't completely light yet. Resting on his elbows James yelled at Moaka over the dogs, "When do we get to the cafe for breakfast?"

Moaka stopped, pointed back toward Nome, and replied, "Cafe," and as he swung his body around to point to the open spaces they were headed for, he continued, "life and knowing."

Getting up and folding the skins, James hollered, "By the damn, Moaka, you're quite the philosopher. We'll hit the cafe on the way back someday."

James carried the skins over to the sled and Moaka handed him some dried meat for breakfast.

As Moaka was checking the dogs' lines, James got into the sled and ate. He watched Moaka walk past each of his fourteen dogs and Anore, his lead dog, checking each dog's condition for the day's trip.

James knew he'd been lucky to locate Moaka. Actually, Moaka had located him and James could not be more satisfied.

As Moaka started returning to the sled, he noticed James in the sled waiting. Barely shaking his head inside of his hood he thought, *Kincaid has no idea about taking care of dogs.* Pausing to touch one of his dogs, Moaka stated, "Soon Kincaid need know dog," as he motioned toward the dogs with his hand. "Moaka teach."

They stopped early that evening to let the dogs get some extra rest, and James got an opportunity to ask Moaka more questions.

The dogs staked and fed, both men settled down beside the small cooking fire. Staring into the flames with their own private thoughts, James broke the silence by inquiring, "How did you learn to speak English?"

Raising his head to look at James he replied, "Missionary." Reaching into the fire to adjust a stick that was not burning properly to Moaka's satisfaction, he continued, "Religious people."

"Where are your parents, Moaka?"

Taking a deep breath and still looking into the fire, Moaka replied dryly, "Dead."

Alarmed, James instantly responded, "That's too bad, Moaka. I'm sorry. How did they die?"

Without any change in speaking tone or facial expression, Moaka replied, "Polar bear kill."

Silence fell over the two men again until Moaka asked, "Kincaid got woman?"

"No, Moaka, I don't have a woman. Do you have a woman?"

Still sitting cross-legged at the fire Moaka raised back and stretched his arms out and smiling proudly replied, "Moaka have wife. She at Teshpuk."

"Where in hell is Teshpuk?" James probed.

Raising his arm, Moaka pointed, "Four day past Barrow, you see."

Lying over on one elbow James inquired further, "What is your wife's name?"

"Kincaid say Tess."

James cooked some seal meat while Moaka tended the dogs. They enjoyed their evening meal with conversations pertaining to hunting, fishing, Native life, and each other's likes and dislikes.

As both men fell silent and eventually the fire died down, both retired for the night in their sleeping skins.

CHAPTER SIX

After sixteen days on the trail, the trip had become long and uneventful, and James was starting to get very tired of seeing nothing but trees, brush, and snow. The country was beautiful and the farther north they traveled the fewer trees they saw as the terrain flattened out much more. They had seen several kinds of animals—foxes, wildcat species, hares, and when crossing frozen rivers the otters were always playing: always staying near their breathing holes in case danger approached. Many times, they spotted deer and elk in stands of timber. Game was everywhere, and almost to the point of being indescribable, there was so much of it. For all the country's splendor and remoteness, the journey was starting to get tiresome.

Just when James thought he could take no more of the rocking and rolling of the sled motion, he heard Moaka hail to his dogs to stop. James felt Moaka step off the back of the sled and heard him say, "Kincaid, be here."

Becoming familiar with Moaka's speech, James understood he was to drive the team. Moaka had told him that one day he would let him drive the team, and much to James' delight the day had arrived. Excited about the prospect of this new experience, he jumped from the sled. James approached the rear of the sled, and Moaka stepped back to let James stand on the runner footpads.

With an easygoing and patient tone, Moaka started explaining to

James how to control the sled and team. James listened intently about turning, stopping, starting, helping push, and riding. Once some of the basics were explained, Moaka finished with, "I ride," and as he was getting into the sled, he continued, "I say to dog."

Standing on the footpads and looking down at Moaka settling into the sled, James felt his hands sweating inside his gloves, and he knew he had to relax. This was going to be a learning experience, nothing more and nothing less. Moaka had explained all the details, what was there to go wrong.

"Kincaid, move sled."

Without further instruction, James jarred the sled loose from the possibility of the runners being frozen to the surface. Moaka hailed the team and the crisp breeze filled James' hood and whipped it off his head, exposing dark, uncombed hair. Quickly he bent down and flipped the hood back into place.

James mentally reviewed Moaka's instructions, turn right—hail the dogs to the right, lean the sled to the right, turn left—hail the dogs to the left, and lean the sled to the left. He could feel the power of the dogs all pulling together, and when little rises occurred he would push with one foot as Moaka had instructed, to help the dogs.

James thought, *Considering everything, driving a dog team seems to be reasonably easy. All I have to do is keep the sled under control. Their speed and direction would be taken care of by Moaka.*

Just ahead James could see where he was going to swerve around some snow-covered brush. A distance before Anore approached the obstacle; Moaka raised his left arm and hailed to Anore to go left. That was James' signal to lean the sled slightly to the left and put his weight on the left runner footpad.

Suddenly, disaster struck. James had leaned the sled too much to the left and the sled toppled over on its left side spilling out Moaka and most of the contents.

Moaka rolled free of the sled and the supplies continued to slide across the frozen snow. Fortunately, Moaka quickly regained his composure enough to see the dogs dragging the sled on its side with James being dragged along. The equipment, supplies, and frozen meat still being bounced out of the laid-over sled.

Moaka jumped to his feet and yelled, "*Nutkarpok, nutkarpok,*" and the dog team stopped.

Moaka hurried to James' side as he was just letting go of one of the sled runners and was rolling over trying to get up.

Realizing that Moaka was standing beside him, James hastily questioned, "Is the sled broken or anything hurt?"

Not being able to keep a straight face Moaka started smiling and replied, "No. Need clean sled."

James noticed Moaka's large grin, and he realized he had been a victim of Moaka's humor. "What the hell are you smiling at?"

Not being able to restrain himself any longer, Moaka started to laugh and responded, "Kincaid, first lesson," as he bent down and lifted the sled upright. "Kincaid okay?"

James began dusting the snow off his animal-skin clothing and responded, "Yeah, Moaka, I'm just fine. I hope that nothing got broken or any of the dogs got hurt. How are you?"

"Kincaid," Moaka said as he started to pick up and sort through the equipment and supplies that had tumbled out of the sled, "Stay sled, I pick up."

"No, Moaka, you may be the guide, and I might be the boss, but you sure as hell aren't my servant." Working together, both men began to pick up the supplies and place them back into the sled.

To James' surprise, once the sled was reloaded and the dogs were settled down, Moaka climbed back into the sled and casually commented, "Kincaid, more."

Breaking the runners loose and tapping Moaka on the shoulder,

Moaka hailed the dogs and the sled jerked ahead. James was determined that he was not going to have any more mishaps while having the responsibility of driving the sled.

They had traveled for only a short distance and James felt his face starting to get cold. He tried to adjust his hood to close more, but he knew he would have to adjust his face piece higher to stop the cold wind on his checks, as he started to appreciate the face cover. He waited until what he thought looked like a good smooth run ahead and then began adjusting his face piece. Holding onto the sled handles with one hand and trying to work the face piece with the other was not working. Leaning down over the sled and trying to hook his elbows on the handles, he attempted to adjust the face cover with both hands. About the time he got his face covered, the sled went over a large bump. James tried to grab the handles, but it was too late, and he was thrown from the back of the sled.

James yelled to Moaka as loud as he could, as he rolled to a stop just in time to see Moaka turn around in the sled and look back at him.

Moaka hailed to the dogs, and the sled came to a stop. Moaka sprang from the sled and ran back to James. Fear showing on Moaka's face, he started yelling, "Kincaid, what do? Okay?"

Still sitting on the snow, James shook his head back and forth and sighed heavily responding, "Moaka I don't know what happened. I was adjusting my face cover when I guess the sled hit a bump, and I went flying off the back end."

"Go wrong today," Moaka replied as he helped James back to his feet. Then he said, "Kincaid do more."

Shaking his head, James laughed and responded, "Damn, Moaka, you think that's a good idea? Next time I might wrap us around a tree or run us off a cliff."

Moaka's only response was, "Kincaid do more."

The team was trotting along at a good, even pace that could eat up many miles in the process of a day, and James seemed to be more aware of the sled movements as it slid over different kinds of terrain. He was also learning the influence he had on the movement of the sled. If he leaned back holding onto the handles he could lift the front of the sled, and if he leaned slightly to the right or left he could feel the right or left runner cut in. He practiced pushing with one foot and then the other to become efficient from both sides. Smiling beneath his face cover, James knew he was learning what he had to know to survive in this country, and Moaka was a fine teacher.

Seeing Moaka raise his arm and hailing the team to stop, James stepped lightly down on the brake. As James looked down at the brake that was made out of antler bone, he wanted to be sure that it dug into the hard surface to stop the sled and keep it from moving.

"I do," Moaka commented dryly as he walked away from the sled to relieve himself. "We come village."

Rolling into the sled, James felt relaxed, it felt good to just lie there and do nothing, and he realized that driving the sled was hard work and tiring after a while. Moaka hailed his well-trained team and they were off again.

Suddenly Moaka yelled, "Kincaid look."

Through the haze, James could just barely make out a flickering light of a campfire. They had been traveling for sixteen days and this would be their first sign of life other than wildlife, and James was excited about meeting more Native Eskimos to learn as much as possible, and as fast as possible. Moaka had already started his lessons in the Native tongue, but the language was very difficult to speak.

Moaka stopped the team a short distance from the small village and said, "Kincaid, stay sled. No live here. I see stay. Say no English here."

Watching Moaka approach the settlement of four skin-covered, small huts, James smiled to himself and thought, *This must be the equivalent of knocking on the door.*

Shortly Moaka returned and excitedly explained, "Kincaid we stay. They have dog. Buy or trade."

Having gotten out of the sled while Moaka was at the little village, James commented, "Go ahead to the village, I want to walk the rest of the way."

Moaka grunted and hailed the dogs for a slow pace into the village.

Dogs, James thought, as he walked toward the village. *Is this where I'm to start getting my team together,* shrugging, *Why not?* James knew that Moaka would help choose good dogs and that would be a big asset. James wondered how old the dogs were and he wondered how many dogs he would need. Moaka had fourteen, and Anore. That seemed to be a lot, but what did he know about it. Reaching the first hut, he saw Moaka already staking and feeding the dogs. Moaka still didn't feel comfortable about him being around his dogs yet, especially during feeding time. Moaka's lead, Anore, was still wary of him.

Moaka finished tending the dogs, and came over to James saying, "Kincaid, when get dog, we say English," as he motioned with his hand back and forth between himself and James, "They no say English."

James stooped down to enter the hut entrance, and upon getting inside a most pungent order slammed at the inside of his head. It smelled something like a cross between dead fish and raw rotting guts. Blowing lightly out his nostrils didn't seem to help, for he had to breathe in again. Being seated in a circle, the members of the group welcomed Moaka and him; no one seemed to mind the smell—not even Moaka. The hut was lighted by small shallow lamps burning some kind of oil, and upon closer inspection, James found that the inside of the hut was lined with hanging meat, raw fish, and drying skins.

An old man began passing a wooden bowl around as each person dug into the bowl with their fingers and passed the bowl to the next person. Moaka passed the food bowl to James and motioned with the bowl for him to follow suit. Smelling the contents before digging in James knew that this was something he had never eaten before, but this was food and it didn't seem to be killing them. Dipping his fingers into the soft, meaty food, he pinched some together and placed it into his mouth. James could not figure out if he was so hungry or the food just tasted good. Savoring the food, James noticed that all eyes were upon him. Smiling and leaning toward Moaka, James enquired, "That's very good, do we get more?"

Moaka replied in a low tone, "Yes, more come," as he motioned with his hand in a circle.

Moaka and the Natives talked as if they had known each other for years. Several times during the meal, Natives came in, had short conversations, and left the shelter. James suspected they were the neighbors. Several times hand motions had been directed in James' direction and Moaka would lean over and explain that they were interested in who he was, what he was doing here, and how long he was going to stay.

The conversation seemed to cease as Moaka leaned over to James and said, "Now dog."

No sooner had Moaka spoken, when one of the men got up and went outside and returned shortly with four dogs; all looked to be a year old or more. They all were well built and looked like little bears with their winter coats on, except one. One of the dogs was larger and seemed to be stronger and stand straighter than the rest. He was a male with a black back, grey sides, and almost a white chest and belly. The animal looked something like a German shepherd, but with a much heavier built chest and front shoulders, and shorter ears.

James leaned over to Moaka and asked, "Can I handle the dogs?"

"Wait," Moaka quickly replied, and he said something to the older Native and made a motion with his hand from James to the dogs and the older Native nodded his head in approval.

Upon getting approval, James held out his hand toward the large male that had caught his eye. Instantly the dog jumped into James' lap, and rolled him backward. All the Natives including Moaka cheered as Moaka proclaimed, "Good Kincaid, good."

James and Moaka decided to get all four dogs and James wrote them a voucher to be collected at Harris' store in Nome for the supplies that were needed for the trade. They didn't understand the voucher situation until Moaka explained, and the price for the four dogs was three metal hide scrapers, five pounds of salt, and a roll of flannel, all of which would be picked up at Harris' store.

The next morning Moaka hooked up his team, and helped James get the newly acquired dogs ready for the rest of the journey to Barrow. James made a non-slip loop collar around each dog's neck out of leather strips and then attached a leader line to each dog's collar, which was then tied to the back of the sled in different lengths. It was hard to believe that all the animals came from the same litter. The three smaller dogs were fighting the lines for all their worth, but the larger male that was tied with the longer leader line stood still, straight, and tall, never seeming to twitch a muscle or whine.

The young dogs hooked to the back of the sled, James and Moaka left the small settlement headed for Barrow, which was about three or four days' journey. At first, the three smaller dogs were dragged along the frozen snow surface, but eventually they figured out that it was easier to trot along, rather than to be dragged. *The large male,* James mused, *was never drug, nor was his line ever pulled tight, as he seemed to have a built in instinct for the movement of the sled.* Several times James rolled to the side to look back around Moaka to check the dogs and he was amazed to see the proud-hearted behavior of the large male. He carried himself tall with a strong even gait and brayed occasionally for no apparent reason. James didn't know much about dogs, but this dog impressed him, at least so far.

Hailing the dogs to a stop, James knew it was his turn to drive and as Moaka stepped from the rear of the sled he casually commented to James, "Kincaid, look," and pointed toward the new large male. "Spirit high, proud."

"Yeah, Moaka, you could be right, he seems well beyond his age." Staring at the new male, James walked over to him and the animal started whining and squirreling around as if he was getting ready to play. James knelt down and reached for the dog, but found himself on the ground as the animal leaped for him to play. James grabbed the dog and they rolled over, and over being tangled in the leash line.

Out of nowhere, Moaka stood over them, grabbing the dog by his neck fur, and held the animal away from James' face. With alarm on his face, Moaka stammered out, "Kincaid, get up."

Struggling to remove the leash line from around him and the dog, James hurriedly got to his feet. Anger swelled inside of him, as he demanded, "What the hell is the matter with you, Moaka?"

"Kincaid," and walking a short ways away while rolling his hands together as if trying to figure out what to say, he turned back toward James, "Keep dog, dog."

"Moaka, I got a feeling that this dog is going to be one of the best leads on these north slopes, and he will be that even with all the playing around I do with him. You will undoubtedly show me many tricks and teach me much about dogs and dog teams, but I don't want you to ever interfere with me playing with this dog again."

Moaka climbed into the sled, sat there without a sound, then commented quietly, "Kincaid say."

The days passed as James and Moaka traded positions driving and riding, and James felt he had started to get the feel of driving the team. Moaka was very attentive to his team and James learned a lot about the care of the dogs. Moaka was very patient helping James tend the new dogs and teaching them the ways of being a sled dog. Anore was always let to roam free after the evening feeding, and he was very curious about the new additions that had been obtained. He didn't seem to pay much attention to the smaller young dogs, other than to approach them as they crouched in the submissive position, but he did challenge the large, new male that was as large as Moaka's lead. Moaka explained to Kincaid that the large male was the only dog that offered Anore any threat. Anore was just making sure that the newcomer was straight on who was the boss in the dog world.

Stopping several times along the way at small communities of three or four huts, and one much larger of about ten huts, they managed to purchase or trade for six more dogs, which made James a team so far of ten dogs. Moaka figured they could get the rest of the dogs in Barrow or Teshpuk.

CHAPTER SEVEN

The sun's blinding rays glistened off the crystal white snow, and the cold air of the afternoon was dangerous to exposed skin. The sound of the runners scraping across the hard, snowy surface, and the occasional barking of the dogs was starting to become monotonous, even though Moaka and James were trading off driving and riding.

Suddenly Moaka exclaimed, "Kincaid," as he pointed off to the right and excitedly shouted, "Barrow, Barrow."

Straightening up in the sled, James could see at a distance a large number of structures. They would finally be able to get away from the sled for a while. His instructions from Nealy and the map sketches were that he was to make his territory east of Barrow as far as he wanted to go. He knew this was to be his jump-off point and his heart was in his throat with excitement. James had already started entering details into his log, including the game they had observed, how the country spread, and weather conditions.

As the sled came closer to Barrow, James turned slightly back to Moaka. "Stop the sled; I'd like to walk the rest of the way. I want to enjoy this and remember my first visit to Barrow for a long time."

Moaka hailed the dogs to a stop, and James rolled off the sled, stretched, and started to walk toward the settlement. Suddenly, the large male started pulling on the lead line and howling and braying as if he were being killed. James turned back to Moaka and asked, "What's the matter with the dog?"

"He want go," and smiling, continued enthusiastically, "he know master," Moaka replied.

James turned and started walking toward the braying dog and stopped beside Moaka who was standing at the back of the sled and without looking at Moaka, James said, "I think I'll name him Bray."

"Bray, strong name."

And so it is, James thought, as he reached down to untie the lead line to Bray. No sooner had James got the line untied when Bray jumped at him, almost knocking him over in his excitement. Staggering and struggling to keep his footing on the slick surface, James looked at Moaka and laughing said, "Damn, he's strong already."

With a quick glance down at Bray, Moaka emphatically responded, "Good lead, big, strong."

When James came close to the settlement, he and Bray stopped. While they waited for Moaka to come along, James put a hand leash on Bray to control him while around other animals and people. Moaka had walked his team in at a slow pace so he would not get to the village ahead of James. Stopping his team so the sled was next to James, Moaka stated, "We go in."

"Well, Moaka, you go and present us, and I'll stand by the dogs."

Smiling, Moaka stated with assurance and enthusiasm, "Moaka know people. No ask. We stay many days. Need get more dog. Come," and waving his arm to follow, he led James into Barrow.

After getting the dogs staked and fed, they announced themselves at one of the larger sod huts located on the outskirts of town, and they were promptly welcomed in. Entering, he and Moaka were greeted with hugging and slapping on the back. Later, James learned that these were some of Moaka's relations, but Moaka didn't elaborate at the time. The evening meal was served as the other evening meals James had eaten with the other Natives, so he was starting to get the hang of some of the mealtime rituals. After the meal, there was talk and laughter of travels and adventures since Moaka's last visit. Moaka had tried to keep James informed, but sometimes the conversation progressed too rapidly. James was also starting to pick up a few Native gestures, words, and phrases, but the language was very hard for him to pronounce and interpret because of the guttural tones.

These are a happy people, James thought, *they have little or no knowledge of the outside world, but they seemed to be doing just fine.*

The next morning, Moaka approached James as he was waiting at the outside cooking fire for his coffee to make, and asked jokingly, "How team?"

Laughing, James responded, "Well, they seem to be full of energy." As James motioned over toward Bray who was standing and wagging his tail, he continued, "Damn fine dog, don't you think, Moaka?"

"Strong dog," Moaka replied. "Need more dog? Barrow has many dogs. Kincaid get team?"

Throwing his hand in the air, James responded, "Of course, but hell, I don't even have a sled or any harness."

Smiling and slapping James on the back and almost spilling the coffee James had just poured, Moaka commanded, "Kincaid come."

James hurried to catch up as Moaka disappeared around a hut. As James rounded the corner of the hut, he was met by two other Natives and Moaka. Waving him on, Moaka stepped aside to reveal a newly built sled. Excitedly, Moaka sputtered out, "It Kincaid."

Walking around the sled and running his hand over the excellent workmanship, James shook his head saying, "By the damn, it's beautiful, it's beautiful. Isn't it Moaka? It's beautiful." Excitement growing in his voice, James could not keep from smiling and almost laughing with amazement. Stammering, James looked at Moaka and asked, "How much Moaka, how much does this cost?"

Moaka smiled and turned to the other Natives and said something, then turned back to Kincaid and responded, "*Aituserk*—Gift."

James, almost yelling with excitement, exclaimed, "Moaka, I can't take this as a gift! I'll pay for it, whatever it costs."

The Natives and Moaka were talking among themselves as Moaka finally said to James, "If buy dog from Sungo, he give sled."

"What about the harness, rope, and whip?" James inquired excitedly, and before Moaka could answer James stammered, "*Anut*—harness and *tiggarut*—whip." James wanted the Natives to think he was quite proud of some of his recently learned Native tongue.

Moaka laughed at James' pronunciation of the Native tongue and the other Natives followed Moaka's lead. Moaka walked over to James, slapped him on the shoulder, and responded with the correct pronunciation. "*Anut* and *tiggarut* give." Moaka, acting proud and as if introducing James, waved his gloved hand toward him and exclaimed, "This man, James Kincaid, is a good man. He has started to learn our way of life and language."

Later that day Moaka informed James that the Natives were a little distrusting of strangers, but word was spread that James wanted to live like the Eskimo, and had even begun to learn the language. Moaka had also told James that everybody would help train the dogs, if any help was needed.

James was impressed with Barrow. It had a supplies store, laundry, post office, small livery for summer use, hotel, small place to eat, couple of saloons, meeting hall, and a church. All the buildings in town were built of rough wood. Holes in the walls were filled with dried mud. The other structures on the outskirts were either canvas or skins tents, sod, or ice igloos. It had been settled by white men as a jump-off point to the northern slopes. The sea route to Barrow was open only from late spring to early fall, but it seemed ample time to receive supplies and drop off mail, miners, hunters, and resident of the area.

"Well, Moaka, as soon as we get the rest of my team and get them trained we should be able to push on to Teshpuk. I figure it will take about a couple of weeks more to get my team set up, at least in the rough anyway. Will Tess be all right till we get back to Teshpuk?"

"She strong," Moaka quickly answered.

James couldn't help liking and respecting Moaka's simplicity. It was plain to James that if the whole world could have Moaka's mindset, many problems could be wiped away. These courageous people in this far North Country didn't need much and they didn't expect much.

During the routine of the next weeks, Moaka and James bought the rest of James' team. Fourteen dogs in all, not including Bray. Moaka explained that it really didn't take that many dogs to pull the sled, but it made it easier on all the dogs to have extra just in case the going got tough. Some of James' dogs were quite young, but they were growing to full strength fast.

James worked hard to discipline his team without using the whip, and he informed Moaka that he wanted the dogs to pull because they wanted to, not because of fear. However, one thing James learned early on was that the dogs enjoyed pulling. It took a lot of patience from him and Moaka and many hours of training, and the Natives thought he was doing it all wrong, but James was convinced his way was the right way. James knew Moaka was also impressed by the way the team was turning out. When they started, Moaka didn't like James' way of training the dogs either, but as time went on Moaka was starting to understand what Kincaid was trying to do. James felt that the way the team was working out that Moaka was starting to have some confidence in him and his abilities for training dogs.

James had wondered why the typical sled dog was not more like a pet, but after being around dogs and Natives even for this short time, he understood. None of the Natives treated their dogs mean, but rather just as another tool, very little affection, very little petting, except for their lead dog.

When James had started harnessing his team in the traces and tug lines it seemed they would never perform as a single unit, but as time went on, and with each day's practice the dogs became a team. James would reward with praise and discipline with scolding, but he never used the whip once. He loved each one of his dogs, and they showed their love for him by performing well every day. Bray was an exceptional animal, and several Natives wanted to trade or buy his lead. James thought, *Bray is the best lead in the country, even better than Anore.* Bray was a natural lead dog and he was quick to learn new commands. Several times James had to break up fights between his dogs, but never with a whip. Scolding seemed to suffice for punishment.

Moaka hailed his team to a walk, and brought Anore up even with Bray, and speaking loud enough hailed James, "Kincaid, stop."

Hailing Bray to a halt, and resting down on the bone spike, James inquired, "What is it, Moaka?"

"How team?" Moaka cautiously inquired.

James gazed out over the backs of fifteen dogs, and smiled confidently. "Moaka, this is the best damn team on the north slopes, and I'd put them up against any team, any time."

"Good, Kincaid. Go Teshpuk tomorrow."

Nodding, James responded, "Do we get supplies today or wait until tomorrow?"

"Get tomorrow," Moaka acknowledged.

* * *

Both teams halted on a small ridge, and James' eyes strained against the sun reflecting off the snow-covered terrain. Blinking his eyes and then closing them tightly, he commented to Moaka, "I guess I'd better put on these damn bone shades you made for me," as he felt several pockets before he located their hiding place. Donning them James continued, "It's incredible how much these things cut the glare from the white shining surface."

"Kincaid, wear. No blind." Moaka pointed slightly off to the right as he continued, "Look far place. Teshpuk there."

From the vantage point they had, it looked to be about ten miles to Teshpuk.

James could sense Moaka's enthusiasm in his voice as he excitedly remarked, "Teshpuk soon, Kincaid."

"That will be wonderful, Moaka. Then I'll get to meet Tess and all her family."

The stop on top of the ridge was not only to see where Teshpuk was, but was also for the dogs to take a breather. Moaka finally commented in a cheery tone, "Dog rest."

James sensed Moaka was getting impatient as he hailed Bray toward Teshpuk. He always seemed to lead out, but that was always the way Moaka wanted it, and it didn't make any difference to James.

Walking his team past the first hut of Teshpuk, he knew that Moaka wanted to come in from the other side of the village so he could surprise Tess without being seen coming through the village. Slowing the dogs down to a slow walk, James marveled at the huts spread about the area. There was a small main passageway or street down the middle of things, but the huts were not all lined up along each side. Rather they were a bit scattered, but there did seem to be a left and right to the place. The huts were all built about the same way, rather rounded on top. Some were larger than others with seemly additions added on to the sides or back. Some appeared to be wood frame, by what he could see, and then covered with sod. There were tents made of animal skins in several places. All had a single entrance and smoke drifting from some mysterious unseen hole in the top.

Not paying particular attention to where he was going as he was looking about the village, James heard someone yell.

"*Nutkarpok.*"—Stop.

Immediately, he saw Bray sitting beside a person on the ground, a woman, a white woman! Moreover, she was trying to get up and brush herself off.

Muttering half-aloud, "What the hell," all he could do was stare. The women that was dressed in Native skin attire, was definitely white, and had the prettiest long blonde hair he'd ever seen. She was small and slender, as best as he could see, and she had very sharp and distinct facial features, which made her appear to be very nice-looking.

"There is no use in cursing," the English-speaking voice returned, this time in a lower tone. "I'm fine. Your lead dog is quite gentle and he didn't try to bite me when he knocked me down. You look as if you have seen a ghost."

"Who are you?" James finally managed to blurt out.

"My name is Suzette Caron, and this is my hut." She pointed to the nearest structure. "I teach school to the local children, and teach English to the adults, at least to the ones that want to learn. Who are you?"

"I'm Kincaid!" he exclaimed as he was starting to feel nervous. "I mean I'm James Kincaid. Moaka and the Natives call me Kincaid, but my first name is Kincaid, I mean my first name is James. The Natives call me Kincaid for my whole name, but it's not. I'm here to study wildlife."

Suzette began giggling slightly as she approached James and asked, "Well, James Kincaid, will you please remove your parka hood."

As James shoved back his parka hood, he felt the cold air bite at his neck and ears.

Stopping a short distance from James, Suzette asked, "Tess's Moaka?" Very excitedly, she questioned, "Is Moaka back from Nome?"

"Yes," James quickly answered. "Moaka and I will be working together for awhile."

Almost jumping off the ground and clapping her hands together she looked to James as if she was about to be uncontrollable. "I've got to go and tell Tess right away."

"Don't bother, Miss Caron, Moaka is probably there right now. He wanted to surprise her and her family with his person and some gifts he bought in Nome."

Calming some, Suzette asked, "How long are you going to be working around Teshpuk?"

"I don't really know for sure, Miss Caron, but it will be for quite some time, maybe even as long as four or five years or even longer. I have hired Moaka as my guide and we'll be working together most of the time. I'm sorry Bray knocked you down, he probably outweighs you, but he just likes to play. I doubt that he would ever bite you; I've made a friend out of him besides a good lead dog, and you won't find that in many sled dogs around here."

"You're right about that, Mr. Kincaid, most of the sled dogs happens to be quite untamed and unpredictable." Hesitating just for a second she continued, "The reason I wanted you to push your parka hood back is that I wanted to be sure whom I was talking with. It's not often I get a chance to talk with someone from down below. I knew you were not Native when I heard you curse."

Shifting uneasily, James lifted his arm and pointed as he commented, "Well, Miss Caron, you won't have to wait much longer to see Moaka. He and someone else are coming toward us now."

Turning, Suzette exclaimed, "That's Tess with him! Don't they look happy together? They are probably coming to look for you."

"Look, Tess," Moaka said, "Kincaid didn't waste any time finding Suzette. I didn't tell him about her. I thought I'd let him find her for himself."

As Moaka and Tess approached, Moaka stated, "Kincaid find Suzette.

"Yes, Moaka, we've met."

Moaka stopped to talk to Suzette, and James was immediately approached by Tess. Stopping her short frame in front of him, Tess strained her neck to look up into James' eyes and rather startled him with, "Kincaid?"

"Yes," James quickly replied, and asked, "And I bet you are Tess?"

"I Tess. You like Suzette? She got no man. Kincaid have wife?"

Feeling quite intimidated and uncomfortable for himself and Suzette, James finally responded, "Moaka, where do I eat and sleep while we are here?"

"Tess!" Moaka exclaimed loudly, and she immediately stepped back and stood next to him. "Kincaid tired. Stake dog, eat."

"Kincaid stay us," Tess answered.

"Kincaid," Moaka explained, "put team," as he pointed, "come eat."

Seeing them turn and walk away, James quietly apologized to Suzette for Tess' bluntness.

"Don't worry about that, Mr. Kincaid," Suzette pleaded, "These Natives are just that way. If they have something to say, they will say it."

"Well, it has been nice meeting you and I hope to see you again," James commented.

"Same here, Mr. Kincaid; I'm not going too far away from this place with the school and all."

Nodding his head, James hailed Bray toward where the team would be staked and fed.

CHAPTER EIGHT

James stood on the back runners of the sled and his thoughts wandered to when he'd first came to the north slopes two years ago as a green Wildlife Biologist. He had been under the impression that a certain territory would be assigned to him and he would work only within that area. Shaking his head and smiling, *that couldn't have been farther from the truth.* Nealy had told him to wander a little, but a person could meander on the north slopes forever and never cross his own path. James kept track of his location for game sightings, and noted unusual landforms and concentrations of wildlife. His main territory lay in the area influenced by the Colville River tributaries from the Brooks Range to the Arctic Ocean. He had been determined to carve a name out, for not only the organization, but himself as well. A man comes to this country and survival is the byword, and reputations and letters of accommodations and the like are not important any more. A man must make do to survive in this great wilderness.

James liked to make early morning runs with the team because he had the chance of spotting wildlife that normally could be not be observed during midday. He had written numerous reports back to Don Nealy about their sightings of wildlife, land, and terrain, and their overall escapades. They had counted *netjerk*—seal in summer, *angutiviark*—birds and *tuktu*—caribou in the spring, and all year long *tireganiersiut*—foxes, *amarok*—wolves, and *nanuk*—polar bears and their cubs. Moaka had shown James many other species of birds that James noted in his reports; he didn't know their names, but rather described them. James also noted many habits and customs of the Native Eskimo. In each report to Don, he had included a rough drawing of a map showing where significant numbers of wildlife were sighted or pertinent landforms existed.

When Don had written back, he had been overjoyed with James' report. He had said he was going to make it up to that big country one day, but recently he had been promoted to the division head at the Seattle station, and he would not be able to make it for a while. Don didn't want James to leave because he was the only one that had stuck it out on the North Slopes.

In most of the villages, a person could find good shelter and lodging for at least one night. Once leaving the protection of the village, your best friends were your rifle, good judgment, and a good dog team.

The Native language was very difficult to learn. Individual words didn't mean one thing, rather one word stood for a thought. James was rather proud of his success in learning at least some of the tongue, and Moaka was always glad to have the Natives see that Kincaid thought enough of the Native culture to learn the language.

Off in the distance, James could see smoke coming over the horizon, gently being lifted skyward toward the blue emptiness of the quiet heavens by the early morning light breeze. This time of year, being about the first part of March, the sun would not show its face for another hour, and then only for about six hours, but the pink glow in the southeastern sky over the Brooks Range was the first encounter of the new day. The thought came to him, *This is a cold, lonely, and wonderful place, all at the same time, and people are special up here; they have to be survivors. They are a happy and joyful people with the determination to accept their destiny as best they could.*

Smiling to himself, James knew the smoke he was seeing was coming from Tess' cooking fire. Tess was a great wife for Moaka. She was a short, stout woman of twenty-seven years, the same age as Moaka, and about two years younger than James. She had very black straight hair like all Natives and she kept it cut short. She could speak sort of broken English like Moaka, but not as good. The Natives learned what English they knew from the early missionaries or Suzette. She was as faithful to Moaka's needs as any wife, and several times, she had asked him what women did or wore in America, but she had not seemed to be too impressed. James remembered she had a problem understanding that Alaska now belonged to the United States, and he still didn't think she had accepted the concept. She acted as though she had everything that was needed to be a good wife, and she hoped to be a mother someday soon.

Moaka had been married to Tess only a short time when the two men had joined up in Nome and Tess had started traveling with Moaka and James on their expeditions not long after they had gotten to Teshpuk. Tess did a good job of being cook and camp tender. She also cared for dogs that had got hurt, tanned skins, and made clothes from hides. Not only had Moaka been a good guide, but also he had become a very good friend. James knew that his success in this untamed land could be credited to how well Moaka had taught him to survive and his determination to be triumphant.

Not taking his eyes from the smoke drifting over the horizon, he thought, *Tess will be impatient to have me return to camp for breakfast.*

Bray had started to bark in anticipation of returning to base camp and the other dogs followed suit. "Damn dog," James muttered aloud. The villager James had gotten Bray from swore him to be the best breed of husky that ever lived or breathed.

"On Bray," James hailed as he broke the runners loose. With a sudden jerk of energy, the dogs and the sled seemed to skim across the hard white flats as if they had taken wings. It had never stopped being exciting to James to ride the runners behind his well-honed team. Adjusting his fur face-piece, he stopped the freezing wind from rushing down and around the back of his neck. The wolverine parka hood would protect his head and face from all angles except head on wind, so it was necessary to have some breaker that would cover the face. Moaka had fashioned him a new pair of bone eyeshades last year, but he didn't wear them much unless the sun was very bright and glaring as it reflected off the snow surface. Besides, they never did fit right. Smiling to himself, James remembered Moaka saying after fitting them on him, "Look like Native."

The dogs were working smoothly together, when he noticed Nel, a large female and his youngest dog, favoring her left front. Hanging on to the rear sled guide handles, he leaned to the left to get a better look at her side. Shaking his head in puzzlement, James could not remember her fighting or getting hurt anytime. He'd have to look at her when they got back to the base camp. The temperature was quite cold, probably somewhere around -15 degrees F and the dog's feet were protected from the cold surfaces with small leather foot protectors that were secured to the paws with leather lacings.

Breaking over the horizon, the camp was just now starting to come into view. The dogs had spotted the camp and James could feel them starting to pull harder. Not having the normal load on the sled, the team was able to increase speed as they came nearer to camp.

CHAPTER NINE

As James' team neared the camp, Anore charged toward Bray. Bray and Anore got alone fine just as long as there wasn't food involved. Sometimes Moaka, as James did with Bray, would let Anore off the stake for a while, and apparently that is what he did this morning because Anore was coming to play.

"Yaw, Yaw!" James yelled, "Get out of here, you stupid mutt!" as Anore swerved off to the side. James knew Moaka didn't like his dogs insulted. Actually, Moaka would sooner have someone insult him.

"Damn that Bray," James muttered, "he's starting to bark at Anore." James shook his head in disgust, knowing that the rest of the team would follow suit. *There they go,* James mused, *each one yapping like they haven't good sense.* The dogs did bark a lot, and James didn't like them barking too much while pulling, because it took too much wind from them.

Hailing Bray around and stopping the sled next to where Moaka was standing, James peered from around the side of his wolverine hood, and yelled over the dogs barking, "Good morning, Moaka." Then he proceeded to walk along his team, quieting them and scolding the ones still barking.

Moaka was getting a kick out of James' irritation, and inquired loud enough for James to hear over all the barking. "Kincaid," he motioned with his head, "what do, in dark morning?"

With a wild slap at Anore, which James really didn't intend to hit him, but to just shut him up, James angrily responded, "Looking, Moaka, just looking. After all, I'm paid to come to this God-forsaken country to study wildlife movement and habitat."

"What see in dark?" Moaka inquired as he put a leash on Anore.

With his eyebrows raised, his eyes wide open, and a slight smile touching his lips, James replied in a low mystical voice, playing on Moaka's superstitions, "What I can't see in the light."

Shaking his head, Moaka countered, "*Kappianartorvik*"—hell. That was about the only curse word he ever used. "Get breakfast, Tess wait."

With a laugh, James waved Moaka on and replied, "Tell Tess I'll be along in just a moment, I've got to check Nel's left foot or shoulder, she favored it some coming in."

"Tess no happy," Moaka warned.

Tess is always worried about me being late, James thought. He really didn't see it as a problem, but she sure did.

James unhooked and staked the team, and checked Nel's condition. Suddenly he heard Bray growl deep in his throat as if some stranger was coming too close. Standing up straight, James searched the horizon, but the small wind gusts were blowing snow around in swirls, making it difficult to see anything very far away. One thing James had learned about Bray, when he growled deep in his throat, he'd better start taking notice and paying attention.

Leaning down slightly to touch the top of Bray's head, James softly responded to Bray's warning with, "Bray, what's the trouble, boy?"

Squinting against the early sun's reflective glare, James figured that Bray must have caught a scent of something. Scanning the horizon in the direction Bray was staring, James could barely make out a shadowed outline. Instantly alarm ripped through James' body as he realized what had alarmed his lead dog. There was a polar bear not more than two hundred yards away from camp.

James bolted for his rifle that was still on the sled, and he pointed in the direction he wanted Moaka to look, and yelled, "Moaka, get your rifle, there's a damn polar bear out there towards the sun!" James knew he wasn't going to kill the polar bear unless he was forced to protect the camp because he didn't like killing unnecessarily.

Out of the corner of his eye, James saw Tess rushing to Moaka's dogs, which had picked up the scent and were beginning to get edgy. Moaka's team being staked and James' still in the harness were now starting to bark after the newcomer threat.

James ran up to Moaka's side with rifle in hand, half out of breath. They searched against the blowing snow for the bear that had ventured so close to camp, and had somehow mysteriously disappeared. It looked to be a large male, and it didn't seem to be too afraid of the men or dogs. With his parka hood thrown back so he could have better hearing and vision, James could feel the movement of the crisp morning breeze biting at his exposed skin. Suddenly the polar bear reappeared just as quickly as it had vanished. The large male had circled, and he was less than fifty yards from camp. James levered a round and took one shot that was aimed low. The effect of the bullet splashing into the snow just in front of the animal quickly deterred any more progress toward camp, and the immediate danger mysteriously disappeared again into the blowing snow.

Silence prevailed between the two men as they both stood against the elements. James could almost feel Moaka's thoughts, as they stood side by side, straining to get another glimpse of the unwanted phantom intruder. Breaking the silence, but not taking his eyes from the snowy horizon James quietly asked, "Did you see him, Moaka?" Knowing all along that Moaka did, James wanted to break the tension that Moaka felt. James knew that Moaka had a built-in hate for the polar bear because of what had happened to his folks. James had never talked to Moaka much about the incident, but he knew Moaka killed any polar bear for vengeance as well as food and fur. That behavior for the Natives was common; these people had been killing and eating polar bear for generations.

Moving his head slowly from left to right, Moaka searched the whiteness for any sign of the animal, and without looking at James he muttered, "White Ghost go quiet. Danger to all."

James responded, "I don't know if the polar bear looked like a ghost, but it's spooky to see a male polar bear in this area, at this time of year."

"Kincaid, say." was Moaka's only response.

Not seeing the bear anymore, James turned back toward camp to pick up where he'd left off tending his team. As he walked back to his team, James remembered the name *Nanuk*, the Native name for polar bear.

Moaka was determined to maintain a negative feeling about the polar bear, whereas most Natives respected them and tried to give the polar bear a lot of room if they were not actively hunting them at the time. James knew the Natives had been hunting polar bears in this country for hundreds of years, and they were used to the habits and movements of the great beast. Moaka had mentioned the incident about his folks only twice, and both times he stopped short of telling the whole story. There was something strange about the incident that Moaka had not seen fit to tell him, at least not yet.

Reaching down to disconnect Nel from the traces, he noticed swelling on her left front shoulder. Removing his right mitten, he softly stroked her swollen shoulder. With a nod of approval, James was relieved to find that it didn't seem to be too serious. The dogs staked out at proper distance to keep them from fighting, he threw each one a small piece of frozen seal meat. The dogs really didn't have their main meal until evening, but they sometimes fed the teams with bits and pieces.

His breakfast had been cooked long past, and James ran smack into the wrath of Tess.

"Late!" she hotly spit.

Smiling, James arrived at the cooking fire and it was always amusing to him to have her get upset. Tess didn't speak much English, but she could spit out what little she did know as she mixed the Native language in with her broken English.

As James sat down on the folding stool that he always carried with him, Tess handed James his breakfast of hot steaming seal meat she had just dipped from the cooking pot, and a corn flour biscuit. Returning to her breakfast cleanup chores, James knew she was unhappy with him. James smiled to himself for he knew that Tess couldn't stay angry with him very long, she was too light-hearted a person. Moaka on the other hand was very serious most of the time, where Tess in many ways was just the opposite.

Moaka sat cross-legged staring intently into the fire keeping his thoughts to himself, as he was thinking about how to deal with the polar bear. He knew that James was against killing any animal unless the kill served a purpose of trading for their supplies, for their food, or for their protection.

Breaking the silence, Moaka looked straight at James, and asked in a quite determined voice, "Why polar bear come close? Dog here."

James hated it when Moaka stared right at him, or rather through him. Moaka was right about one thing, though, if there was anything a polar bear hated, it was dogs. They tried to stay away from any dogs. Seeing the concern on Moaka's face, James knew his answer had to be a believable one. In a reassuring tone James replied, "I'm not sure, Moaka, but it could be a couple of reasons. It might be that he smelled the fish hanging on the drying racks, or he might have just wandered into our area. You know they wander all over the place, from here all the way to the other side of the top of the world."

Not being convinced, Moaka stood up and glanced around, and fired back, "No like; polar bear too close."

Standing, James placed his hands on his hips and bent backward to stretch his muscles as he answered, "If you want, we'll track him for a while this morning just to see what his intentions are." Not wanting Moaka to see that he was also upset about the polar bear's behavior, James added, "And on the way let's keep a lookout for more sightings. I need to send in a report pretty quick, and I'd like to include some more sightings of wildlife if I could." Sensing Moaka's seriousness, he tried to act as if it were going to be routine tracking the polar bear. Sitting back down on the stool, James asked Tess, "Any hot tea left, Tess?"

Tess reached for the pot sitting next to the fire and poured him the hot soothing drink, and then returned to cleaning up after breakfast.

Moaka was getting more nervous with every passing moment, and he kept fussing around with his rifle and the gear he would be taking for the day's trip.

When James had first hooked up with Moaka in Nome he had an old beat-up, Russian-made, single-shot rifle that would hardly work, and on the first trip, back to Nome James had bought Moaka another rifle. It was not new, but it was a lever-action, multi-load 44-40 rifle, and Moaka was proud of it. He showed it off like it was gold, and he always made sure that his friends knew who got it for him.

"Moaka, why don't you sit down and settle yourself. I'll be ready to go in just a minute; you're fussing like an old woman."

As Moaka spun around to face him, James realized he had made a mistake in judgment. Moaka's long strides brought him directly in front of James, and he expounded excitedly, "Bear come close. Dog here. Bear no afraid. Kincaid say!"

Moaka was frozen in the standing position, as he awaited James' response. His hands and arm were positioned stiffly on his sides, with eyes firmly fixed at James.

James realized that Moaka was concerned and truly worried about the passing polar bear.

James took a deep breath and moved his head gently from side to side saying, "Moaka, I don't know. Maybe we'll find out some answers after we have tracked him for a while.

CHAPTER TEN

The day's supplies loaded and the teams hooked up, Moaka walked over to Tess, and asked, "Where is the pistol? I want you to keep it extra close today." Moaka always left a loaded pistol with Tess to ward off any animals that might venture close to the drying racks while they were gone for the day.

"I put the pistol in my pocket," Tess answered.

The farewells said to Tess, who was busy tending a couple of arctic hare skins, both men made last minute checks on their teams for departure from camp.

James shifted his sled slightly to break the runners free and lifted the sled break spike with the toe of his boot. Looking back at Moaka for the all's well sign, James hailed, "On Bray" as his team surged forward. Moaka yelled his normal low grunt to his team and followed James with the same gait.

Approaching two hundred yards from camp James' sled cut the trail left by the polar bear and he hailed Bray to a halt.

Moaka's team halted beside James' and both men put their hoods down for better vision and gazed in the direction the bear had gone. Moaka quietly uttered, "White Ghost."

Seeing Moaka's great concern, James replied sternly, "Moaka, for hell's sake, it's just another polar bear. You have hunted and killed many of them.

The animal might have just been roving around out here on his way to anywhere and just ran into us."

James didn't believe what he had just said because the polar bear was a long ways from the coast. The polar bear should not have been this far inland away from his staple food of seal. Continuing, James commented, "Well, Moaka, if he runs the way he should, we'll let him go, but if he challenges us we'll get us some new sleeping skins or trading goods for our next trip to Barrow."

Still staring down the phantom's endless trail, Moaka said in a very sure and determined voice, "This bad one. Feel bad thing." Moaka's voice tailed off as he flipped up his hood seemingly to shiver under his clothing. "We follow?" Moaka motioned with his arm down the trail the polar bear had left in the crusted snow.

"Yes, for a while," James agreed.

Remounting their sleds, James and Moaka hazed their teams to the left, and they paralleled the trail for about an hour, seeing no sign of the polar bear.

Hollering Bray to a stop to rest the dogs, James sensed that the polar bear was somewhere close. James squinted from the reflected light off the snow as he scanned the white emptiness in front of him. He put all his senses together trying to detect any sound or motion on the horizon. He could not believe that the bear had gotten this far ahead of them. The tracks in the snow showed the length of the polar bear's gait, and it indicated the polar bear didn't seem to be in that big of a hurry to get whereever he was going.

Quietly speaking to his dogs to steady them, Moaka loosened the rifle on his sled, and quietly confirmed, "Kincaid, rifle ready? Bear no hurry."

James was always amused at the way Moaka used the English language. He always seemed to leave out words, but as James began to understand and speak the Native language, he understood why Natives left out words. The Native language used few words that did not contribute to the main thought. Pushing his hood back and rubbing the back of his neck, James replied, "Yeah, Moaka, it's ready."

As James turned around, he scanned back down the trail of the bear's tracks. He could see that the bear was traveling in somewhat of a straight line. That might be good information later if they were going to pursue this animal any farther. "Moaka, where do you think the polar bear was headed? This time of year polar bears should be riding the ice pack hunting seal."

Moaka softly replied, "Kincaid, look dog."

Glancing at both teams, Moaka was right. The dogs could tell a good story. All thirty dogs had their noses pointed the same direction, smelling the light breeze, and he could even see a little hair standing up on Anore.

James waited for Moaka to break his runners loose, and doing the same, hailed quietly, "On Bray."

Not wanting to pass up any surface signs scratched in the snow by the bear, James kept hailing Bray with the command, *pissukpok*—walk, to control the speed of the dogs. Spotting a place in the snow where the bear had stopped and scratched around a bit, James knew they had to be getting close. The tracks had not started to be filled in from the blowing snow. That was a good sign the polar bear was very close.

Suddenly, not more than one-hundred yards away, the polar bear stood up on his back legs challenging the men, and then made a charge. James' heart jumped into his throat. Instinctively, he stomped down on the bone sled brake, and screamed at Bray to hold. Quickly, James glanced back at Moaka, and realized that Moaka was having a hard time controlling his team.

James got his team stopped and ripped the parka hood from his head. He jerked his rifle from the sled holster, threw it into his shoulder, and banged a shot off that landed in front of the charging polar bear. Instantly, he heard Moaka's rifle respond. Just as Moaka's rifle barked, *Nanuk* turned and disappeared over the backside of the small snow ridge they had been traveling in parallel.

Frantically, Moaka ran by James and yelled, "Hold Anore, Bray, I get shot."

Staring after him, James ran to the front of the teams, not grabbing the lead dogs, but just standing in front of them. James trusted Anore, but didn't like getting too close to the dog when he got excited.

James' shot was more to turn the polar bear away from their position, but he knew Moaka's shot was to kill. He probably would not have fired at all, except for the animal charging them; and the polar bear charging them was strange all in itself.

Moaka looked like a wild man as he climbed up the side of the snow ridge. James saw him top the ridge and shoulder the rifle, two quick shots. The picture of Moaka the next instant told the whole story; he dropped the rifle limply down to his side, he'd missed.

He paused for an instant, then came dashing back down the slope pointing and yelling, "Break in ridge. Bear run other side."

Hastily, both men ran back and boarded their sleds. They wildly threw their rifles into their sleds, kicked the brakes loose, and jerking the runners loose, hailed their teams forward. They followed the snow ridge with the dogs running at a wide-open gait. Moaka and his team fell in behind James as the excitement of the chase instantly transferred to the dogs. James knew it was for times like these that the teams and equipment were kept in good repair. The wind stung his face as the dogs pulled the sleds across the snow surface at a frantic pace.

Traveling about a half mile, James signaled to Moaka that the cut in the ridge was coming up. James wanted to stop before the cut and climb up the slope to get to higher ground for maybe a better look. If the bear ran beyond the cut, they would go through the cut to give chase.

It was not hard to stop the dogs this time because of all the excitement and running full out. They set the sled brakes securely into the hard-crusted snow, and both grabbed their rifles and started to scramble up the ridge. Breathing hard because of the climb up the snow ridge, both James and Moaka were just about to the top when the unexpected happened.

The elusive polar bear had paralleled them on the blind side of the ridge, and when they had stopped, the polar bear heard the barking of the dogs and climbed the back slope. When the men got to the top of the ridge, the polar bear made his move.

The large male polar bear did become a White Ghost when the great animal met James and Moaka at the top of the ridge. Standing on hind legs, his huge white body seemed to block out everything behind him; his front paws raised with claws extended as they knifed through the air. His heavy, thick neck and huge head waved back and forth like some kind of a serpent's dance, and with such a loud and aggressive growl that it deadened both men's ears to any other sounds. The polar bear had taken both of the men completely by surprise. They weren't ten feet from his glowing, angry eyes and piercing, three-inch-long teeth that were threatening to rip both of them into pieces.

Instantly, Moaka jerked off a round that went wildly into the air. Slipping, he lost his footing and fell backward.

James fell on his stomach, sliding down the slope rather than falling backward like Moaka. On the way down he snapped a shot right at the bear's head. He wasn't sure he hit the animal, but his shot kept the bear from coming down the slope after them. James finally stopped sliding at the bottom of the ridge, right beside Moaka. Moaka was out cold, but still breathing. James figured he must have hit his head on the way down.

Instinctively, James levered another round into the chamber, and looked toward the top of the ridge to make sure that the polar bear was gone. In his mind's eye, James could still see the giant polar bear meeting them at the top of the ridge.

Moving to a kneeling position, he checked Moaka's condition. James put the gloves back on Moaka's still hands and picked up their rifles, as he looked into Moaka's quiet, unemotional face. James knew they had both been very close to death, and were lucky one of them had not been badly hurt or killed. James hoped that Moaka's injury would result in nothing more a bad headache, but James still needed to get Moaka in his sled and back to camp.

James stood up and glanced at Moaka who looked peaceful lying there. He reached down with a handful of snow and laid it on Moaka's forehead. Speaking in a loud voice, James urged Moaka back to consciousness by shaking him gently and calling his name.

Glancing to the top of the ridge again, James did not want the polar bear coming back for another round, with Moaka down.

Moaka moaned and tried to sit up, but lay back down as his head started to spin.

"Must have hit your head on the way down." James spoke loudly, as he was still trying to bring Moaka out of his dizzy state. "How are you feeling?"

Moaka fought to roll over on his stomach, and with James' help stood on wobbling legs. Shaking his head and rubbing his eyes, Moaka slurred, "Where polar bear?"

With a firm hold on Moaka's parka, he steadied him. James realized that the dogs were just now starting to settle down, and a thought quickly passed through his mind that the barking dogs might have been the difference between the bear stopping at the top ridge or coming down the slope after them.

While Moaka gained his balance and footing, James maneuvered back to the top of the ridge to look to see if the bear was still around. He could not see the polar bear anywhere. Yelling down to Moaka, James said, "Well, Moaka, I don't see a damn thing. The polar bear must have taken off." James searched the entire area and detected no sign of movement.

"What way bear go?"

With a shake of his head, James answered, "Hell, I don't know." Remaining on top of the ridge for a short time, he searched the horizon, but James knew the polar bear didn't have time to run out of sight.

James was privately starting to agree with Moaka. This polar bear was displaying different behavior patterns than normal polar bears.

As James approached Moaka's team, Anore greeted him with his normal growl, but James had learned that Anore would not bite him, at least under normal conditions, and the best thing to do was just ignore him. James went about straightening out the mess they had made of their harnesses.

"Kincaid, get rifle."

James spun around to see Moaka still standing where he'd left him, not moving a muscle. James snapped around to look in the same direction Moaka was looking, and there the polar bear was, standing on top of the ridge. The polar bear was swinging his thick large neck and head like a whip and bouncing up and down on its front legs displaying his ultimate challenging posture.

"Stay right there, you damn beast," James muttered under his breath as he quickly grabbed for his rifle lying against his sled.

Before James realized what was happening, Bray broke for the polar bear with his whole team dragging the sled behind them up the ridge after the polar bear. Startled half out of his wits by his rampaging team, James glanced back toward the ridge just in time to see the bear disappear over the backside like some kind of slow-moving cloud passing behind a mountain ridge. When James' team broke and took off in the direction of the bear, James' first instinct was to grab onto Moaka's team to keep them from breaking and running after the bear in stride with his team.

With a shake of his head in disgust, James had never seen the likes of it. Still kneeling in silence holding his rifle, he let go of Anore and surveyed the whole situation. He remembered he had applied the sled brake, but he wondered why it didn't hold. James looked at his team scattered up the ridge, and realized that they were tangled in a mess of harness.

James glanced over to see Moaka kneeling on the snowy surface where he had been standing a moment ago.

Moaka had removed his hood and was rubbing the back of his head, probably still trying to shake loose the cobwebs from the blow.

"How's your head?"

Moaka was attempting to stand. Still rubbing the back of his head, he answered with slurred words, "*Kungasinerk anernartok,*" which roughly translated meant, "the back of my neck hurts badly."

"Well, Moaka, clear your head and watch for the polar bear. No telling where that critter is right now. I'm going to get my team back in shape. Will you be all right?"

With a wave of his hand motioning to go, he replied, "I see."

CHAPTER ELEVEN

James shrugged to straighten his clothes, and walked toward his run-away team. It was a good thing the sled turned over because that was what stopped his team cold. A well-trained team is taught when the sled goes over, they stop pulling, but Bray was too involved in getting at the polar bear to stop.

The sled turned upright, James started untangling the snarled harness.

While James was rescuing his team, Moaka had come more to his senses, and he seemed to be getting quite upset with the whole affair. Unsteadily, he walked to his sled and began digging through the gear. Mumbling to himself, he finally found what he was looking for and retrieved it from the pile of gear in the sled.

James was leading his team back, and saw what Moaka had in his mittened hand. James commanded Bray to hold as he inquired, "What are you going to do with that thing?"

Holding the leather whip toward James and without facial expression, in a hard, stone-cold, steady tone, Moaka commanded, "Whip Bray."

James' expression immediately changed as he challenged, "Whip Bray, your ass. Why should I do that? Bray ran that damn polar bear off."

Looking James straight in the face, Moaka responded as sternly as he possibly could, declaring, "Bray no hold."

Throwing his hands in the air, James screamed, "No hold!" Promptly

James thought, *I'm even starting to talk like him.* "To hell with he didn't hold. Those damn dogs well might have saved your ass. You better think about that before you get so damn high and mighty."

Still holding the whip toward James, Moaka didn't change expressions, but continued, "No different, Kincaid, Bray be taught. Kincaid got good team. Good training. Kincaid stop?"

James had the sinking feeling that Moaka was right. Bray had been cuffed and scolded from time to time, but he had never been whipped. James knew it would be like using a whip on one of his kids, if he had any. Standing near Bray, James looked to the Brooks Range horizon as the mountain was silhouetted from the waning day's light. "How in hell does this happen?" James muttered to himself, "Nobody got hurt because Bray didn't hold. This whipping stuff is stupid."

Moaka let his arm fall to his side with the whip almost touching the snowy surface. Raising his voice for James to hear, "Kincaid, I no happy this. Brays make polar bear run. No get shot. Must think…," stopping what he was saying Moaka suddenly blurted out, "*nalaktok*"—obey.

Moaka again raised his hand with the whip in it, as if offering it again, and commented, "Kincaid do. Bray be better."

James' sinking feeling returned as he looked from Moaka to his team; not really looking at Bray alone, but at the whole team. Shaking his head James knew Bray had actually committed a very serious crime for a lead dog. It could mean life or death for the sledder someday if the lead dog could not or would not hold.

"Damn," James uttered under his breath. He didn't want to do what had to be done. He was angry with Moaka because Moaka had backed him into a corner. Removing his right mitten, James rubbed his wind-burned lips as he continued looking over his dogs.

Jamming his right hand back into his mitten James turned and proceeded towards Moaka. His steps were slow as he thought about what he had to do. Anger was still within him as he approached Moaka and said coldly, "Give me the damn thing."

Moaka forcefully shoved the whip toward James and replied, "Bray be better."

James grabbed the whip from Moaka. The two men's eyes met— Moaka's glare of determination and James' of frustration and anger. Grasping the whip, James spun around and quickly walked to the front of his team.

Bray lay on the hard snowy surface in a submissive position, not moving a muscle. As James looked down at Bray, he knew in his heart that this was not the way to solve the problem. James looked back at Moaka and muttered, "Damn, I hate to do this."

Whack! The whip cracked as James struck it across Bray's rump, and he just laid there, no sound. Whack! Another blow across his rump, as Bray made no movement or whining sound. James raised the whip again and then let his arm fall limp at his side. This business was all done with at last and James decided he would not whip Bray ever again.

Without a word, James walked back to Moaka and shoved him the whip coiled as Moaka had given it to him. James turned and proceeded back to his sled and boarded. Without looking back at Moaka as he always did, James hailed, "On Bray." Right at that instant James didn't care if Moaka ever came with him or not. James was so angry with Moaka, he thought about stopping the sled, going back, and telling him what he truly thought of the situation. He guessed the reason he didn't was because Moaka was right about Bray not holding, but James couldn't really buy into the idea of whipping.

The trip back to camp was uneventful and very quiet, and Bray seemed to do his job, but the spark had gone from him. His voice had been silenced; his spirit had been broken. James hated himself for whipping Bray.

As the two weary men came into camp, it was getting on toward the time of day when the light in the sky would hide for another day, and Tess was standing beside the cooking fire anxious for their late return. James halted his team and wondered if Bray would ever be truly trustful of him again. After staking the dogs and throwing each one a piece of frozen fish or seal meat, James headed for his tent to prepare for supper and Moaka went to the cooking fire without a word between them.

In a low voice, Tess asked Moaka, as he came closer to the fire, "What's wrong with Kincaid? He didn't even wave."

With a shake of his head signaling despair, Moaka replied, "Kincaid and I had a talk. Bray went after the polar bear and didn't hold the team when the polar bear came in close. I told him that Bray needed the whip to reinforce discipline. Kincaid didn't want anything to do with it, but eventually he did strike Bray with the whip. That's what is wrong with him."

Sighing, Tess quietly commented, "The dogs need constant training. Kincaid should know that?"

"No," Moaka replied. "He is angry at me." Pinching off a small piece of meat that was hanging over the cooking fire, Moaka continued, "He thinks Bray won't love him anymore."

"Well," Tess responded, "don't scold him, Moaka, he maybe doesn't understand. You know he is a good friend."

Nodding his head in agreement, Moaka commented, "Kincaid is a good man."

Inside the tent, James could see that Tess had cleaned things up. The light inside the tent wasn't that good and he had to light one of the candles that he kept on a small folding table setting next to his cot. After looking around the tent, James smiled slightly and mumbled, "She sure has the touch out here in the middle of nowhere." While they were out today, Tess had come in and straightened the whole tent up. Fortunately for Moaka and him, she was a good cook and a good hand around camp. He wondered if she would stick it out, following along with Moaka and him through all their trips.

Sitting down on his cot, James relaxed before going out to the evening meal. He thought about the polar bear and the incident with Bray. He felt bad about whipping Bray. The idea that Moaka was right made him angrier every time he thought about it. He just didn't like to be as rigid as Moaka was about certain things in life. *It wasn't always black or white, right or wrong.* Lying back on his goose-down filled bedding, James stared at the ceiling of the tent, and thought, *This was better than being back in some office somewhere taking orders from the public. Yeah, Moaka was entitled to one mistake.*

As Moaka heard James exiting from his tent, he leaned toward Tess and quietly said, "Let it be. He'll work it out."

Flipping the tent flap closed, and stomping to the cooking fire, James noticed that Moaka was talking with Tess in a low voice.

As James reached the fire, Tess turned to her cooking.

Moaka looked up at James and asked, "Kincaid okay?"

James held Moaka's stare for an instant and replied, "Moaka, I hated to do that out there today, but you're probably right, Bray should have held." Shaking his head slowly, he sat down on his stool. "I don't want to talk about it anymore."

Without a word, Tess handed James a plate of seal meat, fish, and biscuits and stepped back. Squatting on the other side of the fire, Tess questioned, "Kincaid sleepy?"

James looked at her through the fire heatwaves and smiled while nodding his head. "Yeah, Tess I'm tired, but this hot food will go a long ways in making me feel better."

The evening meal finished, Moaka and James silently looked into the fire. Tess cleaned up around the fire and retired for the night.

Breaking the silence, Moaka quietly commented, "Kincaid, Tess say need supply. We low on firewood. Go Teshpuk tomorrow?"

Nodding his head in the affirmative, James replied, "Yeah, we had better, Moaka. I'd hate to get the cook upset with us."

Moaka looked across the fire at James and leaned forward so Tess couldn't hear. He softly asked, "Kincaid, what think polar bear?"

"I don't know, Moaka." Yawning and wiping his eyes James continued, "That crazy animal just didn't seem to be too afraid of us. The thing that puzzles me more than anything else was that he came back for us, even after we both shot at him at close range. The dogs didn't even seem to bother him. Another thing I can't figure out is what that animal was doing so far inland. Their behavior is to hang around the coastal areas or out on the ice pack this time of year."

"Go when Bray ran up ridge," Moaka replied.

"Well, Moaka we'll just have to be on the lookout for the beast as we go about our business. Speaking of that, we've had a busy day and I'm ready to hit the sack."

Moaka pressed again with, "Kincaid, come back here when done Teshpuk? Think bear gone here."

"No, Moaka, we'll probably be going over across the Colville River. Not really sure as of yet, but I'm pretty sure we won't be coming back to this area for some time, and if that crazy polar bear wants to stay here that will be just fine with me. By the way, the bear was a male, right? I need to say something in the log about our encounter."

With a quick movement of his head back and forth and a shrug of his shoulders, Moaka slowly replied, "Think too big for female."

As James walked back to his tent, he realized how really tired he was and how much he was looking forward to getting a good night's sleep. He just hoped that Bray was getting over his whipping. Feeling lowly, as he walked to his tent, James thought, *Moaka was right, but Bray will never feel the whip again.*

CHAPTER TWELVE

During the month of March, the weather is cold with daylight lasting longer to warm the land north of the Brooks Range, and its inhabitants, man and animal alike, try to make the best of the daylight hours. James was the type of person that desired plenty of sleep and this season was to his liking. Moaka on the other hand, did not especially desire to sleep as long as James, and sometimes he would wake James to get the day's work started, which would be much to James' displeasure.

Soon the days would start to get longer and longer and then he would have to grab sleep and rest when the opportunity presented itself. The days were just starting to get a little longer and some nights offered a miraculous show of the most beautiful colors of lights streaking across the dark sky. The *Aksarnerk*—Aurora Borealis was the most impressive sight for the newcomer to this part of the country. James explained to Moaka and Tess what caused the strange lights in the sky, but Moaka told James the story of how the Eskimo believed the origin of the lights happened, and both considered each other to be wrong.

Rolling over in his warm and cozy bedroll, James knew it was morning, as light began to filter through the tent. He could remember several times when they had been studying wildlife behavior that the caribou gave birth in the spring, along with the arctic hare, wolves, lemmings, and foxes. Moaka and he had spent many sleepless hours, and Moaka never seemed to mind spelling him on watch to study the animals' habits when they found a den of fox or a nest of early nesting snow geese, or anything else that needed behavioral documentation. James remembered Moaka's only comment was that he wanted to learn the business so he could do a better job.

James moaned slightly at the thought of getting out of bed. At least the tent canvas was not moving, which meant the wind had not started blowing too much this morning. A chill ran down his spine as he thought of the cold morning, and the inside of the tent that would be at least twenty below zero. Slowly James rolled out of the sack as he heard the familiar sounds of Moaka tending the teams and getting the gear ready for the trip back to Teshpuk. Moaka and Tess were always happy to get back to Teshpuk to be with their friends and relations. They were considered the rich side of the relations because of the jobs they had with the Wildlife Service.

Dressing his medium-size frame as quickly as he could, and running his fingers through his jet-black hair, James looked around the tent to see that everything was ready for packing, and as his head brushed the cold tent canvas, a chill forced him to shiver.

"Damn, this cold could kill a person," James muttered.

Stooping to exit the tent, he scanned the open space to what used to be camp, where now only the cooking fire and his stool existed.

Moaka and Tess must have been up for hours anticipating the trip. Scratching the back of his head and still looking around, James thought, *Moaka must be in a hurry to get to Teshpuk.*

The only thing still standing was his own tent. The drying racks were down and packed, Moaka's tent was down and packed, and Tess had breakfast ready, waiting for him to get out of bed.

Moaka walked over to the tent and said, "Kincaid, morning. How sleep? No worry Bray. Anore and Bray run side by side before sun." Slapping James on the shoulder, he continued, "Nel okay, no swell. She in good spirit."

Before returning to his packing Moaka commented, "Breakfast ready. Go Teshpuk."

No sooner had Moaka finished speaking than they both heard Tess calling, "Kincaid, Kincaid," and both men looked to see Tess beckoning with her wooden spoon for him to come to the fire for breakfast.

As James watched Moaka walking away, he quickly turned toward his team. His attention was immediately directed toward Bray. Bray didn't seem any different and he was whining and wiggling as he always did when James approached him. Kneeling down beside him, James gave him his routine chest rub and stroked the back of his powerful neck. Removing his mittens, James rubbed the coarse hair on the dog's back and neck vigorously. He let his fingers sink deep into Bray's heavy coat to where his skin was warm and firm. Bray tried to turn his head back to look at James and lick him in the face, but James jerked back just barely in time to elude his flashing tongue. Grabbing his snout to close his mouth, James forced his weight upon the dog's body and they went down to the snowy surface in a pile. Rolling repeatedly together in the snow, James knew that Bray was back in good spirits.

"Morning Tess," James remarked as he reached the cooking fire. "How's the best damn cook on the north slopes doing this morning?" He continued cheerfully, "What time did you and Moaka get up?"

"He play," Tess spit hotly as she shoved the steaming breakfast plate into James' hands.

James eased himself down on his stool and started to eat the fresh roasted hare. Laughing to himself he thought, *He play. It didn't seem to be much of a description, but Tess had a way of getting her point across without too many words.* Normally the Native women were not quite as brassy as Tess was, and she never said things like that around anybody else, but she knew she had nothing to fear from him.

"Kincaid, sit *mimerk*—on butt, all day," Moaka yelled, as he started toward the cooking fire to help Tess get the rest of the stuff picked up after the breakfast.

James answered back smiling, "Hell, I'd better not; you'd probably run off and leave me." With that comment, he gobbled down the last bit of rabbit, grabbed his stool, and headed back to his tent, to break it down and pack up.

James hated the ordeal of taking the tent down this time of day. The canvas was cold and stiff as a board. When they got back to Teshpuk, they'd both have to lay their tents out flat to let the canvas dry, because the moisture would rot the canvas if the tents were left folded up for any length of time.

When everything was packed up and tied down, the dog's harnesses checked, and the camp left clean, except for the scorched snow where the fire had been, they were at last ready to travel. James stood on the back runners of his sled, and by swinging his weight from side to side he finally was able to break the runners away from the frozen surface. They had sided their sleds last night, but Moaka had righted James' sled early that morning, enabling the runners to freeze down to some extent.

Tess, who was settling onto Moaka's sled, yelled over to James, "Kincaid, happy go Teshpuk?"

Smiling and nodding his head, James responded, "Could be, Tess, could be."

With hands on the guide bars of the sled, James glanced around at the flat, quiet, white surroundings. A soft breeze had started blowing from the east and some snow had started moving on the horizon, but it was going to be another beautiful day. The temperature was warming up to about fifteen degrees below zero, as the sun was shining brightly against the snow-covered rolling plains of the tundra that adjoined the lower reaches of the northern slopes of the Brooks Range. During his first winter on the north slopes, Moaka had taught him how to tell temperature, or at least close, by the sound of the snow squeaking under foot. When it squeaked loudly, it was below zero, if it squeaked a little it was about freezing, and if it didn't squeak at all it was above freezing; simple system, but it seemed to work, at least for most situations. This information was important because the dogs were fitted with paw covers to keep their feet from freezing when it got cold. After Moaka had gone through the full explanation about telling temperature, James showed him his hand held thermometer that his father had given him. Moaka was impressed with the gadget, but his last word on the subject was, "Listen as walk Kincaid."

James wondered, as he stared off into the distance, if he should be putting on the bone eyeshades Moaka made for him. He decided not to because they were so uncomfortable. Maybe he'd have to put them on later, but for a while, at least, they would be traveling with the sun somewhat at their backs because they would be traveling in the northwest direction to get back to Teshpuk.

Moaka was adjusting his rifle in the sled when Tess motioned toward James and asked Moaka, "What's Kincaid thinking?"

Glancing over toward James, Moaka replied, "Haven't you ever seen a man that was satisfied with life?"

"On Bray," James yelled through his face wrap, and after letting the dogs run hard for the first couple of miles to get them warmed up, James slowed Bray to a good, steady pace. They had a long way to go today, and there was not any particular hurry. It would take the best part of two days to get to Teshpuk, whether they hurried or not.

James scanned the horizon for their best route and any game that he could note in his log as sightings. Then, suddenly, James heard Moaka frantically halting his lead.

Moaka was hailing Anore to stop as loud as he could yell. Stomping on the sled brake, he was screaming at Tess, "Give me the rifle. Will you get off the rifle?"

James couldn't see any problems to the sides of him or ahead, but he halted Bray just the same and looked back to see what Moaka was yelling about, and to his surprise there was an arctic fox cutting their trail about fifty yards to their rear.

Moaka was jumping around his sled like a wild man, yelling at Tess to get off the rifle, and she was returning his scolding. Tess had piled some gear on the rifle and it was hooked up under something on the sled, and Moaka was frantic to get the rifle free.

James knew the reason Moaka was so determined to get the fox, for it was a prize to have the fur. The fur was good trading material for any supplies they needed, and even if a person didn't trade the pelt, it was useful to make linings for *tadluks*—snow boots.

Finally, Moaka got the rifle out from under all the gear and wheeled for a shot. By the time he was able to bead down on the fox, the shot was probably about one hundred yards, and the blowing fine snow was making it hard to see clearly. Moaka quickly leaned over the back of the sled to steady himself and squeezed. His rifle barked as smoke curled from the end of the barrel. James didn't see how Moaka was able to get a clear shot through the blowing snow, but the fast moving fox dropped like a rock.

Moaka jumped into the air, gave out a holler, and throwing the rifle to Tess, he took off at a run to capture his prize.

Half out of breath, Moaka came hurrying back toward the sleds. James could almost feel how proud he was of that fox. Breathing hard and carrying the fox over his shoulder, Moaka puffed, "Kincaid, no buy ammunition long time," as he held the fox high into the air.

As Moaka approached his sled, Tess ran to him, and excitedly exclaimed, "Good shot, Moaka, what a beautiful coat," while she gently stroked the soft coat of the silver white fox.

Digging his knife from under all his clothes, James prepared to help Moaka skin and quarter the fox.

"Moaka, that was a fine shot!" James exclaimed, as he slapped him on the back. "How did you ever see him good enough to get such a good bead on him?"

"Texas wind," Moaka proudly responded.

Laughing slightly, "You mean Kentucky windage?" James joked.

"Kincaid say," Moaka murmured.

"Here Moaka, let me help you." James steadied the hind quarters of the animal while holding the rear legs spread apart. Moaka's sharp knife sliced the skin up the belly just like a surgeon's tool. Just splitting the skin, but not touching the meat. James was always amazed at Moaka's skillful movements with a knife. It took years of practice to acquire such skills and Moaka had a good hand.

Moaka was being very careful so he didn't get any blood on the fur because it would damage the pure white color. Finishing his last cuts, he explained to James, "See large blood," as he pointed to a large blood vessel with the tip of his knife, "No cut. If cut, pinch fast, no blood."

Moaka slowly peeled the soft hide from the fox. Tess took the hide, rubbed her face into the warm fur, and quietly spoke, "Annorarpok nutaralak"—baby wrap.

Moaka looked up at Tess and smiled, then sent a wink in James' direction.

Smiling back at Moaka, James knew that no ammunition would ever be traded for this fox skin.

The fox skinned, quartered, and packed away, they were on their way again.

As the day wore on, they stopped periodically to rest the dogs. The noon meal, as it was so much of the time, would not be a consideration this day. Finally, after a non-eventful afternoon of traveling, the party stopped the teams after the last flickering of light was gone. It was going to be a cold camp, without a campfire. It had been more important to use the daylight for traveling rather than setting up camp. They had lost some time messing around with the fox, but probably it would work out to be time well spent. They staked out and fed the dogs, and this feeding time was going to be a treat for them. Each dog was given a small portion of the fox meat. Tess had cooked some extra meat at the last camp, and they ate it cold. After the meal, they wrapped up in their sleeping skins for the night.

Breaking the silence of the night just before James went to sleep, he heard Tess speak to him. "Kincaid."

"What do you want, Tess?" James answered.

The reply came in the same high-pitched tone as before, "Glad go Teshpuk?"

"Yeah, Tess, I'll be glad to get back to Teshpuk," James conceded. He knew what she was getting at, as she was playing little matchmaker. Rolling deeper in his skins, and peering into the star-lighted sky, James' only exposed body parts were his eyes.

It was as though James had just gotten his eyes closed, when Moaka was jerking at his skins waking him up. It was still dark with only a trace of light in the southeastern sky over the Brooks Range as he peered out from the warm sleeping skins, the cold morning air biting at his face.

Moaka towered over James like a giant. "Kincaid. Want sleep life away."

Almost yelling at Moaka, James quickly responded, "I know it's time to get up." James was about ready to leave his warm haven, when Bray jumped on top of him, and it took James a second to realize Bray was trying to pull his sleeping skins and not Moaka. He yelled at Bray, and noticed Moaka laughing at what Bray was doing. James was finally able to run Bray off, and he looked at Moaka, and yelled, "Damn you, Moaka, the payback is going to be tough on you."

Laughing and stammering at the same time, Moaka finally blurted, "I no take skin, Bray do."

Reluctantly, James crawled out of his only remaining sleeping skin, and he came to a sitting position and finished dressing. He noticed Bray standing about twenty feet away wagging his tail in anticipation of James' next move. Looking right at him James said harshly, "Yeah, and you're going to get yours too, mutt." Instantly, Bray came running over to James wanting to be forgiven.

Rolling up the skins and getting the dogs harnessed, James, Moaka, and Tess loaded the sleds for the last leg into Teshpuk. They all had dried fish for breakfast, so they didn't have to waste any time with a fire, and

James missed his morning ration of coffee or tea, which was about three cups. Tess never drank coffee, just tea, and Moaka would drink tea or coffee most of the time just during the morning meal.

⁂

On one of the stops to rest the dogs, Tess was complaining about the way Moaka's sled was loaded. She was having trouble sitting in the center of the sled to balance the load. Loudly Moaka scolded her, "If you would sit with the gear on the side, you would have a better ride."

Tess hotly responded, "The rifle is in the way. Why don't you do like Kincaid, and make a place for the rifle outside the sled?"

"Do you want to walk to Teshpuk?" was Moaka's final word on the subject. Silently, he stood on the back sled runners waiting for James to hail his team.

James' endless searching of the horizon and his thoughts was interrupted by the sound of Moaka's hollering for him to hold up. He hailed Bray and Moaka brought his team even with James'.

As Moaka stomped down on his brake hook, he glanced around the horizon and said, "Kincaid, need talk, polar bear."

CHAPTER THIRTEEN

James knew this conversation was coming, and he had tried to prepare himself for it by reviewing in his mind the habits and different accounts he'd heard and read about polar bears. This morning he'd seen Moaka scratching his head where he'd taken the bump, and James knew he was still thinking about the encounter. Moaka hadn't mentioned it, but James had heard Tess ask Moaka how his head was feeling because apparently she had felt the bump on his head the other night. Moaka was no fool, and he was well aware of the habits of the great predator that roamed the frozen desert and ice packs.

James knew Moaka wanted to know what the books had to say about the polar bear's behavior. Moaka found it hilarious and always interesting how book learning defined a situation different from how he saw it. James remembered he had explained to Moaka how the Gray Jay survived the long winters; Moaka just could not believe it, and he thought it surreal that a bird could remember where stores of food were hidden.

Lazily walking over to James as Tess was getting out of the sled to stretch and walk around a bit, Moaka asked, "Kincaid, polar bear far from ice? Why bear close to camp? Smell dog and us. No see male polar bear here this season." Shaking his head, and looking toward the horizon while shading his eyes, he continued, "Kincaid, polar bear strange. No like male polar bear here now. No good."

"Moaka, I don't know the answers to your questions. All I can do is speculate on the behavior of the polar bear. I think it was a male, and so do you because of its size. There doesn't seem to be any reason for him to be so far away from the ice pack. We are at least forty miles from the ice pack; and seals, his main food supply are plentiful on the coastal ice pack. I do know that polar bears wander all over the place without rhyme or reason, generally, because that is one of their behavioral patterns. I know that their wanderings have to do with their food supply, but I wouldn't think that much of his food supply would be here on the flats. As far as him coming so close to camp, that's a real puzzle because as both of us know, the polar bear is very illusive and solitary. Even though they are a curious animal, I believe they hate dogs more." Pausing, James continued, "Moaka, I just wonder if we both aren't getting a little too jumpy about this polar bear situation?"

Hardly giving James a chance to finish his sentence, Moaka questioned, "Why bear come back over ridge after we shoot?"

"Moaka, you and your people have been hunting and killing polar bears for many years. When you used to go polar bear hunting, didn't a polar bear ever try to double back on you anytime? I never hunted bear back in Wisconsin, but I can remember hearing some stories the old timers told of when they were hunting bear, and the animal seemed to travel in a large circle." Making a circle motion with his arm trying to illustrate to Moaka, "The bear circling would almost have the effect of who was hunting who after a while."

Moaka sighed and replied, "Polar bear *kanungayok*—too aggressive."

"Moaka, I don't know right now, but there might have been a reason that we don't know about. Nature has a way sometimes of steering animals to do strange things. It could have a sickness, be looking for food, or just migrating to another region and we may never know if we don't see the animal again."

Slowly, Moaka slid back his parka hood and carefully said, "Kincaid, I need say. Good time to say." Flashing a quick look at Tess, Moaka explained his secret to James. "No want feel *kappiasuktok*—afraid. Polar bear act same that kill family. *Kanungayok*—mean. That why no happy this polar bear. Father, mother, me come from hunt. Attack by polar bear. Father and mother fight polar bear. Mother send me away to village. Polar bear kill father, mother, all dog. I run for help, no see again." As Moaka finished his statements, he seemed relieved to have gotten the story told of the ordeal, and raising his hands and arms into the air and letting them fall was the final gesture he made.

Without warning, Tess joined into the conversation explaining, "Moaka, bad dream."

Nodding his head as if acknowledging the reasoning, James replied, "Well, Moaka, I'm glad you trusted me enough to tell me your complete experience. I don't really have anything to say about it right now, but just remember one thing, we are together in this thing until the finish, we have two good rifles, and we have each other. I figure if this polar bear becomes a problem we'll either run him back out onto the ice pack or just do away with him. I hope the incident we had was just a happen chance occurrence."

Slowly shaking his head, Moaka replied, "No think so, Kincaid. Got bad feeling. Polar bear no afraid, man or dog. Maybe see old man, get back Teshpuk. He go many polar bear hunt."

Mounting his sled, and glancing back at Moaka to see if he was ready, Moaka gave the familiar nod, and James hailed Bray ahead.

James was jerked out of his thoughts by Moaka's team coming up alongside of his and he instantly knew what Moaka was planning. They must be getting closer to Teshpuk than James had realized and Moaka wanted to race. Moaka's team had never beaten James', but Moaka was always ready to try again.

As Moaka's sled came even with his, James yelled as loud as he could, "On Bray, on Bray," and the race was on. James could feel the surge of his team straining on the tug lines and traces. Looking over the backs of his team, he could see unison in their movements and times as these made all the hardships worth bearing. He would have liked Don Nealy riding in his sled, just to show him that survival can be accomplished by young officers just out of school.

Moaka was hailing his team in a loud strong voice, *"Tuwawi, tuwawi"*—hurry up.

Tess was desperately hanging on as she was trying to stay in the middle of the sled for balance, and she was urging Moaka's team to run faster in her high-pitched voice. Somehow, her voice just didn't carry as well as Moaka's, but she was getting into the fun and excitement of the race.

James kept hailing to his team, and he could feel their strength pulling hard on the traces. His reward was when his team started to pull slightly ahead of Moaka's, and as James took the lead, Moaka's voice got louder and louder trying to urge his dogs along faster. A dog sled was not an easy thing to ride even at a slow pace, but at these speeds, James and Moaka were constantly shifting from side to side, making adjustment for balance because the sleds were rocking and rolling from side to side, and dipping from end to end.

James glanced over his shoulder, and Moaka was still slightly behind, but by no means out of the contest.

Shifting around on the back of the sled from runner to runner, Moaka quickly leaned down toward Tess and yelled, "Stop moving."

Hollering back at Moaka, Tess replied, "My arms are tired."

Moaka was having such a hard time trying to balance the sled with Tess moving around so much, he probably wished she could be tied down like the rest of the gear on the sled.

A mile into the race, James' team came upon a rise and not far ahead was Teshpuk. The teams were going to be tired after this run, especially having to go full out, but the teams were in good condition and could draw on reserve energy if need be.

As Moaka's team lost more and more ground, James also felt his team slowing down. A race like this one tested the endurance of each dog.

As James' team seemed to fly past the first villager's hut, he knew it was the tradition to go to the middle of the village. Looking ahead of the dogs, he had about fifty yards to go.

As James was approaching to the middle of the settlement, villagers began to stop and look to see about all the yelling. It didn't take them long to figure out what was going on because this was a common practice, and cheers began coming from the Natives in appreciation of a good race.

James hailed his team to a halt and looked to see how far back Moaka and his team were. To his surprise, Moaka was not more that twenty yards back, giving the dogs what for, and trying to get to the finish as fast as he could.

As Moaka pulled alongside and halted his dogs, he waved his arms in the air and hollered, "Good race, Kincaid. Team run like wind. Feed well, need dog speed, strength one day."

Teshpuk was different from most of the other villages on the north slopes. It had been here for some time and had the look of being a permanent place. Teshpuk was located next to the Colville River and was probably set up that way in the beginning, but the settlement stayed and more folks started to move into the village area. The villagers were always friendly and willing to trade for goods and supplies.

James rested on the back of his sled, as he watched Tess roll off or rather roll out of Moaka's sled and started to walk unsteadily toward her cousin's hut.

James elevated his voice as he asked, "What wrong, Tess, you can't walk so well?"

Without looking at James, she hissed back, "No say, Kincaid. You ride sled."

There was a young woman in the village that James had been with several times during the last few visits to Teshpuk. Nothing had ever been established between them other than just being able to enjoy each other's company. She was a schoolteacher and he was a wildlife biologist in a faraway land. Suzette and he were probably the only white permanent residents within one hundred miles.

Not moving from the back of his sled, James let Moaka take the lead from here. Moaka needed to approach Tess' cousin Kirima's hut with a gift, if they were to stay there for the night or for any length of time. The gift didn't have to be anything too big or costly, but a gift of some kind.

James gave Moaka a rabbit's foot to give one time. Tess' relations were all a little puzzled, and a little insulted until Moaka explained to them that Kincaid said the rabbit's foot was for good luck. Half the men in the village wore rabbit's feet hanging around their necks or had them in their medicine bags.

Moaka halted his team and bent over the sled to begin digging through the cargo for a gift. Finally catching up to him, Tess reached under his top garment and began tickling him.

Instantly, he tried to push her away, but Tess grabbed onto his clothes and exclaimed, "It's good to be back in Teshpuk. We'll have a fine visit and get all the news."

Still trying to dig through the cargo on the sled, Moaka calmly replied, "Yes, it's good to be back. How are you feeling?"

Hugging him again and quickly letting him go, she answered, "I'm fine. How long are we going to stay?"

Continuing to dig through the cargo, Moaka shrugged his shoulder and replied, "Kincaid say."

Tess looked over her shoulder to where Kincaid was waiting behind his sled and asked quietly, "Tell him we want to stay for a while."

Moaka rose up and shot a quick glance toward Kincaid to see if he might have heard Tess, and speaking low he sharply scolded her saying, "Kincaid is the boss. He'll say when we go."

Tess smiled back at Moaka and replied, "You ask him. He'll stay longer."

Without answering her, Moaka turned back to the cargo in the sled, and finally retrieving a small spoon that had been carved from a bone he exclaimed, "This is what I've been looking for."

CHAPTER FOURTEEN

The hut Moaka and Tess entered was quite large with a lean-to shed constructed on the north end. A skin and meat drying rack was built outside the structure where the front yard would have been. The dwelling was typical of most huts built in this area, except that it was larger than most because of all the family and relations that lived there. It consisted of a pole frame with skins stretched over the frame. The sides were made of sod placed on the outside for further insulation against the cold, and on top was a thin layer of dirt that grew grass at certain times of the year. These structures weren't too much to look at, but they worked quite well for protection against the elements. Additional snow piled around the sides and on top added to the insulation of the structure. Some of the temporary structures did not have the sod and soil barrier, rather tanned skins stretched over a pole frame covered with snow blocks. There were a few ice igloos built on the edges of the settlement by people that wanted to stay a couple of nights near a settlement, but they were temporary structures.

James loosened his clothing a bit to get more comfortable, because the last time they went through the ritual it took close to thirty minutes for Moaka and Tess to say their hellos, before Moaka came out to get him. James was told that if they were here more often they would not have to bring a gift.

James looked back through the village to see if any changes had occurred since last they came to Teshpuk, and James noticed Suzette's hut had not changed. The last time he was here, she was gone on a trip to some other village farther inland and he had not seen her. She was a real nice person who had shown a lot of intelligence, she wasn't bad looking, and she was about James' age. Her long blonde hair just seemed to go along with her well-shaped, slender form. She was very active in the village functions with the children and never seemed to tire easily. She had been raised by one of the local villagers when her real folks, French missionaries, were killed in a boating accident when she was just a youngster. Somehow or another she got her education training, maybe down south, and started teaching Native children to read and write the Native and English languages. She also taught some of the adults to read and write their Native language and English.

Moaka hailed James as he came out of the hut and walked out to his team. "Kincaid, stake dog and feed. Food ready soon. Good back Teshpuk. All happy we back. Much news to hear."

James nodded his head and casually replied, "Yeah, Moaka, it is good to be back, but let's not get too used to this easy living."

Stopping in his tracks, Moaka turned his head toward Kincaid and, smiling, replied, "What! Do ear lie? You one sit on stool."

Laughing, Kincaid responded, "Yeah, Moaka, you've got to be right."

After taking care of the teams, the two weary men gathered what would be needed for the night, sided their sleds and went inside to join the others to hear James' and Moaka's tales of adventure. Moaka would be the storyteller while James sat quietly and watched the others marvel at the slightly inflated tales that Moaka would spin. When a point of truth would occur, according to Moaka's white lies, Moaka would use James as a verifier to his story, and everyone would nod in approval.

It was quite roomy inside, but, as most Native dwellings, it lacked good ventilation and light. The Natives had a habit of occasionally drying skins in their lodges, and a stranger had to get used to the odor.

Moaka sat down and motioned James to sit next to him and Tess, and as soon as James was seated, Tess' cousin, Kirima, handed him some warm tea. She motioned for him to have more, but James motioned that this would be fine. James couldn't wait for the group to start eating the seal steaks that had been cooked over the fire and smelled as if they had been prepared just right. The rest of the menu included cured caribou, corn biscuits, and dried fish. Most of the cooking was done outside the huts, but small flame pots of animal oil were placed under the warming pots to keep the food warm inside the huts.

Interrupting the conversations in the room, Moaka stood up and presented James to the group. As Moaka was making the individual introductions, James was sure that he had met most of them before, at least several times, but they went through this ritual every time he came to visit. James had learned it was their way of trying to make outsiders welcome. The Natives gave their friendship easy, but they were still very close-knit to their own kin.

When Moaka finished and sat back down, Kirima's husband started to pass the containers of food and steak around.

The Natives were excellent preparers of food, and as the meal went along, large, soft deerskin cloths were passed around to wipe hands and faces. The skin cloths were used by everyone, so a person had to be careful not to wipe someone else's grease on him.

Suddenly, and without apparent reason, Tess reached across Moaka, and hit James on the arm and asked, "Kincaid, happy?"

Leaning forward and looking at her James nodded his head. James fired a quick glance at Moaka for a reading, and Moaka just smiled, shaking his head. James frowned slightly, and he thought, *Now what are those two planning?*

There was a lot of conversation around the circle during the meal, and James had a hard time keeping up with all the different issues. He'd learned a lot of the language, but the room was just too full of many different topics being discussed. James figured he'd better try to stay on track with the people he was talking to, and not try to get involved in others' conversation. Most of the Natives would try to use the English they had learned from Suzette when they addressed James, but their English skills were very limited so the Native tongue was used most of the time.

Missionaries still came to the village from time to time, and tried to indoctrinate the Natives with their religious ways, but the Natives only used what was reasonable to them, which was disturbing to the missionaries.

As the conversations buzzed around the room, James slowly leaned over to Moaka and whispered, "Can you find out if Suzette is around?"

Turning his head toward James, Moaka replied, "Yes, she here. Tess say have no man."

"Does she still live in the same hut?"

James seemed to feel that he was the object of everyone's gaze, as he looked again at Moaka for some type of understanding.

Moaka started laughing and replied in a slurred voice, "Kincaid, all know want see Suzette."

Talking out of the side of his mouth, trying not to be too obvious, James impatiently asked Moaka again, "Does she still live in the same damn place?"

Moaka motioned to Tess' cousin and quickly rattled off something, then turned back to James and, grinning, said, "Same place."

Just then, a child came charging through the entranceway, and started speaking very quickly. James managed to catch some of the conversation, and the name Suzette.

When the child finished, Moaka turned to James and smiled saying, "Suzette like see."

James' heart jumped into his mouth, as he tried to appear calm. He didn't want the folks here to know how eager he was to see Suzette. James thanked Moaka and bid everyone goodbye, at least for a while, because Moaka had asked if they all could sleep here for their stay. Thinking about this for a second, James motioned Moaka outside with him.

Once outside, James quietly explained to Moaka, "I might not be back tonight. If I don't return could you offer my apologies to our host?" Putting his hand on Moaka's shoulder James continued, "You don't think Tess' people will be insulted, do you? What I mean is that you asked for all of us to stay here. I wouldn't want to offend anyone."

Moaka looked down the street toward where Suzette lived, "All know. All like you marry. Native women happy you marry Suzette," Moaka replied.

With that statement from Moaka, James turned away and started walking on what could be called the main street of the village, which would eventually lead him into the middle of the village and to Suzette's hut.

Stopping along the way, James dipped his hands into a pot of warm water that was sitting next to a hut, and washed his face and hands removing the remainder of the evening meal.

Continuing down the street, he thought about what Moaka had just said. *I don't have any particular reason; I'm just not ready to settle down.* James wondered why Suzette stayed in such a place with all the training and talent she had to offer. They enjoyed each other's company, at least he enjoyed hers, and he hoped she enjoyed his as well. In other parts of the world, their relationship would have not been accepted by normal folks. There would have been the question about living together without marriage. James was sure that his parents would question the relationship highly. *Well, they are not here, and Suzette and I are, so let the questions be ended.*

The night air was cold, and the stars were displaying their entire splendor. The sky was black behind the millions of twinkling specks that penetrated the darkness. Shivering slightly, James quickened his pace. The village was very quiet and dark. The moon had not yet shown its face, but the stars gave up their light for the night. As he made his way through the village, the cooking fires had all but died out for the night. The dogs were bedded down, and all the Natives were in for the night. There was no movement anywhere in the village except for an occasional dog stirring. Most of the villagers were already asleep by now, as the Native Eskimo tradition was early to bed and early to rise.

James stopped and took a deep breath as he approached Suzette's hut. He stood at the entrance, closed his eyes, and hoped that their relationship could continue. As he stepped closer to the entrance, he hailed to Suzette inside.

"Come on in, James," sounded a soft and inviting voice within.

He hesitated for just a moment, took a deep breath, and pushed aside the skin door that blocked the entrance. As James entered the hut, the main room was empty. It was warm and comfortable with several oil lamps burning brightly. Padded floor mats were well-placed covering the wooden floor, with extra mats to be placed around the room as needed. Just then he heard Suzette's voice call from the back room saying, "Sit down and make yourself comfortable; I'll be out in a moment."

It was strange to hear proper English being spoken back to him. He stripped off his parka, and settled down on what had to be the softest floor-covering pad in the world. He stretched out and made himself comfortable. Feeling his muscles relaxing, it felt too good. The danger in this soft living was a person could get used to this kind of treatment. As he was checking the room out to see if any changes had occurred, Suzette entered the big room.

Suzette stopped and exclaimed, "James, your face is all sunburned!" Immediately, she crossed the room and picked a bottle of something off the shelf and approached James saying, "Here, let me get some of this salve on you before your skin falls off. I am glad to see you back. I kept track of you and Moaka through the Natives who told me whenever they had seen the Fish Man. I guess some of the Natives started calling you that after you helped them last summer with their fish snares they had set in the river."

James didn't say a word, all he could do was lie there and look up into her radiant, glowing face and her long, blonde hair that hung down as she knelt beside him. He felt her tender, soft hands gently massaging the salve into his sunburned face. It had been more than a year since he'd seen her last, and she seemed to have become more beautiful. As she finished applying the salve and stood up, her robe lay open slightly, exposing a portion of her long, slender leg. Her skin was smooth and unblemished. A portion of her long, blonde hair lay over her left shoulder and it sparkled in the glimmering light of the hut.

Smiling at him, she inquired, "What are you looking at?"

"I'm just admiring a person that I've come to care for, very much. It's sure been a long time since I saw you last. Why don't you come down here and give me a proper greeting?"

Without hesitation, she slowly walked across the room and replaced the bottle, and she returned to where James was stretched out on the padded mats and lay down beside him. "Now what was it you wanted?"

James kissed her passionately and he felt her responding back.

When they finally broke their embrace, James whispered, "I'll bet I thought about doing that a thousand times out on the flats. It is so nice to be back."

"I thought about you many times, and at times I would get very lonely."

James reached up and touched her long, blonde hair. Letting his fingers sift through her hair, he said, "I don't know if you know it or not, but a man gets awfully lonesome out there too. Even though Moaka and Tess are with me, it's just not the same. I don't think I get lonesome for company," he paused for second, then continued, "It's just certain kinds of company."

"And what kind of company would that be?" Suzette teased.

James looked into her lovely oval face and touched her soft, glowing cheek, and replied, "You know what kind of company." She slowly rose up on one elbow and kissed him on the cheek as she got to a kneeling position.

"Are you hungry, James? I've got some biscuits made, and I can get some rabbit warmed up if you want?"

Not answering right away, James just kept looking into her lovely brown eyes; his mind was a whirlwind of activity, thinking about all the possibilities there could be with this person.

"James, why are you looking at me that way? You look as if you're a thousand miles away. Is something wrong?"

He shook his head and smiled. "No, Suzette, there is nothing wrong, but I was just thinking how lucky I am to be here tonight. No, I'm not hungry. I ate over at Kirima's before coming here, but if you have any tea made, I'd sure like some of that."

"I have some warmed up already."

James watched her rise and she seemed to float across the floor to one of the oil heating lamps, where she poured the hot steaming liquid into a cup and brought it back to him. Sitting down beside him again, she asked, "James, do you realize that I haven't seen you in over a year? Couldn't you have made it back before now? I realize that I had to be gone the last time you were here, but I would still like to see you more often. This country is hard enough to get along in without depriving each other of the luxury of seeing someone you care about."

James sipped the body-warming beverage slowly, trying to think of a good or at least believable excuse for his absence. He felt her eyes bearing down on him, and whatever his answer was, it had to be believable. Setting the half-full cup down and turning to her he replied, "Suzette, I really don't have an excuse. I know that Moaka and Tess were here some time back, but when they came here, I had to go to Barrow for supplies. I guess all I can do is apologize to you and hope that you will accept that."

Her response was half-shocking and half-surprising to James. "You foolish man; do you think for an instant that I would not forgive you?

It's just that I missed you, and I tried to keep track of you, but there were long periods that nobody had seen you two. By the way, when you go to Barrow sometime, I would like to come along if that would be possible." Pausing and smiling slightly, she continued, "I don't want to be like Tess, and go with you all the time, but I think it would be a fun adventure to go to Barrow with you some time."

"Are you serious, Suzette?"

"Of course, I think it would be fun for both of us. Don't you?"

"I think it would be fine. I can't think of anything better. Maybe we could plan a trip for this fall, but I've got to warn you, riding on the sled may get tiresome," James explained.

"Don't worry about that, we can put soft mats in the sled for easy riding." Lying on the soft mats next to him, she continued, "Did you know that this hut was built for me by the villagers? I guess they thought it was a good idea having a school for their children."

"Yeah, Suzette, you have a good setup." Reaching down for his cup, James exclaimed, "Damn, I spilled the rest of my tea!" As she started to get up for a cleanup rag, James grabbed her arm and pulled her down to him saying, "Let it be, there wasn't that much in there anyway." Studying her soft, creamy complexion, as if looking for a flaw, but finding none, he whispered, "I don't want to waste any more of our time together."

Molding her body to his, he could feel her every line and curve, and he knew this was going to be a night to remember. As their passion grew, James knew his feelings were changing for Suzette. James didn't know if it was the atmosphere of the room, his loneliness, or was he starting to have the kind of relationship with Suzette that was meaningful?

CHAPTER FIFTEEN

James was awakened from possibly the best night's sleep he'd had in weeks by the sound of Suzette's low humming. He smelled the aroma of breakfast cooking and his stomach reminded him that he had only a small meal last night, and that he was starving. Looking up at the roof of the hut, James could see the rough poles that supported the skin roof sections. Outside, sod covered the skins, and about a foot of snow was on top of the sod, which made for good insulation. These structures could be heated and kept warm with limited amounts of heat, and they would stay warm and cozy inside. They usually had a vent hole for ridding the inside of smoke and fumes, and from time to time, the entrance flap was fanned or blocked open to get rid of stale air, but the inside could be warmed up again very quickly.

Snow was a very good insulator, and when it really got cold out on the flats, he and Moaka built an igloo to ward off most of the cold. The tents were easy to put up and take down, but they just weren't as warm as the igloos, especially during a storm and high wind times.

James was amazed how something built as crudely as these huts could be kept so warm. Nothing was painted because plain and simple was the way here. Maybe that's what he liked about this lifestyle. Even the bed he was lying in was crude. Soft mats made of feathers covered by a layer of cloth, lay on a wooden floor. The covering quilts were made of the same material, but with a softer cloth covering the feathers. It always took some time to warm the covers up, but the bed would eventually become warm and cozy.

James rose up on one elbow and peeked over the covers to see Suzette kneeling over the warming pot. As he gazed at her gentle form, he was reminded of their welcoming rendezvous together last night. She was attentive to his every need, and asked almost nothing in return. Her long blonde hair was tied back with a ribbon as it fanned down her back, like a waterfall.

The warming pot was being kept warm by a small seal oil flame that was slid under the hanging pot and the small flame could keep the contents steaming hot, besides warming the hut.

Suzette had got up early this morning and cooked outside. Last night she had made a mention about him and Moaka staying on at Teshpuk for a while, but he didn't want to spoil the moment of last night by telling her he had to leave again right away. He hoped that she had not prepared too much food for his stay. The aroma that filled the hut told James that it was cooked salmon. James also appreciated that he wouldn't have to eat it with the wind howling down his neck.

As James stretched his neck muscles to get some of the stiffness out, he noticed movement out of the corner of his eye. Sitting across the outer room was the most bewildered looking little boy staring at him as if James had just fallen from of the sky. James guessed that the small boy was not accustomed to seeing a man in Suzette's living quarters. Turning his head in the boy's direction, James looked straight at him and made a funny face. The boy broke out into a big smile, and James knew that he hadn't intimidated the young lad at all. James questioned Suzette, who was in the main room, "One of your students already, this early in the morning?"

Suzette jumped as she was startled, and exclaimed, "You! I'm not quite used to having someone in my bedroom." She let out a short laugh and resumed, "James, I can tell you're not used to sleeping inside. It's already about eight-thirty; this child has been here for about a half hour, because he is waiting for school to start. We don't usually start until about nine o'clock, but his folks had to leave early this morning, so they dropped him off earlier than normal. I hope you don't mind. They had to go to another village some distance away today for some trading, and they needed to get an early start."

With no reply, James started to rise when he remembered he was naked. Looking around quickly and not seeing what he was looking for, he asked Suzette, "In all the activity last night, I seemed to have mislaid my clothes. Do you happen to know where they might be?"

Giggling, she replied, "They're in here. Just a moment and I'll get them for you so you won't have to come out here in your birthday suit. You can get dressed in there. When you've finished, I have some warm water here, so you can shave and get cleaned up a bit."

"I left my bag at Kirima's hut last night," James replied.

Softly Suzette replied, "I went over there earlier this morning and picked up your stuff, you'll find the bag lying at the foot of the bed."

Just then, he saw his bag just where she said it would be. "Thanks, Suzette. That was very thoughtful of you. I'll bet it's colder than anything outside this morning. The only thing is, you're starting to act and sound like Moaka, waiting on me all the time. By the way, has he come around yet this morning?"

Returning to stirring the contents in the warming pot, she responded, "Yes, he announced himself and poked his head in here early this morning. That's who woke me up. I have to get up anyway about seven o'clock, to get ready for the students, but Moaka came calling a little earlier than that."

James smiled to himself and thought, *Yeah, his mental alarm is always set at early or before.* James stood as gracefully as he could, trying to keep the blanket wrapped around him. "Suzette, do I smell tea brewing?"

"You men are all the same, always thinking of your stomach. Of course tea is made."

The still form covered by a blanket seemed to be without life. Moaka silently knelt down and sharply struck thru the covers. At the time of impact Moaka roared, "You're like Kincaid. You would sleep your life away."

Instantly, Tess rolled from beneath the bed covers and scolded, "What did you do that for? I don't hit you when you're asleep!"

Staring at Tess, somewhat drawn back by her aggressive behavior, Moaka quickly fired back, "You are never awake early enough to bother me."

Rolling back beneath the covers, Tess replied angrily, "Leave me alone." Ducking her head under the covers, she stuck her head back out and blurted, "Go wake up Kincaid and leave me alone."

"I tried; Suzette wouldn't let me wake him. She is going to spoil him."

"If you can't sleep, then go and wake up the whole village," Tess continued scolding. As her head ducked back under the cover, she angrily added, "Go away. You have nothing to do today. Go clean out your sled or something."

Slowly rising from Tess' still form, Moaka returned to the warming fire to join the other members of the hut.

As Moaka seated himself with the others, Kirima said calmly, "Let her sleep. Not everybody gets up early like you. Tess was right; you don't have anything to do today." She handed Moaka a warm cup of tea and continued, "Here, have some more tea, and enjoy your visit."

Moaka accepted the cup of tea and again asked, "When did the polar bear come to the village?"

Without hesitation, Kirima answered, "Yesterday sunrise. Why ask about the polar bear? Maybe it's the same one you and Kincaid had trouble with?"

Shaking his head slowly Moaka quietly replied, "I don't know; I can't be sure, maybe." Standing up, Moaka continued, "I'm going to find Karkak and see what he has to say."

* * *

James washed, put on fresh undergarments, dressed, and shaved. He was starving and his breakfast plate was already prepared and sitting next to the warming pot. Suzette had prepared James' favorite breakfast, cooked salmon and biscuits. She remembered that was James' favorite breakfast from his last visit.

Sneaking up behind her as she stood over the warming pot, James gently slid his arms around her tiny waist and squeezed her softly. Tilting her head back, he kissed her on the cheek.

"I remember last night too, but try to remember we have company this morning."

Glancing over to where the Eskimo child was sitting, James answered, "Yeah, unfortunately, I remember." As he looked into the cooking pot, James exclaimed, "Why have you cooked all that seal?"

Turning and wrapping her arms around his neck, she said, "Moaka said you two would be leaving soon and I thought I would make some food for you to take along. I'm also going to make a couple dozen biscuits for you and Moaka."

A worried expression came over James' face as he asked, "Did he say anything about Tess?"

"Moaka didn't seem to think that she would be coming along on this trip," Suzette replied.

"She always comes along, but maybe she shouldn't this trip. Moaka and I will want to travel light and fast. I told him we would talk with some old man about the polar bear, and then maybe see if we could find some sign of the animal."

"Could the old man be Noka?" Suzette inquired. "By the way, has anybody told you that a bear came to visit Teshpuk the other night? Oh, never mind, I'm sure Moaka knows by now, and he'll tell you all about it."

"The polar bear was here? Here in Teshpuk?" James exclaimed. He thought for a second. "Well, what in the devil is going on. Anyway, I don't know his name; Moaka just called him the old man."

She removed her arms from around his neck as James sat down to enjoy his breakfast.

James' thoughts began to wander. *Suzette couldn't ride around on a sled the rest of her life like Tess does. This lady has a lot more going for her than that, and she has a future, if not here, then somewhere else. What would happen if we got married, and I was transferred to some other place? What would happen with this school; ah, it's not worth stewing over right now.*

As James finished breakfast, several children charged into Suzette's hut and stopped dead still just inside the entrance. They were surprised to see a man sitting in the middle of Suzette's school finishing breakfast.

Rising to his feet, James thought he'd better be getting out of everybody's way. Donning his outer layer gear, he didn't figure on coming back and interrupting school for a while.

The morning was cold. The new day was well underway with the villagers performing their daily routines. The sun had been up for a while and would be setting in the early afternoon behind the Brooks Range, but the days were starting to get longer.

As James surveyed the lay of the village, it seemed to have a couple of new huts. James knew that civilization would be here before anybody knew it. The country wouldn't stay primitive much longer. Even now, the small village of Teshpuk seemed to be growing. The Natives didn't realize the potential or understand the full meaning of owning property, and nobody in Teshpuk owned property. If a Native, or anybody else, wanted to build a hut and live somewhere, that's just what they did. Nobody asked permission. The Natives believed that the land belonged to everyone.

James saw Moaka coming down the street toward him, with one of the villagers. James was anxious to talk to the old man Moaka told him about because they needed to try to put more pieces of the puzzle together on the polar bear events. The whole situation seemed to have gotten to Moaka, and the sooner they solved the polar bear situation, the better off Moaka would be. James couldn't remember Moaka ever being as unsettled as he had been since that critter busted in their camp out on the flats.

When the two men drew nearer to James, Moaka gave him the morning greeting, *ublarpalluk,* and added, "Woman make man all."

James sheepishly smiled and said, "You ass, you always have to rub it in?" With a quick motion of his head, James asked, "Who is your friend?"

Slapping the Native next to him on the back, Moaka responded, "This Karkak, village elder. He chase male polar bear yesterday sunrise. Polar bear come village in night, rob meat racks. Polar bear kill two dogs. All village up fast, but dark. No get good shot. One think hit bear in rear, no see blood. Some chase polar bear." Moaka paused for just a moment, seeing that James was doing some deep thinking, and then continued, "What say Kincaid?"

"I just can't figure it, Moaka. That bear was headed in this direction, but it sure came a long ways in a damn short period of time, if it is even the same bear, which it sounds like it could be." Thinking back to when they first got to Teshpuk yesterday afternoon, James remembered that he had noticed the lack of dog teams at the huts. He never thought about it much then, but now it added up.

Karkak turned to Moaka, using quite a few hand motions, as most Natives did, to emphasize his point.

James picked up most of the conversation, but Karkak was talking so fast it was hard for James to keep up. Holding his hands up in the air, James addressed the two in Native tongue, "Karkak speak slower so I can follow the conversation."

"English can say some," quickly responded Karkak.

"Okay," James answered. "Use English if you want, but don't hesitate to speak Native for a meaning. I can understand some Native, and Moaka can help."

Nodding slightly and smiling, Karkak held his hands far apart and continued, "Polar bear male, as walrus."

James knew Karkak meant that the polar bear would weigh about what a full adult walrus would, about one thousand pounds. Nodding his head James asked Karkak, "Was anybody able to get a close look at the animal, if only for an instant, to see if there was something wrong with him, or were there any blood spots on him before they started shooting?"

Karkak thought for a moment, and turned to Moaka for help with what James had just said.

James wondered, *Why a big male would be so far inland, and what was he doing robbing drying racks? There has to be something wrong with that stupid animal, or better yet, maybe he just found an easy source of food. It had to be the same big male Moaka and he ran into the other day.*

When Karkak had finished thinking about James' questions, he answered saying, "Kincaid, no see polar bear good, no see wrong with bear."

In a discouraged voice James answered, "Well, that doesn't help us a hell'va lot; other than the fact that it could have been the same male that we ran into." With a motion of his hand toward Karkak, James thanked him without much enthusiasm for his help as Karkak turned and departed from Moaka and James.

Standing silently together watching Karkak walk away from them, Moaka stated, "Talk Karkak, he say village north here, big male come camp four day back. Kill four dogs, steal meat from racks."

James' mind spun in circles, and he asked rather annoyed, "Why in hell didn't Karkak tell me that? I don't know, but I feel like Karkak somehow didn't trust me very much."

"Karkak elder," Moaka explained. "No think you like talk to him."

Shaking his head, James' quick response was, "That's crazy, Moaka, and you know it. How did he ever come to that conclusion? I've just met him."

"Kincaid," Moaka snapped, "native need eye and eye with stranger."

Knowing that Moaka meant eye contact, James blurted, "Moaka, by hell, I don't have time to think of all the damn rules all the time. Sometimes I get sick and tired of trying to keep everybody happy."

"Be okay, Kincaid. Karkak understand. He hear you true man."

"Well, remind me the next time I see Karkak to thank him again for his help." Pausing for an instant, James continued, "Moaka, I wonder if the polar bear has found himself an easy source of food and doesn't want to hunt anymore? Was it also at night that he hit that other village?"

"I think," Moaka instantly responded. "Bear hit before morning sky. Karkak say same for Teshpuk."

"Moaka, let's go and see the old man you said lives here. Maybe he can shed some light on the whole mess. What is his name?"

As James started to follow Moaka, Moaka grabbed James' arm and said, "Kincaid, Karkak have say for us. He village elder." Pausing for just a second, Moaka continued, "Name Noka."

"Yeah, Moaka, that will be just fine, don't worry about Karkak talking for us. I don't mind and we can work through it."

As Moaka and James caught up with Karkak, Moaka made a quick comment to Karkak about protocol, and they proceeded to the old man's hut as Karkak announced their presence.

Some of the customs that were established in these far away villages always fascinated James. He had been told the reason that someone from the village had to announce a stranger—or anybody had to announce themselves—was so there would be no surprises from unwanted visitors. Smiling to himself and thinking of last night, *I wouldn't have wanted anybody coming into Suzette's hut unannounced.*

Before long Karkak stuck his head out of the entrance and motioned for James and Moaka to come in.

James and Moaka sat across the small, poorly illuminated room from the old man and Karkak, with a single seal oil lamp burning low between them. The air in the hut was stuffy, and it needed to have the roof flap opened more for better ventilation.

Getting as comfortable as he could on the thin floor matting, James waited for Karkak to make the introductions. James noticed that Noka was staring straight at him. Without breaking his stare at James, Noka said something so low and so fast to Moaka that James did not hear or understand. Since they had entered the room and James' eyes had adjusted to the light, Noka and James had been locked into a stare down contest, and James was determined not to break eye contact. James didn't know what the game was, but he was willing to go down to the mat with this old man, if necessary.

Immediately thereafter, Noka got up, walked over to James, and held out his hand. Moaka touched James on the elbow and said, "Noka want see fish badge."

Not looking at Moaka, James questioningly responded as he began feeling his chest pockets, "Why? Hell, I don't even know if I got the damn thing with me."

"Think he want. See way give. You make trade."

Still holding his stare with Noka, James replied, "Hell, we didn't come here to trade, we came here for information," as he kept feeling his outer parka pockets for his Wildlife Officer badge. James' neck felt as if it was breaking, but he was determined to keep eye contact and kept the staring contest up with old man. James could not figure out why Noka wanted his badge.

The old man's short stature towered over James, as their eyes were still locked into a silent battle of wills. Not looking at Moaka, James bumped him with his elbow and questioned, "Why does he want my badge?"

Feeling Moaka's closeness by his breath on his face, Moaka answered, "You important person. Want show important person visit. He give you special gift."

"Well that's fine with me, Moaka." James finally got the badge out of his pocket and handed it to Noka.

Noka finally broke his stare and glanced down at the badge.

James looked at Moaka, and continued, "You can tell him he can have it as a gift." James thought about telling Noka himself, but he thought some protocol would be broken if Moaka didn't tell him. For some reason he had not had the need or opportunity to meet this elder of the village, but he knew years of knowledge lay behind those tired old eyes.

Moaka smiled and motioned as he said, "Kincaid would be honored if Noka would accept the badge as gift."

As soon as Moaka was finished, Noka smiled and returned to the other side of the hut. He knelt down and removed something from underneath the mat, and on returning to James, he handed him a bag made of softened caribou skin, and replied, "It for your life."

"I'll be damned," James murmured quietly, and as he showed it to Moaka, James continued, "the old man just gave me a *kujariwok*—medicine bag." James thanked him for the gift, as he smiled up at Noka. James knew the medicine bag was a special gift because it didn't mean a thing unless someone gave it to you first; then it was up to the owner to fill it with meaningful articles.

Nodding his head in approval, Noka went back to his mat and sat down.

A conversation between Moaka and Karkak began as James glanced down at his newly acquired medicine bag and knew that it would be empty. He thought humorously to himself, *Everybody has his own trinkets for luck*. Opening his coat slightly, he slipped it into his inside pocket, the same pocket that the badge had come from. They did make a trade, but who benefitted the most remained to be seen. He loosened his coat; the hut was hot and stuffy.

Moaka turned to Noka and told him about the polar bear that had been raiding the villages and was possibly the one he and James had encountered.

Noka told a story of many years ago, when he was a child, and his father and older brothers took out after a polar bear that was doing the same thing as this one was doing. Apparently, according to the old man's story, they chased the animal for a week or more, and never got close enough to kill the animal. They chased it so much the polar bear just left the area, and supposedly it went out onto the ice pack and never came back again. He also said that the polar bear attacked their camp one night, when they were chasing him, and then disappeared.

Eh, the old story of who is chasing who, James thought. With a slight nod of his head toward the old man, James cautiously asked, "Did they ever see anything wrong with the animal?"

After some thought, Noka answered, "No."

Slowly and with his best enunciation James asked in Native tongue, "Did the polar bear they were chasing outrun the dogs for a long distance? Why do you think this polar bear would venture so far inland, especially this time of year when its main food supply is out on the ice?"

Noka lowered his head as if going to sleep, but in actuality he was in deep thought, and after a time he raised his head slowly and began another story. "The polar bear that my father and brother chased was a male. He could run far and as fast as the wind. My father said the polar bear came inland because the bear was being guided by spirits. He said the polar bear was protected by spirits and that was the reason they could never kill him."

James looked at Noka and nodded his head as if in agreement, and thanked him for his counsel. He looked at Moaka asked, "Have we dealt with all the particulars of visiting? If so, let's get out of here. We need to set up some sort of plan to get this damn bear or run his butt back on the ice pack, before he ends up killing somebody."

With the proper thanks and goodbyes to Noka, all three left the hut.

CHAPTER SIXTEEN

It was a beautiful clear, crisp day with not much wind as the three exited from the old man's hut. The temperature rose to about ten below, and it felt refreshing to be in the open air again. He could still smell the odor of those rank hides as if the odor had stuck in his nose. James seemed to be able to think clearer outside the stuffy hut, and raising his arms high above his head he stretched, as he turned to Moaka and inquired, "Is there anyone in the village going to Barrow that could deliver a letter?" Before Moaka could answer, James continued, "I realize that Barrow is three or four days from here, but if someone was going, they could get the letter to Barrow and then have it sent on to Nealy in Seattle. I should get a report off to Nealy. I was planning on making the trip to Barrow myself before the spring thaws, but I'm not sure how long this polar bear thing will take."

Moaka scratched the underside of his chin as he responded, "Mail here."

Surprised, James exclaimed, "Mail here at Teshpuk! What in the world are you talking about?"

"Kincaid, what think? Teshpuk civilized." Moaka, sensing that James' mind was working, stood silently.

James pondered, *A mail route from Barrow to Teshpuk...that might change a few things.* Once again turning to Moaka, he asked, "How often do you think that this mail run goes back and forth between here and Barrow?"

Shaking his head as if to say he didn't know, Moaka raised his voice to Karkak who was just returning to the old man's hut after talking to another Native a short distance away. "Karkak, how often does mail go to Barrow?"

Continuing to approach Moaka and James, Karkak replied, "The mail gets here from Barrow about once a month or more. It depends on what comes from Nome and other places to Barrow that will make its way to Teshpuk." As Karkak stopped next to James he asked, "Need help kill polar bear?"

"Thanks for your help, Karkak. I know you want to help with the polar bear. Moaka and I know you have much to give in knowledge and skill. We will call on you if we need any help."

Karkak turned as he heard someone call his name and replied, "Kincaid, I help," then proceeded on his way.

Staring into the cloudless blue sky, James commented to Moaka, "I really don't want a lot of Natives involved in this search for the polar bear, at least not right away. The less people we have involved now the better off we are going to be. We may need the whole village and more before this thing is over, but not right now."

"Kincaid, what in mind?" Moaka inquired.

"You know, Moaka, when we were in the old man's hut there was some conversation about ordering supplies. I didn't think much of it, but now it is making sense. Apparently, some of the villagers order certain supplies from Barrow. It seems that the supplies are limited and a person may not get what he orders, but at least some of them do get a few articles delivered from Barrow." Nodding his head, James continued, "Well, at any rate, if I could get mail delivered here, that is all I want right now. We can talk about ordering supplies later on."

"Kincaid, what in mind?"

As James looked up and down the street of the makeshift village, he almost felt like this was becoming his home. Without looking at Moaka,

James simply replied, "It's nothing, Moaka, I was just dreaming a little."

As James and Moaka watched Karkak enter into his hut, they walked back to the middle of the village to where Moaka thought the so-called mail office was located. As they approached a hut, not unlike the others in the village, James wondered, *Why a mail route? I'd bet there's not two people in the whole village that gets mail on a regular basis. I'd also bet just as quick this mail route thing was a good excuse for getting a supply line set in place.* James knew that with supply lines open and mail routes established, that meant more people and more trading. Eventually, though, it would come to buying and selling everything and trading would take a back seat.

Just before they got to the entrance of the mail office, Moaka stopped James by gently grasping his parka sleeve. "Kincaid make good thought for Noka. He say Kincaid have eye, and heart of the mountain bear. Most no look into old man eye like you. He test you. He thinks badge big medicine." Pausing for a moment and slapping James on the back and laughing, he continued, "Noka say, he only one have power in badge."

James laughed, "Yeah, I figured it was something like that, but I wasn't going to break the stare down first, once the thing got started. But, Moaka, why in hell do the Natives feel like they have to test every stranger they meet?"

Moaka shook his head, and responded, "Not know. Way things are." With a quick look at James and a grin spreading across his face, he added jokingly, "Native, strange people."

They entered the mail hut to find a different atmosphere inside than most huts in the village. Apparently, it was not necessary to announce yourself before entering this hut. It was well-lighted with seal oil lamps and had ample ventilation with no skins hanging on the walls for curing. It had a makeshift looking post office, complete with counter and little boxes for sorting mail. James stood in the middle of the hut, while Moaka explained their wishes to the woman behind the counter.

James was getting more excited about the mail route as time went on. He was mentally working on the assumption that he could actually establish Teshpuk as his headquarters.

Moaka turned back to James and said, "She say letter go Barrow, go Seattle."

"Can I have my mail in Barrow sent here, to Teshpuk?"

Moaka stood staring at James for a second, then broke into one of the biggest grins James had even seen him tote. Without breaking his stare, he commented, "Suzette got you?"

James slapped Moaka on the shoulder saying, "Don't bet on it just yet."

Moaka turned back to the woman behind the counter and they talked for a short time then Moaka turned back to James replying, "She say deliver Nome thirty day in winter by dogsled, and fourteen day in summer by boat."

James and Moaka thanked the woman and both men walked toward the entrance. James held up before they went outside, and commented to Moaka, "I'll have to write a letter this evening, and mail it in the morning before we leave."

Exiting from the hut into the fading early afternoon sun, James and Moaka both knew what they had to do. Somehow, they had to find the polar bear, and either run him back out onto the ice, or kill him. James was not in favor of the latter, but he knew if Moaka got a good shot at the polar bear, he would be as dead as a doornail.

James and Moaka halted about ten paces from the sleds. Looking at each other, they shrugged their shoulders and shook their heads, as James commented, "Well Moaka no time like the present. I don't mind being out on the flats; matter of fact, I enjoy being out there, but I just hate to do all this damn packing up."

Moaka stretched his arms above his head, and commented, "I do."

"Nope," James said discouragingly, "The packing and unpacking is all part of the territory."

They began unpacking their sleds so the sleds could be turned upside down to check the hardwood runners for splits or breaks. About the time

James got the gear off his sled and had it turned upside down he heard Moaka hailing him. James rose up and leaned on the runners, to give Moaka his full attention.

"Kincaid, no tell story how make runner in past. Use driftwood. Carve shape need. Tie leg bone caribou length." Pausing for a moment, he finally resorted to, "*Kresiuyak,*"—rawhide strips. "Driftwood no last long." He was silent for a moment while he ran his hands along the smooth bottom of his hardwood sled runner, then continued, "Hardwood last more season. Sled strong," as he firmly shook the sled. "Haul more." Glancing up to see if James was still listening, Moaka continued, "Kincaid daydream about Suzette."

James stopped his stare at nothing, and half-listening, as he looked at Moaka for an instant, before he pushed off from his sled runners and ran straight for Moaka. Moaka was crouching down, getting set for the weight to hit him. Within four or five running leaps, James hit Moaka's squat body squarely. Grabbing each other, they rolled repeatedly on the snow and ice surface, as both of them were laughing like a couple of school kids wrestling and hanging on to each other for dear life. They both had so many layers of clothes on that it was as though they were rolling on a mattress. Finally coming to a stop, they separated and lay on their backs, still laughing.

James sat up and questioned, "Are you planning on taking Tess with us this time?"

His laughter now subsiding, Moaka rolled up on his elbow and answered, "No Kincaid. Say, Kincaid want go after polar bear, stay Teshpuk. She know, travel fast. Tess good wife." Then he fell silent.

James remembered what Suzette had told him, but he wanted to give Moaka the chance to make that decision. Concern in his voice, James asked, "Will she worry much, Moaka?"

Shrugging his shoulders, Moaka replied, "Maybe. That is way. She people here."

Still resting on the ground, James continued, "You know, Moaka, we don't have much time to do whatever it is that we are going to do. It's getting on into the middle of March and not too long from now the snow is going to start getting soft. The dogs will have to work twice as hard, but more importantly that damn polar bear will really be able to outrun us for sure."

As they both got up and brushed the snow off, Moaka looked at James and asked, "Kincaid kill polar bear?"

"Moaka, I already know what you would rather do, but at this point, I can only say that if the bear keeps running in the right direction, I would like to run him back onto the ice. If he doesn't run, then I'll let you do as your natural instincts tell you to do. If he doesn't run the right direction, I'll help you eliminate him. Nobody wants a dangerous animal raiding the villages and possibly killing somebody."

"Kincaid, remember what Noka say?"

James answered slowly, "Yeah, he mentioned something about the spirits guiding the bear."

Moaka calmly stated, "No judge belief. Noka say, happen for reason. Native hunt polar bear many season. Native say, spirit true. Understand Kincaid."

James nodded in the affirmative, and quietly replied, "I know, Moaka, and I don't mean to say I doubt his or anybody else's belief, but I can't deal with spirits right now. We need to put facts together. I hope you can understand?"

Reassuringly, Moaka responded, "Kincaid, no worry. We okay. What come no easy for dog or us. Polar bear no afraid Native or dog. Him danger to all."

James surveyed the sleds, and continued, "Let's make sure that we have everything that we will need for this trip. I know that we had talked about traveling light, but I'd hate like the devil to be out on the flats and come up short of something."

They both turned back to the sleds and neither one of them had any damage to their runners. As they started reloading the sleds, they kept checking with each other to make sure that they had everything. It was also important to make sure that the sleds would be loaded with about the same weight loads because each team was thirteen strong. They would pick up a few supplies in the morning before they left, but they already had most of the gear and supplies they needed for the trip. Neither James nor Moaka liked to go out on the flats without Tess because she added the touch of stability that a good camp needed, and both men hated to work all day then have to stop and have a cold camp or prepare food.

All the extra rations they needed they could trade for at the trading post, or James could use government credit. He didn't like to use that credit because it took a long time to receive payment, but now that Teshpuk was on the regular mail route, the time element could change.

Straightening up and looking at Moaka, James asked, "Do you think that the polar bear is carrying lead?" Pausing for an instant James continued, "Not only did we get some shots off at him, but so did some of the villagers. It would take a good hit to bring him down, but maybe somebody wounded him."

Moaka answered, "Maybe. Maybe shot before us. Maybe injured can no swim good. Take strong swimmer catch seal."

"No! Moaka, I don't mean someone else shot him, I mean maybe the villagers around here or maybe we put a slug into him. You could be right though. Someone before us could have plugged him. But if he is hurt, it sure doesn't seem to affect the damn animal's running ability."

The question not resolved, they returned to the task of packing the equipment they needed for the chase or hunt, however it turned out.

The sleds were finally loaded for the next morning start. They both walked over to the barking dogs who seemed excited to get going. The dogs were rested and in good condition for the coming journey. James approached Bray's squirming body, and Bray began to whine little noises in his friendly greeting. James knelt down and dug his fingers into the animal's thick, coarse hair on his wide chest. James thought to himself, *The team may really need their full strength on this run.* As James was kneeling down beside Bray, he noticed that Moaka was giving some extra attention to Anore, and was probably thinking the same thoughts.

After checking the rest of the dogs, and feeding them some bits and pieces of frozen fish, James and Moaka headed back to Kirima's hut. As they proceeded around to the front of the hut, they ran into Tess.

She had been watching them get ready and as they approached her, the look on her face told the whole story; she was worried. James had never seen that look on Tess' face before.

Standing directly in front of Moaka, she blocked his path and asked, "What is it going to be like?"

Slowly shaking his head, Moaka responded quietly, "I don't know. Kincaid and I will do what we have to."

Tess' tear-covered eyes gazed beyond Moaka and looked to James as she asked, "Kincaid, say what do?"

Before James could answer, Moaka interrupted. "Tess don't bother Kincaid. We'll be all right. We have good teams and both of us have a rifle."

Her gaze quickly swung back to Moaka and she exclaimed, "I heard the polar bear isn't afraid of Natives or dogs."

Moaka gently placed his arm around her shoulder and slowly walked her toward the hut entrance. Softly Moaka reassured Tess by saying, "We should be back to Teshpuk in a few days. Don't worry, Kincaid and I will protect each other."

Watching Moaka and Tess walking away, James hoped someday to have that feeling for a woman.

It was getting time for the evening meal and James and Moaka had agreed earlier that later that evening they would talk about their plans for the trip. Leaving Moaka and Tess, James proceeded on to Suzette's hut. Nearing the entrance, he hailed for a response from inside.

As James' eyes became accustomed to the golden glow light of the lamps, he noticed Suzette watching him from across the room. She moved across the room and kissed him passionately. Stepping back she said, "I missed you today. Where in the world did you go after breakfast? Don't you and Moaka eat the noon meal anymore?"

Not answering for a moment, James took off his coat, and then slowly replied, "Don't need to eat lunch when I didn't get up until almost the middle of the day." James smiled and gently took her in his arms softly whispering, "I missed you too, Suzette." Releasing her, he moved to sit down beside the warming pot. "Moaka and I spoke with a villager named Karkak, who said that a village south of here got hit by a polar bear the other night. Then we went and talked to Noka about some of the behavioral patterns of polar bears. He was not a lot of help. After some wild tale, the old man ended up with something about the bear being led by the spirits."

Suzette laughed. "You have to accept a lot of that around here. If the Natives don't know or can't figure out any other reason, it's the spirits' fault. Isn't Noka a sweet old man? Many villagers go to him with their problems and he helps them. Not that he is so intelligent, but he listens intently and really finds out what the problems are before he gives his valued counsel."

"By the way, Suzette," James inquired, "When the devil did they start having mail service to this village?"

Surprised, she quickly responded, "About two months ago. Why?"

As he eased himself around to the other side of the warming pot, James leaned back on his elbows and replied, "I didn't think it had been very long. I didn't think there was a post office at Teshpuk the last time I was here."

As James watched her move about the room, he just couldn't get the thought of her out of his mind. James thought, *Would a relationship work? Would she understand my long trips and being away from her for long periods of time?*

As these thoughts crept in and out of his mind, James heard Suzette respond, "There wasn't, James. After all, you haven't been in Teshpuk for some time other than a quick stop for supplies. Before a village can get mail service, it has to be in one place for at least five years, and two months ago Teshpuk had been established for just a little more than that amount of time."

"By the way, why was the village set up here anyway?" James inquired. "What I mean is it seems kind of far from the coast. I understand being next to the river is good for fishing, but I was just wondering."

Suzette's answer was quite matter-of-fact. "The main reason for setting up the village here was this location is near the caribou migration route, and the villagers are still close enough to the coast to get seal or fish anytime they want. Another reason is that during the summer months, this village is located near one of the best fishing areas on the Colville River. You ought to know that."

"Suzette, are most of the people related in this village like most other villages?"

As she moved closer to the cooking pot, Suzette lifted the lid and stirred the contents. "Yes, I think so, but there are more people moving to this village all the time. I can tell that by the way my school enrollment has gone up the last couple of months. Most of the newer folks are not related to the original settlers, but they are welcome here. We've even got a small trading post set up now. I think that also happened since the last time you were here."

"Damn, this place is really growing fast." Laughing somewhat to himself, James continued, "Before long you'll have a food store and a clothing store here and then you'll have a boomtown."

Waving her hand at James, she replied, "Don't be silly. This little village is a comfortable little nook, and that's just the way we like it."

"You've heard of progress, haven't you? Little comfortable nooks have a habit of becoming larger, especially when services are available." Pausing,

James asked, "When can we eat? The reason I ask is that I told Moaka we could meet here later this evening to talk about our plans for this trip."

"You mean hunt, don't you," she said in a rather irritated tone.

"Now Suzette, you can't have any feeling for this damn polar bear. That animal is dangerous. Moaka and I are concerned about this situation because of this polar bear's strange behavior."

Almost bitterly, she replied, "I guess you're right, James, and it does seem awfully strange behavior for a polar bear. But, when the animal was around here, the Natives didn't seem to have any problems running it off."

With a shake of his head, James fired back, "Sure the damn bear will run if threatened enough, but what if someone is alone out there? Damn it! It is strange, and that's not all, this situation has Moaka seeing White Ghosts, as he calls them, around every snow ridge. I'll tell you, Suzette, it's got me a little puzzled too."

"Wash up, James; we're about ready to eat. We are having rabbit, dried fish, biscuits, seaweed, and hot tea. Doesn't that sound tempting? I got the seaweed from the trading post. They said it came all the way from Nome."

James grabbed her and pulled her over on top of him. Kissing her passionately, he released his hold on her, and she didn't seem too interested in dinner now either.

Her eyes looked steadily into his and made James warm all over. Her long, soft, blonde hair fell gently across his wind-burned face as he enjoyed the moment.

Raising her supple female form from his, she exclaimed, "James! You were just saying you were in a hurry to eat; now you're playing around. Isn't Moaka coming soon?"

With an exaggerated sigh, James got up, and as he washed, his mind returned to the problem at hand. He wondered what direction they would take to try to intersect and track the polar bear. James knew it could be anywhere, even back out on the ice pack. Finished, he sat down in front of the cooking pot again and mumbled aloud, "Fat chance of that."

"What did you say? Fat chance of what?"

"Nothing, Suzette, I was thinking aloud."

Suzette baked some small sweet biscuits that had to be the best James had ever eaten. After the meal was over, he leaned over, kissed Suzette on the cheek, and softly said, "You obviously believe the way to a man's heart is through his stomach."

She laughed her typical little laugh and began cleaning up the meal's utensils and just then, they heard Moaka's voice outside of the hut. "Suzette, Kincaid?"

"Come in, Moaka," Suzette responded, as she continued cleaning up.

Moaka stumbled through the entrance, and questioned, "Ready talk trip?"

Before James could respond, Suzette scolded Moaka saying, "Moaka why are you speaking English like that? It doesn't do any good to teach these little ones proper English and then have the adults use a lazy form of the language. You can speak a lot better English, and you know it. I just don't understand why, especially you men, don't try and improve your English techniques." Without hardly taking a breath she continued, "And James, you're just as bad. Sometimes you sound just like Moaka, leaving out words and being lazy with your language."

"Damn, Suzette. I didn't realize it was such a big deal. We'll try to do better if that will make you feel any better."

Without another word, Suzette busied herself with her chores.

Moaka still stood at the entrance, almost as if he didn't know if he was going to be welcome, until Kincaid said, "Yeah, Moaka, come and sit down. We might want to look at the map I have, to lay out a route. I don't know if it will do any good, but at least it may help us with our general plan of what direction to go."

Spreading the sketchy map out on the floor mats, James asked Suzette, "Will you make Moaka and me some more hot tea?" Glancing up to make eye contact with Suzette, James could see that she wasn't any happier about he and Moaka going after the bear than Tess was, but James suspected that the two women's reasons were different. Tess was concerned about Moaka, and Suzette seemed to be more concerned about the polar bear. *That wasn't true, but sometimes it seemed like it.*

Suddenly, James said rather loudly, "Suzette, if you don't want us here, we can go somewhere else."

Clenching her fists in irritation, she responded, "I don't give a hoot what you do! Go ahead and make your killing plans. I'll fix your tea. And, no, you don't have to leave."

Moaka shifted his position, showing his uneasiness. "Suzette, maybe no kill."

"Oh, Moaka, go ahead with what you are doing. Don't mind me."

Not knowing how to respond, James looked back to the map and asked, "Now Moaka, where do you think we should start looking for this critter?"

After an hour or more of discussion about their tactics and different routes, James and Moaka finally came to a meeting of minds on how they were going to attempt to drive the polar bear out onto the ice, or eliminate it. Neither of them were very hopeful of having much success without having to scour the whole north slopes. They knew where most of the larger villages were, and they would concentrate their search between those villages, or in the vicinity. If they didn't find any trace of the animal, they would start extending the search. Nothing was mentioned by either man about how long they would keep up the searching patterns, but both hoped the siege would not last long.

With the discussion over, and their work cut out for them, Moaka finished his last cup of tea, stood up, and turned toward the entrance and said, "Maybe no sleep tonight."

Just before Moaka got to the entrance of the hut to go out, Suzette remarked, "Moaka, I hope that you feel like you are always welcome here. I want to say I'm sorry for scolding you about your English. I just wish you men would try harder to use proper English, especially around the little ones. It is so important for them to learn properly."

Nodding his head in the affirmative, Moaka replied, "Suzette say. It important for children to learn. "

Just before Moaka left James stopped him with, "Moaka I probably won't sleep a wink either. The sooner we get started the better off I'll be." As Moaka disappeared through the entrance, James turned his full attention to Suzette.

"Suzette, I've wanted to tell you something all day. It's just that I haven't had time to explain it properly. I'm rather excited about the whole thing."

As she was cleaning up the rest of the cups from their tea, she replied, "Well, the way you and Moaka have been so busy getting ready for tomorrow, I wonder that you have had time for any other thoughts of anything else. The polar bear seems very demanding of your time right now."

"I know, but now is the time for us to have each other alone for a while. Anyway, I've had my mail routed to Teshpuk, instead of having to go to Barrow to get it. That means that I will probably be able to be around here more often. What do you think?"

Speaking with a trace of shyness in her voice, she asked, "I would like to ask you the same question, what do you think?" As she finished cleaning up she continued, "What I mean is, did you have your mail changed for the fact that you don't have to go to Barrow, or could I have anything to do with your decision?"

She shook her long, silky hair with a seductive shrug, as she reached to pinch out the wick on the closest lamp. The room became considerably darker as she crossed the room toward James and lay down by his side. Snuggling closer to him, she asked, "I didn't hear an answer yet."

"Suzette, you know that I care for you very much, and if things were different, well things might be different. One thing I don't want you to forget is that you are very special to me, and I care for you very much."

Softly she whispered, "I guess I can settle for that right now."

As they lay snuggled in each other's arms in the softly lit room, James felt he could have been in the fanciest hotel, and it would not have been any more enjoyable. James knew that he was getting more involved with this person, but right then he didn't care.

CHAPTER SEVENTEEN

Suzette sat quietly in the large outer room with a single seal oil candle burning which lit her immediate area so she could see to darn a hole in one of James' socks. Dropping her darning into her lap, she thought of the early times of her life when her parents brought her to this great country. Although just a child, she could still remember the Russian domination, and the Russians thought that the missionaries would not promote the Russian government or policies. Smiling to herself, she silently answered, *And they were probably right.* She also thought about her parents, and how much they would have liked James. Sighing lightly and returning to her darning, she retraced the events since James had returned to Teshpuk. James was an influential man and everybody liked him. He seemed to be able to listen to everyone that had something to say. Many times, he never did anything about some of the requests or questions, but people respected him because he listened, and the more Native he became the more the Natives loved him.

Suzette knew that she was hopelessly falling in love with this stupid Scotsman from Wisconsin, but she couldn't help it. Thinking, *James seemed to care for me and be somewhat attentive to most of my needs.* Staring at her darning, Suzette knew that she wanted to close the trap as soon as possible.

Putting her darning down, she rose and woke James, because she knew both men wanted to get an early start.

The dim light of the lamp in the outer room seem to cast strange images on the exposed rough pole beams of the ceiling as James closed his eyes again and felt the warmth of the covers around him. He snuggled deeper, knowing that before long Suzette would call again. He was determined to lie in the warm bed as long as possible.

The sound of Suzette's footsteps rustling across the mats into the sleeping room was the last peace James would have that day. "James Kincaid!" she exclaimed, "What are you still doing in bed? Moaka is going to be ready to go and you'll still be in bed."

Slowly opening his eyes, James turned his head just enough to see a large, dark form towering over him. The lamp in the next room gave off just enough light to outline her shape. Closing his eyes again, he asked, "What time is it?"

Without answering, she knelt down beside him and kissed him softly on the cheek. Feeling the covers being disturbed around his neck, James never had time to react before he felt an ice-cold hand sliding down his chest. Grabbing her intruding fingers, he rolled sideways and he instantly felt the coolness of the air on his exposed skin. James looked back over his shoulder, to see her giggling like a schoolgirl. Sitting up, he declared, "Suzette, do you understand that the payback is always greater than the deed?"

Jumping up, she laughingly stated, "Right now you don't look like much of a threat to me."

"Yeah, I'll give you threat." James grabbed for her foot, but missed when she quickly jumped back.

With a laugh she turned to go back into the front room saying, "You better not lay there too long. I've got some warm water for you to shave with, and breakfast will be ready pretty soon."

Still sitting in bed half covered, his thoughts turned to Moaka and the job they were going to try to do today or over the next couple of days. Moving his head slowly from side to side, stretching his neck, and shrugging he thought, *What the hell, we'll do what we have to do.*

James shaved and dressed. He ate a hasty breakfast of sliced salmon, and biscuits, and while drinking his last cup of tea, he commented to Suzette, "I don't know how long we will be gone, but it shouldn't be more than a couple of days. I hope that we can find this polar bear and push him out onto the pack."

In a questioning voice, Suzette asked, "And if you and Moaka can't run him out onto the ice?"

With a shake of his head, James answered, "I don't know, maybe he's gone already and we won't have to do anything."

Setting his cup down, James stood up and donned his outer garment, and softly kissing Suzette goodbye. He started for the entrance.

Reaching for his arm, she halted his progress while handing him a tightly wrapped package of food for their trip. Using a voice so full of sincerity that it almost scared him, "Come back to me, James."

James nodded and replied, "Don't worry, Suzette, with Moaka and me guarding each other's backs we will be all right. By the way, thanks for last night. We will talk when we got more time." Still looking into her eyes, James winked, and then disappeared through the entrance.

* * *

It was early morning, and the sun was just starting to shower the sky with gray light, as it had not yet shown its face over the Brooks Mountains, and soon the sky would be colored with purple and blue streaks with a hint of yellow and red, marking the arrival of the new day. Early mornings were peaceful. Most of the villagers had not started their daily routines, and the dogs had not started their morning ritual of barking at each other.

Not moving from the entrance of the hut, James pulled back his parka hood to feel the crispness of the morning. He looked up and down the main road of the village and was glad that Teshpuk had finally become a permanent settlement. He almost felt like he'd established a home base after all this time. He really didn't know exactly why because he didn't own anything here, course neither did anyone else, except the hut they were in and their own personnel belongings. It must be the feeling of being close to Suzette.

Just as he was getting used to feeling at home, James heard a familiar voice. "Kincaid, what standing there looking, need find bear."

James smiled to himself, and slowly proceeded to where Moaka was just getting his team ready to go. He was savoring the idea of being established and belonging somewhere. He had lost that feeling when he'd left home from Wisconsin. As he approached Moaka he asked, "This village we are going to first, does it have a name?"

Being busy with his dogs, Moaka didn't look up as James drew nearer, but replied, "Native there for caribou hunt. No village. No name. Need name for book?"

"It would be nice, Moaka," James replied, "If I could identify at least some of the places that we visit during our travels. We wander around out here so damn much I doubt anybody could realize where we've been. It won't mean much to anyone else if the journals just state approximate locations." Not getting any reply, James approached his team and started hooking the dogs up. Bray was so full of energy; he would not settle down until James took some time and rubbed his chest.

"Hey. What time does that trading store open, Moaka?" James inquired.

Moaka rose up and looked to the sky, and then smiling and nodding his head he replied, "Now."

"You don't know!" James hazed. "But if you're right, we can get the supplies we need on the way out." James finished hooking up his team, and he walked over to Moaka saying, "Let's walk up to the trading store and bring the supplies back here and pack them. After thinking about it, I'd just as soon not have to stop in the middle of the village when we're ready to leave."

Smiling at James and slapping him on the shoulder, Moaka mocked, "Kincaid need woman, why no marry? Suzette fine woman. Have many children."

"Damn it, Moaka, I'll marry her if and when the time comes, and when and if the situation is right for both of us."

As Moaka finished hooking up his team, they headed for the trading store. It was hard to walk fast in the bulky caribou skin boots that were worn, and James was getting more impatient to leave with every step. Arriving at the trading store, they went in as they had at the post office, not needing to be announced.

Ducking low and passing through the entrance, they entered into a hut that was filled to the roof poles with so much stuff that it was hard to see or move around. Surprised, James asked Moaka, "Was this place here the last time you were here?"

Moaka never stopped staring at all the supplies the store had to offer. He slowly replied in amazement, "No. Many trip to Barrow. Here since I here."

James glanced at Moaka and commented, "This must be part of what is meant by getting Teshpuk put on the map."

Moaka looked back at James and with a smile replied, "Yes, Karkak say. Teshpuk be place make home. Good trade. Food all year. People for talk, mail," pausing just for a moment, Moaka continued, "Kincaid, in middle territory."

Quickly responding, James said, "I don't have a territory. It seems to be where I am at the time." James looked down one of the several aisles in the trading post, and commented, "Well Moaka, we shouldn't have any trouble getting what we need here."

As Moaka continued his exploration, James started doing a little of his own. Moving slowly through the aisles he was amazed at all the stuff. They had barrels of salt and tealeaves, traps of all shapes and description, and all kinds of ropes and cords. James wondered how they got all this stuff here from Barrow. Somebody had been busy, for quite a long time. He wondered who owned this outfit. As he stopped for a moment, a curved bladed knife hanging on a leather strap caught his attention. Sliding his hand under the blade, but not lifting it from its hanger, he examined the workmanship. The knife was well made with a strong bone handle.

They took their purchases to the Native behind the counter, and Moaka pulled out several skins that had been tanned by Tess. The snow-white arctic fox skin was not in the bunch of skins, as James knew it wouldn't be.

The Native's eyes lit up like diamonds. He was more than happy to trade the goods for tanned skins of good quality.

Moaka and the keeper talked for a while, and then Moaka turned to James and said, "We go, worked deal."

Loading the supplies in their arms, James and Moaka exited the hut. Moaka said, "Kurac," as he motioned back toward the hut they left, "Owner of trade place. We make good deal. He say, like skins. Bring in more."

James could almost read Moaka's mind, as James quickly replied to Moaka, "That's not going to work. We can't go into the hunting business because we both are paid to protect and foster wildlife, not kill it for profit. That's all I need is to have someone down south find out that I'm trading furs, and it would be all over for me and you. No, Moaka, we'd better not take any more furs in for trade, but we can still take game for our own use though." Walking silently for a short distance, James asked, "Were the skins enough to cover all these supplies? Also, will Kurac take government credit for payment?"

Moaka casually answered, "Make good deal. Cousin of Karkak say, skins worth more than supply. He owe us."

Quickly James commented, "Moaka, you better stop shortcutting your English. I got a feeling that Suzette was serious about the adults around here setting the example for learning and using proper English now that this place belongs to the United States, even though it doesn't seem to make a lot of difference to some folks around here."

"Kincaid, states no matter to Native, all same."

Silence fell between the men as they made their way back to the sleds. Finally, James commented, "Moaka, I'd just as soon you didn't try to get the rest of the credit due to us. We got what we needed and that's good enough."

"What problem, Kincaid," Moaka said as he looked at James in puzzlement, "Tell find on trail, already dead."

"You know better than that, Moaka," James answered, "and so does everybody else."

Moaka packed up the rest of the supplies, and they were about ready to get under way when their attention was caught by another team and sled charging toward them. James glanced over at Moaka to get a reading, and just barely caught a faint smile coming on his face.

Hesitatingly, Moaka answered James' questioning look. "James, it Karkak, he want go."

Irritated, James snapped, "Hell, Moaka, we can't have everybody stringing along after us. Does he even have a rifle? How well will his team hold up?"

Quietly and calmly, Moaka responded, "Leader of village, he have right. No stop him."

Hailing his dogs to a halt, a distance from their teams, Karkak approached Moaka. Some quiet conversation took place between Karkak and Moaka and then Moaka motioned to James, saying, "Karkak say he help get polar bear."

Glancing at Moaka then over to Karkak, James asked in Native tongue, "Karkak, do you have a rifle?"

Karkak smiled and replied, "No, throw spear far."

James knew that was quite an honor here in these parts, and it would not do to insult one of the leading men of the village, especially since he was planning to make this place his home base.

Turning away from his own team, James walked over to Karkak and asked, "Is your team strong and well-rested, and do you have enough food for them for at least four days?"

Karkak quickly responded, "Yes."

Desperately, James searched his mind for something that would keep Karkak from coming. It wasn't that he didn't want Karkak along, but the bigger the party sometimes the slower it makes the progress. He couldn't think of any logical reason why Karkak couldn't come that would make any sense, or would not insult Karkak, so he smiled broadly at Karkak and said as he slapped Karkak on the shoulder, "We welcome Karkak, and we will be thankful for his knowledge and strong arm."

As James proceeded back to his own sled, he passed Moaka standing at the back of his own sled. Moaka quietly commented, "Kincaid, say good."

With Karkak on his sled and Moaka on his, James hailed, "On Bray," and they were on their way. They had never gone out with the intentions of doing anything in particular, other than checking out wildlife, their behavioral patterns, and generally being around to see what was to be seen. What they didn't get done today, they'd get done the next day, but this polar bear changed the situation and now it was a completely different story. This trip would be more challenging, traveling light and fast with danger lurking around every corner, or as the case may be, around every snow ridge.

The teams pulled hard on the tug lines, and as usual, they were let run hard for the first mile or so, then settled down to a good even pace. James glanced back around his wolverine hood just to make sure all the teams and sleds were not having any problems, and that Karkak was keeping up. James didn't like the situation, but there was not a thing he could do about it. He knew that Karkak was a good man, but he felt the party had one too many members.

When James turned back, he just happened to glance down at the snow that was rushing by along the side of the sled. Excitedly hailing Bray to a halt, he stomped down on the sled hook, and he could hear Moaka and Karkak hailing their teams. James walked back to Moaka, and Karkak came rushing up to meet them at Moaka's sled.

"Look around," James commented as he used his hands to motion looking around on the snow, "I thought I saw a track flash by on the ground."

Within just a couple of minutes, Karkak had located a track.

James and Moaka rushed over to the spot where Karkak was, and kneeled down to examine the somewhat obscure tracks. Letting Moaka and Karkak examine the tracks closely, James noticed that if Karkak would have kept coming, his sled would have wiped out the tracks altogether, maybe a stroke of luck already.

"How old is the track?" James inquired.

With a shake of his head, Moaka replied, "No say for sure."

Karkak added, "Snow hard crust. Lucky see. Lucky track no full snow."

As James looked down at the most visible track, it was plain that it was the right front; by the way, it was turned in. All bear's front feet more or less leave a track as if they walk pigeon-toed. Looking across the open spaces toward the direction the bear had gone, James wondered, *How far ahead is he? Is he held up somewhere, or is he still moving?* James knew this was starting to become a tactical game of man against beast.

Slowly Karkak moved around to the other side of the tracks, and said something to Moaka. James caught just enough of what he said to understand that the bear was not moving fast. As James kneeled down, he asked, "Karkak, what do you think."

Not saying anything for a moment while he let his fingers trace the track in the snow, Karkak finally replied, "Kincaid, track two-day, bear walk, no hurry."

James studied the blowing snowy horizons. As he peered from beneath his wolverine hood, his eyes caught the movement of the blowing hairs on the hood rim. Placing his hand alongside of his windburned face to help shield his eyes from the glaring sun's reflection, James couldn't see a thing except the swirling wind blowing the snow. Thinking, *Two days, that was just about the time the polar bear had been around Teshpuk.*

Turning his attention back to the track that the three men were surrounding, as if the imprint in the snow was in some way going to get away or vanish, they agreed that the track was made during the raid on Teshpuk two days ago.

Settling what was to be the next move, all three men headed back to their sleds. Looking back to Moaka and Karkak to see if they were ready, James hailed Bray on and hazed them around to follow the direction that the polar tracks were heading. It really didn't make any sense to James at the time because it wasn't much of a lead. Those polar bears wandered all over the place, but they could not afford to ignore any possibilities. It was in the general direction of the other village that had been raided.

As the caravan of sleds skimmed along over the snow, like boats on water with a rhythmic roll, James' team was performing at peak level. All the dogs seemed to be pulling evenly, and the ice on his runners was holding up in good shape because of the cold temperatures. The only noise that a person could hear was the occasional barking of the dogs, and the scraping of the runners on the ice and snow. These noises could be blocked out after a time, and all was quite silent. As James scanned the horizon, the blowing snow seemed to play tricks on his eyes, seeing something one second then, after blinking, the image being gone. This was a demanding country and it took demanding men to live here, and James liked the way of the flat tundra, with its low rolling hills that blended into the base of the north slopes of the Brooks Range.

After traveling for about five hours with a couple of rest stops for the dogs, James was starting to detect his team slowing down some, so coming upon a small rise he decided to stop and give the dogs a longer rest. Moaka and Karkak came up even with him and nobody really had anything to say. Along their travel, they had detected only a few scratches in the snow to support their direction of travel. All three of the men stood on their back sled runners scanning the rolling white terrain ahead of them as they were looking south toward the foothills of the Brooks Range.

Squinting slightly, James looked far ahead of their present location. Shaking his head slightly, James pondered, *I'm supposedly the leader in this search, but where can I lead them now? Trying to find a single particular polar bear out here was crazy.*

Moaka raised his arm and pointed to Bray, and commented, "Bray bark?"

Not noticing Bray barking until Moaka mentioned it, James hollered at Bray to be quiet, but Bray paid no attention.

Walking up to him, James could see that Bray was very excited, and seemed to be barking at something over the side of the downslope. On James' right, the edge dropped off quite abruptly. Unable to see the bottom of the slope, he walked a short way, and a shocking, frightful sight lay straight ahead of him. A sick feeling instantly came to the pit of his stomach. Not thirty yards away at the bottom of the slope was a horrible sight.

James yelled, "Moaka and Karkak come over here," as he carefully made his way down the slope.

Both men topped the ridge and stopped immediately, staring in horror.

CHAPTER EIGHTEEN

James continued to pick his path as he moved down the slope and approached the gruesome massacre. There was no doubt what had taken place. He looked to the top of the rise just in time to see Moaka and Karkak freeze in their tracts. It was a terrible and shocking sight to witness.

Moaka swiftly spoke to Karkak, "Go take care of the dogs. Settle them down."

Once Karkak was dispatched, Moaka cautiously eased down the hill, half sliding, and half walking, with small snowballs rolling in front of him. Turning his attention back to the horrible sight, James couldn't believe what he was seeing. He shook his head, thinking, *They didn't teach this in school.* Stopping just short of the scene, James just stared at the unbelievable sight in front of him. *How in the hell could anything like this happen?*

James knew the polar bear had just crossed the line. This beast had turned man killer, and now had to be stopped. Once an animal learns that man can be easy prey, there is no stopping him, except to eliminate him. This could no way be described as normal behavior for any animal.

Moaka and James stood silently and looked at the eleven dead dogs, the sled that was torn apart, and the native that was badly mutilated. Two of the dogs were half eaten and the rest were disfigured from the fight. The dogs were all twisted in their traces and tug lines, with white hair wedged between their projecting teeth. Frozen guts were strung around over some of the dogs like lengths of purple and blue rope. Wild, staring eyes peered from several of the dog's eyes as if mirroring the terror of the fight. The bodies of most of the dogs were twisted in unnatural positions, as if they had been struck hard enough to kill them instantly and crumpled in the snow, tangled in their traces. Dried blood was splattered everywhere. James had never seen such a sickening sight before, and he was beginning to realize the power and fury of one of those great wild beasts.

James turned and made his way toward the Native who was hanging over the back of the sled. Unexpectedly the Native groaned slightly.

"Moaka, get over here, the Native is still alive."

Rushing to the Native's side, James and Moaka gently turned him over so they could get a look at him.

The Native was still barely breathing, although he was badly mauled. His broad facial features were accented by his high cheekbones that were slightly windburnt, not unlike other Natives. Down the right cheek of the Native were a couple of large deep gashes made by the bear's claws. Holding the Native's upper body in his arms, James heard the Native groan again. James cautiously removed the hair of the parka hood from the gashes that had stuck with dried blood. The Native was a young man about thirty, which would be in his favor if he were to survive this traumatic ordeal.

Moaka exclaimed, "Know this one. He from village near big water! See at contest."

Knowing Moaka meant the Arctic Ocean, James asked, "I wonder what he was doing way out here on the flat?"

Just then, the Native muttered something that sounded like spear, and fell back into unconsciousness.

Moaka blurted out, "Luck of damn," as he slammed his fist down on the sled frame.

"What is it, Moaka?" James asked excitedly.

Moaka quickly replied, "Got problem. Native maybe spear polar bear. Maybe wound animal."

They turned their attention back to the Native, and James could see that the man had been batted about because his clothing had been slashed by the polar bear's long front claws in numerous places. On his left side were teeth marks through the outer layer with traces of blood present at each hole. Carefully cutting open his clothing, James discovered three puncture wounds that had stopped bleeding, and the blood had caked around the wound area.

"Moaka, do you think that Karkak could take him back, I mean to his village?"

As both of the men tried to make the Native more comfortable without moving him too much Moaka answered, "Karkak do."

James instructed Moaka, "Go and get a blanket and the wound wrappings off my sled. We'll carry him back up to Karkak's sled after we bandage him up, so Karkak can try to get him back before he damn well bleeds to death."

Moaka clawed his way up the slope, and in short order returned with Karkak helping to carry the blanket and dressing bandage.

Karkak wrapped the wounds as best he could while Moaka held the Native in a sitting position. Once the dressing was applied, they eased the Native down to a flat position on the blanket.

They slowly carried him up the slope to Karkak's waiting sled and securely fixed him atop the gear that Karkak had flattened out. When they got him strapped on the sled, the Native regained some consciousness.

James turned to Moaka and said, "If you can get him to say anything, ask him when the attack took place."

Moaka began to question the Native about the attack. After some slow and deliberate questioning, Moaka turned to James and Karkak and replied, "From Three Rivers Village. Attack last night before camp."

James asked Karkak, "Do you know where Three Rivers Village is located?" In his excitement, James had forgotten that Karkak could not understand much English and he had to repeat what he had just said in Native tongue.

Karkak, nodding his head in the affirmative, responded with, "I know, I take. How find after?"

"I don't think there is a chance in hell you can find us, Karkak," James explained. "You'll be doing your part just to get the Native back to his village. The way I see it is that we are going to have to be moving fast and not staying long in one place. Don't you agree?"

With a quick nod, Karkak answered, "Yes, warn villagers on way."

"Good idea, Karkak."

With the wounded Native settled on Karkak's sled, and final instructions given to Karkak by James and Moaka, he began his trip back. James hoped Karkak would not run into the polar bear on his way, especially since Karkak did not have a rifle. A sled loaded with supplies and a man on it would not be able to out-run a polar bear.

James and Moaka stood silently watching Karkak disappear through the blowing snow, and James heard Moaka mutter under his breath, "White Ghost."

Impatiently, James asked, "What did you say, Moaka?"

Shaking his head, Moaka replied, "No say."

James grabbed Moaka's parka sleeve and yelled with exasperation into Moaka's face, "If you are talking about believing in White Ghosts, no, but if you are talking about a polar bear that has gone wrong, then yes, I'll believe in that."

Jerking his parka sleeve away from James' grasp, Moaka hotly responded, "Gone wrong, Kincaid, now wounded!"

James and Moaka stood looking at each other and neither one of them were willing to give mental ground to the other. Two strong-willed men giving each other the respect of silence. A moment passed as tensions eased.

James broke the silence with, "I wonder if we made camp here, if just maybe we could get a shot at this thing if he comes back to feed on its kill? We could set up camp not far away, and then we could take turns lying on that knoll," as he motioned with his hand, "Overlooking the site during the night?"

Moaka swept the parka hood from his head, looked around the area, and responded, "Good plan, if return tonight. No need cover our scent. Native scent here."

Laying his hand on Moaka's rounded shoulder, James stated, "Moaka, I can't help thinking that the polar bear got chewed up quite a bit taking on all those dogs. Did the Native say where he hit the polar bear with his spear?"

With no expression in his tone and no change of facial expression, he continued staring at the dead dogs. "No."

Not moving from their position on the knoll, James methodically searched the surrounding area for a suitable site for their camp that should not be far away, but not so close as to keep the bear from returning. They never knew when either of them would need help, because they would be separated. With James or Moaka in camp, and the other on lookout, they would have to relieve each other from time to time. James remembered the last words he'd spoken to Suzette, "With Moaka and me covering each other's backside, we'll be just fine." *Well,* James thought, *that didn't last too long.*

Seeing a small depression not more than fifty yards away, James pointed to it.

Moaka looked and nodded his head in agreement.

Before they returned to the sleds James asked, "How long would it take you to run from here to where we are going to make camp?"

Moaka turned toward James with as slight smile came to his face, "Maybe what chase me."

Slapping him on the back, James half chuckled and replied, "Yeah, me too; fat chance of outrunning a polar bear. Let's get back to the dogs and get things set up. Now it's up to us to try and stop this killing machine before it has a chance to do more harm."

Returning to the sleds, they drove their teams to the area where they decided they would make camp. They hailed their teams to a halt, and Moaka walked over to James' sled and suggested, "Kincaid, spread dog this night. Polar bear maybe take on dogs."

"Good idea, Moaka," James responded. "If he does wade into them, hopefully he'll only get one or two, before one of us get him." James didn't know why, but the thought of the polar bear only getting two or so of the dogs was relieving as long as one of them was not Bray. He knew that the polar bear could get them all if the situation was right, and that had been proven already.

Both men staked their teams spreading them out farther than normal. They pulled both the sleds close together, trying to set things up for a long and dangerous night. They unpacked some fish for the dogs and a little food for themselves, and the rifles and ammunition.

When their meal of boiled seal meat was eaten and the pot secured back into the sled, they made plans for the night.

Sitting cross-legged on the snow, Moaka inquired, "Kincaid, bear come tonight?"

Ignoring Moaka's question, James suggested as he stood from his stool, "Let's walk around, and learn the terrain from here to the top of the rise, where one of us will be during part of the night."

Walking side by side, each of them carried his rifle as they carefully took notice of any irregular features. Each man knew that the terrain would look different at night, but it helped to get used to the lay of the surfaces that might have to be crossed, maybe in a hurry. They reached the rise that overlooked the massacred team, and they looked back to where the makeshift camp was set up. It was out of sight, and if they could keep the dogs quiet, they would have a chance to surprise the polar bear, that is, if he did return. All the reports were that the polar bear hit the villages in the dark, but the Native who was ambushed was hit in the daylight. "Do polar bears ever get rabies?" James asked.

As Moaka peered out across the white wilderness his eyes squinting in the sun, he asked, "What rabies? Is sickness?"

"Yes. It is a sickness that makes animals behave in strange ways, and often makes them damned mean before they finally die. Also, the sickness can be passed onto most other animals through bites or eating on the same carcass."

Moaka reached up to scratch his forehead, and replied, "Sickness maybe Noka's spirits."

"Maybe," James answered.

The wind was blowing gently across the front of James' parka hood, and he could hear the noise it made moving through the wolverine hair. Scanning the horizon, he did not catch any trace of movement across the open whiteness.

Moaka's voice broke the silence, "Kincaid, no answer question, bear come back?"

James looked straight at him and replied, "I don't know, but at least we'll be ready for him if he does show up. I'm sure polar bears return to their kill just like any other bear. It's a behavioral pattern."

"Think maybe, return," replied Moaka calmly.

They proceeded back to the camp, and it was now starting to get dusk. The sun had gone over the horizon, and the golden rays in the southwest sky were disappearing into shooting rays of purple. The blackness of night would be surrounding them soon.

Without breaking his stride James commented to Moaka, "I'll take the first watch on the rise, if that's all right with you. Give me about two hours, and then you can come and relieve me. I know that will leave the dogs unprotected for a short period of time while we make the switch, but it can't be helped."

As they arrived back at the camp where the sleds were pushed together, James walked over to Bray who was about half-asleep in the snow. Stopping just short of him, James tried to imagine him lying there with half his guts torn out. Approaching Bray, chills ran down his spine and he shrugged slightly beneath his clothing. He knelt down and touched

Bray's coarse hair. Bray instantly rose up and started his little whining routine as he greeted his master. James dug out his pocketknife and leaning over Bray, cut the leather tie collar half in two and then proceeded to rub up Bray's wide chest until his hand was warm from the friction. James was putting his knife away when he noticed Moaka watching him. James proceeded to check the other dog's leads and stakes and ended up meeting Moaka beside the sleds.

"Give Bray edge?" Moaka asked smiling.

With a grunt, James replied, "You don't miss much. If that damn bear hits this camp, I want Bray to have a fighting chance and not be tied down to a short chain lead. He'll be able to break the collar, now that it's been cut."

Moaka nodded his head, and said, "Bray maybe hold polar bear till we get shot."

With loaded rifle in hand, James started for the rise to stand his watch over the dog carcasses, hoping that he would get one good shot. James found a suitable location just at the crest of the ridge. He hollowed out a place in the snow where he was able to see the dead dogs, but be down far enough not to be silhouetted on the skyline. He did not see Moaka or the camp location, but James had no doubt that Moaka was on the job, just as he was, on the ridge. Smiling, he was thinking, *The one reason why me and Moaka had hung together these couple of years was that we could always depend on the other to hold up his end of the bargain and protect the other's backside.*

Lying on his stomach, with his gun barrel pointing down the slope, James barely made out the forms of the mutilated dogs and the shredded sled in the snow below him. The sunlight was completely gone. There wasn't much twilight in this country, especially this time of year. Last night there was a half moon, and it would be the same tonight. There would be moonlight when the moon rose over the Brooks Range, but not for a while.

He hoped that Karkak had made it back to Teshpuk in time to save the native's life. The man was torn up pretty bad, and a dog sled wasn't the softest thing to ride on. Tess and Suzette would be imagining all sorts of things after seeing the injured native.

Just before Karkak left with the injured Native, Moaka asked him to notify the people of Teshpuk, or any other village, that all caution should be taken when traveling while the marauding bear was still on the loose.

James' vision was starting to play tricks on him. Objects looked so much different in the night than they did during the day. James figured the different perspective was because of the different light reflection. He could have sworn the Native's dead dogs moved from time to time. *Hell,* James thought, *I know they're not moving; it's just a play on the light. If I keep thinking about that kind of stuff, I'll be seeing all kinds of things running around out there.*

Shivering slightly, but not really feeling the piercing cold, James wondered what time it was getting to be. He figured it to be a long night and very cold. He didn't hear a sound, and the quiet was almost deafening. He couldn't think of any place he'd rather not be. Shaking his head, he thought, *I could be back at Teshpuk in the arms of a warm, caressing lady.*

Hearing scraping noises behind him, James flipped over on his back and was relieved to see Moaka slowly easing up to him on his hands and knees. Moaka was staying low in order to keep a low silhouette, although the moon was not up high enough yet to cast much light across the white blackness.

In a whispering tone, Moaka asked, "Anything move?"

"Sure, a couple of greenhorns and one old polar bear." By the gray cast of the moonlight, James saw Moaka crack a grin. "Hell, Moaka, if I'd of seen that bear, you would have known it, and it would have sounded like a damn war going on over here. No, this gives me the creeps, and this silence is terrible. I think it's making me jumpy. I thought you would never get here."

CHAPTER NINETEEN

Quietly, the two men traded places, and James hurriedly made his way back toward their makeshift camp while Moaka settled himself in the depression James had made. He was eager to take his turn watching over the scene below, and hoped for a clear shot at the polar bear, which would put an end to these strange happens that reminded him so much of his past.

Moaka's thoughts wandered back to Tess. *She wanted to have a baby, but what would Kincaid think?'*

Moaka realized he and Tess had fallen into a good thing with the strange white man who couldn't speak the Native tongue so well, but someday he would. One day soon Moaka knew he would have to approach Kincaid with the thought of leaving Tess at Teshpuk with the child. Kincaid liked to have Tess along as a cook, but maybe they would have to hire someone else.

* * *

Walking on the crisp snow crust, James knew he was making some noise, but it wasn't creating a problem right then. It had only been dark for a couple of hours, and the pattern of this animal was to be active toward the early morning hours, although this was coming back to a kill not a raid. Neither James nor Moaka had bothered to put on their snowshoes, and when breaking through the crust they would sink only halfway up to their knees, but most of the time the hard crust held their weight. It was easy walking if the crust didn't break through.

Halfway back to the makeshift camp, James stopped to listen to the night. He slid the hood of his parka off, letting it fall gently on his back. The cold night air bit at his ears and the back of his neck. His rifle cradled in his arms, he stood silently and listened for the slightest sound. Squinting his eyes slightly, he tried to penetrate the dimly illuminated darkness. As he moved his head from side to side there didn't seem to be anything unusual. He lifted the parka hood back in place and slipped off his right mitten, and rubbed his chilled face with the warm palm of his hand. His face was starting to get rough again. James knew he should be using the salve Suzette had given him to keep his face soft and from being chapped.

As James approached where the first dogs were staked, he heard a low growl and stopped to speak to them. Once they recognized his voice, they settled down and all was quiet again. The dogs were well spaced, and he began circulating through Moaka's team and his own, checking everything out and reassuring himself that all was as it should be. He didn't want to leave anything to chance this night. Once all the dogs were checked, James circled wide of the camp and approached from the far side.

* * *

Rolling to his side, Moaka sighed slightly and looked to the heavens to stare into the star-studded sky. The blackness of the sky was broken only with the twinkling stars and the half moon. Returning to his position on his stomach, Moaka strained to see anything unusual about the scene in front of him, and nothing had changed. Closing his eyes, he thought of Tess back at Teshpuk. *She must be worrying a lot, but she would have to be strong.*

Moaka remembered when Kincaid had come to him as a greenhorn. Moaka and the north slopes had trained Kincaid. Kincaid had been easy to teach because he was so determined to succeed. The language was hard for Kincaid to learn, but he was learning slowly.

* * *

Bray was becoming fidgety. He was standing and whining a bit, displaying his uneasiness.

James walked over to him, trying to offer assurance, and he knelt down beside Bray and spoke softly to him. As James rubbed up his chest, Bray seemed to settle down.

If something happened, he knew they would have to move fast. Smiling to himself, James thought, *Hell, who's fooling who? If we had to get moving in a hurry, the dogs would be the worst of our problems. Gear doesn't jump around, fight, or bark like hell when there is excitement in the area.*

Quietly muttering, "Stupid dogs."

James remembered when he and Moaka were in Barrow on one of their supply runs, and they got themselves entered into a contest. It consisted of staking out your team and standing back one-hundred feet. The signal was given by the starter, and all the contestants had to run to their teams, remove them from their stakes, harness them up, and then get across a finish line a short distance away. His team was quite new at the time, and he remembered that he didn't do so well, but he had a great time watching everybody else. Never had he seen the like. Men running after loose dogs, dogs getting into fights, and teams getting all tangled up in their tug lines and traces, like being caught in fishnets. What would it be like in the middle of the night? Shaking his head he thought, *We'll do what we can as fast as possible.*

As he moved cautiously around the camp, James began to notice how bright it had become, especially with only a half moon or maybe he was just getting used to the light. He could see all the dogs and they looked like piles of brush laid on the snow. He looked down at his 32-40 shining in the moonlight. There was sense of security carrying a rifle around, and

James just hoped that if he did get a shot, that he'd be good enough to down the polar bear. James was well aware it was a completely different experience to be squeezing off a round at a seal for meat, than to be trying desperately to find your target by moonlight with the target rampaging toward you. Not even to mention the fact that if you missed, you might be eaten. Turning the rifle so the wooden stock picked up the moonlight, he could see the hard use. Several dents and scratches were present, and he remembered when most of them had happened.

Assured that the camp was secure, James went over to where Moaka put a few sticks of firewood together and had added a little bit of seal oil for quick starting. If they'd have time and the situation was right, one of them would be able to throw a match toward the firewood, and maybe lighting if off, to give them some shooting light. *Actually,* James thought, *all anybody had to do was to get the polar bear to look into the fire and shoot right between the two red eyes,* and he mumbled to himself, "Fat chance of that." There was a problem with that; *dog's eyes reflect red also.*

James shivered slightly. The temperature was way below zero and he was glad there was no wind. The wind would make it much colder and impair their hearing somewhat. A light wind blew in the daytime most of the time, but at night it was very still unless there was a storm.

James stretched his neck muscles, and he looked to the south into the blackness of the Brooks Range. He'd only been to the top of the mountain range one time, and that was during the warmest month of July. Moaka and he paddled up one of the tributaries of the Colville River, and they had taken several of the dogs for pack so they didn't have to carry so much weight. They had a good time up there, but he'd hate to try it this time of year, even by dog sled.

With his rifle cradled loosely in his right arm, James slowly walked over to where Bray was curled up. He knelt beside him and began rubbing his chest as Bray rolled over. Without a word, James patted him on the chest and circulated through the other dogs.

James sat down by his sled and leaned back against the frame, and it felt good to get off his feet. The dogs would let him know if anything was coming close. Slipping his hood back and uncovering his ears, the piercing cold immediately became present. It just might give him an edge of hearing any little sound that he might have otherwise missed.

It was about time to relieve Moaka on lookout, and he slowly made his way toward Moaka's location making as little noise as possible on the ice-crusted snow. As he walked across the rises and through the lower ground, James realized that the moon was getting closer to the southwestern horizon. He could barely make out the faint eerie shadow of his body that was being cast on the white surface. As he closed on Moaka's position, James got down on all fours and crawled the rest of the way.

As James neared the still form of Moaka lying in the snow, he hailed him in a low voice. Not turning toward James, he lifted his hand in recognition. Easing close to him on his stomach James asked, "Enjoying the show?"

Moaka turned his head toward James and replied, "Okay. How dog?"

Both of the men spoke in a whisper as James replied, "Everything is quiet at camp, it might be awhile before we see anything, Moaka."

Whispering back to James, Moaka responded, "I no like waiting. White Ghost can say where and when."

"Moaka, stop worrying about ghosts," James urged. "This thing is only a polar bear that probably has something wrong with it. We know the where, and if he comes tonight, we'll be calling the when."

Moaka didn't offer any response, but silently crawled away. James could have predicted that reaction from him. He didn't have to worry about Moaka, and when the time came for action, Moaka would know what to do and how to do it.

Settling himself down in the hollow he'd made the first time he'd been on watch, James positioned his rifle toward the native's twisted dog team. *What did the Native think when that polar bear jumped him out here on the flats. Probably didn't even have time to get over the shock before the battle was over.*

James wondered how many years the man had put into building his team. Building a team was never finished, because from time to time animals that can better fit in the team were found. James had one small female that should be replaced, but he'd gotten to know her, and he just hated to let her go. Moaka always accused him of treating his dogs like children, but James had found that a little affection went a long way, and made the animals work that much harder for their master.

A dog bark from the camp! Another! Now more! James' alertness instantly came alive. He didn't hear any shots. He didn't hear Moaka yelling. He didn't hear anything that sounded like fighting, just wild barking.

Just then he heard Moaka's yelling over the dog's barking, "Kincaid, come here. No hurry."

Jumping to his feet James quickly glanced toward the native's sled and wasn't sure what Moaka had meant. He knew the stake-out had been ruined or at least not gone according to plan. He hurriedly started making his way toward Moaka's position, as he could still hear the dogs barking wildly. He could not figure out why he didn't hear any shots, for Moaka must have been able to see the polar bear the way the dogs were getting so excited. *No, that didn't make any sense,* James thought. *Moaka had hollered, and said to come, but not hurry.* Nearly stumbling over a small drift, he kept pushing hard. Finally reaching Moaka's side, half out of breath, James could see by the moonlight what caused all the commotion. Not thirty feet away from where they were standing, he could faintly make out the forms of a dog team hooked up to an empty sled, not of equipment or supplies, but of a rider.

Finding the security of humans, the spent phantom dog team lay down in their traces. James and Moaka slowly walked around the dogs and approached the sled with caution. They looked as best they could in the moonlight for any sign of what could have happened, or why the dog team was out alone in the dead of night. The moon gave off just enough light for them to see most of the outlines of the dogs and the sled, but they had to get closer to see details.

As they approached the sled, Moaka broke the silence. "Kincaid, what think?"

James didn't answer him right away; he couldn't see anything wrong with the rig or dogs. "It doesn't look like there is anything out of order," James commented. "Everything looks as though it is still packed up. There is one thing, Moaka; I don't see any weapons on this sled. Usually, the Natives carry several different sizes of spears or knives strapped to the sides of their sleds, and I don't see any of that kind of gear."

"Kincaid, dog come long way. They tired. Lay in harness. They need food. Know sled or dog?"

Sleds were more or less all the same to him, but James did know what Moaka was talking about when he mentioned the dogs. A team maybe will have one or two dogs that will stand out or you remember among the rest. Either in color or size, there always seemed to be at least one dog that is worth remembering. Nevertheless, by moonlight, he couldn't see any distinctions. "Moaka, let's light the damn fire and get the team closer, so we can look things over. Maybe then we can find some clue to what happened."

Surprise in his tone, Moaka quickly asked, "What about polar bear?"

Somewhat irritated and upset with the whole situation James snapped, "What about it? We've made enough noise and commotion to run off ten polar bears." As James ended his statement, he spun on his heel and stomped off toward the unlit fire and proceeded to get it started.

Moaka turned back to the lead of the lost team, and as he approached the dog, it made a grab for him. Moaka yelled something in his Native tongue, and grabbed the dog and threw it brutally to the ground. The dog yelped in pain and whimpered as Moaka's frame towered over him.

"Kincaid, dog no taught. Hope no train dog for owner."

James knew that Moaka would have the team doing what he wanted in short order, and by the sounds of things, Moaka and the lead were getting acquainted very rapidly. The fire was burning well and illuminating quite an area. Moaka brought the team in, half dragging the lead, with the rest of the dogs pulling the riderless sled.

Moaka halted the team in front of the fire and commented, "See how team hooked, Kincaid."

Slowly, James moved away from the warmth of the fire, walked over to where the dogs were, and studied the harness. James turned back to Moaka saying, "They are hooked up in a fan, instead of a parallel tug line."

"Good Kincaid! Does mean anything?"

Hesitant about answering Moaka because James felt he was being tested, he replied, "Well, Moaka, I think that it means that this team has come from somewhere farther to the east of here. I've only seen one other team hooked up like this, and that was about two years ago, when we ran into that trader from over Yukon way."

Moaka asked, "Kincaid, what now?"

As Moaka came back to the fire, James replied, "Hell, I don't know, but right now let's bed down all the dogs, and then you and I should get some shuteye. We might see things different in the morning. Look and see how much meat for that team is on that sled. We should probably feed them. No telling how far they have come since their last meal. I'm going to try, if they will let me, to look over the team real quick to check their condition."

Straight away James and Moaka got to the task of staking out and feeding the phantom team. Their own dogs started settling back down, and both men met back at the fire, which was now starting to die down.

Finally breaking the silence, James asked, "Moaka, where do you think the driver of that team is? Moreover," before Moaka could answer, James continued, "I don't think he was a Native."

Moaka lifted his gaze from the fire, and through squinted eyes looked across the darting flames at James. "Why think Kincaid?" as his gaze went back into the fire.

"Well," James slowly answered, "for one thing, the sled doesn't have any of the standard weapons on the sled that Natives carry. For another, the sled is loaded down with food for the dogs. Whoever the driver was, he was planning to go a long distance without many layovers. Almost as if he knew he was going to be in a big hurry to get somewhere. As far as the team getting away from him, hell, he might have stopped to take a leak and the damn dogs ran off."

Again, Moaka raised his head, looked at James through the flames licking the frigid air, and then replied, "Wish knew for self. Maybe White Ghost.

His eyes filled with tears from yawning, James stood up and said, "I don't know about anything else, but I do know that I am damn tired. I won't be worth a damn tomorrow if I don't get some sleep." James walked toward his sled, while Moaka remained by the fire. He paused, turned around, and asked, "Moaka, are you going to go back over to watch for the polar bear?"

"No want miss if come back."

"Well, wake me up in about an hour or so," James slurred. "You need to get an hour or so of sleep before daybreak too. Let the fire go. I added some wood awhile ago and it should last until first light."

CHAPTER TWENTY

James was disturbed from his short nap by the sound of barking dogs. He rolled over, half out of the animal skins he used to sleep in, and tried to sit up. The chill in the air instantly bit at his exposed skin, as his body shivered in reaction to the cold. He sat in the twisted sleeping skins trying to come fully awake. The early morning light was starting to show over the mountain peaks as he caught a glimpse of Moaka walking back from the direction of the massacred dog team. His makeshift bed was down on low ground, and all he could see of Moaka was his head bobbing up and down. Smiling and shaking his head he thought, *Reminds me of a lemming bobbing in and out of a hole.*

James knew Moaka would be in a bad humor this morning because of his lack of sleep. "Damn it," James murmured under his breath, "why didn't he wake me up earlier?" James fought to a standing position as the sleeping skins fell to the snowy surface. He stretched his arms above his head and tried to get his body parts working again. It felt colder than normal this morning, which made moving even harder. He could finally feel some warmth generate through his body as he shook himself from head to toe.

Moaka finally made his way to the camp, and inquired, "How sleep Kincaid? Bear be close, he hear you snore."

James smiled and retorted, "Yeah, Moaka, that's my first line of defense when I'm sleeping. You've been walking around this morning; what's it looking like out there?"

Moaka waved his arm back toward the massacred team, replying, "Same as yesterday, only dogs are frozen stiff. No sign anything around to feed on them." Moaka noticed that James was looking down at his bedroll, and questioned, "What see, Kincaid?"

James raised his head and commented, "Moaka, you know what I would like to do?" and before Moaka could respond, James quickly finished, "I'd like to take the phantom team, the wounded Native's sled, and go back to Teshpuk. We almost need to start over again with a fresh start. We're so damn strung out now with all this extra gear, we can't even function. Besides that, I'm hungry and about half frozen to death. Let's get the damn fire started and get something to eat."

A couple of quick steps forward and Moaka was right by James' side. Moaka slapped James on the shoulder, and exclaimed, "Good idea, Kincaid! Load all sled same. No-rider team have easier time if load less, team tired after trek. I take phantom team, hook behind me. Think pull okay. Native sled you pull," and pausing momentarily, Moaka continued, "Kincaid, okay?"

Without a thought, James smiled and nodded his head in the affirmative, and they went immediately to the tasks of building a fire, feeding themselves, feeding the dogs, and getting the loads distributed on the sleds. Most of the entire morning was spent getting some of the phantom sled's load distributed to James' and Moaka's sleds, and the Native's sled hooked behind James' sled after it had been repaired enough to pull.

It would be a long time before James forgot the frozen, mutilated dog team. He just couldn't shake the image he had in his mind of the wild staring eyes of those dogs. They didn't try to save any of the blood-soaked traces or tug lines of the mutilated team. Since they were so entangled in and around the frozen dogs it just didn't seem worth the effort. There wasn't any problem with leaving the dogs there because they would be eaten by wolves, foxes, or other critters. James knew that food never went to waste on the tundra.

Moaka finally got the lead dog of the phantom team hooked behind him on a short lead. James had the Native sled hooked behind his sled, and the whole procession looked like a disorganized caravan. All Bray could do was stand around and growl at the intruders that had mysteriously showed up in the middle of the night.

Everything put to the ready, James shook his head slowly in disbelief and looked to Moaka for the okay. In sheer determination to get this mess back to Teshpuk, James hailed, "On Bray," and they were off. They were so hampered with all the mess, they couldn't do anything else but regroup before their search for the polar bear started anew.

James glanced back over his shoulder and, to his relief, Moaka wasn't having too hard a time with the lead of the phantom team to come along. The lead dog was hooked directly behind Moaka's sled, but the rest of the team wandered all over the place, as they were hooked up to their sled in the fan formation. With a wave of his hand, Moaka motioned back that all was well, at least for the time being.

Without a broken stride, James displayed confidence of practice as he stepped onto the back runners of his sled to take a break from running alongside as he scanned the horizons along their route for any obstructions that may be ahead. Their teams were in good shape after the rest at Teshpuk, and they pulled well. However, James knew the phantom team was spent. James didn't want to push them too hard, especially since it was not necessary. Neither he nor Moaka had any idea of when the phantom team had gotten away from the musher, or how.

Concern showed on Moaka's face as he studied the phantom lead dog that was tied behind his sled. He was concerned about how they pulled together. Moaka wasn't sure how the rest of the team was pulling, but the lead was a strong dog and doing well. He noticed that the other dogs were starting to close the fan, which made pulling easier for the whole team. He knew that James would hold the pace of travel slow because of the different teams involved.

Turned half around, James watched Moaka's team perform, and they were doing just fine. He saw that Moaka looked back at the lead often to check on the dog, but the lead seemed to pull steadily, and James knew that Moaka could bring the trailing team along.

James looked over the backs of his team and knew there wasn't a better team on the face of these slopes, and most folks knew it. They would be well spent by the time they got to Teshpuk, having to pull both his sled and the Native's sled that was filled with the Native's gear.

James detected a strange darkened object somewhat a distance away, but it was hard to tell what it was for the swirling blowing snow. He hailed Bray to a halt and, standing on his sled brake, he waved to Moaka to hold up. His eyes strained for vision against the bright sun's reflection, and he shaded his eyes and squinted. He was sure he had seen something in the distance. He eased his rifle from its place and walked to the head of the team. James motioned for Moaka to stay put. He looked again for the obscure darkened figure and finally spotted the dark figure again, but still could not distinguish whether it was man or beast. At his feet, James noticed Bray lying down. His lead must have not seen or scented the intruder.

Ready and prepared for anything, James finally made out not only the figure of one man, but two, as they walked toward James and Moaka. He doubted the men had seen them yet, because they walked bent over looking straight at the ground, and one man carried a rifle. James pointed his rifle toward the sky, and fired one shot into the air. The strangers froze in their tracks and they looked one way then the other. Finally seeing James, one man waved his rifle in the air, and they started in James' direction. The sound of James' rifle aroused Bray, and he was up and growling. Patting Bray's head, James spoke softly to him to calm him.

When James looked back to Moaka, he was surprised to discover

Moaka almost up even with him, with the phantom team behind.

Moaka halted the teams and quickly proceeded to James' side. With a shake of his head, Moaka asked in a puzzled tone, "Who be, Kincaid?"

"I don't know for sure, Moaka, but I bet we are about to find out. It's not every day you find a couple of fellas wandering around out here with no gear or mode of transportation." He glanced at Moaka and then back to the strangers that approached, and James continued, "I wonder if we haven't found the owners of the phantom team?"

Moaka laughed loudly and commented, "Kincaid, Native say. No control dogs, no control woman."

James looked at him, smiled, and responded, "Oh bullshit, Moaka, one doesn't have a damn thing to do with the other. That's a dumb saying."

As Moaka rolled his head around on his shoulders to loosen up his neck muscles, first to one side and then the other, he responded, "They say, take or leave. Native believe. Think about. It make sense."

The figures approached, and James was not surprised to see that they were not Natives, but white men. As they came closer, James removed his right mitten and moved to meet them, offering his hand in a greeting. "Hello, I'm James Kincaid."

One of the other men followed suit, and replied, "I'm Ralph Tone. I see you found our team and sled."

James then introduced himself to the second man in the same manner, and did not feel that the second man received him well.

James brought them back over to where Moaka was and said, "Moaka, this is Ralph Tone and Drake Simmons. We apparently have found their team for them."

Sheepishly, Ralph answered, "Mr. Kincaid, I sure do want to thank you for finding and holding onto our team for us. It was very strange how they got away from us. In the first place, Drake and I are coming from a little village just this side of Chamberlin country. We need to get to Barrow as soon as possible, and late yesterday afternoon we came across a polar bear that seemed more interested in us than we were in him. To make a long story short, we stopped the team and Drake and I rather worked around him to get a better shot at the bear. All we wanted to do was just scare him off. We weren't any more than thirty yards away from the sled, and those damn dogs took off like a whirlwind. Anyway, this polar bear came right for us. I fired a quick shot, and the round blew snow up in front of him, stopping him in his tracks. We turned to go back to go our sled, and here comes the bear after us again. This time I took good aim, I think I hit him, but I never brought him down because he turned and went the other direction. By the way, was there a rifle on the sled under some gear when you found it? Drake here," as he motioned with his hand, "left his rifle under some gear on the sled."

Drake jumped into the conversation with, "Stupid damn dogs—I should shoot every one of them. No more brains than a rock, and now I've probably lost my rifle."

In the short time that James had known Drake, he was getting more irritated at him by the minute. And he had a bad sense about the fella already. Clearing his throat, James commented, "Well, Drake, it wasn't the dogs fault you lost your rifle. Besides that, one of you should have stayed with the team with that polar bear around."

Drake responded with, "Well, that doesn't make any difference. I don't suppose you fellas did find that rifle?"

James slowly turned back to Moaka and with a questioning look. Moaka just shrugged his shoulders at James with no response.

"Don't seem to have located your rifle, Drake."

Abruptly Moaka jumped into the conversation, quickly inquiring, "How big bear you saw?"

Surprised, Ralph directed his attention toward Moaka and declared, "I don't know! It was a polar bear! If I might say so, he acted awful brave, that is until we scared him off with the rifle."

Quietly and with sincerity, James asked, "Ralph, what in the devil are you two fellas doing way out here? What I mean is that neither of you appear to be men used to driving a team cross country, especially all the way to Barrow."

Ralph shrugged his shoulders and slowly responded, "We're not, Mr. Kincaid."

Interrupting Ralph, James commented, "Just call me James, please."

A flash of a smile crossed Ralph's face as he continued, "I will if you call me Doc; that's what everybody else calls me. I'm a doctor and Drake here volunteered to accompany me, and we need to get more medical supplies to a small village where many people are coming down sick. We need to get the supplies back to them before the sickness kills them all. Now the way things turned out, we've lost a day losing our team, which isn't either one of ours. Thanks to you two men we can be on our way, hopefully not losing more time."

"Not your team!" Moaka exclaimed.

"What Moaka means, Doc," James explained, "nobody should jump out across country with a team they don't know."

"I understand all that gentlemen," Ralph explained, "but I had no choice in the matter. Drake and I are the only adult males that have not been affected by the sickness, so he and I lit out. I left instruction of what to do while I was away. It was either that or just sit there and watch the whole village die."

CHAPTER TWENTY-ONE

James sighed in frustration and shook his head as he commented, "Doc, it's crazy how some things turn out. Why don't you two come with us to Teshpuk? It is a small village less than one day run from here, and once there we can put you on a fast sled with a driver that can get you to Barrow and back in short order."

Turning to face Drake, James continued in a stern tone that left Drake with no choice, "Drake, you will stay in Teshpuk till Doc gets back from Barrow, that way your team will be well-rested for the trip back to your village." James looked at Doc, and added in a normal tone of voice, "Maybe we can even help you get back to your village in time to do some good."

Moaka perceived James' suggestion and nodded his head in agreement, as he responded, "Yes, Doc. Can help to Barrow then back Teshpuk. Know man in Teshpuk, he help."

Handing Doc the lead line of his team, Moaka helped him get the dogs up for the start. Moaka studied Doc just for an instant and decided that he was a good man. Moaka could not put his finger on it, but he didn't trust Drake. *Both are white men and both are strangers, but somehow Doc was okay, but Drake didn't seem trustworthy.*

As Drake walked back to the sled, one of the dogs growled as he walked by, and he lunged forward and kicked the dog, to which the animal responded with a loud yelp and cowardly lay flat on the ground.

James had seen Drake's motion out of the corner of his eye, and the dog's yelp in pain brought all of James' attention directly at Drake. He stared at Drake with cold, hard eyes and scolded, "What the hell did you do that for?"

Drake stuttered something under his breath, so no one could hear.

James quickly continued, "Mister I think while you're around me you better lay off those dogs. They never did a damn thing to you. You're the one that left your rifle on the sled, and if the truth was known, somebody should kick you in the ass. And I'm here to tell you, you touch those dogs again around me and I'll be that somebody." James continued to challenge Drake Simmons with his cold stare before he added, "You got anything to say?"

All three men could see the anger in Drake's face, but he never responded, rather he slowly shook his head and turned to climb on the sled.

"Gentlemen, gentlemen, we don't have to fight among ourselves," Ralph pleaded in a compromising tone. No one said anything further, but went about their business of getting ready for the trip back to Teshpuk.

Everyone mounted. James looked around to check to see if the caravan was ready to go as he hailed, "On Bray," and his team strained on the tug lines all together. If he kept this pace, they would be into Teshpuk late that evening. He hoped that Doc's team could keep the pace.

I wonder where and how Doc got hooked up with that ass Simmons. Simmons doesn't seem to be of the same cut as the Doc. The Doc seems like a sensible and likeable fellow; not too many smarts about dog teams, but a sensible sounding guy.

James realized this had been an empty run, and Suzette would probably be happy they didn't get a shot at the damn thing, but on the other hand, Doc Tone was able to, and by Doc's description, it might be the polar bear they were seeking. At least they would have a starting point when they went out again. They would have to talk further with Doc before he left and see if he could give them a closer location where he sighted the polar bear. It couldn't have been too far from where they had met him, a man walking without snowshoes just didn't make good time.

Moaka looked in front of him to Doc's team, and they seemed to be keeping pace, even with Drake in the sled. Moaka's thoughts wandered. *I can't understand why Drake was even along on the trip with Doc. What good did he do? Maybe Doc didn't want to make the trip alone and that was probably it. I got to approach Kincaid soon about Tess' baby, maybe after the polar bear is taken care of, because Tess is impatient for me to talk to Kincaid.*

The caravan made their regular stops to rest the dogs without incident. James and Moaka talked to Doc on several of the stops to get a better idea where the polar bear had been sighted. Drake didn't seem too interested in any of the conversations and about all he did was get in and out of the sled and walk around when they stopped. He wasn't concerned about the dogs because he didn't help check the condition of any of the dogs during their stops.

James and Moaka were reasonably sure of the location that Doc sighted the polar bear, and they were satisfied that they could pick up or cross the trail when they went out again the next day. That is, if the tracks weren't blown in by the swirling snow. James also got a chance to have Doc tell about how he came to be in the North Country.

Doc explained, "I met a trapper from the far north iceberg country while I was working in the lower states. He told me about the fast money that could be made in furs, but when I arrived in the far north, I found that folks would pay highly for good medical attention. I didn't really want to go into the fur business anyway, so I decided to stay with the medical trade. The money was good for a while, and then I got to feeling guilty about taking folk's last furs or money as payment. Now I'm lucky if I get food in return for my services. Oh, I don't mind, just as long as I can make a living and help out some of these poor Natives."

"Well, Doc, that was interesting," James remarked. "Sometime I'll have to tell you how I got here. It's quite a story, and sometimes I don't even believe it."

"Are you working for the American government?" Doc inquired.

James answered, "Does it show that much," as both men laughed. "Yeah, I'm a wildlife biologist." James suspected that Doc had been bitten by this country and its people just as he had. James thought, *A person either loves this country or can't get out fast enough.*

The four men and teams arrived in Teshpuk late in the evening, and the dogs were just about spent. It was most important to have a team and driver set up for Doc so he would leave before first light. Another question that popped into James' mind was, *What is to be done with Drake while Doc is gone to Barrow. The Doc would be gone about six to seven days. Maybe Moaka would know somewhere Drake could stay while Doc was away.* Right then, James didn't really care if Drake stayed or left, but he should let Doc's team rest.

All was dark when James halted his spent team in the middle of Teshpuk. The village was peaceful and quiet except for the normal barking of a few dogs of the village welcoming the new arrivals.

Moaka announced, "Find team, driver, for Doc."

James nodded his head, and he and Drake staked the dogs and fed them while Doc got his personal stuff off the sled. As they finished tending the dogs, they were joined by Moaka and a villager who would take the Doc to Barrow.

Moaka introduced James, Doc, and Drake to the local villager, and they all went into Kirima's hut to plan the trip to Barrow, then the return trip from Teshpuk back to the Doc's village.

The chain of events happened so fast, that nobody had time to visit much, until the plans had been laid. Doc and Drake were to spend the night with the driver and his family in their hut. Tomorrow morning before light, Doc and his driver were to leave for Barrow. Drake was to go to Three Rivers Village, a village next to the coast sometime tomorrow to wait for Doc's return. Drake said he had a friend there that would put him up. Three Rivers Village was more on the route back to their village than Teshpuk so that would work out well. Doc thought Drake and he would make it back home without the driver once they got back to Three Rivers Village. All plans laid, the Native driver, Doc Ralph Tone, and Drake Simmons left Kirima's hut to prepare for the trip and get some rest.

Just before leaving the hut, Doc quickly turned back to James and Moaka and replied, "You two guys make a strange pair, but you've both got my deepest thanks. I don't know what we would have done out there today without you two coming to our rescue. If either of you are ever over in my part of the country, stop in and visit. And by all means, if you ever need help, Doc Tone is always on the job." Doc smiled, raised his hand in farewell, and not giving James or Moaka a chance to respond, they disappeared through the hut entrance into the night to the Native driver's hut for the night rest.

Once the early morning travelers left the hut, Moaka slapped James on the shoulder and asked, "See Suzette yet?"

Rising from the circle of Tess' relations, James replied, "No, hell no! You know better than that. I've been with you all evening, but I sent word to her that I would be around soon." Fastening his parka, James continued, "I'd better get along though, and, Moaka, I'll see you in the morning and not too damn early."

Quickly Moaka asked, "What think Drake Simmons?"

Shaking his head, James replied with a disgusted voice, "What an ass. I don't like him and I don't want to be around him, and I'm glad he is going to Three Rivers Village tomorrow."

Moaka nodded at James and then returned his gaze to the seal oil lamp in front of him and simply commented, "I say."

As James turned to go, Tess quickly rose and grabbed his arm, and cheerfully said, "Happy back, Kincaid."

James smiled at her, and gently squeezed her shoulder, then quickly disappeared out of the hut.

Outside the hut in the pale moonlight, James let the night's cold air bite at his uncovered skin as he glanced up and down the main road of Teshpuk. A few outside cooking fires still glowed in the night with hot ambers, but nobody was outside. The whole village looked deserted and lonesome. He thought, *what a primitive place.* James was learning that primitive was relative to what perspective a person established.

As James started for Suzette's place, he knew he would be satisfied to make Teshpuk his permanent headquarters. He really didn't think anybody was going to mind a whole lot, just as long as he was willing to stay up here. *Neely just didn't know how good it really was living up here. It is cold and barren in the winter, but the other seasons are enjoyable. There are more birds and animals in this country than anybody could count, let alone hunt.* He mumbled, "Hell, some of the wildlife hasn't even been named yet."

⁂

Moaka and Tess sat beside the seal oil lamp. Tess leaned over and hugged Moaka asking, "Tired? You and Kincaid look tired when you came in."

Moaka nodded his head and lazily replied, "Yeah, we're tired. Kincaid got two hours' sleep, and I didn't sleep. I wanted to watch for the polar bear, but it never returned."

Alarmed Tess quickly responded, "Why didn't you wake up Kincaid?"

"It doesn't matter, Tess. How do you feel?"

Beaming with a wide smile, Tess answered, "I am fine." Pausing, Tess continued, "Are you hungry?"

Moaka answered, "Yes. We ate earlier today, but I am hungry."

Tess had prepared some food beforehand, and almost before Moaka finished answering, Tess started to prepare a meal for him.

Moaka saw her having trouble, and questioned, "Are you okay? Are you having a hard time getting up?"

Tess giggled slightly, and responded, "Don't be so silly. I just sit too long. Did you talk to Kincaid yet?"

"No, I'll talk with him pretty soon," Moaka quietly responded. "We have had quite a bit to think about lately, but I will get a chance before long."

❋ ❋ ❋

Halfway to Suzette's place, James stopped in the middle of the road. He turned around to look back toward Kirima's hut, and he suddenly had the strangest feeling. It was like a feeling of complete satisfaction. Moving his body around underneath the loose fitting clothing to rid himself of a sudden chill, he was puzzled at the unfamiliar sensation. *Maybe it's satisfaction that I know where I'm going, and that I will be welcome. Maybe I feel that way because I have good friends here. Maybe… have something to do with my affections for Suzette?*

James arrived at Suzette's hut, and hailed, and she called for him to enter. He stooped low to get through the entranceway, and stumbled and clumsily rolled into the main room of the hut. James had so little sleep, and he felt run down and tired of all the conversations, that all he wanted do was lie on the floor quietly and go to sleep.

Startled, Suzette exclaimed, "I've had men fall for me before, but never like this!"

James never moved a muscle as he slurred, "I'm tired, Suzette, dead tired. I need to get a good night's sleep tonight. I know that it is damn short notice, what I mean is, you're not running a hotel or something. I didn't want to sleep over at Kirima's because they have too damn many people over there as it is. I didn't have much choice."

She peered down at his motionless body, and looking quite put out, she asked, "Well! And if you would have had a choice, where would that have been?"

"Oh Suzette, I don't know, I don't want to talk, if you can see your way to it, I would like something to eat." Closing his eyes James continued, "So I can lay my head down and get some shuteye."

Without warning, he felt Suzette's body land squarely on top of him,

180

as she quickly reached inside his parka top and started tickling his ribs. Throwing her off from him, he rolled over to pin her down to the floor mats. For just an instant, he stared into her dancing brown eyes before passionately kissing her. His passion temporarily satisfied, James rolled off her slender, soft form and lay silently beside her.

As she rose to one elbow Suzette disappointedly replied, "Well, James, after supper, you will feel better. The bed is all made up and you can climb in when you're ready." Jokingly, she asked, "You don't look like you have enough energy even for a short wrestling match."

Without looking at her, James slowly answered, "Suzette, I'm serious, I've got to get some sleep. I hardly got any since Moaka and I left yesterday morning. My eyes are burning, and they feel like someone's been walking around in them."

Suzette sat next to James and stared at his prone frame, and she knew she was developing a serious attachment to this Scotsman. He had come into her heart, and she knew she would not be able to rid herself of him. She knew that she wanted a close, lasting relationship with this person more than anything else.

Suzette pushed away from the floor mats to stand, and noticed that James had sunburn around his eyes, and half asked and half scolded, "Have you been wearing the bone snow shields that Moaka made for you and have you been putting on the salve for your face?"

Without opening his eyes or his voice having little expression, James slowly replied, "Oh those damn things blind me worse than wearing horse blinders."

"Well, James, they do help keep the sun from blinding you. The Natives have been wearing them for generations. If you don't start wearing them your eyes won't last because the sun's glare is too bright coming off the snow, even when it's cloudy." Turning away to fix a meal, she continued, "Well, get washed up, and I'll fix you something to eat. The bed will be there when you're ready. I'll be in later because I have some things to do for school."

CHAPTER TWENTY-TWO

The next sounds James heard were the hushed voices of Suzette and Moaka. He couldn't understand what was being said until he rose up on one elbow and slightly leaned toward the outer room. He blinked the sleep from his eyes and tried to come fully awake as he heard them talk about the dog sled that had been attacked. He could just barely hear Suzette tell Moaka how worried she and Tess were when Karkak brought back the Native and they had kept each other company most of the time. Suddenly, coming alert, he thought he heard something about it being due.

Instantly, James rose to both elbows and in a loud enough voice to be heard inquired, "What's due or who? What are you two talking about?"

No sooner than he had finished, than Suzette came into the sleeping room and questioned, "What in the world are you saying in here sleepy head?"

James tried desperately to rub the sleep from his eyes. Muttering he asked again, "Whose due or what."

She started to laugh and replied, "Worry not your heart and mind James, it's not me."

James fell back down on his back with a sigh of relief, and muttered under his breath, "It's a good thing. That's all I'd need right now."

From the outer room James heard Moaka inquire, "Kincaid, sleep all day? I feed dog, they think you gone."

Rolling to his side James growled back, "No I'm not going to sleep all day, but if you keep giving me a bad time about it, I just might. It doesn't sound like a bad idea. What time is it anyway?"

As Suzette turned to leave the sleeping room she responded, "Well if you're going to be that way, I might not tell you how late it is getting."

Instantly, James sat up, grabbed his trousers, and groped for the right front pocket. He found his badly worn pocket watch, which read eight-thirty. Before Suzette could say anymore, James responded, "Never mind the time, it's not important anyway."

James lay back down, and enjoyed the warmth of the bed. He felt under the cover across the bed where Suzette had slept last night, and he knew she hadn't been up very long because the spot was still warm. He sat up once again, threw the covers back, and stood up, putting his inside layer on. He finished dressing, went out into the large room, and was greeted by Moaka's smiling face and cup of hot tea that Suzette handed him.

James sat down by the seal oil warming flame and crossed his legs. He slowly sipped the hot tea and commented, "Moaka it just doesn't get any better than this," as he waved his arm around acknowledging the room with the other oil seal lamps burning for light and warmth and the softness of the room. He smiled at Suzette and he motioned with his cup for a refill, and replied, "Thanks, its sure is nice to have you fix my first cup of brew in the morning." Quickly James looked about the room, and inquired of Suzette, "No school today?"

With an outstretched hand Suzette patted his unshaven face and replied, "Not today, James. We all need a day off once in a while."

Moaka raised to his feet and motioned toward James, and commented to Suzette, "He up now, get gear ready." Moaka waved farewell and smiled at Suzette, then disappeared through the entrance.

"I wish Moaka would not speak like that," Suzette stated. "I know he can speak English more properly than that. I swear I'm never going to get these children around here to speak proper English if their parents don't even try."

"I wouldn't be too hard on Moaka," James replied. "He just doesn't feel like it is that big a thing right now. After all, he doesn't have any children at home and none planned as of yet. I bet he will make a big change when he and Tess decide to have little ones."

"Well, boy do you have a surprise coming!" Suzette exclaimed. "Tess is going to have a baby. Moaka was a little afraid to tell you about Tess, and Tess wasn't sure until you and Moaka returned from this last trip. Moaka knew last night as soon as he got in. Tess is happy, as are the other members of her family." Smiling at James she continued, "I told Moaka not to worry about you; I'd take care of that."

"And just how did you figure to take care of me? Why should I care?" James inquired jokingly. "Hell, I'm happy for them."

"Well, Moaka wasn't sure what you would think, and you know he worries about things he is not sure of," Suzette explained.

As James finished his second cup of tea, he inquired, "I am supposed to let Moaka come to me on this matter?"

Suzette responded with, "He knows that I will tell you, but he didn't want me to. He felt he should be the one to tell you, but I told him that was foolishness."

James chucked to himself, and asked, "And what did he think of being called foolish."

"Don't be silly, James, he never thought a thing about it," she commented as she handed him his shaving gear, which Moaka had brought in from his sled for him. "You had better take care of Moaka; he has become one of your best and most loyal friends."

With a sigh, James responded, "Yeah, I know it. He tries to anticipate my every need. Sometimes that bothers me though. He almost makes me feel like I am as helpless as a babe. I might have been when I first came up here, but he has done a good job of training me, so I wish he'd lay back some."

With a quick wave toward his shaving gear, she asked, "Didn't you want your shaving gear this morning?"

"Yes, Suzette, yes, but damn it, I could have gotten my own gear."

After shaving, eating, and putting on his outside layer, James started for the entrance. He stopped and turned back to Suzette who was still standing in the middle of the room looking after him. Moving back to her, he took her in his arms, and kissed her gently. "Moaka and I should be back within a week or so whether we get the polar bear or not. I'll try and stop by just before we leave."

"Oh, by the way, Tess will probably have the baby sometime in November."

James smiled at the good news, gave Suzette one more quick kiss, and left the warmth and security of her hut.

Outside the hut, the cold air seemed to try to find any opening it could to get to James' bare skin. He shivered slightly and looked southward to the Brooks Range. The sun's face was just starting to appear over the mountain, and the day was clear and crisp. The Teshpuk area had not had a storm for several days, and that didn't hurt his feelings. When the wind started blowing in the snowstorms, man and beast might just as well hold up until it's all over.

The villagers were well under way with their normal daily activities, and there were a lot more folks around these days. Dog teams hooked up in front of hut, villagers in and out of the trading post, villagers helping each other fix or rebuild their huts, and several men up and down the street repaired sleds or their other equipment. Just a short time ago, this place consisted of about seven or eight huts and all of the people were related. James could not believe the village of Teshpuk had grown so much.

As James approached his staked team, Bray started whining, and it reinforced James' love to have contact with his dogs. His favorite thing was being around and handling his team. Somehow, it gave him a sense of accomplishment. He started checking the gear on his sled, knowing they were not going to need to get much more gear or supplies for this trip because they didn't use much from the last trip.

Just then, Moaka came out of Kirima's hut, and headed over to where James was checking gear. "Good morning again, Moaka, we all packed and ready to go?" and before Moaka had a chance to answer, James continued, "Talking about going, I didn't get a chance to ask if Ralph Tone got on his way this morning. Also, did that Simmons get gone to Three Rivers Village?"

"Ralph Tone go. Simmons still bed," and in an irritated tone of voice, "he be up soon. No hurry, Three Rivers Village no far."

"Yeah, Moaka, but he's not the kind I want to see around here," James dryly commented and inquired, "Are we packed and ready to go? We need to get started sometime today."

"Kincaid need talk."

By the sound of his voice, James knew that Moaka had something important to say. He stopped fooling around with the sled and replied, "Okay," as he leaned back against the sled. "I'm ready to listen."

"Kincaid, think how get bear in trap."

Calmly James responded, "Moaka that would be quite a trick if we could do that. What have you got in mind?" He detected an element of excitement in Moaka's voice, and James wanted to make sure that Moaka was not overly excited before they had talked out this new plan.

Enthusiastically Moaka continued, "I speak old man. Remember Noka? I told him problem. He counsel how kill polar bear."

James' facial expressions told on him.

Moaka put his hand on James' shoulder and stated, "Kincaid listen?"

Quickly James responded, "Yes, Moaka, I'm sorry, I just got lost in my own thoughts; seems like lately I've had a hard time concentrating for any length of time."

As Moaka continued, "No think much of idea, until old man say how work. Say build igloo."

"What!" James exclaimed. He looked at Moaka in bewilderment and sputtered, "Build an igloo!"

Moaka waved his hand in the air as if to say wait. He continued, "Kincaid, old man say make igloo, roof push up." Moaka demonstrated as he pushed up with his hands, then continued, "Make fish rack close. Wait polar bear come."

"If we are inside the igloo, how will we know the right time to lift off the igloo roof and shoot?" James asked impatiently.

More excited with every word, Moaka demonstrated by poking his finger and responded, "Make hole in wall, so can see."

"Where will the dogs be, Moaka?" James questioned, as he probed the old man's apparently well thought out plan and quickly thinking to himself, *Noka probably worked this little trick when he was a young man.*

"Staked," Moaka hastily replied. "Fish on rack, no go for dog. Old man say, I trust his say."

With a shake of his head, James slowly replied, "And so do I, Moaka," and hesitantly he finished his statement, "to some extent."

His own interest and excitement starting to build, James thought, *It seemed so elementary, these Natives have to be respected for their experience and knowledge about this country, course they have only been living in it almost forever or so.*

As James felt Moaka's hand hit his shoulder, he heard Moaka's words echo through his brain, "Kincaid, what think?"

Jarred from his thoughts, James looked through squinting eyes into the clear, cold, blue sky and coldly responded, "The old man may have a good idea, Moaka."

James looked at the dogs, but really didn't see them, as he visualized jumping out of the top of an igloo like some sort of jack in a box, and a smile appeared on his face.

Moaka asked, "Kincaid, what smile?"

"I was just thinking about popping out of the top of an igloo," James answered. "You know Moaka; we could give that bear the shock of his life."

"No care give bear shock of life," Moaka fired back, "care kill him. Native need us take care bear."

James nodded his head, and agreed, "Yeah, Moaka, I know they are depending on us to spearhead this operation, but you have to admit we've had some exciting times with this polar bear. Have you lost your sense of adventure?"

In a rather irritated tone, Moaka responded with, "Kincaid, make say, like fight polar bear."

"No, Moaka, I'm not, but if things work out the way we've got them planned, we will sure have something to tell our grandchildren." Pausing, James could see that he wasn't going to get a rise out of Moaka, so James continued, "Okay, Moaka, I know we need to get more serious; where do we start?"

James watched Moaka survey the sleds, and James knew that Moaka was excited about the plan. Silently, James stood by and waited for Moaka to make up his mind about what to do with the sleds.

Finally, after some thought, Moaka replied, "Kincaid, no think will do all sled. We move gear, strap poles for fish rack on side of sleds. Keep," stammering for an instant, Moaka blurted, "*kotsiktok*—high, no jamb in snow," as he demonstrated by keeping his hands about three feet high off the snowy surface.

James asked Moaka to go over to the trading post and get the supplies they would need, and Moaka showed James what he had in mind for the fish poles. When Moaka left for the trading post, James started on the sled arrangement.

As James was about to finish the work on the sleds, he loosened his parka a couple of loops. The temperature was about twenty degrees below zero, but the body could sweat easily the way they were dressed in several layers of skins. Nobody could afford to get their underclothes damp, and everybody knew the first rule of keeping warm was staying dry.

When James had finished moving gear around on the sleds, he went for the poles. As he returned with the fish rack poles, Moaka returned from getting the supplies.

Moaka walked over to James' sled and helped adjust his rifle sheath so the poles would not get in the way.

Half the fish rack poles were strapped on James' sled, and half on Moaka's. They loaded the rest of the supplies that Moaka had picked up, and it was pushing noon already, but that didn't matter. They were going to get to the sighting location, or close to it, by nightfall and hope the bear would still be in the area.

Once the dogs were hooked up and the traces checked, James turned to Moaka and said, "I have one more thing to do before we get out of here, and so do you."

Moaka looked at him questioningly as James started for Suzette's hut, and when James was about twenty feet away from him, he heard Moaka reply, "Kincaid say."

As James approached Suzette's hut, he hailed and she returned his call. Once inside, he was surprised to discover that the main room was full of children. Uncomfortable in the arrangement of all the children, James hurriedly said, "I came in to say goodbye, but it looks like you're a little busy. I thought you said you weren't going to have school today?"

She walked over to him, and gently took his hand and led him into the sleeping room and kissed him passionately. Parting from their embrace she whispered, "You be careful, James. I want you back in one piece." She slowly moved away and said with forced joviality, "By the way, this is not school, but just some little ones who came over just because they wanted to."

After their private good-byes were completed, they left the small sleeping room and went back into the larger room. The little ones giggled and were quite aware of what they couldn't see, but suspected what was going on in the next room. At the door, James paused, and looked back and smiled at the children, and shot Suzette a parting glance, then stooped to go out the entrance.

As he walked back to Moaka, James thought to himself, *Suzette always smells so clean and her lips are always so soft and tantalizing. I wonder if I could somehow settle down with her. I know that she would not want to travel around on my sled as Tess does on Moaka's, but I wonder how often I could get back to Teshpuk. How often would I have to come home to have a good marriage? The way I was raised to think about marriage was the husband and wife were together all the time, or at least most of the time. That was the way it was when I was home. Maybe to make this particular situation work, some of the rules would have to be changed somewhat to fit the circumstance.*

Moaka approached James after his good-byes and asked, "Kincaid no want leave?"

James smiled with tongue in cheek and with a quick shake of his head, looked at him and replied, "No I don't, Moaka, and neither do you."

With a quick slap of his hand on James' shoulder, Moaka remarked, "Kincaid say."

"How in the world could it work?" James confessed, as Moaka listened intently. "I'm gone for too long a time, and I couldn't ask Suzette to ride around on my sled all the time like Tess does. She has her school to take care of, and besides I don't think she would want to stay out on the flats as long as we have to sometimes. Marriage would be tough."

"Marry work, Kincaid!" Moaka emphasized. "Suzette no care, people marry all difficult. You and Suzette make good life, many children."

James quickly stepped to the back of his sled, and thought about what Moaka had just said, and smiled to himself. He turned to check Moaka and hailed, "On Bray," and they were off, on what he hoped would be a well-planned expedition. Little did he know at the time it would almost end in tragedy.

After letting the team run for the first mile or so to loosen them up,

James slowed them down to a good steady pace, as he hailed Bray over to a route that would take them southeast of Teshpuk. That was the last reported sighting of the polar bear they'd received from Doc. His mind wandering, James thought, *That crazy Doc. He was headed for Barrow with a strange team. I have to admire a man like that for his courage and dedication to the sick folks of his village. Few men would have taken that risk. I'm glad we were around to help them out of their bad fix. Those guys could have wandered around for days before coming upon someone or a village.*

CHAPTER TWENTY-THREE

Karkak returned to Teshpuk from taking the Native to Three Rivers Village, unaware that James and Moaka had left Teshpuk shortly before. He pushed his team hard from Three Rivers Village to get back to Teshpuk and possibly help get the marauding polar bear. He stopped his team in front of his hut, set the sled brake, and proceeded to Suzette's hut to see if she had any information. Halfway to her hut, Karkak saw at least seven or eight little ones come out of the entrance. He thought, *Suzette must be letting out school.* As he approached the entrance, she exited the hut.

Startled, she jumped and gasped in surprise. "Karkak, you scared the devil out of me." In native tongue, she continued, "How is the native?"

Karkak laughed because he had frightened Suzette, but he suddenly became solemn and replied, "He died."

"That's too bad, Karkak; you did everything you could for him. I'm going over to the trading post; do you want to walk along?"

Karkak shrugged his shoulders, and answered, "Yes, we can talk as we go."

Walking side-by-side toward the trading post, Suzette asked, "Do you need something, Karkak?"

Hesitantly he asked, "Where Moaka and Kincaid?"

"Oh Karkak!" Suzette exclaimed, as she felt some compassion for him, "They just left here not long ago to try and get the polar bear again."

He murmured under his breath, and asked, "Did they say when they would be back?"

"I'm not really sure, Karkak. James didn't seem to think they would be gone that long, maybe a week or so. Is there a problem, Karkak?"

Karkak continued in a dejected voice, "I hoped to get back to help out."

Suzette saw the look on Karkak's face, and she decided to tell a little white lie and quickly added, "Karkak, I am sorry you missed them, but James and Moaka both asked me if you got back from Twin Rivers to have you handle things around here. If the bear was to come back to Teshpuk, they said you would be the one that would know what to do. I hope you understand what they meant?"

Karkak did not respond, but a broad smile appeared on his face as they continued on their way to the trading post. Approaching the trading post entrance, they both entered the close quarters. Inside they went their own way; Karkak stopped at the counter to talk with the owner, and Suzette made her way through one of the narrow aisles filled with goods brought from Barrow.

The aisles were very narrow, which allowed for more supplies to be arranged in the hut. Suzette held a sample of sewing material toward the oil lamp to see well enough to examine the cloth. The inside of the trading post smelled of cured skins, leather, and dried meat. It was well supplied with the basics of life, for this far country, and she was glad Teshpuk was an established village, and would probably be here for a long time, if not forever.

Unexpectedly, she heard an unfamiliar voice ask, "Hey, sweetie, where did you come from?"

Suzette turned quickly to see a medium-sized man with a grizzly, uncut beard, who looked to be in bad need of a bath and clean clothes. Alarmed at the man's forward manner and tone, Suzette quickly dropped the cloth she was holding, and turned to hurry back to the front counter where she had left Karkak. She did not know this man, and all she wanted to do was get away from him. He was not of this village and she was afraid of him.

Pain instantly shot through her left shoulder as the strange man grabbed her. She could feel his hands roam all over her body as she fought to break loose, but only succeeded in being pinned against one of the aisle racks full of skins. The man's body odor was that of someone unclean and her face burned from his beard rubbing her face. His hand cupped one of her breasts, and she jerked away, but not out of his grasp, knocking over a small display of pots.

Gruffly, the rude stranger mocked, as he reinforced his hold on her and clasped his rough hand over her mouth to keep her from calling for help, "What's wrong, sweetie, you only like stinking Eskimos? We need to play around before you take me to your hut."

Startled by all the noise, Karkak hailed to Suzette, "What are you doing, tearing up the place?" Disturbed when he didn't get an answer Karkak slowly moved from the counter to look down the aisle where Suzette had gone. Rage instantly ran through him. Screaming at the stranger to let go of Suzette, he instantly charged the man.

With closed fist, Karkak slammed the back of the stranger. Drake yelled in pain and, turning, shoved Karkak to the floor, and immediately went back to renew his fondling of Suzette.

Karkak came off the floor with his knife in hand and quickly slid the knife under Drake's chin as if he were going to cut the throat of a seal.

The encounter ended as quickly as it had begun. Drake quickly let go his hold on Suzette and dropped his hands down to his sides. Karkak grabbed his left arm and applied pressure on the man's throat with his knife blade, while he shoved the man out to the front counter.

"Get a rope," Karkak commanded the Native owner. In bewilderment, the owner jumped to Karkak's command. He quickly got some small lashing rope and stood at the ready for more instructions.

"Don't just stand there," Karkak yelled at the owner. "Tie his hands."

Frightened because of Karkak's stern orders, he immediately began to follow Karkak's direction and began to secure Drake's hands behind him. Quickly Karkak checked the tie-up job, and released his hold on Drake. Karkak removed his knife from Drake's throat, and took the knife from the scabbard at Drake's side. Stepping back he angrily inquired in native tongue, "Who are you, and where are you from."

Drake's puzzled expression told Karkak right away he didn't speak the language and he may need Suzette to translate. Fortunately, Suzette came from the aisle and began translating every word with equally demanding expressions as Karkak used.

After some questioning, they found out that his name was Drake Simmons, and he had come from the Chamberlin country located east of Teshpuk. He was supposed to take the dog team and go to Three Rivers Village while he waited for Ralph Tone to return from Barrow.

After the interrogation, Karkak stepped up to Drake and stuck the point of his knife into Drake's throat as a drop of blood oozed and determinedly stated, "No come Teshpuk, I say, cut feet off, feed to dog. You stay from village for life."

Karkak stepped back and continued to stare into the frightened eyes of Drake Simmons. Karkak asked Suzette to tell Drake what he had said. Although Karkak used broken English, Suzette knew he wanted to be sure that the intruder got the message without error.

As Suzette spoke to Drake in English, Drake started nodding his head and repeating, "No, I won't come back. No, I won't come back to this place, ever."

Karkak cut Drake loose and motioned him outside. Karkak also told the owner to follow Drake to make sure he got out of the village as soon as he had his team hitched up, and if there were any problems, seek help and Drake's feet would be cut off and fed to the dogs.

After the owner and Drake left the trading post, Suzette almost fell into Karkak's arms, sobbing, "Thank you, Karkak. What would I have done if you hadn't been here? I will always remember what you have done for me this day. James was right; you do know what has to be done."

Easing her away from him he gently questioned, "Are you okay?"

"I'm fine," Suzette quickly responded through sobs and tears. "There was no time for him to do anything before you came."

Putting his arm around her tiny waist, Karkak helped her out of the trading post and walked her to her hut. Stopping at the entrance, Karkak sympathetically inquired, "Do you want me to get Tess?"

As she bent down to enter her hut she tearfully responded, "Yes, I would like to have her with me right now. If you could get her for me I would like that." With that, she disappeared into her hut.

❊ ❊ ❊

James hailed Bray to a halt so they could rest the teams, since they had been out for about two and a half hours. This trip would not be a long one if the bear could be quickly lured into the trap.

The snow crunched under Moaka's feet as he came up behind James inquiring, "What think, Kincaid? Go where polar bear spotted, maybe stay back? No answer last night when talk."

Quickly responding, James replied, "What I would like to do, Moaka, is move around out here for today and check for signs, and move closer to where we're going to build the igloo tomorrow. Maybe by moving around in the general area, it may also let the bear know that there may be some easy pickin's close by. I know that it is a long shot, but right now, I think that's the best thing to do."

Moaka nodded in agreement and replied, "Kincaid say, move slow, make sure." As Moaka remained standing next to Kincaid, Moaka was thinking of another possibility. Touching James on the shoulder, Moaka asked, "Kincaid, when get where polar bear seen, drop fish in trail, lead polar bear to us."

"Moaka!" James quickly exclaimed, "that is a hell'va good idea," and

James hit him on the shoulder as he continued, "That way we are looking for him; at the same he will be looking for us. Did Noka tell you that?"

Moaka's face turned into a large smile as he hit his chest with an open hand and answered, "No, I think."

"Well, Moaka, be proud. I can't see any reason not to; it makes all kinds of sense to me."

Unpacking some frozen fish to bait the trail when they picked up some sign, they were soon on their way again. The horizons were always changing, and they always seemed to move with the swirling, blowing snow, and create weird images in the distance. James guessed that visibility was not more than one-half mile. The sun's reflection off the whiteness was relentless, and James hated to wear the bone eyeshades Moaka had made for him, but he knew they were necessary if one was to see for very long when the sun conditions were as they were now.

Moaka watched Kincaid alternate on and off the sled runners as smooth as anyone. Moaka smiled to himself and he knew that Kincaid had come far in his knowledge of this country and the people. Kincaid was an excellent student because he really cared about this land and its people and animals. Moaka pondered the next encounter with the polar bear as his thoughts wandered back to his father, who had been killed by such an animal. *I'm not about to go by the same fate.* He was sure that Kincaid would be cautious and careful because it was just his nature. He had learned a long time ago that Kincaid was not stupid. Kincaid learned fast and remembered well. A slight grin came over Moaka's face as he remembered the first time he had seen Kincaid. *What a* chechahcos— greenhorn. Kincaid had been dressed in clothes that seemed to be so tight that they restricted his movement. Reaching up to adjust his hood and face wrap, Moaka knew that Kincaid initially didn't want to kill the polar bear, but now there was little or no choice.

As James ran beside his sled and then on and off the rear runners, he thought, *A polar bear's keen sense of smell was their greatest asset. They could smell food miles away. If the polar bear was around the area, it would pick up the odor of the frozen fish. They just needed to start seeing a sign before they baited the trail with the fish, and when the polar bear got close to the trap, he would scent the thawed fish on the fish rack.* Hopefully they would be lucky enough to draw him in, but they would have to be patient.

James glanced back over his shoulder at Moaka through his hood, and it always reminded James of looking through a tunnel. James signaled Moaka to hold up and hailed Bray to a halt, and as he stepped back off his sled brake, he slid his rifle from its scabbard. He turned and started to walk toward Moaka as Moaka approached him. When the two men met, James asked, "Would you stay with the dogs while I make a circle around in close? I can't help thinking that we're missing some sign. I don't know about you, but I can't study the surface good enough while moving on the sled."

"Good Kincaid. I same trouble. Sign hard see, even walking. Sign two day pass."

James started on his way, and he mentally heard Moaka's words again, sign two day pass. James knew Moaka meant that any track might be as much as two days old. James was confident he had been around the Natives long enough to understand what they were saying. It was very logical to the Natives; they just left out words that didn't have meaning to them.

As James got ready, he heard Moaka warn, "Dark two hour Kincaid. No good in dark."

Lifting his rifle into the air to check the sighting, James answered, "Point well taken Moaka, but I don't think I'll be out that long."

James walked past his team, and Bray began to whine and wiggle because he wanted to go. James stopped and looked down at him, then started to walk on again. *Ah, what the hell,* he thought. Turning back, he decided to take Bray with him. As he leaned down to unhook his lead, Bray seemed overjoyed to be able to go. James straightened and waved to

Moaka, as he and Bray were off on their scouting expedition.

A half hour into their scouting trip, James became disheartened. The frozen snow crust supported most of his weight, but he still sunk in slightly, which made walking a bit of an effort. He had snowshoes on the sled, but he didn't feel like he needed them. As he stopped to loosen his parka, Bray also stopped, and came back to see what he was doing. That was always a trait of Bray's that nobody had ever taught him. Bray always stayed close and always, well usually, came back to James if he stopped. Bray never seemed to get more than twenty yards away from him when they walked.

James hadn't cut trail or anything since leaving Moaka, and it was as if everything had disappeared from this area. He hadn't seen any game or any sign at all. That was peculiar; he wondered if that could mean the polar bear was still in this area. Starting on his way again, it was starting to get dark and he was beginning to doubt if he would ever cut a trail.

Suddenly, Bray stopped, and a low growl came from deep within his throat. James stopped and desperately tried to see what caused Bray to growl. He walked up to where Bray stood, and he could see the hair on the dog's back stood straight up. James knelt down beside him to get a better look at what Bray was looking at, but he couldn't see anything. James rubbed Bray's wide chest, and strained through squinted eyes searching the horizon in the direction of Bray's stone cold stare.

Bray's growls subsided, and James could feel his muscles beginning to relax beneath his hand buried deep into the animal's course hair. James continued to search the horizons ahead, and whatever it was, it seemed to alarm Bray. While still kneeling beside Bray, he eased the rifle bolt open to check for a round in the chamber. He rose from Bray's side, and they proceeded slowly in the direction that Bray had been looking when he became alarmed.

The packed snow surface was hard and it made signs hard to find. They went no more than twenty yards when James detected in the waning light a slight impression in the frozen snow. He leaned down to inspect the track, and Bray came back to James to have a sniff for himself. It was definitely the track of the polar bear. About the only part he could make out was half of the rounded paw impression and two claw marks, but that was enough. James moved ahead in the suspected direction of travel, and he found traces of more tracks. Again, he moved ahead and each track was examined, and he was sure of the polar bear's travel direction. He looked around the area, and half expected to see the polar bear disappear over the horizon or down into a low spot.

James searched the surrounding terrain, but he couldn't see anything. The bear traveled in a southwest direction. *Damn,* James thought, *that was inland again. That bear had no intention of heading for the coast, at least not by the track he'd left here.* He leaned down to reexamine the track, and he figured it was about one hour old. The blowing snow could cover tracks or any sign in a short time, but he thought it had only been here for about an hour because there were still sharp edges around the outside of the track. He figured if he and Moaka headed southward from where Moaka was, they would come close to intersecting the area where the polar bear might be heading.

The Brooks Mountain Range was pitch black and the sky above them had about lost any reflective light and James was apprehensive about getting back to Moaka at after dark. Moaka and he would have to travel at night to get to where they should be by daybreak, but that's the way it would have to be; if they were to have any chance of making contact with the marauder.

James started back to Moaka's location at a fast pace, trying to make up some time, but he soon realized that the light would soon dissipate. He hoped that Moaka would have a small fire lit as a beacon. He stopped to rest for just a minute, and thought, *Damn, why wasn't there more twilight this time of year.* Moving out again he maintained a fast pace, and finally saw the flickering of Moaka's fire.

As the dogs started barking to sound the alarm, James saw Moaka stand up. With his rifle in his hand, he moved away from the fire, not knowing what to expect from the dogs' warning.

James hailed as he and Bray approached the camp.

Moaka returned his call saying, "Kincaid dark two hour."

Smiling, James knew Moaka was jabbing at him for being late. Stopping long enough to hook Bray back in the traces, he then proceeded to the fire where Moaka had his stool set up, waiting for him.

Impatiently, Moaka asked, "Kincaid, see sign?"

Out of breath, James panted, "Yeah, I did. The only problem is that we are going to have to travel all night to get into position for that polar bear. Let's hope the crazy thing won't be traveling at night, at least not this night." James finished explaining the situation, and closely watched Moaka for a reaction.

As Moaka shook his head, he looked straight at James, and replied apologetically, "Kincaid know how feel travel night."

"Moaka, I don't understand. You can get up before daybreak and travel early in the morning or you can travel late into the evening, but yet you can't travel in the middle of the night?"

Moaka had never told James the reason for this belief, but James always figured he would when the time came.

It was silent, and James knew Moaka had to decide what move he was going to make. James knew Moaka could not be pushed easily.

James gazed into the fire, and waited patiently for Moaka's decision. He did not press him for a quick response.

Moaka knew they had to get to the area ahead of the polar bear to set up the trap. Still pondering the situation, Moaka noticed James patiently sitting on his stool, gazing into the fire as he waited for his decision. Moaka also knew that whatever decision he made, that James would honor it.

Only a few minutes passed when Moaka asked, "Need travel now?"

James nodded his head, and replied, "I don't know that for sure, but right now would be my best guess. Hell, we might travel all night and get set up and the damn bear won't come at all. This move is only a gamble, but I think he will stay on the same line of travel because it lines up with another village location."

"Fear no reason, no travel night," Moaka snapped.

Quickly raising his eyes from the fire's darting flames to meet Moaka's glare, James answered, "Didn't think that it was, Moaka."

"Knew you no think. Must go for time, and then can go."

As Moaka rose from the fire and disappeared into the darkness, James vigorously questioned, "Where the hell are you going?"

Moaka stopped and turned back slightly so the fire reflected his bronze colored face, and stared intently at James responding, "Make mind and spirit one."

Not fully understanding what was going on, James felt a little frustrated, and asked, "Is your team all right?"

"They okay. Feed team you gone. Bray need feed." Then without another word, he disappeared into the darkness.

The conversation that he and Suzette had about having to accept many of the Native beliefs started to mean something to him. Moaka had never talked about believing in such things as religious or native spirits, but Moaka thought Native, and Moaka was an excellent representative of his race.

James moved away from the small flickering fire to check the dogs, and feed Bray. With a shrug of his shoulders to rid himself of the night chill, James buttoned up his parka, and walked back to the small fire for the night cold was upon them.

Relaxed on his stool, James tried to rehearse what might happen when they finally caught up with the polar bear. His chin resting in the palm of his hand, his thoughts wandered as he stared intensely into the fire, which constantly moved, changing depth, and height, and never seemed to take the same path skyward. He felt a sense of peace come over him as he stared into the yellow and white flickering flames.

Just as suddenly as Moaka had disappeared into the night he reappeared, and stood silently beside James as he stared into the fire.

James looked up at him and softly asked, "You made up your mind?"

Without expression, Moaka rubbed his hands together to warm them up and finally responded, "Made mind before left fire. Had make all one. Ask one thing."

James stood up and stretched, and questioned, "And what would that be Moaka?"

"I lead while travel in night."

Relieved to hear such a simple request, James instantly responded, "Of course Moaka, I have no problem with that. You have led before. Why did you think it would have been a problem at this time?"

As if James had taken a load off his mind, Moaka almost cheerfully answered, "I lead, Kincaid say lead, now Moaka say, lead."

With his back to the fire, James rubbed his rear and upper legs while he stared into the blackness of the night. "Yeah, Moaka," James said, "I see what you mean. Well don't let that bother you, and from now on you can lead anytime you want."

"Okay," Moaka responded. "Kincaid, how far, what way?"

James realized that Moaka had now satisfied himself that everything would be all right. He seemed to be his old self once again. James picked up his trusty and much appreciated stool, and pointed due south saying, "That way for about four hours should take us close to where we want to be, I hope."

"You hope!" exclaimed Moaka.

"Yes, I hope," James responded some annoyance. "I'm not sure how fast that damn polar bear is traveling or for sure what direction. The only thing I can do is just do some guessing and hope it is close."

"No get...how you say?" Moaka stammered, "yes, no get anger. I make fun."

"I won't, Moaka, it's late, and I'm really not sure of the situation," explained James.

As James glanced at Moaka, he detected a smile that assured him all was well.

With a seriousness befitting only of Moaka, he said, "Be slow go, Kincaid, stay close. Want Bray hook my sled?"

"No," James responded, "I'll keep close."

As both men hazed their teams up, they rechecked the sled packs and started on their night journey, with Moaka in the lead.

As James followed close behind Moaka, he listened to the runner's scraping sound as they slid across the hard, crusty snow. He tried to figure out why Moaka thought it so important for him to follow so close behind, or even what his big concern was about traveling at night or even taking the lead.

The night was very dark, with starlight as the only source of light. Soon, the moon would show its face over the Brooks Range, and there would be more light, at least to see some distance, as it reflected off the crystal white snow. James could remember nights in the past when the moon shone so brightly and its light was reflected off the snow so much, it was almost like daylight.

Listening carefully, James thought he heard singing through the scraping of the sled runners. He jerked one side of his parka hood back away from his head to hear, and then realized that Moaka was chanting some kind of verse. As he turned his head sideways to make sure he was not imagining things, the cold air cut into his neck and down his chest, and the piercing cold instantly took its toll, and he quickly straightened his parka hood into place and readjusted his face cover. James' thoughts instantly jumped to the conclusion that this chanting had something to do with Moaka making peace with himself. *What the hell,* James thought, *it doesn't make any difference to me if Moaka wants to ride a sow sidesaddle to where we're going, that's fine, just as long as he keeps moving.*

They had traveled a good distance at a slow, even pace, when James heard Moaka hailing Anore to a halt, and he followed suit with Bray. Leaving his sled and approaching Moaka, James asked, "Why are we stopping?"

Without looking at James and rather staring off into the night, Moaka replied slowly with concern in his voice, "Look at night."

Resting his mittened hand on Moaka's shoulder, James inquired, "What are you worried about, Moaka?" James knew by Moaka's tone of voice that he had some concerns. James knew that Moaka didn't like this whole business of traveling at night. "If you would tell me what your problem is, I'm sure I'd be able to understand better."

Almost with a whisper, Moaka responded, "Night hold danger, Kincaid. My father, his father, no travel in sacred time. You believe, sacred time, just middle of night. To Native, believe time of peace and unity. Belief of some Native, not all. Things need time make energy for life, spirit. I say chant, part of make energy for life, spirit. Stay close, get energy from chant."

"Moaka, that's wonderful," James instantly responded. "I'm not kidding, that's wonderful. I get such enjoyment out of hearing you tell me of such Native beliefs, and I understand not all Natives believe. That reasoning makes sense to me, Moaka; I wish you had shared that with me long ago. I've always wondered why you didn't like to travel at night, now I know and can understand better."

Slowly removing his hand from Moaka's shoulder, James explained, "We have traveled for about an hour so we need to keep pushing on for another three hours. In two more hours of travel, I want you to start throwing out a fish occasionally. It may not do any good, but it won't hurt anything. That just might bring the polar into us."

Noting a quick nod of Moaka's head in the growing glow of the dull moon's indirect reflection, Moaka answered, "Kincaid say."

James waited for Moaka to hail his lead, as James looked into the darkness. The moon was not up over the Brooks Range yet, but it offered a pale glow of light over the mountain peaks, and the blackness had not been removed yet. No landmarks could be seen, except the black rough form of the Brooks Range far to the south. He couldn't read his compass without striking a match, and the silence just made it all the darker. The only real compass now was the moon. Shortly, James heard the familiar sound, like a grunt, coming from Moaka's throat. He followed suit and hailed Bray and they were off again.

Through the depth of the darkness, James glanced toward the southeastern sky and noticed that the Brooks Range was just starting to become illuminated by the rapidly rising moon. The north face of the mountain was still black, but the far away ridgelines could be faintly seen. The light rays drifted across the snowy surface that created eerie shadows and made things seem to appear and disappear that were never there. James could see Moaka quite plainly, and Moaka was tossing a frozen fish occasionally as he was alternating off the runners, and on the runners, as James was doing, trying not to load the dogs down too much.

After several more stops for the dogs to rest, they were finally getting close to the location where James figured that they could intercept the polar. *Damn*, James thought, *I hope my calculations were right. Not that Moaka would say anything if I was wrong, but I sure want to get that polar bear and real soon.* The polar bear wasn't going back to the coast, so they were going to have to stop it from raiding villages, and possibly killing somebody else.

Finally, after what seemed like forever, they hailed their dogs to a stop and Moaka walked back to James, asking, "Kincaid, here?"

James looked up into the sky, and checked the moon's position and considered their time of travel, then replied, "Yes, I think so," and to be sure he dug out his pocket watch and verified the travel as being about four and one half hours. "I sure hope that I'm right in my guess that the animal will come in this direction."

"Kincaid say, Moaka say."

With a head motion to signify agreement, James responded, "Thanks, Moaka, that makes me feel better. I just hope that we are both right. Did Noka make any suggestions about where and how to set up the igloo in relationship to the fish rack?"

Shaking his head, Moaka replied, "No. Say in open."

Stretching his arms above his head and sighing deeply, James declared, "Well, Moaka, this looks like home, so let's get started building our trap."

CHAPTER TWENTY-FOUR

"Kincaid! Say crazy thing," Moaka exclaimed, as he shook his head in wonder, and continued to sputter. He added, "No like Teshpuk home."

James laughed, and responded, "Moaka, it's only a saying. I know this doesn't look like Teshpuk, but this will be home for a while; I just hope it's for a damn short while."

James and Moaka stood in the moonlight and pondered their plan of attack, or rather their plan to make the trap and wait to be attacked. The dogs were tired, because they began to lie down and curl up for the night, still in their traces without being fed or staked out. James thought to himself, *They need an extra ration because of the long day's pull.*

"Moaka, I sure hope that bear comes in contact with the fish you dropped and comes this direction. At least maybe it will help get him to this area, and then he will smell the fish rack. How long will it take to get the igloo built? I mean one of a temporary nature, with a top that can be quickly pushed off."

Moaka turned his head to look upward toward the shining moon, and replied, "Two hour. If moon not in cloud."

"Well, Moaka, while you're doing that, I'll unload the sleds and build the fish rack. By the way, when I spread those upright poles out for height, how high should I make the top pole for the fish to hang?"

"*Pingasunik*"—eight feet, Moaka replied. "Want bear stop; reach high for fish, better shot at middle."

"One thing I want to do before we get started is to take care of the teams. They have put in a long, hard day and no telling what will come during the next few hours or so. I think we are ahead of the polar bear and the dogs will be able to get some rest, but my thoughts are to let them get as much as they can."

Both men nodded their head in agreement, and parted to stake their dogs and feed them a well-deserved extra ration of meat. When James had finished staking his team, he walked back to Bray to say a quick hello. Most of the Natives didn't try to make pets of their teams as he did, but he'd always tried to be close to all his dogs. Some he'd had luck with, and some always seemed to be leery of any human contact. Regardless of the wary dogs, James seemed to believe his dogs worked better individually and together for it. James knew there were many Natives that did not agree with that philosophy.

James walked back to the sleds for the frozen seal meat they had brought from Teshpuk, and he met Moaka also getting meat for his team. James commented as he glanced around the area, "It's amazing how you get used to seeing in the dark, especially if there is a slight moon for light."

With a disapproving grunt, Moaka commented, "Kincaid, look down gun barrel this light, no see."

"Oh Moaka, look on the bright side of things for once, it's a beautiful night." James had done some night hunting and he knew just what Moaka had meant, and he replied, "Yeah, I know, but if you got a target as big as a polar bear you just point and pull the trigger, right?" Looking at Moaka out of the corner of his eye to check his reaction, Moaka just grunted and picked up the meat for his team and walked away.

James fed his team, and met Moaka back at the sleds. They started unloading gear trying to get the poles free, and, James suspected that Moaka was looking for his *panar*—long knife. To James it looked like a machete, but it was effective for carving out the blocks of snow needed for an igloo.

Moaka, finally finding his long knife, raised it above his head, saying as he looked down the blade into the moonlight, "Father kill bear, one of these. Story told many time at fire, when I boy."

"Moaka," James replied, "I didn't know your father, but he sounds like a real rounder. What I mean is that he was able to do it all, if he had a mind to. Your description of him sounds a lot like my own father." James stopped unloading for a minute, straightened up, and continued, "Isn't the memory a funny thing? We remember all of the good things about our folks, but not so much of the bad. I've often wondered about that. The bad things almost seem to be funny now that the years have passed. But at the time they were hell on earth." Laughing, James slapped Moaka on the shoulder and asked, "Don't you think so?"

"Yes Kincaid. Father good," was the only comment Moaka mentioned.

A picture passed through James' mind of Moaka' father; James knew he would have liked to have known Moaka's father. Shrugging with nothing else to say, James continued unpacking his sled to get the poles for the fish rack, while Moaka started cutting blocks out of the frozen snow for the makeshift igloo.

James walked about thirty paces from where Moaka worked on the igloo, and laid the poles down. He looked back at Moaka, and raised his voice loud enough for Moaka to hear him and questioned, "About here should be all right? The sun and moon should be more or less at our backs when we shoot from the igloo."

"Okay," replied Moaka.

James arranged the poles, tied them with cured sealskin strips, and in no time at all, he had erected a versatile and strong fish rack. He stepped back to look over his finished work by the cloud-covered, dim moonlight, and James could see why the structure was so popular with the people of this land. It was easy and quick to put up, and quite sturdy. He knew it would not support a thousand-pound polar bear, but that wasn't its intended purpose.

Moaka must have noticed James looking at the rack, because he commented, "Kincaid, admire work?"

With a quick grunt and laugh, James answered, "As a matter of fact I was, Moaka. No wonder the Natives like it. Once you get it up you could use it for anything. You can hang meat on, or just throw some skins over it or you could have a temporary shelter, or hell you can even hang your hat on it."

Moaka chuckled just loud enough for James to hear him, and then declared, "Kincaid, you crazy. Say dumb thing. People in village say, you happy. People in village say, you learn good." Pausing, Moaka continued, "They know I teach you."

Just then, James figured he had been the brunt of one of Moaka's jokes.

Moaka had about two rows of ice blocks set together, as James started scraping up loose snow and filling in the cracks and responded with, "Yeah, I learn well, but I did have a good teacher." Silence fell between the men and within a short period, they had the igloo finished. They didn't put a fancy entrance on, so Moaka cut a hole near the bottom, on the opposite side from the fish rack, just big enough to be able to get in and out.

As both men stepped back to look at the finished product, James slapped Moaka on the back and chided, "I see you're admiring your work?"

Moaka smiled from around his parka hood, and chuckled, "Kincaid say."

They both chuckled, and began to loosen a couple of the blocks in the roof, for fast removal. Moaka went inside and sliced up through the ice blocks with his long knife. He cut through the roof and made two rounded pieces that could be removed from the inside, by a light upward pressure on them. The knife's moonlight reflection disappeared and Moaka came back outside saying, "Dark inside. No see hand at face. Cut hole in top again soon, freeze together. Cut hole better, wait daylight."

The southeastern sky was garnished with the grayish-purple rays of the new day, and the Brooks Range would be silhouetted shortly. James motioned to Moaka and commented, "Be getting light pretty soon." James noticed the moon was still high in the sky, but had lost all of its reflecting power. That was excellent; it should be the same way tomorrow night, if they had to stay here that long.

Daydreaming, James thought about when he and Moaka had spent several days atop Brooks Range last year. They had been on a routine game count expedition and hunting trip. James remembered looking northward from the top of the mountain, and imagined he could see the sea in the far distance north. He recollected trying to lock the vision into his mind.

"You know? Moaka, I think that I'll move my team to the other side of the igloo. Don't know why, other than the fact that if things go wrong, I would just feel better about the dogs being well spread out and by having yours on this side and mine on the other side, it seems to be more...well, balanced." James looked at Moaka for some kind of response, and James noticed him looking around the area. Impatiently James asked, "What are you looking for Moaka?"

With a chuckle he replied, "Just look, Kincaid, just look."

James gave Moaka a shove on the shoulder, and jokingly sputtered out, "You ass, what do you think about me moving my dogs?"

"Kincaid say! Moaka say," as Moaka answered as he tried to stop his laughter.

They had just begun to move James' team and sled to the other side of the igloo when the sun started to shower its golden light over the Brooks Range horizon. James peered into the sky's red and orange rays climbing over the mountain. The rapidly changing colors could only be caught with the naked eye and never in a painting. The ball of fire continued its upward progress, but it had not yet shown its golden face to this part of the world.

James rubbed his stomach, and commented, "Moaka, my stomach just growled, and I just realized how hungry I am. Let's get a fire going and have breakfast, and start thawing the fish so they will create a stronger order."

With the fish rack built, the igloo almost completed, and the dogs spaced out, James felt satisfied that they were just about ready. The only things left to do were have breakfast, get the fish thawed, and get them hung on the rack. They both went to the sleds and began to unpack. Moaka broke out the fish while James got some firewood and a little seal oil. They got the fire going, and James went back to his sled for his stool. He never could get used to sitting on the cold, hard, snow-covered ground, like the Natives.

"Kincaid," as Moaka shook his head he continued, "be greenhorn long time, no get rid stool. Some say you, *akrittok mimerk.*"

Roughly speaking it meant, man with a soft butt. "Well, that's all right Moaka, let them say what they want, I don't care. Besides being more comfortable, my legs don't get cramped as bad when I sit on my stool."

His steps unsteady, Moaka approached the fire with a full armload of fish they had also picked up while in Teshpuk. Laying them down, he began to break them apart, and commented, "Hope bear good smell today."

"The polar bear has never raided a camp in daylight," James remarked, "at least not that we know about." As he scanned the horizons as if half expecting the bear to come charging in at any time, he continued, "I just wonder if we will be able to entice him into the camp in the daylight?"

Moaka sat back on his heels, peered over at James and replied, "Maybe wait dark. If bear close, will grab at fish. Fish, seal, best food," pausing, Moaka continued, "this easy fish meal."

James thought about what Moaka had just said, and began to laugh and sputter, "You're a real philosopher, Moaka; I didn't know you had it in you, but you're right, Moaka, this is the easiest fish meal around, and we'll just have to wait and see how long it takes the polar bear to get here."

"What philosopher?"

"A philosopher is a person that can understand the past, know the present, and can sometimes predict the future based on the past and present."

"Like Noka."

"Yes, just like Moaka." James reached into the food bag and pulled out a large piece of frozen seal meat. He held the meat in front of him, and asked, "Moaka do you want a piece of this now or after I thaw it out?" As he gazed at the frozen hunk of meat, James thought, *It resembles a hunk of red rock.* He tapped on the meat with his finger; it felt just as hard as a rock, and it was difficult for him to realize they were going to be eating it very soon.

His head to the side, Moaka replied, "Kincaid put on fire. No easy eat froze."

James smiled, knowing that nobody would really eat frozen meat unless there was no other choice. Fortunately, Suzette had cooked some seal meat for them to take, but it had to be thawed first before eating. A lot of Natives ate raw meat, but James really never did figure out why, other than the fact that maybe fuel for cooking fires was sometimes hard to come by. Moaka, and other Natives like him, oftentimes said they liked the flavor better when the meat was uncooked. James, from time to time, ate raw fish, but he never could stomach eating raw seal; he somehow couldn't get it past his nose. Fish always tasted like fish, but raw seal didn't taste the same as cooked seal. The raw seal tasted too much like blood for James.

"Okay, Moaka, we'll be eating like kings in about twenty minutes," James commented, as he placed the seal meat in the skew basket and placed it over the fire. The meat adsorbed the heat quickly and began to drip almost immediately. He reached behind his stool to get the other bag that Suzette had prepared for them, and the stool slipped out from underneath him and scooted right into the fire. James jumped up and kicked the stool out of the flames, and he glanced at Moaka who was having quite a laugh at his expense. As James had frantically kicked the stool out of the fire, he had also accidently kicked the seal meat out of the skew basket, and it went sliding across the snowy surface. The meat tumbled over near Bray, who was about to have his third meal. James yelled at his lead, "Don't even think about it, Bray!" and as Moaka continued laughing, James yelled, "Damn it, Moaka, sit there on your ass, laughing it up, you could help out here?"

Slowly, Moaka got up to retrieve the meat Bray kept his eye on. As Moaka approached the meat, Bray growled low in his throat.

Instantly, James stood squarely in front of Moaka, grabbed Bray by the back of the neck, and shook him vigorously. Never hurting the dog, but letting him know that he was not happy with that kind of behavior. James then told Moaka, "Pick up the meat and don't hurry about it, let's see if he has learned a lesson about who is friend and who is foe."

Moaka leaned over slowly and picked up the meat, and Bray didn't move a muscle or growl. Both of the men returned to the fire, and Moaka reset the meat in the skew basket, as James got his stool back underneath him. James knew he didn't have to worry about Moaka, he would have dealt with Bray, not a problem, but James needed to reinforce some authority, and also reinforce who was the leader of the pack.

"As I started to say," James continued, "before the crap hit the barn door, let's see what Suzette has fixed here in this bag." Examining the contents, he found some *sigalarallak* inside. "Moaka you're going to love these. Suzette has made us a whole bunch of those sweet biscuits you like so well."

His eyebrows rising and a yellow-toothed smile coming over his face, Moaka responded, "Good! Need picking-upper. Fall off stool, raise spirits. Give good laugh, that good."

"Moaka the saying is 'picker-upper', not 'picking-upper,'" James corrected.

"Kincaid know I say."

With a grunt, James handed him three biscuits to set beside the fire to thaw; he took the same for himself. Soon the two men were eating their meal fit for a king.

James looked across the fire at Moaka, and he knew that Moaka was unaware of his knowledge of Tess' condition. Casually James asked,

"How's Tess feeling nowadays?" and before Moaka could respond, James continued, "I doubt that she will be coming with us for quite some time, or maybe not at all after the baby? I sure hate to lose a good cook."

Moaka's head jerked up and his facial expression revealed total surprise. He quickly answered, "She fine. She come, after baby. How know she with baby? Suzette say?"

"Yes," James answered as he waved his right arm into the air. "Hell, I don't care, Moaka, and it might be nice to have a little one around. A child on our routine trips will make them more enjoyable. I like to watch other people's children romp and have fun. The child would not be able to go on all trips, but could be left with the family while we were gone. Sometimes Tess and the child could be left behind if we weren't going to be gone for very long."

"Good, Kincaid. Tess worries what Kincaid say. Native way, children stay with parent, to teach. Before Suzette teach, parent teach, what need know. Suzette know Native way. Parent like children be at Suzette." Moaka smiled at James across the fire, and continued, "Native say children very good in life." Moaka chuckled to himself, as he smacked his lips and wiped the last remnants of seal oil off his mouth with the sleeve of his outer garment, and as he finished chewing his last bite of seal meat, commented, "Native say eat good in life."

Wanting to discuss the issue of Tess and the baby further, James backed up to his first statement. "I wish if she had been so worried, she or you should have let me know instead of fretting about the situation."

"Kincaid, I say to Tess, I tell Kincaid."

"Damn it, Moaka, don't hold back on me; if we have a problem let's get it out in the open, as soon as possible." James wiped his knife free of seal grease on his pant leg, and explained further, "There is never any need to worry about decisions that have to be made between you and me. I've always thought we could work any problems out between us." Leaning forward slightly on his stool, James inquired, "Don't you agree, Moaka?"

216

Moaka raised his head and squinted as he peered through the red and yellow flames, and responded, "Kincaid last say."

Despair began to creep into James mind. He shook his head, saying, "Moaka, you can't even remember the last time I said anything about having the last say."

Silence fell between the two men as they finished eating. Except for the crackling of the dying fire, it was silent around the camp. After they had cleaned up from breakfast, both men straightened the gear on the sleds and began hanging the thawed fish up on the rack.

They hung the fish about eight feet off the ground by throwing a line of dried seal gut over the top rail and tying them off. The thawed fish would freeze again soon, but at least they could get the odor on the wind and circulating around the area. A polar bear could smell these fish from as far away as five miles or more, so if he were in the area or even downwind he'd be along. The task completed, they returned to the dying fire, and James rekindled it with small bits of wood. Once the fire was burning again, James put on a pot of snow for tea. The small amount of water from the snow boiled quickly, and then James poured two cups of hot water and added the tea leaves for Moaka and himself. They sat beside the fire silently scanning the horizons for any movement that would tell them that the polar bear was approaching.

Moaka broke the silence, asking, "How long, Kincaid?"

Shaking his head, James sighed and replied, "I sure wish I knew, Moaka. It could be right away, sometime tonight, or hell, it might be tomorrow. I do think that we are ahead of him, and I'll bet he's hungry. I never saw a polar bear yet that wouldn't eat anything anytime." Pausing for a moment, James continued, "Moaka, one time I watched a polar bear eat an old boot that had been discarded. I mean he torn it in pieces and ate every bit of it."

Moaka stood up from his sitting position, and slowly looked around the surrounding area. Not seeing anything different or unusual, he asked,

"Kincaid, why bear be hungry? Maybe, make raid."

"Well, Moaka, put it together this way. There are no villages in the area he's been in for the last two days. Before that, there was just the attack on the native's sled, which didn't give him much of a meal, because not many of the dogs had been chewed on. Yeah, I figure him to be looking for an easy meal right about now. Remember Moaka, we don't know what is wrong with this polar bear. He should be out on the ice right now hunting his favorite food, seal. Why he is not out there right now is anybody's guess."

In an irritated voice, Moaka suddenly inquired, "Kincaid, where rifle?"

Shocked by his tone, James quickly answered, "Well, hell, over by my sled somewhere. I guess I should keep it a bit handier during times like these." James went for his rifle, and noticed Bray standing and staring straight at him. Retrieving his rifle, he hailed back to Moaka that he and Bray were going to look around.

He walked over to Bray and rubbed his chest for a minute, and he could feel the animal's coat was so heavy and thick that he could barely get his fingers down to the warm skin. Unleashing Bray, James waved to Moaka and they began their walk.

"How far go Kincaid?" Before James could answer, Moaka continued, "See bear, come back. No fight alone."

With a quick circling motion of his rifle barrel above his head, James yelled back, "Don't worry, we're not going far. I just need to stretch my legs and take Bray for a short walk; we'll just circle the camp some distance out."

Moaka watched Kincaid walk away from camp with Bray, and thought, *If Kincaid had been correct in thinking the direction the polar bear would be coming, then the trap was set up properly.* Moaka watched the fish swing slowly back and forth on the rack. *I hope this trap will lure in the polar bear, and we can be finished with this craziness.*

Bray enjoyed these times and James saw that he jumped around as he used to when he was a pup and so full of energy. Moving his eyes from Bray to the horizon, it looked like they were in luck. The wind had lay down a little and the snow wasn't swirling so much. Stopping now and again to study the flat white emptiness, scattered brush outcropping, and a few small rolling hills James set a course to circle the camp from about three hundred yards away. As they slowly walked along, Bray kept grabbing at James' leg coverings and pulling, wanting him to play. One of Bray's favorite pasttimes was for James to get down on the ground and wrestle with him. Normally the sled dog was not born nor bred to be playful, but James had played with Bray ever since he was a pup. Moaka gave Anore some extra attention sometimes, but he never played with his lead, as James played with Bray.

Maintaining the circular route and scanning outward, James couldn't see a thing, except the white, gentle rolling hills of the low lands, which lay between Brooks Mountain Range to the south and the ocean to the north. James didn't see any tracks of game, and that might be because of the polar bear being in the area. There was not a lot of game on the flats this time of year, but on several occasions they had spotted arctic hares, wolf, fox, and artic hens.

James chuckled to himself, and thought, *In just a short time from now this area will be a living paradise for all kinds of animals and nesting birds. Caribou will be here and passing by the thousands, the rivers will be thawed, and fishing will be good.*

The change of seasons had its own requirements. The teams would be tied up all summer, all except for Bray and Anore, until they were needed the following winter, but a few of the dogs would be used as pack animals to haul supplies. They traveled in summer on the rivers or walked. They had built a large boat of driftwood and sealskin and it served the purpose for river travel. He and Moaka always kept Anore and Bray with them to help pack through the summer months, and they both hired a local native to feed and exercise the teams while they were away from Teshpuk.

Looking toward the camp, James could see Moaka going in and out of the hut probably making the peek holes they would need later on. Completing the circle of the camp, James and Bray leisurely started making their way back.

Suddenly, Bray stopped and the hair raised straight up on his back, as a low growl came from deep within his throat. Kneeling beside him, James looked in the direction Bray was warning, but James couldn't see a thing. Bray must have picked up a scent. James stood back up and finally got a glimpse of the faint blurred outline of the prize, the polar bear. He was following their trail, probably feeding on the fish Moaka dropped. Instantly reaching down and grabbing Bray by his leather collar, James nearly had to drag him to the camp.

Moaka saw them coming in fast, and by the manner James was holding on to Bray, he knew that they had spotted something. James drug Bray to his leash stake, and hooked him securely.

Moaka was ready to go into the full swing of action, as soon as he knew what the score was, and excitedly he asked, "Polar bear?"

"Damn right, and it looks like he is headed straight for us and bringing hell with him. You'll be happy to know he is following our trail, feeding on those fish. Moaka, I'm going to check my dogs one more time and you should too, just in case one might have jerked something loose."

Quickly parting company to check their dogs, all James could think about was the Native who had been caught off guard by that polar bear, but that would not be the case this time. They were ready for him.

Both of them were out of breath when they met back at the igloo. They looked around for a final time to check everything, and then ducked into their ambush station. Getting settled inside and looking out through the peek holes Moaka had made, James could see Bray and a couple of the other dogs of his team standing at alert and barking—giving warning to the intruder.

Not taking his eyes away from the peek hole, James asked, "Are your dogs up and barking?"

"Yes, they bark at polar bear, and then look for us."

"Think they will be all right Moaka?" James asked nervously as he looked over at him.

Quickly nodding his head, he responded, "They tie good, no problem. Kincaid, you see polar bear?" Moaka asked excitedly as he quickly peered out one peek hole, then another trying to see the polar.

James quickly moved to several peek holes, and to his surprise the white giant was well within visibility. "Yeah, Moaka, but the damn thing is just standing out there waving its huge neck and head back and forth like a snake ready to strike. He's out too far for a shot, and if I did try a shot, I'd probably just scare him away. The only respect he seems to have is for the sound of a rifle."

Jumping to James' side of the igloo, Moaka quickly peered through one of the peek holes saying, "Kincaid no shoot, let come in. Need best shot can get."

"Don't worry, Moaka; I know that we have to hit him hard."

"Kincaid, he scent fish. See how hold nose in air?"

Still peering out one of the peek holes and not bothering to look at Moaka James replied, "My guess is that he was coming this way just like we thought, and just happened to scent the fish trail on the way. That's kind of how we planned it, right?"

"You say, Kincaid." As Moaka continued to peer out one of the peek holes on James' side of the igloo, he said in disgust, "He no come, Kincaid. He smell trap. Dog bark too much."

James jerked back from the inside wall, and looking at Moaka, quickly asked, "How can you say that with such confidence?"

Without taking his eyes from the peek hole, Moaka replied, "He stop. He no sure. Head stop high. Head swing, nose in air. Mean he smell fish. Daylight, dog keep him away."

"You're probably right, Moaka, but we can't shoot the sun out." Turning back to observe the polar bear movements, James couldn't have agreed more. The polar bear was just staying out of range and deciding for itself what he was going to do. "Moaka, have you seen this behavior from a polar before?"

Moaka slowly replied, "Yes. With father on ice pack. He and other hunter lay dead seal on ice. Wait polar bear come. Bear come, no close take seal. My father and other hunter want kill polar bear for fur. Father say bear smell wrong."

"Do you think that we will lose him?" James questioned.

"Maybe," Moaka answered.

Irritated, James demanded, "Maybe what?"

Out of the corner of his eye, James detected movement from Moaka, and Moaka's reply was, "Maybe come in or no."

Pulling back from his position, James looked at Moaka and knew that he'd been a victim of one of his mild jokes. Slapping Moaka on the shoulder, James blurted out, "You're no damn help, and you call yourself a hunter." Chuckling together, they both resumed their positions at the watch.

CHAPTER TWENTY-FIVE

The polar bear started moving in a path that would circle the camp. The path was similar to that James and Bray took, except about fifty yards closer to the camp, but still out of range for an accurate rifle shot. Moving around to the other side of the igloo, James spotted the polar bear continuing his circling path and marveled, *What a magnificent animal, and no natural enemies except man, he is surely the king of his territory.* Each step the polar bear took seemed to be sure and calculated, his fur was shimmering white in the bright sunlight, and his gait was slow and easy. James guessed he was going to make sure of things before he made his move.

Moaka moved around James to pick up the bear on the other side and said quietly, "Kincaid, polar bear no come, maybe later."

"I think he will wait until dark." Rolling away from the wall, James suggested, "Why don't we take shifts watching him circle us. We didn't get any sleep last night, and the way it looks, we are probably in for a long night tonight. Are the dogs' occasional barking going to bother you?"

"No Kincaid. Need sleep," Moaka mumbled under his breath, just loud enough for James to hear.

The dogs were not barking as much now, but three or four dogs always kept up the warnings to the polar bear. Inside the igloo, their barking was muffled, but the different tones of each dog made it hard to get some sleep.

Moaka rolled over on his side with his back to James, as James tried to stretch out his legs while still peering out the peek holes to keep an eye on the polar bear's movements. The problem was that the bear kept stopping, and then would retrace his path for a few paces or more and then he would start circling again. Whenever he'd stop his circling, he'd stick his black nose in the air, wave his huge head back and forth sniffing the air for any change in scent, and continue again. Occasionally he'd stop and throw his head in the air, bouncing up and down on his front feet, as if he were challenging someone to come out and fight. James marveled at the magnificent beast, and he figured the polar bear would weigh in over a thousand pounds. James wished there was another way to deal with this critter, but he had turned marauder and had to be stopped.

Quietly watching from inside their small enclosure, James listened to Moaka's rhythmic snoring. Thinking of another way, *What would be the chances of sliding out of the igloo, hooking up my team, unloading the sled some, and taking out after the polar bear? Would the animal stay and fight or would it run? If it stayed and fought, I'd have him, but if he ran, there is a chance of losing him for sure. The polar bear could outrun the dogs in a long pull. If the polar bear ran, I would have to catch him right out of the chute. No, that's not a good plan. I better sit tight.*

As the time slowly passed, James noticed that the sun's rays shining through the peek holes kept changing positions from the snowy floor rising up the walls as the sun was going down. It was late afternoon. Not long from now it would be getting on toward dark, and James hoped that the moon would shine as well as last night, and with the sky being mostly clear. He peered out of one of the peek holes toward the sky, and it was clear. The sky had never been more blue or peaceful looking and the wind wasn't blowing as hard today as sometimes it could.

Nudging Moaka with his foot, James woke him up to take over the next watch.

With a grunt, Moaka slowly struggled to a sitting position. As he tried to wake up, James commented, somewhat mockingly, "Talk about my snoring, Moaka, you shook the whole inside of the igloo. I'm really surprised it's still standing."

Still trying to dislodge the cobwebs of sleep, Moaka replied thickly, "First defense. What bear do?"

James thought for a moment, and then explained, "Well, Moaka, I'll tell you, that polar bear circles some and stops and then retraces some distance then starts circling again. Often, he stops and throws that big head around and jumps up and down on his front paws then just stands there waiting, until he decides to circle again."

With an expressionless tone Moaka stated, "Bear challenge us."

"We'll let him challenge, Moaka; I'll shoot his eyes out if he comes any closer!" James exclaimed.

As they chuckled, James tried to stretch out as Moaka had, but he was just about three inches too long, and he lay back the best he could. It was not hard to relax for he was tired and his eyes felt like they had sand in them. With his parka hood pulled down over his eyes, James asked Moaka, "You ever do this before?"

Moaka replied, "Kincaid, be quiet, go sleep."

The last thing James remembered was the sporadic barking of the dogs; and how he could not have cared less, whether they all barked or not.

The igloo was small and Kincaid's body seemed to fill more than his half. Moaka knew he would have to maneuver around inside to look out the peek holes without climbing all over the still form, now sleeping soundly.

Moaka noticed the sun drifting toward the southwest ridgeline of the Brooks Range, and when the moon came over the mountain, he knew the moonlight would let them see out of the peek holes, but nothing like daylight.

As Moaka shifted his position, he realized that the polar had stopped, and had lain down. Slowly shaking his head, Moaka could almost feel the thought pattern of the beast. He wanted to come in for the fish rack, but his instincts told him something was wrong.

Sighing slightly, Moaka's thoughts strayed back to Teshpuk and Tess. *She is with child and that could add some problems to the relationship between me and Kincaid. What if the baby got sick? What if the baby cried a lot? Would Kincaid understand or would he be irritated by such things? Kincaid likes things to be the way they are supposed to be, without confusion. He is a simple man with simple wants, but most of all he is fair. He is fair to himself and fair to others, just as long as everybody carries his own load.*

The inside of the igloo was now getting dimmer. The sun was just about ready to dive behind the horizon and the red and orange rays were streaming across the sky in many shades. Moaka peered out one of the holes that faced the southeast and imagined the moon that would soon be making its march across the southern night sky. Leaning to the other side of the igloo, Moaka suddenly became frantic. He could not see the polar bear out any of the peek holes on that side. Shifting positions, he scanned all directions in an attempt to locate the polar bear, but Moaka could not find the polar bear through any of the peek holes. He suddenly realized that the dogs were not barking. The worst thought came to him in a flash that the polar bear had left.

Despair instantly came over him as he again hurriedly searched through the peek holes. He was about to wake Kincaid up when suddenly the unseen reappeared. The animal was still interested, and with a sigh of relief Moaka tried settling himself down by breathing deeply. By now the dogs had gotten used to having the polar bear around, and they barked only sporadically, but were still uneasy and on guard.

More alert now for any changes of the bear's behavior, Moaka kept very close watch on the polar bear's movements. Moaka knew it would be dark soon, and they would have to depend upon moonlight for all reflective light off the snow. Although the moon would not give much light, it would be all they had. Moaka realized they would be almost blind inside the igloo for at least a couple of hours, till the moon cast it light over the Brooks Range, and that's when that polar bear might try for that fish rack.

Finally, Moaka nudged James awake and James heard him say almost in a whisper, "Quiet Kincaid, almost dark."

Sitting up and rubbing his eyes, James tried to get the world back in focus. The inside of the igloo was as black as a hole in the ground. Fighting the bulky parka hood off his face didn't seem to make any difference. He felt around and finally located his rifle, and asked, "Is the moon up yet?"

"No," was Moaka quick answer.

Feeling a nudge on his arm, James heard Moaka ask, "Kincaid hungry?"

"Hell, I don't know. I just woke up." As James reached up with his bare hand to scratch his head, he asked, "What have you got to eat?" He didn't really need an answer to that question because as soon as the words were out of his mouth, he realized the igloo was reeking with the odor of dried fish.

Almost in a whisper, Moaka replied, "Fish."

"I would have never guessed, Moaka. It only smells like the inside of a fish's gut in here. Yeah, let me have some." To James' surprise, he was getting used to the shadows in the igloo. "How's our polar bear doing? When was the last time you saw him?"

"See now, he on your side. Stay same distance." Moaka explained carefully, "He stop circling some. No see one time. He disappear, he back short time."

Slowly chewing on the dried fish, James realized that the dogs' barking had turned to growling. Chewing his last bite of fish, he looked out one of the peek holes, in the direction of the fish rack. To his surprise, he could still see the outline of the rack. James moved back to his original position, and said, "Won't be able to see the rack much longer until the moon comes up. The light is fading fast."

After a moment of silence Moaka replied, "I make position by sled. Maybe shoot polar bear from two ways."

Not saying anything right away, James thought of what would happen if the bear got directly between them. He replied, "Moaka, let's ease outside and see what it looks like. I want to know exactly where your location is; besides that, I've got to take a leak."

With rifles in hand, they quietly crawled out of the low entrance, as James noticed that a few clouds were starting to roll over the horizon.

Moaka noticed the clouds also, and commented, "Cloud hide moonlight Kincaid, tough time see anything."

James responded, "Damn it, I know." Keeping a low profile, he went a short distance, and relieved himself, and as he finished, he thought, *Nothing like taking a leak in an icebox.* James rejoined Moaka who was squatting down at the entrance of the igloo studying the situation for the night's ambush.

"Now Moaka, where did you want to set yourself up?"

James saw Moaka's arm motion, and he said, "Kincaid follow." They crawled toward Moaka's sled, and stopped just short of it. Quietly Moaka said, "Be beside sled. Sled, me like same."

As James rose up to check the position of the polar bear, he used his rifle to brace himself. Not visible right away, James raised up higher still until he was able to see over Moaka's sled and spot the polar bear. He crouched back down and commented, "That crazy polar bear is still out there. He's not going anywhere. I think he will make a run for that fish rack when it gets good and dark, before the moon comes up."

James surveyed the area, and said, "That sounds good to me, as a matter of fact, that sounds better than being in that damn igloo. One thing to remember though, we have to keep our positions and know what direction we want to fire. What signals are we going to use; the same old ones?"

Moaka knew what signal James wanted to use. It was a noise made by puckering the lips up and sucking in. The sound wasn't a whistle, but rather a sound like rushing air through a small hole. They had used it a lot in the past when they had to do night spotting of game. The noise didn't seem to spook most animals.

"I wish I was going to be out here with you, but I'll have a much closer shot when I stand up through the top of the igloo, and maybe I'll be able to see to get a better shot at the vitals."

Grabbing onto James' sleeve as he turned to leave, Moaka instructed, "Kincaid, stand up in igloo, roof fall. Make roof thin," as he held his hands together closely signifying thin.

"Yeah, I'll remember," James assured him as he crawled back toward the igloo. He looked up at the sky again, and noticed the way the clouds were forming. It was going to be tough enough to get a good shot off in the dim light, but next to impossible if it grew any darker. James could see the teams spread out on the snow, and they were on edge, and kept getting up and moving around. Bray must have seen movement around the igloo because he barked once, but that's all James heard from him.

James checked the immediate area for one final time, and disappeared inside the igloo. Once inside, it was dark as coal, but soon his eyes adjusted, and he could at least see his hand in front of his face. Positioning himself so he could get a good view of the fish rack, he settled in for a long night. James hoped that Moaka being outside would not spook the polar bear when he got close.

One man outside the igloo would increase the scent of man, but James didn't think that would deter the polar bear's confidence to come in. *Oh what the hell,* James thought, *the critter will make his move regardless. He hasn't stuck around this long to just walk away.* The smell of man hadn't seemed to discourage him before now.

Luckily, the polar bear had not seen fit to make his move, although the moon had recently risen above the mountain ridges. The dim moonlight was being obstructed somewhat by the passing clouds, and the vision out the peek holes was not clear, but James could see the faint outline of the fish rack.

James changed positions several times, as the hours drifted by, and his thoughts wandered. *Suzette would not be up yet, but soon she would be up getting ready for school or mending something. Seattle headquarters is going to question me about changing home base locations from Barrow to Teshpuk, but I can justify the move from Barrow because Teshpuk is in the center of my so called territory.*

Last year when he was in Seattle, all they could talk about, including Don Nealy, was the good job James Kincaid was doing. How the reports he sent were so much help to their work in getting more funding for Alaskan exploration and development. James told them, "Hell, you guys don't realize how big that country is up there. Sometimes it takes me a month and a half or more just to make my routine rounds."

Smiling to himself, he recalled what one fellow from Washington, D.C., commented, "Well, you stay in Barrow, and send the Natives to look for the game and take the counts?"

"Fat chance of that," James had told him. "Documentation of game movements, count, and behavior has to be orderly and consistent or the information wouldn't mean a damn thing to anyone. The individual Native is quite reliable, but if you assign a different Native for each area the information would probably not come out the same." That's when Nealy jumped in the conversation and showed his support for the program as it was being handled.

James could just barely see Moaka's concealed position. His form beside the sled was just as if it was part of or attached to the sled.

Carefully Moaka laid his rifle on the snowy surface and slid his right mitten off. Rolling to one side, he placed his bare hand inside his clothing. The night air was starting to take effect. Moaka glanced at the clouds slowly passing overhead like puffs of windblown smoke, and the moonlight only partially penetrated the clouds.

Suddenly, the dogs went crazy. Moaka jerked the hammer back on his rifle, jumped to his feet, and desperately tried to pierce the darkness with all senses alert. In an instant he realized that a dog, it looked like Bray, had broken loose when the polar bear came in. Bray had not backed off, and James' lead and the polar bear were going at each other just in front of the igloo. Moaka heard snarling and growling, and sounds of jaws snapping shut, as fangs missed their mark.

At the top of his lungs, Moaka screamed, "Kincaid, Bray loose. Fight polar bear."

The two animal warriors were fighting to the death, and Moaka snapped a quick round in the darkness at the marauder. Moving the rifle barrel with the quick movement of the bear's motion he couldn't get another good shot off without endangering Bray. They clashed together, and then fell apart. Bray hit and jumped away, probably sensing he was out-matched. Just as Moaka was about to pull the trigger, Bray would be on top of the bear again. Finally, in desperation, Moaka fired two quick shots and hoped that one would slow down the raging white shadow. The polar bear reared up and fell backward and Bray was instantly on top of him snarling, growling, and snapping his strong jaws.

James jumped to his knees, and the commotion he heard outside the igloo sounded like a gigantic dogfight. He had just checked all the peepholes not thirty seconds ago and everything seemed to be quiet. Desperately, he moved from peephole to peephole trying to see what was going on. The dogs were making so much noise that the polar bear had to be right on their doorstep. *What is Moaka doing? Where is he? Can he see anything?* James could see a shadow appear in front of the igloo, and then gone, then back. He heard Moaka yelling something, then a rifle shot. It sounded like Moaka yelled something about a dog getting loose. *The hell with this igloo,* James thought, *I'm getting the hell out of here.*

Just as he started to stand and push the top upward, he heard two quick shots. Then the world collapsed on top of him, as he was pinned down flat to the frozen surface by the weight of the snow and struggling bodies above him. James instantly realized the polar bear was practically inside the igloo with him, and that some of the dogs were trying to take on the polar bear. Just for an instant, an image flashed through his mind of long frozen purple guts lying in the snow.

The affair ended just as quickly as it began. Desperately trying to drag himself from under the pile of snow, James felt Moaka's strong hands grab his parka, and pull him from underneath the snow blocks.

Moaka shook James vigorously, and screamed in his face, "Kincaid! Say! Say!

"Moaka, take it easy," James yelled, "I'm fine. What the hell happened?"

The excitement still affecting the tone in his voice, Moaka yelled, "Bear come in. Bray fight polar bear. Bray and polar bear move fast. No get good shot."

Not being able to speak plainly yet, James sputtered, "Did you hit him, Moaka?"

Digging snow from around the inside of his parka's hood, James yelled, "Where the hell is Bray now?"

"No here Kincaid," Moaka yelled. "Went after bear."

"What!" Almost screaming, James questioned frantically, "What direction did they go, Moaka?"

Without waiting for an answer from Moaka, James hurriedly kicked snow around where he was standing and finally found his rifle in the rubble of the igloo. Again almost yelling, "Damn it, what direction did they go?"

Moaka, pointing toward the other side of the fish rack, answered in a somewhat lower tone of voice, "I see go that way," and, "Bray biting butt of bear."

James quickly turned and started in the direction Moaka had pointed, almost at a run. He yelled back to Moaka, "Stay with the rest of the dogs," as he disappeared into the darkness.

James didn't have to go very far beyond the fish rack before he saw a still, dark figure lying on the snow about twenty feet ahead of him. Dashing to the side of the dark shadow in the snow, James was relieved to find that Bray was not dead. Yelling for Moaka, James tried to examine Bray in the moonlight. He could not feel any broken ribs, broken legs, no warm blood, and no sharp, protruding broken bones.

As Moaka came running at James' frantic call, he knelt down and quietly said, "Kincaid, let me do." Moaka's gloveless hands moved more slowly over Bray than James' did just a few seconds ago, and James knew that Moaka was probably doing a better job of trying to locate any broken bones, deep bites, or other problems.

Moaka calmly said, "Turn Bray over." As he finished his examination, Moaka advised, "Take Bray to camp."

James and Moaka carefully picked Bray up and carried him back to the area where the sleds were, and they eased Bray down gently. James knew he was hurt bad somewhere because he hadn't tried to move since they found him. James told Moaka, "Build a fire."

Hesitating for just a moment, Moaka asked, "What about bear?"

Irritated that Moaka would be thinking about that polar bear, James hollered, "I don't give a damn where that polar bear is, Bray needs help, and by the damn, help is what he is going to get." James hurried to his sled to get a blanket and a drinking cup and somehow he felt he had to get some warm liquids in Bray and keep him warm. Moaka got the fire built in record time, and before long both men were reexamining Bray next to a warm, bright fire.

"Kincaid, no think Bray hurt badly," he said as he rose up from the dog's side. "Bear in hurry to go. He hit Bray side of head. Bray be sore. Feel no broke bone, see no blood. Bray maybe bleed inside. Not know for time."

Looking up at Moaka, James slowly replied, "He'd better be all right, Moaka, this dog means a hell'va lot to me. If this damn dog dies I'll spread that polar bear's guts all over this damn North Slope, and that's a promise."

"Hard see dog inside hurt."

James didn't respond to Moaka's last remark. He had to get some hot fish broth down Bray and wrap him in the blanket. Moaka helped get Bray taken care of and all they could do was wait to see the results.

By the time Moaka and James had finished with Bray, the moon dropped behind the mountains and the darkness closed in on the firelight. James knew they would not see the first signs of sunrise for another hour or more. They walked around the camp area, and by the flickering firelight, they could see that the igloo was destroyed. It looked as if a team of horses had run through the thing. It was hard for James to believe that at one time he'd been under all that snow with a thousand pounds of bear floundering around next to him. Moaka's team and sled were placed a short distance on one side of the destroyed structure and his was placed about the same distance on the other side. The fish rack seemed untouched.

Moaka moved to James' side of the fire and asked, "Kincaid, keep fire going? Maybe polar bear be back."

With a puzzled look on his face, James questioned, "Do you think he will? Be back I mean?"

As Moaka shook his head, he slowly replied, "No, Kincaid."

James nodded toward the sled, and asked, "Have we got enough firewood to keep the fire going until daylight?"

A slight smile crossed Moaka's face as he responded, "Yes, can use fish rack."

"Hey, take it easy on my fish rack, but by the damn you're right. That's the first one I ever built, and now you want to burn it up." Silence fell over the camp as both men turned serious again.

"You know, Moaka, that we're going after him," James committed. "In the beginning I kept looking for some reason why the animal behaved like he did. Was it sickness or maybe an injury? But hell, there is nothing wrong with that polar bear. I even told Suzette he had to be destroyed, but down deep, I was looking for something, anything that could possibly fit into the pattern that would make this animal behave as he had in the past.

I guess Noka was right, the spirits must have touched this great beast." James really didn't believe that, but he thought, *What the hell, right now it's as good as any explanation.*

With a flick of his wrist, Moaka threw a small stick into the fire. His gaze locked on the knifing flames, as he remarked, "Kincaid care about life. Make Kincaid good man. No want waste anything. People come, take, no give back. Native know Kincaid, not way. Native respect you. Old man know Kincaid way. You go his home for council. He tell story to all. He help Fishman kill spirited polar bear. Be big medicine. Native take his council no question."

The crackling of the fire gave Moaka a sense of calmness and its warmth penetrated through his open outer garment into his undercover clothing. He would have quite a story to tell about Kincaid being underneath a pile of snow, and having Bray and the polar bear fighting as they ripped through the igloo. He could also build his story further by telling how he squeezed off two rounds at the bear without hitting Kincaid or Bray. Smiling, he thought, *Yes, be good story.*

James rocked back on his stool, and commented, "I'll bet that polar bear really thought he jumped into a hornet's nest when he came in here tonight. He must have hightailed it out of here in a hurry. I'd of given anything to be standing off a distance and seen the whole thing."

"Yes Kincaid, maybe polar bear no travel fast."

James' gaze moved from the fire to Moaka's face, and inquired, "You think you hit him?"

Nodding slowly, he answered, "No see how miss. Be short distance. See good. Look for blood, when light."

As James rubbed his slightly chapped lips, he inquired further, "Did you see him come in?"

Quite abruptly, Moaka replied, "No, see Bray go at polar bear. Be proud of Bray. He jump in, then out. Strike like lightening. Bray no afraid, he protect you."

James looked across the fire at Moaka, and mentioned, "It will be light soon." James stood, stretched, reached for the sky, and commented, "We won't be leaving too early in the morning. We'll see how Bray is doing."

James leaned down and gently touched Bray on the shoulder and said, "You get well, boy."

As James unpacked one of his sleeping skins, he could see a trace of light showing in the distant east. He commented to Moaka, "I am going to lie down beside Bray for a while. If I go to sleep, wake me up when the sun gets above the mountain. You might try to get some rest also. We are not going anywhere until I know how Bray is doing."

CHAPTER TWENTY-SIX

Moaka let the fire die down to embers, and yawned long and deep, and thought, *It been long night.* He had dozed sitting at the fire, as the sun shone its face over the Brooks Range, and that was when James wanted to get up. The first part of the night had been very exciting, but the last hours had passed slowly for Moaka. He had checked on Bray several times that morning, and James' lead was doing fine. Moaka sat cross-legged on the snowy surface looking into the glowing embers as he quietly thought about what they were going to do next. He had seen anger in Kincaid before, but never had he seen the rage in him that was brought about by the possibility of losing Bray because of the polar bear's attack. Moaka knew that Kincaid was more than ever determined to get the polar bear. It had taken Kincaid a while to realize the bear had to be destroyed, but Moaka also understood that Kincaid thought all wildlife deserved a chance to live in their natural way.

Moaka stood, stretched, and looked skyward, and he was glad the night was gone. The fresh day promised to be clear and cold with little wind. He bent down and picked up part of Kincaid's handiwork, as he laid another piece of the fish rack pole onto the glowing embers as the morning air bit every exposed part of the body.

Moaka broke the silence of the early morning with, "Kincaid, stay bed all day." By calling Kincaid to get up, several dogs started to stir, and

237

Bray lifted his head slightly. The movement attracted Moaka's attention and he walked over to Bray. He knelt down and patted him gently. The dog's eyes were clear and Moaka knew that was a good sign for recovery. "Kincaid," Moaka called again, as he walked over to where a form lay under skins upon the snowy surface. Nudging the covered form, Moaka called once again, "Kincaid, get up, take leak, world on fire." Smiling, Moaka remembered that Kincaid had taught him that little saying.

James lay quietly under his sleeping skins trying to figure out the intrusion. Finally, he realized that Moaka was trying to wake him up.

"Kincaid, you still alive?" Moaka hailed again.

"All right, Moaka," James complained, "I'm awake. I'll be up in a minute. As James slowly laid back the skins and sat up, the cold morning air surrounded him. A cold chill dashed through his body as if someone had thrown ice water on him. Jumping to his feet, James grabbed his outer clothing and stood next to the fire that Moaka had burning brightly.

The coldest part of the day was upon them, and James' bare hands and face stung from the piercing chill. James moved closer to the fire, and he noticed that Moaka had already torn apart the fish rack and had used some of the material to keep the fire going. They would not use all the rack wood and they would take what was left with them.

Sitting on his stool and still half asleep, James watched the flames sweep into the air and the tea water start boiling. Straightening up on the stool, he peered through the fire to check Bray who was still lying on the other side of the fire wrapped in the blanket. Raising his voice slightly so Moaka could hear him, he asked, "Did Bray move any while I was sleeping?"

"No, give broth hour ago."

Bray was wide-awake looking up at James through clear, sharp eyes, but not moving a muscle. Slowly James moved his stool beside Bray and reached down and uncovered him to check to see how he doing. To his surprise, Bray immediately stood up slowly and stretched. He didn't seem to be hurt in any way and he moved off to relieve himself. James saw him heading toward Anore and called him back to the fire. James gently rubbed up his chest until his hands were warmed by the friction and as he stroked Bray's back, Bray whined slightly. James again lightly stroked Bray's back. This time Bray did not complain. James knew he had found a sore spot.

Moaka watched James rub down Bray, and they both agreed that Bray should be put in harness. "We'll see how he pulls this morning," James commented, "that will be the test." With a pat of James' hand on the blanket, Bray lay back down. Studying him for just a moment, James decided not to cover him up again, since he didn't show any signs of being cold or in shock.

Sighing slightly and crossing his arms on his chest, James' thoughts returned to the problem at hand. *This whole affair is about ready to drive me into the ground. Sleeping on the run; eating on the run. Not being able to do what I want to do or accomplish what I'm supposed to ... observe different kinds of wildlife, document habitat, study migration habits, and any number of a hundred other things.*

Moaka's attention was drawn to a couple of his dogs who seemed to be getting restless. One of the dogs in particular was cleaning the ice from between its toes. The ice could freeze the dog's feet and possibly damage them for life. By licking the ice from between their toes, they could actually dry their feet. All sled drivers who cared about their dogs carried with them, as standard equipment, small moccasins, or socks for their dogs' feet. These small socks were slipped over the dogs' paws and tied on when the snow condition became very icy or when ice crystals formed on the top layer of the snow. He had seen dogs' feet cut very badly and worn raw by ice crystals that had lodged between the toes and was left unattended.

Earlier that morning, Moaka had set out some seal meat next to the fire for the dogs. He leaned over, checked the meat, and stated, "Meat thaw, feed dog. Easy for them eat."

"Here, Moaka, let me help," James volunteered, and both men set to feeding their teams. Bray was next to the fire so James fed him before he took care of his other animals.

The animals fed, James and Moaka returned to the fire to have a quick breakfast of leftover seal meat, dried fish, and seaweed.

Moaka motioned toward Bray and said, "Bray be fine."

"I think probably you were right about him," James answered. "He seems to be a little stiff this morning, but I don't think he's hurt any. He did get up once and walk around earlier this morning."

Pointing to the varied colors skyward, Moaka commented, "Kincaid, in Nome, see picture, same thing. Want money for picture. Who pay money for picture?"

James exclaimed, "I thought you would have bought the picture!"

"No Kincaid, no want picture."

James moved off his stool and walked over to where the bear had caved in the igloo. He was trying to put together what had happened last night and see if he could spot any bloodstains in the snow caused by Moaka's shots. Bray had gotten up and followed James to the igloo and James noticed that he seemed to be moving okay, and James felt relieved.

James looked all around the wrecked igloo, and he couldn't find any bloodstains anywhere. If Moaka did hit the polar, he didn't start bleeding right away. That was common, as some wounds didn't bleed much for a while.

Moaka had walked out a ways toward where the polar bear had made his exit. Suddenly, he called to James in an excited voice, "Kincaid, come."

Hurrying over to where Moaka was kneeling examining the snowy surface, James could see a faint trace of blood that had almost disappeared into the snow. Anxiously, he asked, "How bad do you think he's hit, Moaka?"

"No say." Moaka responded slowly.

James walked on a bit further and found where the polar bear and Bray had battled again and found another spot of blood. As he walked on, he saw another spot, but just traces. Calling for Moaka to come and look, James commented, "Doesn't look like he is losing much blood."

Moaka knelt down and put his finger on the spot of blood and it disappeared with no trace on his finger. Moaka looked up at James and responded slowly, "Think hit under skin, blood thin. Bullet deep, blood be thicker. This blood thin. Go away fast in snow."

With a disgusted tone, James questioned, "Then that's not going to slow him down much is it?"

"No Kincaid. No think so. He stop bleed soon."

As James turned back toward camp he angrily replied, "Well, hell, Moaka, let's get packed up and get after him. We can stand out here all day and speculate about where and how he is hit, but we need to start putting the pressure on him now."

Once back at the make-shift camp the two men loaded the sleds, including the rest of the poles from the fish rack and the frozen fish, checked the dogs feet, hooked them in their traces, and took a final look around to see if they had everything packed. Satisfied that all was done, James looked sideways at Moaka for the ready and hailed Bray onward in the direction they'd last seen the polar heading.

Hazing Bray in the direction to follow the polar bear's tracks, James noticed that Bray seemed to move out as if nothing had happened. The dog was very lucky not to be lame or dead going up against that polar bear. Letting the dogs run only a short while, both men kept eyeing the snowy surface for some sign that the polar had still come this way. Slowing the dogs down, it was easier to watch the surface, although it was still tough to pick up signs from a moving sled. Fortune was with them, because James soon caught a glimpse of a scratch in the snow. He hailed Bray to a stop and Moaka let his team come up alongside before stopping. Quickly, James stepped off the back runners of his sled, and he waved Moaka over to have a look.

The light breeze had started to blow, and Moaka seemed to float through the swirling snow as he hurried back to James' side. He knelt down to get a closer look at the track, and without saying anything, he moved forward a short ways and waved James to him. "Kincaid, he move slow. Claw mark no dig in." Rising up, they both moved on just a little farther, and saw another spot of blood in the snow. Moaka knelt down once more and put his finger on the spot. Looking up at James with a slight smile on his lips and just barely a trace of blood on his finger, which he held up for his inspection, he said, "We closer, Kincaid."

James folded his arms across his chest, "You know Moaka, we've been traveling around out here for a couple of days and we've cut a lot of directions and we have made it pretty hot for that bear, but unless I miss my guess, that damn polar is headed for the coast, and Teshpuk is right in his path."

Before saying anything, Moaka looked around the area and then answered, "Yes, he wounded. Try get back ice area. Kincaid yes. If travel straight, Teshpuk be in path."

As James and Moaka stood together, they carefully scanned the horizon in the direction the polar bear's tracks were heading. Shaking his head, he commented, "That damn wind, Moaka. It's getting stronger and it's going to swirl enough snow around that we're going to lose his tracks soon. We'll lose him, Moaka, that's for damn sure, so we had better think of a plan to maybe outrun him to the coast, or better yet, outrun him to Teshpuk."

"Polar bear no travel fast, Kincaid. Think, even hold up. Chance beat to Teshpuk. Leave pole. Dogs work hard, we chance."

With a quick shake of his head, James replied, "If we head straight for Teshpuk, we've lost the hot trail, not that we are going to have a hot trail for long anyway. I just hate the thought of going back to Teshpuk empty-handed."

Impatient with James' attitude, Moaka explained, "Kincaid, I say.

Native help search. Look area Teshpuk, maybe get shot. No catch, think went back ice. Hope no come back."

"You might be right, Moaka; there aren't any more villages around this area except Teshpuk and some closer to the coast. If he's as hungry as I think he is, he might try for a quick meal at Teshpuk. I'm sure that the polar bear will not try a raid in the daytime. He will probably lay low until tonight or even tomorrow early. That should give us plenty of time to get things set up back in the village."

Moaka excitedly stated, "Think five Native have rifle. Need use all Native. All Native want help. Some have spear, Kincaid no say, no want help."

"Well, Moaka, we can't do anything about some having rifles and some not. We'll just have to get everybody together, and let them know what they are up against. Maybe we can pair some of the Natives that don't have rifles with some that do. I know it is important not to slight any of the Natives, but we need to let them know that they're not messing around with the regular run-of-the-mill polar bear. This particular animal has had enough contact with humans to be a little smarter than most polar bears they have run up against before, and that's what worries me more than anything else, Moaka. The polar bear seems to have a sense of danger, and that could be problems for anybody who tries to take him. Another possible danger is that the animal's wound is not healing and he could be in pain, making him twice as dangerous." Pausing, James asked, "How long do you figure it will take us to get back to Teshpuk?"

Moaka looked toward the sun and shaded his eyes, and replied, "One day. Team be tired, they okay."

"It will be dark by the time we get there," James commented, "Which will make setting things up at Teshpuk all the more difficult. As we're traveling back, I'll try to think about formulating a plan for stopping the polar bear at or around Teshpuk. I'd like you to have some input if you think of anything. That is if we are correct in assuming that he will pass that way."

"Native help, Kincaid," Moaka said assuringly. "Native do what Kincaid say."

"I'm not worried, Moaka, they are a brave and courageous people, and I never did doubt their ability or courage when the chips were down or any other time, for that matter."

Solemnly Moaka replied, "Karkak want hear Kincaid say."

With a long sigh, James replied, "Yeah, I didn't really give him a chance, did I? There just didn't seem to be time. I'm going to remember to get back to him; that's the least I can do." Turning back to his sled James continued, "Well, let's get to it, Moaka. Let's dump most of this stuff off the sleds; we can come back and pick it up later if the need arises. We need to make the pull as easy as possible for the dogs because we're going to be traveling hard and fast, and they are going to need all the help we can give them. We've got a long way to go before we can rest ourselves or the dogs, except for short rest stops." Shaking his head, he thought, *What a hell'va time for Bray to be hurting. He is worth two dogs any day on a hard pull. We'll just have to see how the hard pulling affects him.*

After they unloaded the poles and retied the rest of the gear down, taking all nonessentials off the sleds, James stepped onto the back of his sled. He glanced back to Moaka and hailed, "On Bray." They were on their way again, but this time they were not concerned with following tracks. By now, all tracks and blood drops were probably consumed by the relentless blowing, twisting snow.

CHAPTER TWENTY-SEVEN

Moaka signaled his team forward with his familiar deep-throat sound. He felt good about his team. His team was not as fast as Kincaid's, but he was assured that his team would hold up in hard times. Unlike Kincaid, he picked his dogs for toughness and durability instead of speed, although Bray was about the toughest and biggest dog he ever saw. Adjusting his bone sun shields, he wished that Kincaid would wear his more often. Once Kincaid had gone sun blind and hadn't been able to see a thing for two days. Kincaid wasn't stupid, just stubborn.

Detecting that Kincaid was slowing his team, he followed suit. He was breathing easy and followed Kincaid's lead, pushing with one foot for a while then changing runners and pushing with the other the same as Kincaid was doing ahead of him.

By a lucky chance, James caught a blur of red on the snow. Hailing Bray to stop, he stood down on the sled brake and came sliding to a halt, with Moaka's sled sliding to a stop a short distance behind.

Moaka called, "What say, Kincaid?"

Quickly motioning with his hand, James replied, "Follow me, Moaka." As James walked back about twenty feet, he sighted the red glaze on the snow.

Moaka was instantly beside him and stuck his finger into the reddened mess. Raising his finger from the blood, a smile crossed his face. Rising from a kneeling position, he carefully scanned the horizon and softly and mysteriously said, "White Ghost close Kincaid. Blood string out. Wound no close, blood no freeze." Pausing for a moment, he continued, "Blood no *stiyok*—firm. Stop rest, lick wound. Many scratch mark here. Dig snow for drink."

Both of them stood and strained to see through the sun reflections and the swirling snow on the horizon, but neither could see anything. They looked down at the snow around them and it was evident that the polar had stopped here to rest. James commented, "This might change things a bit. If he has to stop and care for himself that will slow him down considerably. Maybe we can spot him as we go, although he seemed to be wandering."

Moaka looked across the horizon again and he stated, "No keep moving. He hurt, need rest. He hold up. Maybe till stop bleed."

Just as Moaka stopped talking, a swirling gust of wind blew a deep layer of snow across the blood spot, and it was as if it had never been there. In surprise, James looked up at Moaka and exclaimed, "So much for that!" As he threw his arms into the air, they both shook their heads in disgust. They turned slowly and returned to their sleds. James hailed Bray, and they were on their way again.

Scanning the horizons in case he happened to spot the menacing polar bear, James started formulating a plan based on what Moaka had said earlier about the villagers doing anything he wanted.

As the cold wind started to chill his face, James reached up and adjusted his face shield, as he tried to put the pieces together on a plan. Chuckling slightly and quietly murmured to himself, "Damn, it would be dangerous, but what an adventure to tell about." His mind kept trying to settle the chain of events that must happen when he and Moaka got back to Teshpuk. There would have to be many instructions given to the Natives.

The teams were stopped for a rest as Moaka trudged forward, and asked, "Kincaid, what plan?"

With surprise in his voice, James asked, "How do you know I've got a plan?"

Smiling slightly, Moaka answered with, "Know Kincaid."

"I'm not altogether sure yet, Moaka, but as we've traveled, I've been sorting out a few things and trying to find the best way to kill that polar bear, without endangering any of the villagers. One person that we know of has been seriously injured, and possibly killed, and we can't risk that happening to anyone else. The next attack may be on a village that cannot protect itself. If that happens, more people will die, or be injured." As they parted for their sleds James asked Moaka, "How is your team holding up?"

Without turning back to James, he just raised his hand and grunted, "Okay." Stopping for a second, he turned back and asked, "How Bray?"

Quickly James responded, "He's doing just fine."

The day wore on and darkness came. Several times, they made rest stops for the dogs and discussed what has to be done when they arrived at Teshpuk. It was dark and no one was expecting them, and the only commotion from the village as they traveled down between the two rows of huts was a few dogs that barked their alarm. The teams were so beat they never even returned the village dog's alarm. It had been a hard run and James hoped that the polar bear would keep coming this way and give them another chance at ending this nightmare.

Half stumbling and falling from fatigue they unhooked and staked the dogs and once all the dogs were staked they returned to each animal to check their feet for injury. Finding the teams in good condition, they fed them with good rations of seal meat. They removed from the sleds what they would need for the night, and after getting their gear, they both sided their sleds, and headed toward the huts.

Slowly making their way to Kirima's place, they stopped in front of the entrance and James commented in a low tone, "Let's get something to eat and then see if we can get a meeting going to set things up. Where would be the best place to have this meeting?"

Sniffing and rubbing his nose, Moaka thought for a second, "Old man hut. No want keep Kirima's hut from sleep."

Questioningly, James asked, "Don't think we'll put Noka out any, do you?"

Abruptly Moaka answered, "No, be happy choose his hut. Maybe want help."

With a heavy sigh, James responded, "Very well, Moaka, then let's plan to meet at Noka's hut in about an hour. You're going to have to ask him first, aren't you?"

"Meet old man hut Kincaid," Moaka declared. "I tell villagers," he said as he ducked into the entrance of the hut where Tess was staying.

Kirima's hut was warm compared to the outside temperatures, and some of the family members were already in bed for the night, although it was not very late, and others were preparing to do the same. Tess and Kirima were at the warming fire speaking in low tones so as not to disturb the rest.

Standing erect after coming through the entrance Moaka waved slightly and mouthed, "*Unnuk*"—hello, to Kirima and Tess who looked shocked to see him back so soon. Slowly he removed his outer layer and quickly made his way to sit. As he approached Tess, she raised her arms up to him and hugged him. He sat down beside her and explained, "We had a little trouble and needed to come back. Everything is okay." He had to calm Tess down because she was starting to get a worried look on her face. "Kincaid and me missed the polar bear again. I'll tell you the whole story when everybody is here. We're going to have a meeting at Noka's hut later on."

"Noka will be asleep by now," Kirima stated.

"Yeah, I know, but we need to meet somewhere and he won't mind." We need to set the plan up to keep the polar bear from Teshpuk, and maybe get rid of him."

Surprise in her voice, Tess kept her voice low as she inquired, "What do you mean keep the polar bear from Teshpuk? I thought he was roaming around somewhere out there." She motioned with her arm, pointing to the open spaces.

"He is, Tess," Moaka replied quickly. "But his wandering may lead to Teshpuk. Don't worry, Kincaid thinks we may have a good chance keeping the polar bear away from the village." He paused, knowing he had told a small lie about Kincaid's so-called plan. He began taking off some clothing because the inside of the hut was quite warm, and asked, "Is there anything to eat? I'm hungry. We haven't eaten since morning."

Starting to get up, but then sitting back down, Tess' tone turned serious as she put her hand on Moaka's knee and stated, "Suzette was roughed up by that Simmons guy when you and Kincaid were gone."

Alarm jumped within Moaka, and he angrily questioned, "Where is Simmons now?"

Quickly putting her hand to her mouth signaling for Moaka to be quiet, she quietly answered, "Karkak stopped him from doing any harm." Pausing to giggle slightly she continued, "He told Simmons to get out of Teshpuk, and never come back, or he would cut his feet off and feed them to dogs."

Again, Moaka asked angrily, "Where is Simmons now? I'll go find him and do it myself."

"Moaka, he is gone from here. He went to Three Rivers Village to wait for Doc Ralph Tone's return from Barrow. He won't come back again. Karkak made sure of that. He made a banish judgement from Teshpuk on him."

Shaking his head slowly, Moaka commented, "Kincaid won't like this. He didn't like Drake Simmons from the start and this will make it worse. Kincaid will probably go to Three Rivers Village and slit Simmons's throat."

Thinking for a second, Moaka commented, "But, I think Kincaid will understand that Karkak did the worst that can be done, to be banished from a village."

"Moaka," Tess pleaded, "don't tell him this thing happened. Suzette is fine and she never got hurt. I saw her after it happened. She is a strong woman. She was upset after it happened, but she settled down good."

"I think I should tell Kincaid. We don't keep secrets from each other," Moaka explained.

"Honor," Tess angrily murmured. "If you don't tell him, Kincaid won't hear it from anybody else, at least not right away."

"You speak like a woman that doesn't understand. He should know a thing like this because he is a man of principles and honor. If he understands that Karkak dealt with the situation with one of the harshest punishments, he will accept the punishment. Karkak is the leader of the village and he already punished Simmons, and Kincaid will accept that. Was she hurt?"

"No, she is okay. I hope you know what you are doing to tell Kincaid. Suzette will be the same when Kincaid sees her. Simmons didn't get a chance do anything before Karkak jumped in."

Silence fell over the room, as Tess slowly stood up and quietly asked Moaka, "Are you still hungry?"

Nodding his head, Moaka finally replied, "Yes, I am hungry. Pretty soon I'm going to talk to Noka and some other men to set up a meeting for Kincaid so he can tell them what we want to do."

* * *

Not realizing how tired he was until they'd stopped, James slowly continued toward Suzette's hut, which was in the middle of the village. Stopping at her entrance, he sighed slightly, and thought, *Where is this relationship going? I'm getting more and more attached to her, and I'm finding that I'm enjoying her company more and more; I even look forward to seeing her.* He remembered Moaka's words, "You won't decide, it will just happen." Grunting to himself, James almost felt that he should have some say in his own destiny. Quickly he glanced around the darkened village and suddenly felt a stab of loneliness. It was a very dark night with the moon hidden behind a few drifting clouds. He didn't see anybody out this evening and it was almost as if everybody had all just disappeared off the face of the earth. Within three or four steps through the entrance, there would be a completely different world. It was late in the evening, but it still seemed strange, and with a quick shrug of his shoulders, he hailed Suzette.

In a surprised tone Suzette answered, "James, is that you?"

"Were you expecting someone else?"

In a demanding tone, she ordered, "Get in here."

Wearily pushing through the flap and moving into the large room in the hut, Suzette was waiting for him. Once he rose back up, she was instantly kissing him and asking all kinds of questions about the polar bear at the same time.

Trying to set his gear down, James snapped, "Hold on, Suzette. Let me sit down and relax a bit and I'll tell you the whole story when there is time. Right now, I would like to clean up some and shave before I have to go to a gathering at Noka's hut in about an hour."

With eyebrows raised, she asked, "What kind of gathering is at Noka's?"

James responded slowly saying, "A meeting on how we're going to keep the polar bear away from Teshpuk, because I'm sure he's headed this way or at least hope he is, and maybe get rid of the animal for good." As he scratched his head and unsnarling his black hair with both hands, his feeling of tension and fatigue eased, as he lay flat on the padded floor. "I've never seen such an animal before, Suzette. That damn thing seems to have a sixth sense about humans. Can you get me something to eat and I'll get some water warming up?"

Even before he'd finished talking, Suzette was moving around the hut getting things set up for James to take a quick bath. Watching her through half-closed, tired eyes, James thought to himself, *What a woman. I come in out of the night and ask her to drop everything just to wait on me.* Shaking his head, James counted his blessings. Finally building enough energy to move from his prone position he broke out his shaving gear and patiently waited for the water to have the chill taken off so he could get an overdue shave.

Once he was finished shaving, James undressed and used the rest of the warm water and a soft cloth to wash up as quickly as possible.

As he nearly completed his quick washdown, Suzette snuck up behind him and slapped him briskly on the bare cheek of his butt. Stepping back quickly, she giggled slightly and hastily commented, "I just couldn't resist. That baby soft butt sticking out there was too much to pass up."

"Suzette! What the devil are you doing? Do I have to bring Bray in here to protect me?" James exclaimed. "That stung. I'm sure that you're aware of the consequences of your actions, and this means that I get a free one on demand."

"Oh James, did that hurt the poor little boy," Suzette snickered.

"I'll poor little boy you. Just wait till this polar bear thing is over and we'll see what this poor little boy can do."

Continuing to prepare supper, Suzette's last comment was, "Okay James, I might just hold you to it."

Ready to eat, James noticed Suzette had biscuits, caribou meat, seaweed, and a small bit of smoked salmon on the side. He looked at all the food in front of him, and called Suzette over and kissed her gently; he thanked her for her attention, and apologized for snapping at her when he first came in. In his own mind, he knew that their relationship meant a whole lot more than that, but they didn't have the time right now to get involved any further.

As she sat down beside James, Suzette inquired, "Everything all right, James?"

James was just starting to sample the cured salmon, which was delicious, as he replied, "Suzette, you sure know how to get to a man through his stomach. Everything is perfect here. To answer your question, nothing is right; we lost the damn polar again. I tell you what, this thing is going to end soon, or both Moaka and I are going to be strung out as tight as a drum. This eating and sleeping on the run is not the way to go."

Smiling she said, "Well if you would be around here more often you might get used to eating this kind of meal on a regular basis."

James looked into her soft brown eyes, and commented, "Ah, Suzette, maybe someday that will come to pass. By the way, something I have wanted to do is to thank you for the biscuits that you sent along on this last trip. Would you teach Tess how to make them so she could cook them for Moaka? He'd sure be in your debt. He loves your biscuits." Pausing James looked harder at her and asked, "Is your face chapped?" as he pointed to the same spot on his own face.

Quickly laying her hand alongside of her face, Suzette's heart jumped a beat. Gaining composure, she slowly replied, "Yes, it could be."

Suzette folded her hands in her lap, and sat patiently beside James, waiting for him to finish eating. Her mind in turmoil as she remembered how her face was scratched, she was determined not to tell James. What would be the use? She had not been hurt physically, emotionally yes, but not physically.

Breaking the silence, she casually answered James question about the biscuits, saying, "Yes, I would be glad to show Tess how to make the biscuits. I know Moaka would never ask me."

Nodding his head he quickly replied, "You're right there."

Not eating all the food, James announced, "Well Suzette, I've got to be going because it's just about time for that get-together to start." Slowly getting up, he put on his outer layers and continued, "We are going to get the rest of the villagers to help put the final blow to this polar bear, I hope. By the way, did Karkak get back from taking that wounded Native to his village?"

"Oh yes!" Suzette exclaimed, as she briskly stood up, "but the Native died soon after Karkak got him there. He got back to Teshpuk right after you and Moaka left the other day."

With a slap of his hands together, James angrily responded, "Damn it that cuts it. That polar bear, White Ghost, as Moaka calls it, has to be destroyed. Moaka probably knows by now, and is just as anxious as I am to put an end to this rogue. Bad thing is the polar bear is now wounded, and he will be all the more aggressive. I just hope that nobody else gets in his way and gets hurt."

Alarm showing on Suzette's face, she asked, "Is there anything I can do to help?"

Irritated James replied, "I don't know right now. Listen, I have to go. I'll see you when I see you." Starting toward the entrance, James stopped and looked back at Suzette, "When this thing is all said and done, I would like to have a long talk with you." Stepping back to her, he leaned down, kissed her softly, and disappeared through the doorway flap.

CHAPTER TWENTY-EIGHT

Suzette's hut had been warm and inviting and James didn't relish the idea of stepping out into the sharp cold night. The moon's phases had shrunk the sphere to less than half, with millions of twinkling stars that decorated the darkened sky forming the Milky Way. It was just as dark and cold as when he'd first gone into Suzette's, but the short rest, wash down, and good meal seemed to have done wonders for his attitude. Stretching his arms and legs as he reached into the sky, James thought, *It sure feels good to be shaved and reasonably clean again.*

As he moved slowly away from Suzette's hut, he passed some gas that had been building up since he'd first entered Suzette's hut. Every time he could fart like that this time of day, his grandfather's words seemed to echo back at him, "Takes a good horse to fart at the end of a hard day." *I wonder how home is doing with the green fields, the thick woods, and the clear, cool water of the stream that runs not far away from the house? What is everybody doing right now? What time is it there? Is everybody still in good health? I'll have to take the time and go back one of these days.*

His mind went a hundred miles an hour, trying to work out how he was going to tell the villagers at the meeting about his plan, as he scratched the back of his head, which was concealed under the parka hood.

As he approached the hut, James hailed to Noka, and Moaka's voice came from within, "Kincaid, come."

255

Once in the main room, he straightened his six-foot frame, and as he looked around the inside of the hut, he instantly realized that he was front and center. All conversation had stopped, all eyes were focused squarely on him, and each person anxiously waited for James to tell them what he wanted them to do. Apprehension filled James. He feared Moaka must have really pumped them up for this because there were more men in the large hut than he'd ever seen in the whole village before. The room was hot and crowded as James could feel the tension of his audience. Reaching up with his right hand, James pushed his parka hood off and could feel moisture forming on his brow as he let the hood fall softly behind his head.

James moved away from the entrance, as Moaka motioned him to sit beside him in a place that had been saved for the guest of honor. Joining Moaka on the far side of the room, James sat down and took off his parka. Instantly someone handed him a container of hot tea. With a nod of his head, James smiled and offered thanks. *Hell,* James thought, *this is all I need, hot tea when I'm already about to burn up.*

Taking a small sip, he soon realized that it was tea all right, but it had a little something in it to warm the soul. Swallowing, James looked up and realized that everyone in the room was watching for his approval. Raising the cup into the air while nodding his head, James exalted the drink, "*mamartok, mamartok*"—good to taste. Smiles came to all their faces and conversations around the room started up right away. Actually, not being much of a drinking man, it tasted terrible, but James wasn't about to let them know that he didn't care for the drink.

There was only one man in the room who knew James was putting up a front. Moaka knew he hardly ever touch alcohol, but it was important to have the best possible relations with the natives right now. James learned a long time ago that little things like this went a long way with these Native people. Besides, he always figured he would make the best of any situation as long as he didn't hurt someone's feelings. Natives were not any different from other folks; they just figured everybody should like what they like. Sitting uncomfortably next to Moaka, James leaned sideways, as he removed one of his outer layers, and whispered, "Have you told them anything yet?"

Without looking at him, Moaka quietly replied in English, "Say need help. Polar bear come this way."

Still talking in low tones, James and Moaka finally made eye contact, "Do they know that the Native died who was attacked?" James inquired.

"Yes." With idle conversation still buzzing about the room about the day's activities, Moaka explained to James, "Karkak back from Three Rivers Village say Native die. He say to others, Native attack by polar bear. Six rifle in village, no count ours."

James grasped Moaka's shoulder, and quietly said, "That's good, Moaka, we'll need every one of them to work my plan. It will all depend on when and if the polar bear comes this way."

Finally, James figured this was as good a time as any, and got the attention of the group by clearing his throat and coughing slightly. In his mind, he really didn't know where to start and he knew that Moaka would maybe have to interpret a few words. That bothered him just a bit because he didn't want any loss of meaning, but James knew Moaka would do a good job of translation if it was needed. Glancing quickly around the room, he could see that everyone was anxious for him to start.

James cleared his throat again and thanked all for coming as he used the Native tongue. He told them that he would be honored if any of them would volunteer any information that would help make his plan more worthy. When James had completed all the required opening statements he then proceeded to describe his plan in detail: "I would like you to pair off with at least one rifle between two men. Spread out along a line south of the village that will run east and west. You need to set up your stations by building a small fire at your location for your own protection, and so you can see the polar bear coming through or by your position.

Just make sure the stations will not be spread out more than one hundred paces between them and always make sure to keep watch for the polar bear. Moaka and I will help set up the station locations and we will bring wood to your station when needed." Stopping for a few seconds to see if anybody had any questions, one Native asked something about eating. Not being able to catch the whole thing, James immediately turned to Moaka for help in translation.

"What was the question," Moaka asked.

The Native asked again and Moaka replied, "Yes, you can go eat, one at a time. We hope it won't take that long."

Continuing James explained, "I believe the polar bear will be coming this way, but I don't know for sure, and I don't know when he will be coming. It shouldn't be too long."

Moaka commented further with, "We wounded him, and the wound might have slowed him down."

All questions answered and the pairing off complete, they found that eight villagers could not pair up with someone who had a rifle.

Saving the day was Moaka when, knowing they could not be insulted, stated calmly, "You that do not have rifles, take the four stations directly south of the village." Everybody seemed to agree with the suggestion so the situation worked out.

Overall, there were enough men to make up ten stations and two men to take care of the woodpile, with James and Moaka going from station to station with their teams to check that everything was going as planned, and to make sure that each station was kept with a good supply of firewood. Also by Moaka and him moving up and down the line of stations, they might be close enough to the area where the polar bear was sighted to get some shots off. The group decided that the signal to be used, if a bear sighting did occur, would be a shot from a rifle. For the men who didn't have a rifle, the signal would be the beating on a tin pan with a stick, or just yelling.

Karkak signaled Moaka from across the room that he wanted to speak. Moaka slowly reached over, touched James on the sleeve, and commented, "Karkak want have say."

Looking across the room at Karkak, James replied, "By all means Karkak, we will be honored to listen to your counsel."

Moaka motioned to Karkak that he had the floor.

Karkak began to speak. His easy manner and soft-spoken speech was being delivered as if by one who was used to being listened to, and everyone in the meeting sat quietly and listened intently. James was working hard to catch every word that Karkak uttered in his Native tongue.

"I feel the plan to protect Teshpuk," Karkak explained, "is a good plan and it will work if the polar bear comes this way. We've learned the animal has a wound, and a wounded animal will behave strangely. We must all be alert and watch for him to come from any direction. I would like us to make some torches to light the village, so the polar bear could be seen if he might run through our line. Women can bring food during the night to the men watching the fire, and that would be a good thing. Anybody would feel terror if they were alone and were attacked by a rogue like this, but some among us have seen terror close. The villager from Three Rivers Village died because of this animal's deed, and it would be good for all of us to be aware of the polar bear's destructive nature. Also if there is success in killing the polar bear, all will share in the meat and the one who kills the polar bear will get the hide."

James had never in his life, ever heard a more eloquent speech given by anyone. Karkak was truly well self-educated in ways of speaking.

Karkak's words of wisdom were well taken as the group nodded their heads. They all agreed everyone should to keep alert and watchful.

Final instructions given and the tailing questions answered, James rose and started toward the entrance, as did the other villagers. He spotted Karkak across the room coming his way and before he left the hut with the rest of the Natives, James commented, "Good to have you back

Karkak, we will need good men like you before this is over."

Quickly stepping toward James, Karkak peered up at him through weathered, but shining, eyes. Toting a large smile, he replied, "Good man, Kincaid," as he slapped James on the shoulder. Both men gazed into each other's eyes, and both men accepted mutual admiration.

Once outside, James asked Moaka, "You want to take the east side or the west side?"

With a shake of his head, he responded, "No care, Kincaid."

James gestured in a westerly direction, "All right, Moaka, I'll take the west side. Just make sure when you set up the stations, that the Natives without the rifles are closest to the village, and don't let the stations get too spread out." Stopping Moaka for a moment, James explained further, "Moaka, you'll have five stations, but the closest two to the village will not have rifles. I'll have five stations on my side and the two closest to the village will not have rifles either, just like on your side. Just as a reminder, if the polar bear comes through the middle of the line there will not be any rifles in that area, but you or I might be close enough to fortify that area."

"Where you be Kincaid?" Moaka abruptly asked.

"Hell, Moaka, I might be in where it is warm, like say in next to Suzette."

"Huh," Moaka retorted, "She kick you out."

As they laughed together, James quickly replied, "Yeah, you're probably right."

James realized that Moaka was thinking about something, and inquired, "What is it Moaka? Do you have a question?"

"One hundred your pace, mine?"

Quickly James slapped Moaka across the shoulder and exclaimed, "Hell, I don't know. I guess you had better take a few more. You mashed-down fellas need to do that."

Instantly Moaka fired by, "Tall man, take less."

Amused, James continued, "Well, what the hell, Moaka, kind of a bad situation not everyone having rifles, but it will work out. Let's go get our sleds unloaded and load them up with firewood. I hope we don't have to supply the stations all night. But, just in case that critter decides to raid the village during the night, on his way to the coast, we want to be ready for him."

Once they arrived at their sleds, they unloaded the gear, and staged it beside Kirima's hut. It seemed darker than the night before, and James was having a hard time seeing what he was doing.

Suddenly, he picked up the knife from the gear that he'd had been looking for and thought he'd lost. Jokingly he had even accused Moaka of borrowing it and not giving it back. It was one of the few useful things issued to all the conservation officers when they started their field duty. He raised it up and let the moon's dim light reflect on the blade, and commented to Moaka, "You know that knife that I couldn't find for so long. Well, here the damn thing is; I found it at the bottom of all this damn junk."

Moaka turning to look, replied, "No take knife. Kincaid no think where put stuff." Chuckling together, they resumed their task as silence again fell between the two men.

Moaka's mind was being turned and twisted as he tried to decide whether to tell Kincaid about what had happened to Suzette. He knew he wanted to tell him, but what would Kincaid's reaction be? Would he respect Karkak's punishment? Karkak was one of the leaders in the village and his authority should not be challenged. Kincaid should understand that. About to approach Kincaid, Moaka heard Suzette's voice through the darkness.

Hearing someone walking up behind him, James turned around and saw Suzette standing about ten feet away. He could barely see the outline of something she was holding in her arms.

She stepped forward and handed James a rifle, saying, "Here James, I thought you might need this for one of the villagers tonight. I don't know what you guys are going to be doing, but I know that some villagers don't have rifles and, well, I just thought this one might be of use somewhere."

She handed James a box of shells, as he gently took the rifle from her. Examining the rifle in the pale moonlight light and then looking at Suzette he asked in a puzzled tone, "Where in the devil did you get such a fine old weapon? This looks to be an old Henry 44."

With a sad, low voice, she replied, "It was my father's rifle. It's about the only thing I have to remember him. He always considered himself a fine shot and proved it many times."

Holding the rifle up in the air, and not realizing Moaka could not see what he was holding, James asked him, "Do you think Karkak would like to use this rifle tonight, Moaka?"

The crunching sound of snow signaled James and Suzette that Moaka was coming closer. James could hardly make him out until he was right beside him.

"Yes." Taking the rifle and looking closely at the piece he asked, "What kind rifle?"

"Moaka, I believe it to be a Henry 44. That model was popular about thirty years ago. There are still a few around, but not too many."

"Kincaid give to him," Moaka emphasized.

James replied, "Thanks, Suzette. If you don't mind I'll take it to Karkak."

Moaka handed James back the rifle as James said, "I'll be back in just a minute, Moaka." Wrapping his arm around Suzette's waist they walked back to her hut and on the way back, she asked, "What was it you wanted to talk to me about, James?"

As they stopped at the entrance to Suzette's hut, James was not prepared to have a long discussion right then. Softly he replied, "It can wait until this ordeal is over." Patting her on the back and kissing her gently, he proceeded on his way. James knew that she was full of anticipation about the conversation to come. *She probably guessed what it was going to be about, and will play coy when the time comes.*

Finally coming to where Karkak lived, James met him coming out of his hut. Surprised to see James standing there, he greeted him with a slap on the back and an excited hello. James asked him if he was just about ready, using Native tongue, because James was not quite sure how much English Karkak really understood, and this night was not the night to get things screwed up because of language problems.

Enthusiasm ringing in his voice he responded, "Yes, Kincaid. I ready."

"Good," James responded. Holding the rifle toward him he asked, "Would you like to use this tonight?"

In the golden glow of the torch light that had just been lit in the middle of the village, James could see a look of amazement come over his face.

As he slowly reached for the rifle, he began to smile. Looking up into James' face, his only comment was, in his best English, "Kincaid good man." The rifle now in Karkak's possession, James handed him the box of shells that Suzette had given him.

Hesitantly James stood next to him for just a moment, and then asked, "Do you know how to load and use this rifle, Karkak?"

Quickly pointing to the magazine tube under the barrel, Karkak's smiled and replied, "Yes, Karkak take good care."

* * *

"Are you hungry, Moaka?" Tess asked from the darkness.

Jumping around as if being shot, Moaka scolded, "Tess, you scared the devil out of me. No, I'm not hungry. What are you doing here?"

"Where is Kincaid?" Tess inquired as she stepped closer to him."

"He went to take an extra rifle to Karkak."

"Where did Kincaid get an extra rifle?" Tess inquired.

"Stop with the questions," Moaka irritatingly scolded.

"Moaka, I'm worried." In somewhat of a concerned voice she continued, "What if the polar bear doesn't come? Are you and Kincaid going after him?"

Resting his hand on her shoulder, Moaka consoled her, "Don't worry,

Tess. Let's see what happens. You can help take food to the firewatchers tonight, if you want. I'll get something to eat when I get hungry."

"Okay." Concern growing in her tone she sputtered, "I don't like this Moaka; what's wrong with that stupid polar bear? Did you tell Kincaid about Suzette?"

"No. I didn't have a chance. We've been too busy," Moaka slowly answered.

In an unsure tone Tess responded, "I hope you know what you're doing telling him."

Moaka hugged her gently, and explained, "Don't worry. I think Kincaid will respect Karkak's decision.

As Moaka looked around the village, he commented, "Tonight everybody will be okay. The torches are burning and all the guard fires will be lit soon. Everybody will be awake in the village tonight. We won't be surprised Tess, and there are plenty of rifles."

By the time James got back to Moaka, he saw Tess was standing beside him talking in low tones. Apparently, she had come out to see what was going on and to talk with her husband. His arrival interrupted their conversation and Tess walked over to James and said, "Kincaid, be awake."

Gently laying his mittened hand on her heavily clothed shoulder, James softly responded, "You bet. This could be the night that we put an end to this crazy situation."

James watched Moaka's and Tess' forms fade away into the golden glow of the village torches, as James thought, *Tess' loyalty and devotion to Moaka is unending. She and Moaka deserve a child. They waited a long time, apparently waiting for the right time, if there is such a thing.*

From somewhere through the darkness, James heard Moaka hail loudly, "Kincaid stand there all night?"

Abruptly, James was shaken from his trance, and he started making his way through the shadows cast by the torches. Arriving at the sleds, he discovered Moaka had finished staging the gear from both sleds near

Kirima's hut.

"Karkak take rifle?" Moaka inquired.

"With open arms," James responded jokingly. "Yeah, he was both pleased and proud to get it. It really surprised me when Suzette came wandering out here with the rifle, I'm not even sure she knows how to shoot. Although she did say it was her father's, I wonder if she would be willing to sell the thing to Karkak? " Shaking his head he continued, "Probably not, I guess, it being her dad's."

James walked around the other side of his sled, and commented, "Thanks for taking care of all the rest of my gear." Pausing he continued, "Did you find any more stuff that we've been missing?"

Barely able to see Kincaid's darkened face looking over at him, Moaka questioned, "No think lose more gear."

"Oh, hell, Moaka," James responded, "I was just kidding. Now, where can we get this firewood that the villagers were talking about?"

CHAPTER TWENTY-NINE

Moaka could feel himself getting more nervous as he thought he must tell Kincaid about Suzette before Kincaid accidently heard about it from someone else. That someone else may not be able to reason with him, and Moaka felt that he and Kincaid had a strong relationship. Maybe he could use that to help influence Kincaid to accept Karkak's decision. Licking his lips and taking a deep breath Moaka slowly and coldly stated, "Kincaid stop. Need say."

James halted almost in mid stride, as he immediately knew by Moaka's tone of voice that he had something to say that was important.

Moaka saw Kincaid turn his full attention toward him, and he continued, "No easy what say. No easy you hear."

Irritated because Moaka was beating around the bush, James sternly questioned, "What the hell are you trying to tell me?"

Breathing deeply once more, Moaka slowly and clearly stated, "Simmons rough on Suzette, we no in Teshpuk."

Anger instantly built within James as he almost yelled, "What the hell do you mean roughed on? Did he hurt her? Where is that worthless piece of crap? I'll shoot that idiot right here and now. Where is he, Moaka?"

Quickly jumping to Kincaid's side and roughly grabbing his parka, Moaka spun James around and quickly responded, "Suzette no hurt. Karkak punish already."

"What the hell do mean punish already? Did he shoot that no-account?"

"No, Karkak banish from village."

Waving his arms wildly into the air, James loudly retorted, "So what the hell does that mean? The idiot should have been shot."

Still holding firmly to James' parka, Moaka was afraid to let go of him. He somehow felt if he still had hold of James's parka that he would still have some control over Kincaid. In low tones Moaka quickly explained, "Most severe punishment, except death. Need do Karkak's decision. He one of leader of village. Kincaid, need know, Simmons already punished."

"Punished, my ass. Who the hell is Karkak to make those kinds of decisions for me, and how in the hell did he get involved in this?"

Still standing squarely in front of Kincaid with a firm grip on the front of his parka, Moaka sternly replied, "Karkak fought Simmons off Suzette." Not giving James time to break in, Moaka continued, "Karkak back from Three Rivers Village, after we left Teshpuk. Karkak, Suzette go trading post. Simmons roughed on Suzette in trading post. Karkak put knife to Simmons' throat. Karkak say, Simmons leave Teshpuk, no come back, for life. If come back Karkak cut feet off."

Feeling Moaka's hold relax on his parka, James sighed deeply and more calmly asked, "Where is Simmons now?"

Quickly Moaka shook his head, and responded. "Go Three Rivers Village wait for Doc Tone. Let be Kincaid," Moaka commanded as he renewed his hold on James' parka front. "You see Suzette. She no hurt." Letting go of James once more, he continued, "Let Karkak's say be. Simmons got what come to him."

"Would you let it go, Moaka?" James fired back.

"No say for sure. Suzette no hurt. Simmons got punish."

Straightening his parka, James sighed deeply and declared, "If I ever catch that worthless individual out in the open he'll wish he'd never been born." Shaking his head slowly, he continued, "Okay, Moaka, I'll accept things for right now. I guess I owe Karkak thanks. Did Karkak really say he was going to cut off Simmons' feet if he returned to Teshpuk?" James knew well what that meant to some Native groups. Actually, it was worse than being dead. It meant a person of no feet could not live a normal life and would have to be taken care of forever, and he could not be a person in the fullest terms.

As Moaka sensed Kincaid relaxing, he answered, "Kincaid be right. Let Karkak decision be."

Quickly shrugging his shoulders, James sighed deeply again and calmly commented, "Yeah, I've trusted your judgement before, Moaka, and I guess I'll do it again. You've always had my best interests in mind, and I can't see why that would change now."

"Good. Say to Tess, Kincaid good sense."

The night seemed to devour Moaka's last comment as silence came between the two men.

Finally James asked, "What kind of shape do you think our dogs are in, Moaka? They really haven't had a full rest since we came back."

Still standing in front of James, but several paces away, Moaka replied, "Be okay, Kincaid. They rest, eat since get to Teshpuk."

James didn't bother to reply, but just moved slowly away from Moaka and started hooking up his team. Bray wasn't anxious to get back into the traces as were the other dogs, but they were a good lot and he didn't have any problems with them. Although he did notice that Moaka had to convince one of his dogs to cooperate. As James got his team hooked up, he glanced over to where Moaka was just finishing up, and replied, "I'll meet you at the woodpile, and if I don't get another chance to say it, good luck."

He hailed Bray and his team headed in the direction of the Noka's hut. Once James had maneuvered his sled up close to the woodpile, there were two villagers ready to load all the wood he wanted to take on. Thanking them, he started out to help locate his line of stations on the west side of Teshpuk, and deliver their first supply of wood. James could see his crew waiting for him, by the light of the torches they were holding in preparation for starting the big fires. James set the first station just west of the middle of the village. Moaka would set his first station just east of the middle of the village. These two middle stations would be set apart about the same distance as the other ones. From there on, he set a station about every one hundred paces with instructions to build a fire and keep it going all night. James also explained the best he could, that he would be supplying firewood to them during the night. He didn't know how well they understood him, but they all knew the plan and before he could make it back to the village there was a neat row of fires burning brightly, on James' west side. No one needed to supply the two middle stations with wood because they were close enough to the woodpile to get their own.

Hailing Bray to a halt at the west edge of the village, James thought, *The whole idea is to head the polar away from the village, and maybe, just maybe get a shot at him. The latter being only a guess, but still a possibility. If anybody spots the bear, Moaka and I, with possibly others, could start early in the morning and track him before the winds start to blow the snow too much. With any luck at all, we could possibly overtake him and do what has to be done.* Shaking his head, James knew he was considering a whole lot of possibilities. At least old *Nanuk* would not bother the village of Teshpuk this night. With the well-placed torches set in the village and the roll of fires getting started along the southern side Teshpuk, the area was covered with a soft orange glow with dancing shadows reflecting off the snowy surfaces. As James started to hail Bray onward, he stopped short. An inner alarm started to make him feel uneasy. Sighing heavily James asked himself, *What if we don't see the polar tonight? What if the bear died somewhere? What if he's not dead, but just held up some place getting over the gunshot wound? What if it changed direction to the coast and would not even come this way? We'll just have to take things as they come.* Moaka was probably asking himself the same questions and maybe even a few of the other villagers were, too.

James thought to himself that he should get over and see how Moaka was making out, and he finally hailed Bray on. Immediately, James noticed that the team did not have the regular snap that he was accustomed to seeing in them, and why should they? His team had just gone through a long pull of ten hours.

* * *

Anore and the rest of Moaka's team showed their weariness by lying down as soon as Moaka hailed them. Glancing to his right, Moaka could see two figures starting to set up where they would build the fire. They weren't in the right place exactly, but it was close enough without having an argument with them. This was his last and farthest station and he was concerned about the men at this station. During the meeting of the villagers, these two seemed to question what all the fuss was about, and although they didn't say anything, Moaka felt they disliked Kincaid being in charge. He knew only one of the men, and really didn't care for him because Moaka thought him to be an *illitsuitok*—a stupid person. His partner he didn't recognize, but if he was a friend of the stupid one, Moaka didn't care to know him either.

Slowly dismounting from his sled, Moaka loaded up an armload of wood and carried it to the two Native men standing in the golden darkness. Bending down and laying the wood on the snowy surface, Moaka commented, "I'll be back later with more. You need to keep the fire burning brightly."

The stupid one quickly stepped forward and sharply replied, "You come as an *arnakoaksak*"—old woman, "telling us what to do. Only an old woman takes orders from *kabluna*"—white man.

Pouncing like a great cat at the stupid one, Moaka grabbed the front of the man's outerwear and swiftly threw him to the hard-crusted surface, and as soon as the man hit the ground, Moaka's foot found his rib cage. Instantly straddling the thrown man, Moaka leaned down and shouted into his face, "You stupid person! Kincaid may be white, but you need know he is concerned for the safety of the people in village. We tracked and trailed the polar bear for many days, and we saw what the bear has done. If you were half the man of Kincaid, you would thank him for his help. Kincaid is trying to the do right thing, I say! You're stupid!" Spinning away from the bewildered man lying on the ground, Moaka returned to his sled with nothing else being said by either of the men. He left them to start building their fire.

Once back to his sled, Moaka hailed back to them, "Get the fire burning and stay awake. I'll be back later with more wood."

When James arrived at the middle of the fire line, he decided to wait there for Moaka to come by him, on his regular rounds.

Not having to wait very long, Moaka came sledding up out of the golden light night to join him. James noticed right away that Moaka's dogs were as tired as his because they began to lay down in their traces, just as his had done a short time before, and Anore and Bray never even looked at each other.

"How's everything going, Moaka?" James asked and continuing, "Everybody keeping alert and on the lookout?"

In a matter of fact tone, Moaka responded, "Good, Kincaid. All villager want see bear first. Ready shoot any move in dark, maybe look like polar bear. I say, make sure what shoot. I say, make sure target." Not wanting to mention his encounter with the two men, Moaka let it pass. They would get over it and there was no reason to concern Kincaid with such stupid behavior, especially after what he'd just told Kincaid about Suzette. The night would be long enough without having to worry about whether everyone agreed with the plan, and they would do as told. He would deal with the stupid one and his friend.

"The villagers on my side are anxious also," James commented. "The only one I really talked to was Karkak just for a minute, and he thinks that polar bear is going to come right at his position; at least he hopes that anyway. I guess he's a little excited, what with having a rifle tonight. Are we going to have enough firewood for the night?"

Pausing, Moaka asked, "Talk Karkak about Suzette?"

"No, I'll do it next trip. It didn't feel right awhile ago. It was just too busy, but I'll chat with him later."

Answering James' question, Moaka replied, "Firewood no problem, plenty. My side no need any long time. Kincaid think bear come close fire?"

"Well, Moaka, I don't know for sure." As James reached up and rubbed his chapped lips he continued, "It kind of depends on how bad he is hurt and how hungry he is. The animal will scent this village and he may make a run at it. I don't think he will just run up to or through the fire line, but he may get close enough for someone to get a shot at him, or at least close enough so we can spot him as he passes. Then come morning, before the wind picks up, maybe we'll have a chance to track him down."

"Well," Moaka commented, "White Ghost no raid village tonight."

James sensed despair in Moaka's voice, and he called for Moaka to join him, "Moaka, come and sit for a minute and maybe I can put this thing in focus for you, and possibly for myself." As James watched him set his sled brake and slowly walk over to him, he could see that Moaka was somewhat discouraged, or maybe just as dragged out as he was.

Speaking calmly and slowly, James wanted to make sure to say what he was feeling and thinking. Readjusting his position on the wood, he began, "This is the way I see the situation, as it stands right now. Somewhere out there in the dark of the night there is a wounded polar bear. How bad wounded, neither one of us know. I think right now he is holed up, but you or I nor anybody else, can be sure of that. That's why we're doing all of this and like I said, I don't think he is coming in tonight, but we have to be ready for him if he does show up. If he does show up at all, it may not be until early tomorrow morning. I'll bet he only has one thing on his mind, and that is getting back to the coast because that is his natural habitat, and he knows how to survive best there. When he does decide to move, I do believe that this village is in his path, and if he doesn't change directions again, I'd be willing to bet that if we see him at all, it won't be until morning, but you and I know that this polar bear does not always do what is expected of him." Pausing for a second, James continued, "Now, I have told you everything I can think of, at this time. Oh another thing, he is probably hungry about now. He just may try for a quick meal at one of the drying racks."

There was silence for a moment, before Moaka replied, "Kincaid, you say right. Maybe bear no eat. Think he hit good? One my shot straight in. No miss him! We trail him, he slow down. Bad luck snow cover trail. Kincaid maybe right, he holed up. I say polar bear come before light. Teshpuk in path, no change direction."

"Do you think he will try to come into the village for food?"

Moaka reached up and scratched his forehead before answering, "Maybe, Kincaid. Maybe he go around," as he waved his arm in a rounding motion. "Maybe come in village by north. What stop him? Villager no see before get in village."

"Yeah, Moaka, that polar bear would have to be pretty desperate to try a stunt like that, and I think all these fires on the line and the torches in the village will have a tendency to scare him off. He would be able to see all the villagers around the fires and with all of that combined, we'll just be lucky to spot him passing, and with even more luck we'll maybe get a shot or two off."

Cheerfully Moaka added, "Think he more hunger every hour. Think got him where want him."

With a nod of his head, James replied, "Yeah, so do I, Moaka, so do I. I just hope that when he does come, we are able to kill him off, or run him down at first light and get this affair finished. I think we can do that, and the odds are in our favor with every hour that passes toward morning that he doesn't show up."

Their teams looked as if they were down for the night. They had a hard run back to Teshpuk trying to beat the polar bear, but now it didn't seem as if the hard run had been necessary. On the other hand, they couldn't have taken that chance.

Slapping Moaka on the back, James commented, "Let's check our lines again, talk with the villagers some, and meet back here in about two hours." With that, Moaka walked back to his sled and James mounted his.

Hailing their teams, they both had trouble getting them to their feet, let alone to start pulling. Finally, they were on their way to load up with more wood, and then head to their respective stations to resupply firewood and to check things out. James' concern was not that anyone would go to sleep, but that they would start seeing polar bears all over the place, and start firing in all directions, which could cause a chain reaction, and someone could get hurt. These Natives were very dependable once they set their minds to buying into something, and they could be very superstitious at times and work themselves into believing anything if the situation presented itself. *Course,* James thought, *anybody could do that, given the proper set of circumstances. Yeah, these people are very solid and I don't know why I even worry about such things. These folks are survivors up here, and they don't accomplish staying alive by being careless and ignorant.*

As James approached his first station, he hailed Bray to a halt and motioned with his hands, asking them if they needed any more wood. One of them shook his head no, and waved James on. James didn't figure they would need wood being so close to the village, but he figured he'd check them out anyway. These two fellows did not have a rifle, but he noticed that they had several long knives and spears stacked against some of the wood. They probably thought that they had enough weapons to take on anything that happened to come along. It was amazing what one good rifle could do for protection or hunting for food in this country.

Nearing the station that was manned by Karkak and another Native, James knew he had to stop and thank Karkak. After all, Karkak was fighting for him as well as Suzette. Hailing Bray to a halt, James stepped down on the sled brake and walked over to their fire. As he approached, they waved and Karkak turned to reach for something behind him. As James got closer, Karkak handed him a rather large piece of firewood and said, "Kincaid, sit."

James laughed and slapped him on the back, and took the piece of firewood for his stool. Positioning himself on it, a parlor chair would not have been better, and James glanced up to Karkak and said, "Thanks Karkak, I needed to sit down for a while."

In broken English, Karkak responded, "Moaka say to Karkak, Kincaid come fire, he want sit-down."

Sitting on his makeshift stool, James stared into the fire, lost in thought, when Karkak inquired, "Kincaid, how old?"

Slowly turning his head around to look at him, James replied, "Thirty-one."

With a shake of his head and pointing to his hands Karkak said, "Show hands."

Taking his mittens off, James held up ten fingers three times, and then held up one finger.

Without hesitating a bit, Karkak declared, "Missy make good wife."

Slowly nodding James smiled at him, and replied, "Yes, Karkak."

Questioning further, Karkak asked, "Why no," and turning to the other Native and mumbling something, Karkak continued, "Why no catch Missy?"

Resting back on his makeshift chair and smiling, James slowly replied as he nodded his head, "Maybe so." Breathing deeply James continued in Native, "I want to thank you for helping Suzette. I will always be in your debt and if there is anything I can ever do to help you, just say the word."

"Don't talk Simmons, he no good person." Then his face returning to the familiar smile, continued in English, "Missy strong woman," and as Karkak paused for a moment, "Missy have more baby."

Silence fell over the fire and James thought about what Moaka had said about all the women in the village, and their wanting him to marry the schoolteacher to rid them of a good-looking single woman in town. He just wondered if the last statement Karkak had made had anything to do with that.

The fire flickering into the night with the golden flames licking high into the darkness, Karkak once again broke the silence, "That good lead," as he motioned toward Bray.

As James looked over at Karkak, he saw him motioning toward Bray. He smiled, then nodded and replied, "Yes, Karkak, but right now he is a little tired. How many dogs do you have?"

"This many." As he spoke, he started making marks in the crusted snow. James counted the marks that Karkak was making and discovered that Karkak had the same amount in his team as he had in his own, fifteen.

Putting his mittens back on, James stood, bid Karkak and his partner farewell, and walked back to his sled. As he stepped on the runners, he turned around and Karkak was still staring after him. James motioned to him, asking if he needed any firewood yet.

Walking over to James' sled, Karkak looked up at James and cheerfully stated, "Kincaid, I like you cut," in the most understandable English James had ever heard from Karkak.

Amazed, James had not heard that saying since he had left home. Still in wonderment, James inquired of Karkak, "Where in the world did you hear that saying before?"

"I say to Missy," and hesitating for just a second he continued, "how say good thing to Kincaid?"

"Karkak," James expressed, "I don't think anyone has ever complimented me with as high of praise as you have just done. Thank you for your help and ideas, and by the way Karkak, I kind of like your cut also."

Both men laughed as Karkak picked up a small armload of firewood and returned to his fire, and James hailed Bray to the next station at a slow pace.

Shaking his head, he could feel his eyes were starting to get sandy from lack of sleep and his arms ached from hanging onto the guide bars. He knew his body was running out of steam and he realized that his team was starting to shut down.

* * *

Moaka finished the delivery of wood to his last station, and was headed back to the middle stations, when he decided to stop and watch the fires. Hailing Anore to a halt, he felt like he could lay down on the snow and go to sleep. Slowly removing his mittens, he rubbed his eyes that were starting to burn like the fires he watched. He had been tired and sleepy before, but that wasn't really the problem. The last few days had drawn down his strength, but he knew he would have to keep on going. After all, Kincaid would not quit, so he knew he had to keep the pace.

* * *

After making his rounds, James decided to get some more firewood, and then returned to their meeting place. It would be a little early for him to get there, but he could wait, besides, the team could get some extra rest. He just hoped that all would be paying attention to the darkness because the bear may just come close and then fade off into the blackness of the night.

CHAPTER THIRTY

As James traveled along at the back of the fire line, he kept his team at a slow walk. It was a pretty sight to see all the fires in a row, with their golden flames reaching up into the darkness, and the lit torches in the village. Sometimes the fires burning brightly, then waning until more wood was added, and James just hoped they didn't run out of wood at the woodpile. As he neared the edge of the west side of the village, he could see not only his fire line, but also the fire stations that Moaka was in charge of over to the east side. The reflection of all the fires on the snow lit up the whole area with a golden glow. Shadows across the snow seemed to dance and jump with every flicker of the flame.

Slowly moving through the village and keeping the dogs at a walk, James saw someone come out of one of the huts. Strangely, the person looked like they were coming from Suzette's hut and was just standing there as if waiting. As he neared the silent figure, he realized it was Suzette. Hailing Bray to a halt as his sled came abreast of her, he made a sound like a half laugh and a grunt and jokingly asked, "What are you doing out here in the cold? You should be in your nice warm bed by now, and by the way, how is your face feeling?"

Alarmed, Suzette retorted defensively, "Why do you ask that? My face is fine."

Immediately James responded, "Don't play games with me, Suzette; I know about what Simmons did to you."

"Oh, James," Suzette instantly responded, "I didn't want you to know about that because he didn't do anything to me. Karkak took care of the situation before anything serious could happen. You should have seen Karkak fly into action; he was in the middle of Simmons before I knew what was happening."

Moving from the back of his sled in silence, James slowly went to Suzette, and took her in his arms and held her gently.

Sensing James' sincerity, Suzette slowly moved her head back and kissed him gently. Moving from his embrace, Suzette softly spoke, "I'm fine, James. He didn't hurt me and he will be gone forever from Teshpuk." Giggling slightly, she continued, "Karkak even told him if he ever came back to Teshpuk that he would cut off his feet and feed them to the dogs. I guess that convinced him because he sure lit out of here in a hurry."

"Well, Suzette, it should have never happened in the first place."

"I know, James, but no harm was done, at least not to me. Karkak scared the devil out of Simmons, with a knife at his throat."

Stepping back from Suzette he asked in a much lighter tone, "What in the world are you doing out this late?"

Eagerly she replied, "I thought I might be able to help out in some way. I can't sleep anyway." In a mocking tone she continued, "Who can? Moaka and you have got everybody up running around looking for a lonely polar bear."

"Come on, Suzette."

Hurriedly exclaiming, "Oh, James, I was only kidding!"

"Well, I hope so; you made it sound as if I was the entire fault for this night's activities. There is a matter of a rogue polar bear running loose."

"James, you are taking this thing too personal," Suzette explained. "Actually, no one is blaming you at all; the villagers are saying they are glad you are here to help get the beast out of the way. Ever since this has started some of the Natives won't travel alone out on the flats, and

I don't blame them a bit after what happen to the Native from Three Rivers Village."

Taking a deep breath, James said, "Yeah, Suzette, I imagine this whole affair has upset some peoples' lives." Pausing, as he turned his head and squinted trying to see up the street, James resumed with, "Yes, Suzette, by golly you can help. If you would make Moaka and me some hot tea that would be great to warm us up some. I'm going over to fill up with wood and I'll be back in about ten minutes, if that will give you enough time."

Happy that she could be of help, she responded, "That will be plenty of time because the water is already hot and all I have to do is let the tea steep for a few minutes."

Boarding his sled, James hailed Bray forward and quickly glancing back to Suzette, he thought, *That is one fine woman and if I don't ask her to marry me pretty soon some other fellow is bound to come along and realize the same thing.*

The woodpile was going down fast, but James thought they would have plenty for the night. The two villagers assigned to the woodpile helped him load his sled, not that they would need much more wood before daylight. He was soon on his way back to pick up Suzette. As he returned to Suzette's hut, she was waiting patiently at the entrance. James stopped his team, and stepped on one side of the back runners and let her stand on the other, and quietly he hailed Bray forward to the meeting place that had been arranged with Moaka. Seeing that Suzette was having trouble handling the container of tea and cups while holding on at the same time, James took the container from her asking, "Isn't that a little better?"

With a nod she answered, "Yes, James, thank you. I didn't want to ask for help, because I know that you need both hands free to control the dogs and the sled."

Smiling at her he replied, "You're right, and most of the time I do, but just now the dogs aren't in any mood to give me any problems or break any speed records."

Moaka had not showed up yet when Suzette and James arrived at the meeting place, and halting the dogs, they both stepped from behind the sled. He moved around to her side and they made themselves comfortable sitting on the wood waiting for Moaka to show up. Setting the container of tea down beside him, James commented, "I'll wait for Moaka to come before I have any, he should be along shortly."

Suzette reached over and gently touched his parka sleeve and asked, "James, you and Moaka have become very close friends, haven't you?"

Not answering right away because he was thinking about his answer, he finally replied, "I think Moaka is probably the only man I know that I can share my total thoughts with, no matter how dumb or stupid they may be, and he will either laugh with me or be sad with me. That's just the kind of relationship we have established. People don't try to make that kind of relationship; we didn't set out to establish that kind of relationship, it just happened between us. Just like two people falling in love, it just happens. You understand what I mean?"

Slowly shifting her position to turn toward him, she replied, "Yes, James, I understand, you and Moaka are always watching out for each other so much and that's wonderful. I think it would be great to have such a relationship with someone and I don't think it would have to be another female, but it would have to be someone I trusted."

Nodding his head, James noticed the tail end of her sentence with, "Yeah, it's pretty nice to know that you have someone covering your backside all the time, and always looking out for your best interests. Speaking of relationships, Suzette, I think we need to discuss ours. I hate to keep taking advantage of your hospitality and attention all the time and never give anything in return, except maybe bringing food and giving you stupid furs that you can use or trade. Somehow, that makes me feel guilty, and I don't feel like I'm doing my share. I've already told you that I'm trying to establish my home base here at Teshpuk, but I can't see myself staying at your place all the time. I'm sure that Moaka and Tess want to see me established here, and everything seems to be pointing in that direction. I just can't keep putting you out. You have your school to maintain and you have a hard enough time of it, living alone and all, without having an occasional boarder around; especially when I pop in and pop out with the wind, so to speak." Shifting his position on the wood, James inquired further, "Do you understand my concerns, Suzette?"

Softly in almost a whisper she answered, "Yes, James, but I feel that if two people have a sense of togetherness, then they can work out any problems they may have and arrange, so to speak, as you say, a mutual longlasting relationship."

With a jerk of his head, James gazed into her soft brown eyes that were being brightened by the golden glow of the fires and almost sputtered, "What did you just say, Suzette?"

Before she could answer James' question, Moaka came out of the night to join them. Hailing his dogs to a halt, he slowly made his way through the golden light to join James and Suzette, and seeing Suzette he commented, "All up this tonight," as he motioned with his hand toward Suzette.

"Here, Moaka," James said, as Moaka came close enough so James could see his face. "Suzette has fixed some hot tea to help us make it through the night." Pouring large portions of tea out for James and Moaka into the tin cups, Suzette returned the container of tea to the top of the wood stacked on James' sled.

The steaming cup cradled between his hands, Moaka replied, "Thanks. Help keep warm. Air go through clothes. " He chuckled as he took another large gulp of tea, and commented, "I say, hard leave fire."

Gesturing with his outstretched arm toward Moaka's side of the fire line, James asked, "How's everything over on your side?"

Before Moaka could answer, Suzette announced, "I think I'll leave you guys to the night and go back to bed. It is cold out here, and besides, I still have school in the morning, you know. Just set the cups and container down on the old box next to my hut entrance, and I'll pick them up in the morning." As she started to turn away, she stopped and asked, "James, do you think the polar bear will come tonight?"

Taking a deep breath and with a sigh, he replied, "I wish I could tell you for sure, either way. Don't you want a ride back?"

Without moving from the spot she quickly added, "No, James, I'll walk. But, James I would like to finish that conversation we were having, as soon as possible."

Smiling at her, he responded, "We will, Suzette, we surely will."

Without another word, she turned and walked away into the glowing light of the village.

James watched her fade away, and thought, *What did she say just before Moaka come out of the darkness? I swear I'm getting turned around on this relationship.*

As soon as Suzette was out of earshot Moaka jokingly chided, "Finish talk." Chuckling Moaka persisted, "What about, Kincaid?"

"Oh shut up, Moaka. You can ask Suzette, but I don't think I can tell you. Hell, I'm not sure myself. That woman seems to have me all tied up in knots. She always seems to have the last word."

Laughing as he slapped James on the shoulder, Moaka declared, "Need marry, Kincaid."

"I don't know what the answer is Moaka." James shook his head and slowly reached up and rubbed his lips with the palm of his hand.

Silence fell over them as Moaka poured some more tea and slowly drank the warming liquid. It sure did feel good going down, and he was glad Suzette had brought it out. The night was cold and it didn't help not knowing where that bear was keeping himself. Moaka moved to sit where Suzette had been and idly commented, "Kincaid, think caribou migration. Plan go get caribou. Tess need skin for hut and can use meat. Think do us good. No need count animal all time. Tess worry baby come, no place of own. No want stay relation. Kirima's hut many people."

Seemingly to come back alive, James exclaimed, "That would be great, Moaka! I can't think of anything else I'd rather do than help get a lodge built for you and Tess, and that new baby. How many caribou would it take to get a first class hut built? We'll want to cover it with sod and moss for insulation. In addition, I have a new idea for an entrance I saw over in Barrow. A way that is really good for going in and out without letting in the cold so much, and best of all, a person doesn't have to almost get on his knees to go in and out."

Moaka turned toward James, gesturing with his hands, as if to hold back his words, as he exclaimed, "Hold Kincaid! Depend make Teshpuk home. Boss say, yes. Then need skin for house. Tess and baby be with us, if boss say no. I like stay here. Tess like stay close, her family, make own place. She come on trip maybe. Good for all. Lot not know maybe."

"That's true, Moaka, there are some unknowns, but I don't think that I'm going to have any problems getting the people in Seattle, especially Nealy, to buy into it. After all, I'm still only about four days out of Barrow. All they're concerned about is that my reports of the weather conditions, resource discoveries, and wildlife in the area keep coming into their office on time, and now that the mail is being delivered here, I don't think that we are going to have a problem." Running through his mind was the aspect of all this happening. *Tess' new baby, establishing headquarters at Teshpuk, and possibly marrying Suzette.*

"Yeah, Moaka, I think you've got an idea about going caribou hunting. I'd like the chance to tan out some hides and maybe get Tess or somebody to make me some new clothes. Better yet, I'd consider it an honor if I could help you build Tess the best hut in the village. With the help of some of the others we could really do it up in fine fashion."

With a smile and nudge from his elbow, Moaka jokingly responded, "Make one for Suzette and Kincaid?"

Looking straight at him as he nodded his head, James responded, "You might be right Moaka, but only time will tell that."

"How old Suzette?" Moaka inquired.

"I don't know, I never did ask her. I think she's about my age. Around thirty years I think. Why do you ask that?"

As Moaka slid off the wood that was stacked on James' sled and shrugging his shoulder, he answered, "Go check fire."

"Wait a minute, Moaka," James retorted, "you sure are fascinated about getting me married off. What makes you so sure that Suzette and I are going to get hitched up?"

Moaka stopped sharply in his tracks, and turned back to James and asked, "What *facinted* mean?"

James laughed, and replied, "Moaka, I'm sorry. The word is fascinated, and for your purpose it means, wants to know badly."

Without expression in his voice and sounding very confident, Moaka answered James' question, "Tess say."

"What? What!" James exclaimed, "I don't believe this, Moaka. How does Tess know all this?"

Slowly lifting his foot to rest it on the wood, Moaka answered, "Kincaid, she say."

In a very serious tone, James explained, "Moaka, any day I could get orders to report to Seattle and be shipped off to who knows where. I don't think that is going to happen, but would Suzette come with me? She loves this place and she loves the people. I don't think she would ever want to leave here, and I can't say I'd blame her. She is doing what she wants to do, right here."

"No worry, Kincaid," Moaka assured, "She go. Seattle or where you go. She strong woman. Make change need."

Not responding, James turned slightly and looked toward the eastern sky, and commented, "It's going to start breaking light pretty soon. Then what?"

Shaking his head, Moaka muttered, "Need wait, Kincaid."

As James slid off the wood stacked on his sled, he declared, "All right

Moaka, let's go check out our stations for the final time and I'll meet you back here just at first light. With a quick glance and nod toward Moaka's sled, he continued, "Looks like you need to go get a bit more wood."

"Need go." Stopping and turning slightly back to James, he continued, "Kincaid, if get White Ghost, boss no say Kincaid go. Think villager have say. Natives want Kincaid, no want new person." Smiling at James, he quickly turned and walked back to his sled.

James smiled to himself and thought, *Yeah, you got a point there, Moaka.* Hazing his team up, they seemed to be a little more energetic. Actually, they had been able to get quite a bit of rest during the night. Hailing Bray onward, they had about an hour to kill before the whole situation would change, either for the better or the worse. That would be just about enough time to swing by all his stations, resupply them with wood if needed, get back to meet Moaka, and figure out what they were going to do next.

Slowly walking his team through the village, James noticed that a few of the villagers had already begun to start their daily routine. One woman was cleaning out her cooking pot, probably getting ready for the morning meal and another old woman was feeding the family dog team, which was staked beside her hut. Leaving the village and heading for his first station, he adjusted his wolverine face cover, as the crispness of the morning air was starting to sink into his bones. It always seemed to be colder this time of day than any other. He'd guess that the temperature was somewhere around twenty below zero, and at this temperature the dogs had to be watched to make sure they didn't lose their rawhide sox that protected their feet from freezing. *Tough place to be this time of year,* he thought. *Desolate and cold, but this country could sure grow on a person.*

Once James arrived at his first station, which was located in front of the village, he hailed Bray to hold up. He knew they wouldn't need any wood, but he just wanted to stop and make sure things were all right, and it never hurts to give moral support. The Natives greeted James with big smiles and offered their fire for warmth. James accepted just to be friendly, and he soon was on his way. James left them and continued to the next station where Karkak was located. The thought came to him as he was making his way, *Those guys at the first station, and all the rest, were depending on Moaka and me to make the right decisions. The stories of this polar bear had already started circulating and it had gotten some folks a little jumpy. After all, I'm supposed to be the expert in this field, and if the truth be told, these villagers probably knew more about the animals in this area and their habits than I do.*

Karkak had a bright fire going, but as James arrived, he was putting on his last bit of wood. James nodded his head in greeting to Karkak's partner, and commented, "Not long now, Karkak. It'll be breaking light soon." As James motioned toward the eastern sky, Karkak noticed what James was talking about right away. His partner came to the sled and picked up a small armload of wood and struggled back to the fire.

Slowly Karkak approached James and inquired, "Kincaid, what you think? Light soon, no *Nanuk*."

As James watched the other Native kicking small pieces of firewood back into the fire, James responded, "I don't know," as he shrugged his shoulders. "We'll just have to wait and see."

Karkak stepped forward and gently squeezed the top of James' shoulder and replied, "Be okay Kincaid. Moaka say to Karkak, he kill polar bear for father."

Nodding his head slightly, James echoed Karkak's thought with, "Yeah, he has carried his father's death around with him for a long time, although he had nothing to do with it, he felt he was robbed for not having his parents." Bidding Karkak farewell, James remounted his sled and was off to check the other stations that were further out to the west. With a quick stop at his next two stations, he made his way out to the farthest western station and unloaded just about all of his wood. As James was walking back to his sled from their fire, he happened to look at his sled. It looked strange with hardly anything in it. His rifle was still in its scabbard, but nothing else except a little firewood. He had even taken off some of his leather lashings so they wouldn't be tangled in the firewood and the sled seemed to have taken on a different appearance.

Swinging Bray back around, he headed for the middle of the village to meet Moaka. Finally, a dim light was starting to make visibility a little easier, and looking over the backs of his team, he could see the sun's rays just starting to lighten the entire sky. The colors seem to jump over the top of the mountain and change with every passing moment. Now the dark purples were present, later the dark reds and light yellows would appear. The entire area was calm and peaceful this time of the morning, and in many ways, this was the time most enjoyable to James.

CHAPTER THIRTY-ONE

Their meeting place behind the fire line was deserted. Moaka had not arrived yet, but James could see him coming as the early light of day streamed across the mountain turning the high clouds into a blaze of fire. Looking back through the village, the villagers were moving about and looking around, and wondering if the polar bear had ever come during the night, but realizing very soon that everybody was still waiting for the sighting. The plan was for the men on their stations to keep the fires burning until the sun had shown the top of its head over the mountain. Solid plans had not been discussed if Moaka's White Ghost failed to show up.

Not having to wait very long, James could now see Moaka quite plainly coming closer; he was at about his second station out. He wasn't stopping at his stations, so James knew he would be along presently. Still standing on the back of his sled, he cursed and spit. He was somewhere between being angry and depressed. *Where could that damn polar bear be? I thought for sure the stupid thing would have come this direction, and I thought it have been here by now. Now what in world are we going to do? Moaka and I, and the others just can't go running off into nowhere. Nobody even knows where to start anymore. If that polar bear don't come by here, we'll just have to forget it until something else happens to give us another good lead.*

Moaka stopped his sled a short distance from Kincaid's and as he waved his arm toward the eastern horizon hailed, "What think, Kincaid?"

With a shake of his head in disgust, James hopelessly looked to the sun starting to show rays of light yellow in the sky. "Well Moaka, I don't know. I thought we would have seen him by now. Do you think Tess has any tea on yet this morning? At least we could warm our insides and try and figure what our next move might be."

"Yes," Moaka replied dryly, "Tea made."

Lazily, James stepped onto his sled runners, and in a dejected tone replied, "Well, hell, Moaka, we might as well go get something to warm us up some, we sure the devil aren't doing any good out here. The villagers will probably let their fires go out and then come on in."

Hazing their teams forward, they stopped in front of Kirima's hut. "Let's not unhook the dogs now," James commented as he thought, *The polar bear may come yet.* Siding their sleds to keep them from freezing down, James paused before entering the hut and asked Moaka, "Are you tired?"

Moaka turned his head toward James, he responded, "Yes Kincaid, tired. Long night."

Suddenly the early morning dawn's silence was broken by the sound of an echoing gun shot, then another, suddenly it sounded like a war was going on. Firing glances at each other, James screamed, "Damn, Moaka, he's here! He's here!"

Breaking for his sled, as Moaka ran for his, James yelled at the top of his voice, "Grab your rifle, and ride with me."

James quickly flipped his sled upright scattering whatever wood was left in it, and frantically tried to straighten the sled with the dogs. Moaka rushed back to James' sled with rifle and shells in hand and kicked the front of the sled to help straighten it with the dogs, just as he jumped into the sled. At the same moment, James yelled at Bray as loud as he could. The dogs were up and began to bark feverishly, getting as excited as the two men were.

Everything was happening so fast it became a blur. There was no time for thinking or planning, just going on instinct. The team frantically strained at the traces, and no sign of tiredness was apparent, because they were up and snapping the traces like a whip. James screamed at Bray as he hailed him around, heading through the village to the west side where the shots were coming from. Flying through the village, James stood as high as he could on the sled runners, straining to get a glimpse of the polar bear between the huts. At a passing glance, he noticed the villagers were scattering from their path as they raced through the village. Finally breaking out past the edge of the village into the open, they got their first look at the polar bear as he retreated from the villagers' rifle fire.

Moaka's hand hurt from griping the sled side rail so tightly, but he knew he had to try to keep his weight in the middle of the sled to help the dogs. Cradling the rifle between his arm and body, he knew the end was near. He had confidence that Kincaid's team could run down the polar bear, and this time it would not be a cat and mouse game, but a straight on fight to the finish. Suddenly, Moaka wished his father could see him. He had not thought about his father in that way for many years and the determination to kill this beast for his father seemed to build rapidly within him.

Glancing down at Moaka, James could see that he was holding on for dear life trying to shift his position with the movement of the sled. James knew that he must let Moaka take this animal to settle the old score.

With frantic yells of encouragement to his team, James urged them on as fast as they could go. Pulling no more than five hundred pounds, including the sled, the team was going at full gait.

James screamed, "You got that damn rifle loaded?"

Through his parka hood Moaka screamed, "Kincaid, get close, I show."

The villagers were still firing, and it was too late to try to stop them. James just hoped that they had enough sense to stop firing, when they saw the sled coming into view. Cutting between his second and third stations, James was still screaming encouragement to Bray and the rest of his team. He felt a sudden extra pull on the sled and realized the dogs had seen the polar bear, and now the race was on. There wasn't much need to keep yelling at the team, but Moaka was so excited that he continued to urge the dogs on.

Pulling as hard as he'd ever seen the team pull, James was proud of them. Somehow, he knew that the dogs would outrun the polar bear; they had to. The wind cut deep into his face, and this parka hood ballooned behind him. He was aware of the chill of the wind, but the chilling effect only seemed to add excitement to the heat of the chase. Straining to look beyond the team through tearing eyes, James saw the polar bear clearly. He did look like a "white ghost," as Moaka had commented many times. Watching the bear closely, he finally realized that the polar bear didn't see them coming yet. The beast was so concerned about getting away from the rifle fire that he wasn't looking their direction. Because the villagers had started firing too early, the bear had been out of range, and wasn't taking any chances. That seemed to be normal for this animal, who only respected rifle fire.

With a quick glance down at Moaka, who was still adjusting his weight for the balance of the sled, James yelled, "Moaka, I'm going to try and get within one hundred yards before I stop. You're going to have to bail out and shoot as fast as you can. I don't know how long the team can keep up this pace."

Nodding his head in agreement, Moaka continued urging the team and Bray onward, although the dogs didn't understand him. As they frantically pursued the marauding polar bear, there was no need to adjust course because Bray was headed straight for the critter. Then it happened, the polar bear turned sideways and spotted them coming at full gait. Seeing the animal adjust his course and turn straight away from the on rushing team, James knew that the polar bear would give all he had left to escape the barking dogs. A slight smile came to James' cold lips as he thought, *We've got him on the run and by the damn we're going to win, finally, we are going to win.*

Out of the corner of his eye, James caught movement, and turning his head slightly was surprised to see the villagers at all the stations, jumping into the air and yelling as loudly as they could. He could just barely hear their voices with his head turned toward them.

Moaka also saw the villagers and raised his rifle in the air as a quick salute, and yelled, *"Akkerartorpok opinnartok"*—revenge is marvelous, and then Moaka started yelling at the team again. It must have been quite a sight from where the villagers stood and Moaka was proud to be in the middle of the action. Moaka's friends had a ringside seat at possibly the most exciting thing that had happened around here for quite some time and many stories would be told. Quickly Moaka concentrated on performing what he dreamed of doing, downing the animal that had been touched by the spirits.

James' attention was well-focused again toward the polar bear and he guessed that they had picked up about fifty yards on him. Through eyes still tearing from the cold wind, he could now see a reddened spot just below the animal's right hip. *Yeah, he's hit,* James thought. Moaka thought for sure he'd hit him, and by the appearance of the blood spot, he had been right. Although the surface of the snow looked smooth, the faster the sled went the rougher the ride got and Moaka was having the ride of his life. The sled was rocking and rolling just like riding the rapids of the Colville River.

The team still seemed strong, the feverish barking had stopped, and all of the dogs' energy was being spent to chase after the polar bear. Their pace did not slacken, so James was more confident than ever that the team would be able to put Moaka in a position to have a good shot soon. Polar bears weren't notorious for running long distances at full gait, but this animal seemed to be the exception to the rule. Confidence growing within James, he knew it would come down to who could out last who, and he was confident his team would win the battle.

He figured that they were now about two hundred yards behind him. The bear's gait was starting to slow, his strides got shorter, and it looked like the wound was probably starting to have its effect. They were closing fast now, and James could see his magnificent coat shimmering with every bound. His powerful shoulders were pulling hard with every running leap. It was a shame to have to kill this magnificent animal, and James still wondered what went wrong inside the animal's head to make his behavioral patterns change. Closing to less than one hundred fifty yards James yelled at Moaka, "Get ready, Moaka!"

Turning his head and yelling out of the corner of his mouth, Moaka screamed, "Now Kincaid, now."

As James heard Moaka's response, he got the shock of his life. The crazy animal had stopped, turned around, and was now charging them. Screaming at Bray to halt and stomping down on the sled brake, James nearly turned the sled over. Yelling again at Bray to halt, his lead and the rest of the team finally came to a dead stop and started their feverish barking. Instantly, Moaka piled out of the sled and knelt down behind it, to use it as a steady rest.

The polar bear was now about one hundred yards from them and coming fast like a charging bull. There was blood in the eyes of that polar bear, and he had all intent and purpose of ripping the team and both men to shreds as he had done to the other Native. He had come to the end of his rope, and this was his last effort to protect himself and survive.

Horror instantly came over James as he saw that his rifle was not in the scabbard. Thinking, *it must have flipped out of the rifle holster when the sled was quickly turn upright.* He would have felt a whole lot better having a backup right now. Seeing the critter coming at them with all his strength, he thought, *Come on, Moaka, come on, what are you waiting for?* It appeared that Moaka was savoring the moment before he dropped the animal. Frantically he thought, *Come on, Moaka. Come on.*

Moaka suddenly relaxed. The sled didn't make a good rest because the dogs were jumping around so much that they were jerking the sled and moving it slightly. Lifting the rifle ever so slightly off the sled rail, Moaka knew he could take this White Ghost anytime he wanted.

This just wasn't a regular polar bear to him. This animal's death would be revenge for his parents' deaths. James knew Moaka didn't hate polar bears, but this one was for his father and mother. When the polar bear was no more than fifty yards away and James was about to grab the rifle from Moaka's hands, the rifle sounded.

The polar bear dropped to his haunches, then regained his footing, and started to charge them again, this time staggering and half falling.

Chambering another round, Moaka's rifle sounded again. The large white form lay without movement.

Still standing on the runners of the sled, James realized that his hands were cramped from squeezing the guide bars so tightly. Silence fell over the whole area as the dogs barking stopped, and the villagers were too far away too be heard, if they were even yelling at all. Both men's eyes were fixed on the dead animal that lay just thirty yards away. What a great beast. Soon the villagers would have him skinned and carved up into pieces. James knew that was the way of it. The only thing that James could hear was the breeze blowing past his parka hood, and Moaka seemed to be frozen in position, for he had not moved a muscle since he'd shot the last time.

Catching movement from Moaka, James looked down at him, as Moaka said, "Take care of dog Kincaid, maybe need their speed."

They smiled at each other and then they both started to laugh. James realized it was a good way of relieving tensions, and they were both very relieved to be done with this whole affair.

"Kincaid, what do tomorrow?" Moaka asked very nonchalantly.

Not replying right away, James knew Moaka was trying to ease the tension. James wiped his lips, and answered with, "I believe we should go polar bear hunting because we have some good experience."

Moaka reached up, slapped James on the shoulder, and responded, "Think good idea. We know."

Laughing together again and grabbing each other by the shoulders, they shook each other vigorously. James noticed the villagers, who had been manning the stations, were running out to meet them. Karkak got to them first and began hugging and slapping first Moaka and then James. Moaka and the rest of the greeters proceeded on to the fallen polar bear. James remained behind his sled just letting the event all sink in. Other Natives came from the village with sleds to haul the polar bear back in pieces. Everybody would be eating polar bear this night and Moaka would be awarded the pelt.

Quietly, James called to Bray and the lead swung around, heading back toward to the village. As he approached the west end of the village, he saw Suzette standing near the last hut. Shaking his head, James wondered if what he was about to do was the right thing. *Would it be fair to her? How could he be sure he was ready to settle down? Was she really in love with him or was she just lonely and he satisfied that loneliness? Just a short few days ago, he would not have even considered marriage. He was still James Kincaid, Wildlife Biologist. He'd be gone for long periods. He could even be transferred or moved to another area.*

Hailing Bray to a halt with his sled stopping right alongside her, James asked, "You need a lift to your hut?"

With a dash Suzette rushed into his arms and half knocked him off the sled runners, as she excitedly exclaimed, "You and Moaka were magnificent! I didn't see it all, but I saw enough to know that this tale will be told around many warming fires for a long time to come."

James' arms encircled her, as he savored her closeness, then he gently held her away from him, at arm's length. He looked deep into her dark brown eyes and saw only trust and happiness. He really didn't know how to go about this, so he just blurted out, "Suzette, will you marry me?"

Instantly jumping back into his arms she almost yelled, "James Kincaid,

I've been waiting a long time to hear you ask me that. I'll marry you, right now if you want."

Gently James held her close, "No, Suzette, I'd like Noka to give you away, if that's all right with you?"

Finally breaking their embrace, she excitedly replied, "That will be fine with me, James. Tess can be my matron and Moaka can stand up for you."

Slowly turning away from her, James looked off into the distance at the villagers who were quickly dividing the polar bear meat. A feeling of sadness passed over him, followed by a sense of accomplishment. He smiled to himself, turned back to Suzette, and asked, "Lady, do you still want a ride back to your hut?"

Be sure to look for the next adventure-filled
historical novel by this exciting new author!

RELEASED IN THE SPRING OF 2012

ABOUT THE AUTHOR

BEING A NATIVE OF IDAHO, Curtis has always been close to wild game, good fishing, and high mountains. He traveled extensively throughout the world while serving in the Marines and later in life as a tourist, during his working years and after retirement. In each country he visited, his interest in the country's cultures and traditions were of the upmost importance. For many years, he has worked closely with the Idaho Fish and Game protecting and establishing wildlife habitat, and has given numerous presentations concerning best management practices of rivers and reservoirs. Alaska has always sparked his interest, especially during the period of time just after the initial purchase from Russia. Having traveled broadly in Alaska and being inquisitive about the ancient traditions of the Eskimo people, Curtis was driven to write about the opening of the new frontier.